D1744865

The Rebels of Psiere

Book Three in The Mystery of the Makers Series

By

K. Aten

FLASHPOINT
PUBLICATIONS

FLASHPOINT
PUBLICATIONS

Copyright © 2023 K. Aten

All rights reserved. No part of this book may be reproduced, stored in a retrieval system, or transmitted in any form or by any means, without prior permission in writing from the publisher.

Paperback ISBN: 978-1-61929-526-1

Hardback ISBN: 978-1-61929-525-4

Flashpoint Publications First Edition: December, 2023

Printed in the United States of America.

Cover design by TreeHouse Studio

www.flashpointpublications.com

All rights reserved.No part of this publication may be reproduced, transmitted in any form or by any means, electronic or mechanical, including photocopy, recording, or any information storage and retrieval system, without permission in writing from the publisher. Parts of this work are fiction. Names, characters, places, and incidents either are the product of the author's imagination or are used fictitiously, and any resemblance to actual persons, living or dead, business establishments, or events

Dedication

This novel is for my mom.

I'm sorry I didn't finish in time for you to read it.

At the end of the day,
when I stare into my memories,
she's there smiling and laughing.
A daughter, sister, and mother,
this long-time friend I dearly miss.
I see my mom and her light.

Her legacy is honesty and kindness,
a lifetime of perseverance.
I'll carry that torch onward
with her laughter spilling forth.
And tomorrow, I'll feel her loss
with each and every breath.

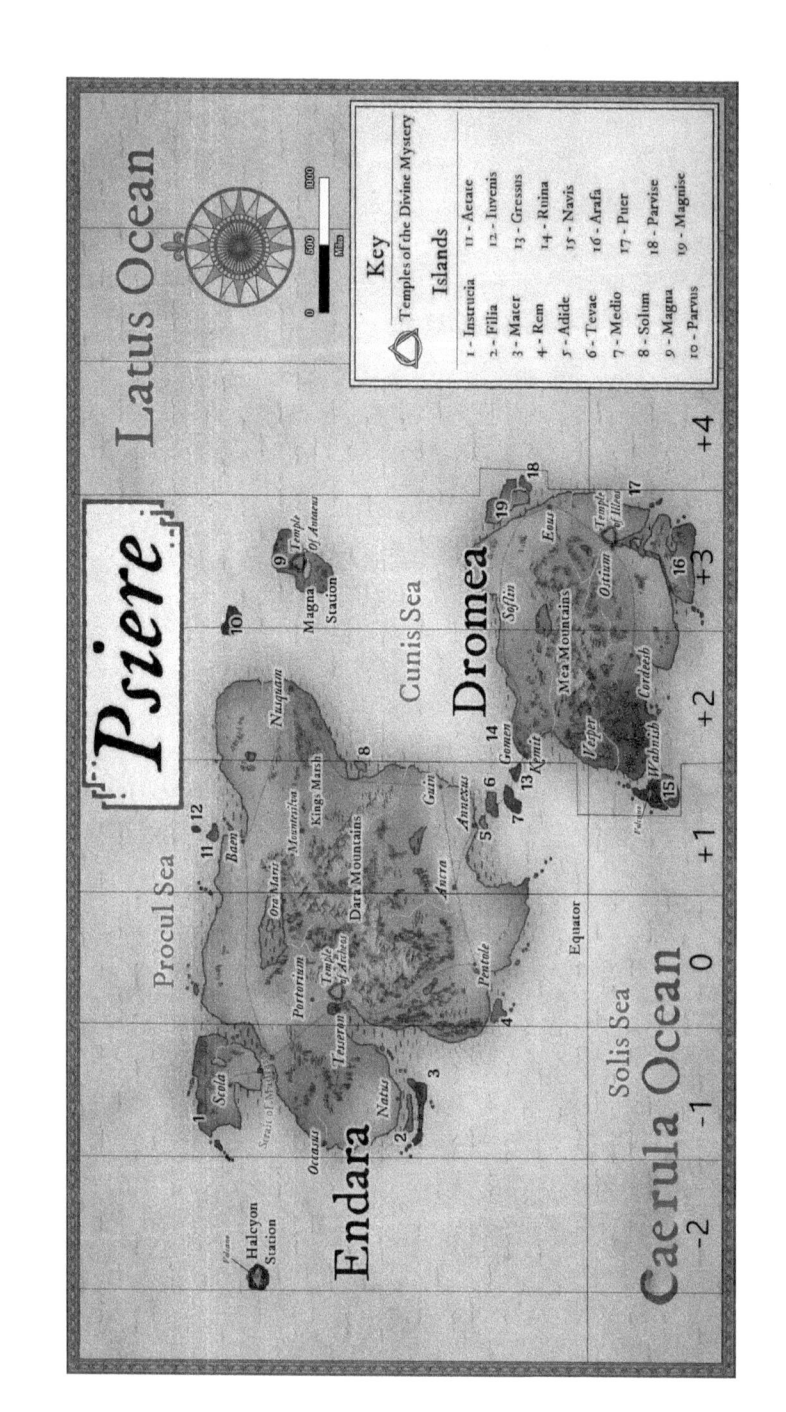

Psiere Glossary

Academy [Society] – Sole location for all secondary education in Psiere. (university) There is also a separate smaller part of Academy that deals with advanced officer training. All other education before Academy is done locally.

Adminstre [People] – Administrator, assistant, scheduler.

Adventurist [People] – Someone whose career is discovering ancient Maker artifacts all over their land in order to advance current technology and aid Psierian lives.

Aeons [Measurement] – Ages, eons, a long time.

Aether [Natural] – Enhanced radiotope gas that is produced by archeostones and illeostones. Archeostone aether reacts with illeostone mineral and charges the illeostones. Illeostone aether is emitted and used to power gadgets and machines. The Archeostone aether changes babies at a genetic level while in utero. The more exposure the more power.

Aetherkinesis [Channel] – The ability to sense and physically manipulate aether, with the mind.

Aft [Transportation] – The back, or stern of a dirigible.

Amita [People] – Family. Aunt, female sib of parent.

Animal Empathy [Channel] – The ability to communicate and read emotions mind to mind with animals. (Soft Channel)

Antaeus [Planetary] – Exploded moon, source of the Archeostones and half source of the fused Antoraestones.

Antoraestone [Planetary] – Pieces of powerful fused rock created when the asteroid Torae collided with the moon, Antaeus. The power imbued within a full-size stone provides 10x magnification of illeostones or Psierians.

Apportation [Channel] – The ability to instantly physically move objects within your sight from one point to another, with the mind. (Hard Channel)

Apree [Measurement] – Second lune (month) of the roto (year).

Archeos [Planetary] – Larger yellowish-orange sun, first to rise in the morning. Part of a binary stars set.

Archeostones [Planetary] – Fist size and glow yellowish orange, very rare. These charge illeostones with two days of exposure.

Armicruste [Natural] – Giant aggressive armored crabs sent by the Atlanteens. 3000 lbs.

Arslick [Society] – Expletive, curse. Derogatory term for someone of ill character.

Atlantee [People] – Race of humanoid fish people who live in the seas and hate the Psierians. Cannot survive on land any more than Psierians could survive under water. They have telepathy and empathy, but no other known channels.

Atlanteens [People] – Psierian name for the Atlantee.

Automaton [Mechanical] – Robot powered by a single illeostone. Controlled by a specialized soldier programmer.

Avi-amita [People] – Family. Great aunt, sister of grandparent.

Avia [People] – Family. Grandmother, mother of parent.

Avu-patrus [People] – Family. Great uncle, brother of grandparent.

Avus [People] – Family. Grandfather, father of parent.

Barde [People] – Writer, poet, storyteller, and more.

Bollux [Society] – Expletive, curse. Balls! Like, shit or damn.

Bosair [Society] – Bra, brassiere.

Bovid [Natural] – Large hoofed stock mammal, primarily for eating.

Broadrep [People] – Broadsheet representative, reporter, news agent.

Calla [Natural] – Beautiful.

Cathedress [People] – Title for the Queen, the ruling sovereign, the current seat of the Divine Cathedra. (throne)

Chemistrae [Natural] – Chemistry.

Clairvoyance [Channel] – The ability to gain information about an object, person, location, or physical event. (Soft Channel)

Coacas [Natural] – Coconuts.

Connate [People] – Immediate heir.

Consor [Society] – Marry.

Consorage [Society] – Marriage.

Consoral [Society] – Married.

Copere [Natural] – Copper.

Corm [Finance] – Money, currency delineation = 1 corundem.

Corma [Finance] – Money, currency delineation = $1/10^{th}$ of a corm or ten cred.

Cormi [Finance] – Money, currency delineation = $1/10^{th}$ of a corma, segmented to break into halves or quarters.

Corundem [Natural] – Super hard precious stones found in blue, red, and white. Used for mining, communication, jewelry, science, and as a base for the Psierian financial system due to its value in all parts of society.

Coz'n [People] – Family, child of an aunt (amita) or uncle. (patruus)

Cred [Finance] – Money, slang general term.

Credit [Finance] – Money, general term.

Cycle [Transportation] – Two-wheeled vehicle 120 mph standard max. (prototype 150)

Dae [Measurement] – Day.

Decaroto [Measurement] – Ten years.

Deka [Measurement] – Tenth and last lune (month) of the roto. (year)

Dextra [Transportation] – When looking forward toward the bow of a dirigible, this is the starboard, or right side of the ship.

Dir [Planetary] – Lake.

Dirigible [Transportation] – Air zeppelin filled with heliopus gas, powered by aether driven props. Max speed 40 mahls per oor. Max distance at full capacity of illeostones is 1400 miles. (*Quaesitum*/black bladder = 60 mph, *Vestigo* is 65 mph, distance only limited by supply need)

Divine Cathedra [Society] – Royal throne. Set with two Archeostones. The throne has existed for the entirety of written Psierian history. The Divine Cathedra can only be held by female sovereigns of the family and is inherited by the first-born Dracore woman of each generation. It can be held in regency by a male, if no other female heirs exist, until the next female in the royal line is born. (There is a secret compartment within the throne only known by sovereigns and no one else)

Doctore [People] – Doctor. Psi with advanced training in all healing techniques.

Dolpheens [Natural] – Dolphins.

Dowsing [Channel] – The ability to sense the location of water. (Soft Channel)

Dromea [Planetary] – Southern continent. Population: 11 million. Sq. Miles: 1.5

Eidetic Memory [Channel] – The ability to perfectly recall the details and image anything that it seen. (Soft Channel)

Empathy [Channel] – The ability to communicate and read emotions mind to mind. (Soft Channel)

Endara [Planetary] – Northern continent. Population: 19 million. Sq Miles: 2.5.

Enhanced Awareness [Channel] – A superior ability to sense and react to every physical thing around you in faster than normal time. (Soft Channel)

Enhanced Memory [Channel] – A superior ability to store and recall all information you are exposed to. (Soft Channel)

Divine Mystery, The [Society] – Origin of life on Psiere. Who were the Makers, where did the Makers go, and why is there no history for Psierians beyond a few hundred rotos?

Ferrokinesis [Channel] – The ability to physically manipulate iron, with the mind. (Hard Channel)

Foot [Measurement] – 12".

Git [Society] – Expletive, curse. Derogatory term for someone who is an unpleasant or contemptible person.

Gozen [Natural] – Goose/geese.

Grav [Natural] – Gravity.

Guardian [People] – This is a soldier serving in the Psi Shield Corp, placed in protective duty of a sovereign.

Halcyon [Planetary] – Island that is home to the Halcyon Station, the location of the last Tau Ceti (Watcher) on Psiere.

Hand [Measurement] – 6".

Hauler [Transportation] – Six-wheeled vehicle for supplies = Max speed 100 mph.

Humore [Society] – Humor.

Illeos [Planetary] – Smaller blueish-white sun, second to rise in the morning. Part of a binary stars set.

Illeostones [Planetary] – Mineral that releases aether in the presence of water. Size can vary from larger down to microscopic elements that can be found within the bodies of all living things on Psiere. The stones glow blueish white when emitting aether and are fairly common. Full Illeostones release aether which powers machinery and other devices.

Imperium [People] – The elected body that rules Psiere in conjunction with the Queen. The Queen has the majority of the power. The King is an automatic member of the Imperium and is responsible for presenting the Queen's agenda as well as breaking voting ties when enacting new laws and governing Psiere in general.

Ince [Measurement] – 1"

Instrae [People] – Professor, researcher, teacher, instructor, etc.

Interpretists [People] – Citizens whose sole career is translating ciphers, ancient artifact schematics, and other texts of the Divine Mystery.

Intinerist [People] – Scheduler, administrative assistant.

Intuition [Channel] – A superior ability to understand something immediately, without the need for conscious reasoning. (Soft Channel)

Judex [People] – Judge.

Juni [Measurement] – Fourth lune (month) of the roto. (year)

Karillite [Natural] – A viridian (green) gemstone native to Psiere.

Laeva [Measurement] –

Leviathan [Natural] – Giant squid, a beast of the Deep, controlled by the Atlanteens. Has an average weight of 5000 lbs, tentacle length of 140 foot, and a 12" eye. The tentacles are covered in suckers with jagged teeth ringing the inside, and feature claws along the edges of each appendage that can rotate or even retract.

Levitation [Channel] – The ability to physically lift yourself, with your mind. (Hard Channel)

Lune [Measurement] – Month. (Marte, Apree, Maia, Juni, Quinta, Sexte, Septa, Octobra, Novea, Deka)

Mahl [Measurement] – Mile, 5280 foot.

Maia [Measurement] – Third lune (month) of the roto. (year).

Makers [People] – The Psierian name for the Tau Ceti.

Maman [People] – Family. Mother, informal like mama.

Mamanar [People] – Family, Mother-in-law.

Mamano [People] – Family. Mother, informal like mama. 2nd mother in same sex parent couple.

Marte [Measurement] – First lune (month) of the roto (year).

Medican [People] – Medical professional.

Meen [Measurement] – Minute, 60 meens in an oor.

Mir [Planetary] – River.

Moto [Transportation] – Four-wheeled vehicle for passengers, average max speed of 100 mph.

Mous [Natural] – Mouse.

Novea [Measurement] – Ninth lune (month) of the roto (year).

Oath of Consorage [Society] – Betrothal.
Oathing [Society] – Betrothing.
Obsidae [Natural] – Obsidian.
Octobra [Measurement] – Eighth lune (month) of the roto (year).
Oor [Measurement] – Hour.
Operae [Society] – Opera.
Ova [Natural] – A mature female reproductive cell. Egg.
Papan [People] – Family. Father, informal like dad.
Papanar [People] – Family. Father-in-law.
Papano [People] – Family. Father, informal like daddy. 2nd father in same sex parent couple.
Par [People] – Family. Spouse.
Paren [People] – Family. Parent.
Parsib [People] – Family. Sibling through consorage. Brother-in-law or sister-in-law.
Patruus [People] – Family. Uncle, male sib of parent.
Pelma [Natural] – Palm tree.
Polycyclon [Society] – Truth serum in gas form, nut derivative.
Portea [Planetary] – Port, distilled wine.
Praefectus [People] – Continental governor.
Prescience [Channel] – The ability to know something before it takes place, foreknowledge. (Soft Channel)
Preservist [People] – Salvo Corp personnel. Search and rescue, fire, life guard, and more.
Psera [People] – Madam, honorific.
Psero [People] – Mister, honorific.
Psi [People] – Citizens of Psiere, Psierian.
Psi Academic Corp [Citizen Corp] – Instructors, and teachers at the Academy, as well as all other local primary education facilities in Psiere.
Psi Codice Corp [Citizen Corp] – Psi that deal with Psierian law in some capacity. Telepath/ psychometry teams, executioners, security specialists for the islands, judex, and judiciary reviewers, etc.
Psi Defense Corp [Citizen Corp] – Soldiers and officers that are tasked with defending home and country. Military corp.
Psi Divinity Corp [Citizen Corp] – All professions related to solving the divine mystery. Adventurists, interpretists, engineers and other professions assigned to adventurist teams. Funded

partially by the government and partially by the schematics, inventions, and artifacts found on their expeditions.

Psi Engineering Corp [Citizen Corp] – Psi whose responsibility lies within public service works, roads, bridges, inventions, schematic adaptions, research, etc.

Psi Medi Corp [Citizen Corp] – All medicans. Doctores, caretaker, therapist, etc.

Psi Politia Corp [Citizen Corp] – Imperium officials, governors, representatives (all elected). Kings have the option to transfer to Politia Corp upon ascendency to King, or they can decline and remain in their original Corp. Elected Politia help define problems in regions and potential solutions. Organize all the other corps.

Psi Resource Corp [Citizen Corp] – Psi that work with all parts of the resource industry such as mining, for stones, gems, minerals, as well as wood and other building materials. Also responsible for illeostone recharging and recirculation throughout Psiere.

Psi Salvo Corp [Citizen Corp] – Preservists. Fire and rescue, cross-over medicans and caretakers for rescue missions.

Psi Security Corp [Citizen Corp] – Law enforcement in the towns and cities across Psiere. First enforcers of Psierian law.

Psi Service Corp [Citizen Corp] – All other customer driven industries, such as art, entertainment, eateries, shoppes, and more.

Psi Shield Corp [Citizen Corp] – All personnel related to sovereign security. The military Corp personnel with the highest and most varied training of all others. Best of the best.

Psi Stock Corp [Citizen Corp] – Responsible for all Psi involved with food harvesting. Farmers, Fishers, hunters and more.

Psiere [Planetary] – Planet and country name.

Psychometry [Channel] – The ability to discover facts about an event or person by touching inanimate objects associated with them. (Soft Channel)

Pund [Measurement] – Weight measurement, pound.

Pyrokinesis [Channel] – The ability to physically create and control fire, with the mind. (Hard Channel)

Pyrs [Measurement] – Degrees, Fahrenheit.

Quaesitum [Transportation] – The first adventurist dirigible captained by Seema Velten. 60 mahls per oor top speed, 1400 mahl range. Larger than standard. Features new black kevlan bladder that is semi-impervious to damage and flame.

Queen [People] – Divine Cathedress, Her Royal Highness, Supreme Sovereign. She is the head of Psiere with an overall say in government decisions and direction, but she leaves the day to day running of the nation to the Psi Politia Corp.

Quinta [Measurement] – Fifth lune (month) of the roto (year).

Railer [Transportation] – A Train fueled by aether, with supplemental carts attached to hold illeostones and water. Passenger and goods conveyance on two rails sent on the ground. Max speed 100 mph.

Roto [Measurement] – 1 Year (10 lunes).

Sculptiste [People] – Artist, sculptor. In the Service Corp.

Sea squim [Natural] – Shrimp.

Sec [Measurement] – Time measurement, second. 60 per oor.

Seg [Transportation] – A shortened form of segment, slang.

Segment [Transportation] – A single car of a railer.

Seme [Natural] – Male reproductive fluid.

Septa [Measurement] – Seventh lune (month) of the roto (year).

Ser [People] – Military honorific, Sir.

Sexte [Measurement] – Sixth lune (month) of the roto (year).

Sharc [Natural] – Shark.

Sheddech [Society] – Curse. (explicit)

Shell [Mechanical] – Metal bullet fired from a pistol, rifle, or rail gun.

Sint [Society] – Curse. Derogatory term for someone of ill character.

Sonal Ocilloscope [Mechanical] – Sonar using sound for depth measurement. Sonal ocillator with scope.

Sonica [Mechanical] – Radar, frequently used in dirigibles to scan around them and below.

Sovereign [People] – Any member of the royal family with a direct line to the Divine Cathedra, including both the Queen and the Connate. Technically, only females of the Dracore line care the sovereign gene. (familial line was genetically created to rule by the Tau Ceti)

Stele [Natural] – Steel.

Sturgeous [Natural] – Sturgeon, giant fish, and common food source.

Sub-Connate [People] – Supplemental or secondary heir, not in line for the Divine Cathedra.

Sub-Instrae [People] – Assistant, lower level. Also, an instructor.

Tau Ceti [People] – Small, gray aliens that crashed their damaged interstellar ship on Psiere. They are the oldest known race in the universe and collectors of other species. They were responsible for genetic engineering the people of Psiere, creating the pyramids, laws, and all the artifacts and documents found by adventurists.

Telekinesis [Channel] – The ability to move and manipulate physically objects, with your mind. (Hard Channel)

Teleo [Mechanical] – Wired communication device, like a telephone.

Telepathy [Channel] – The ability to communicate and read thoughts and words mind to mind. (Soft Channel)

Teleport [Channel] – The ability to physically move yourself from one point to another point that is within sight, instantly. (Hard Channel)

Telesana [Channel] – The ability to physically heal the body, with the mind (subtle vibrations that speed bone repair, blood flow, disease eradication). (Hard Channel)

Telesthesia [Channel] – The ability to see a distant and unseen target using extrasensory perception. Far sight. (Soft Channel)

Templar [People] – Specialist who devotes their life to the Divinity Corp and the temples, higher level than interpretist.

Temple Charging Rooms [Society] – All expended Illeostones from around Psiere are returned to the nearest temple and sealed into a room with the Archeostone to charge. Five days in room with max capacity, about 3000 stones. (Small room 500 stones takes 2 days) Charged stones get shipped out to the entire continent as discharged ones are brought back in. Each temple has 4 stones.

Temple of Antaeus [Society] – Lost pyramid of unknown origin on the island of Magna. (Created by the Tau Ceti after crash landing. Standard procedure for extended stays on an unexplored planet)

Temple of Archeos [Society] – Great pyramid of unknown origin near Tesseron, the capital city of Endara. (Created by the Tau Ceti after crash landing. Standard procedure for extended stays on an unexplored planet)

Temple of Illeos [Society] – Great pyramid of unknown origin near Ostium, the capital city of Dromea. (Created by the Tau Ceti after crash landing. Standard procedure for extended stays on an unexplored planet)

Tempyrature [Measurement] – Temperature.

Therapeutist [People] – Medicans who specialize in mental and emotional therapy.

Tinkerist [People] – Hobby inventor. (usually with an engineering sub-degree)

Tracker [Transportation] – Treaded and armored military vehicle that can go nearly anywhere.

Tun [Measurement] – Weight measurement, ton (2000 punds).

Vectis [Society] – Tax on wages to pay for medican services and academy training.

Vectura [Transportation] – Transportation or vehicle.

Vestigo [Transportation] – The second adventurist dirigible captained by Seema Velten. 65 mahls per oor top speed, unlimited mahl range with an archeostone chamber aboard. Larger than the Quaesitum. Features new black kevlan bladder that is semi-impervious to damage and flame.

Vineo [Natural] – Wine.

Vinier [People] – A vintner, or person that makes portea and other vineos.

Voteo [Mechanical] – Wireless communication device, like a walkie-talkie but longer range.

Weaslet [Natural] – Something like a weasel or ferret.

Weke [Measurement] – Week (6 day).

Whal [Natural] – Whale.

Yord [Measurement] – Distance measurement, yard (3 foot).

Chapter One

Shells exploded all around them and the ship shuddered beneath Olivienne's feet. The air was acrid and thick from a nearby fire, choking her. Another large, black dirigible swung into view and the sharp retort of rifle rounds was interspersed with the louder whumps of the other ship's rail guns. She was left exposed and unable to duck for cover in time. A body collided with hers at the last sec, taking the shells that would have ended her life. Olivienne screamed and clutched at the black clad soldier, tilting her chin just enough to see Castellan's dead eyes staring back at her.

"No!" Olivienne thrashed her head in denial even as her screams pierced the air.

The terror was real, the anguish beyond anything Castellan had ever felt through their empathic connection. She gently shook Olivienne to wake her from the recurring night terror. She hated that dream, seeing her own dead face from Olivienne's perspective. "Wake up, 'Vienne." She didn't rouse so Castellan tried again with a mental nudge. "You're safe, my love. Let's see those violet eyes, hmm?"

Olivienne gasped as she awoke and frowned until her eyes met Castellan's. Then Royal Sovereign Connate, Olivienne Dracore, promptly burst into tears. Great, gasping sobs tore from her and all Castellan could do was hold on and promise to never let go.

They remained abed long after the crying ceased. Castellan could tell Olivienne wasn't sleeping and continued to rub her back in comfort. Her voice was quiet in the darkness. "Do you want to talk about it?"

"No."

Six lunes had passed since they stood in the Temple of Antaeus and oathed to one another, yet the pall of war made it seem more like as many rotos. Attacks from the Atlanteens and southern rogues seemed never-ending and everyone was mentally and physically exhausted. Each weke brought new horrors to the Psierians split by a violent rebel uprising. Despite the passage of time, Olivienne had yet to move on from the loss of their long-time lieutenant, Gentry Savon. Nor had she properly dealt with what she'd done when Savon lay cold at her feet, and she stood heartbroken with mythical antoraestones clasped tightly in her hand.

Castellan sighed. "You have night terrors more often than not. 'Vienne—you cannot keep going like this, witnessing my death again and again."

"How do you know?"

"Some of the dreams are so powerful that I see them with you."

"I'm sorry."

"It's fine. But you need to address your fear because it's eating you from the inside."

Olivienne pulled back, anger raging to the forefront in a matter of secs. It was a classic sign of mental trauma that Castellan Tosh knew well after spending so many rotos battling the Atlanteens and such.

"And what am I to do about it, hmm?" Olivienne lifted a hand from beneath the coverlets and gestured to her own head. "Just scrub it all from my memory? We both know that's not possible. Instead, his death, and all the ones I caused, are like the blackest of stains."

"I know, love. I know." And Castellan spoke true because she had her own mountain of guilt from that dae. "But I've had rotos and training to learn how to deal with that thing you bottle up inside. It will fester if you don't let it out in a healthy way. I spoke with Gemeda this past weke—" She paused when Olivienne turned her head enough that the lights from outside their dwelling shone upon her angry countenance.

"What were you telling other people about me?"

Olivienne's volatility was uncharacteristic and it gave Castellan pause, but she continued anyway. "I told our friend that we're having difficulty coming to terms with the battle of King's Marsh. She suggested that anyone who is struggling should speak with a professional therapeutist, but we both know that would be a difficult task for you with things the way they are right now. Gem then suggested that if a professional can't be acquired, to find someone who can be trusted, even if they're not of the correct career corp. Select a person you feel comfortable speaking with so you can, at the least, get your emotions out in the open to be dealt with."

Olivienne still wore a stormy look and Castellan rushed on. "I'll understand if I'm not someone you lean on in this regard. Our backgrounds are too disparate. But perhaps you know someone else who has been through trauma and is not a soldier? Maybe they can listen and give insight. Perhaps your maman or papan?"

"I—" Olivienne threw herself backward onto the pillow from where she'd been propped up on her elbow. She sighed and ran a hand through the top of her hair in an attempt to untangle the inky tendrils. Fingers through the hair was a sign of frustration that Olivienne had picked up from Castellan. "I'm sorry. I know you're right that I can't keep on like this. I'm exhausted each dae, never getting enough sleep." She turned to look at Castellan. "Can you believe I missed three of ten bullseyes on the target yesterdae?" She scoffed. "I haven't done that since I was naught but a child!"

"It seems out of character."

"You think I should speak with someone?"

"I do, for both our sleeps and sanity."

Olivienne smiled and shoved her. "What about you?"

Castellan turned onto her side so she faced Olivienne fully. "I have been speaking with someone twice a weke for the past four wekes. I am under mandatory orders by Renou to see a corp staff therapeutist because of my role in the civilian casualties."

"Is, um, is it helping?"

Castellan pulled her close, so that Olivienne's head lay flush with her breastbone. A move she knew often soothed her love. "Yes."

Olivienne whispered back, voice slurring with

drowsiness, "Okay. I'll ask my papan for suggestions after our meeting tomorrow." Castellan had drifted to sleep meens later when she woke again to Olivienne's voice. "Thank you."

Castellan kissed the top of her head and slid into slumber.

Faces around the table in the queen's private meeting room were grim, but then civil war could be seen as nothing less than such. Olivara Dracore leveled a piercing gaze at Guldaat Sendae. "Engineer Sendae, what is the status of the new dirigible yard in Occasus, and of our fleet?"

"Nearly finished, my Queen. We are awaiting one final railer shipment of kevlan from Baen to complete the final ten dirigibles in production. The manufacturing facility is fully operational but we are still building infrastructure for the people stationed there. As Instrae Keeley Greene here can attest, we've shunted many newly graduated and some final roto engineering students to Occasus in an effort to aid in production."

Olivara smiled at the highly decorated, older woman. Castellan knew it was a boon to the sovereign cause that Guldaat had come out of retirement just to head up the northern dirigible production facility when they realized they'd lost the one down in Soflin. "Thank you, Gully. I appreciate all you've sacrificed for this. I'm expecting Templar Zane Aislyn at any time. Can you inform whomever is guarding the door to send her in as soon as possible? And don't forget to pick up your escort on the way back to your quarters here in Tesseron. I believe they've already selected your security detail."

Engineer Sendae stood and bowed. "I will, my Queen." She picked up her tablet and glanced around the table. "Good dae to the rest of you."

Before she could open the door, Zane Aislyn pushed her way inside. "Sorry I'm late. I had a last meen review with the secure interpretists before heading over here. Traffic through the city is a snarl right now with the roads nearest the bay closed off." Everyone nodded in understanding as the head of the Divinity Corp took a seat in Guldaat's empty chair and placed a stylus and book of vellum sheets on the table in front of her.

Olivara waited for her to settle, then turned her gaze to the next person down the table. "Keeley, how many final rotos do we have left to spare? I know it's not an ideal work training assignment, and I regret so many have to cut their in-class education short. Unfortunately, war knows no schedule but its own."

Instrae Green frowned. "Not many, I'm afraid. We sent off quite a few of them from all corps to aid in defense and preparation, per Leniste's request. The assignments were mostly based on channel talent rather than corp selection. We have many with ferrokinesis helping with weapons and shell manufacture. Those and the telekinetics were also assigned along the southern border to aid construction of rail gun lines and defense walls. Leniste can probably give you a better report about assignments since much falls under the jurisdiction of emergency placement right now. The academy halls on Instrucia are fairly picked clean."

"I know they are, and I've already seen the many assignment reports from defense. I regret having to send Psierians who are so young into something large and dangerous, but all of Psiere needs to help quell this uprising or we will fail as a society. Even a ten percent loss of life is too much. I wish we weren't so in the dark as to what's going on down there!"

Everyone in the room knew that even if the country was split on the queen, Olivara would never be split on Psiere. They were all her people, to the final psi.

"My Queen, if I may?" General Germaine Leniste's low voice cut into the mood of the room. Olivara nodded for him to continue. "I received word from Dromea just before this meeting and I've got fresh intel to share with the group."

Castellan raised a pale brow. "Reliable?"

General Leniste smiled at her. "Only if your word is to be believed."

"Come again?"

The barrel-chested man laughed and shook his head.

"It seems our lost bird has come home to roost. First Lieutenant Sinta Cando showed up in Annexus two daes ago, a little worse for wear."

After a sec of shock, multiple people spoke at once.

"But—"

"How is that possible?"

Leniste held up a hand to stay the questions. "Cando spent lunes doing reconnaissance around Dromea when she realized she was cut off from the north. Then, the blasted woman took it upon herself to make the long journey beneath the bottom of the railer line where it crosses the Solis Sea, refreshing herself at each island."

Castellan shook her head and smiled. "I'm not surprised she'd do such a thing. Cando showed a lot of promise when I was her lieutenant commander. And what news?"

"Pon Havington's forces are not as united as we thought. Cando says that Havington started the takeover slowly and quietly. She overheard her commanding officer talking to others of the upper ranks about Havington's plan."

"That would be Lieutenant Commander Seevert Bello. He replaced me in Ostium. Fairly useless was my impression of him."

Leniste grimaced. "Yes, well, according to this Bello, only a few of the top ranks were persuaded to Havington's side. For those that weren't, they were either replaced, or had at least one family member taken to a prisoner camp on a large island just north of Gomen."

"If it's the one I'm thinking of, that would be Ruina. Smart decision."

Everyone looked at General Camen Renou. She gestured around the table. "Think on it. If you have limited resources and want to keep people in line, you'll only take as much as you can guard. After all, consider your own families. What would you do for the most precious person in your life?"

"Blast, but she's right." Leniste scratched at the scruff along the side of his jaw. He sighed and continued with his original dispatch. "Anyway, Cando reported that the rebels have General Tenet for sure, but from what you've indicated, Tosh, he and Havington have been in each other's pockets for rotos."

"Yes, ser."

"So, we have top leadership that's either cooperating willingly with Pon, or they're being coerced through fear for someone in their families. Most folks are still going about their dae-to-dae lives. Havington has two main cities where the rebels are concentrated, Ostium and Soflin, but they have key players in all the main cities of Dromea. They also have the shards of Antorae as an added threat to keep the civilians in line."

Olivara raised her hand to interrupt. "Even with the shards, how are they keeping control with so relatively few people? The population on Dromea is nearly that of Endara."

He shook his head. "Havington is smart. One thing he did straight-away was take control of transportation. Every railer has a small contingent of rebels, and the rebel dirigibles are thick as illeostones in a charging room down there. They've taken over the transportation hubs, which encompasses all means of mass conveyance for citizens and supplies. That blasted man also set up checkpoints on the speedways heading into and out of the four main cities."

Control of transportation and resources was key when you didn't have everyone swayed to your side. Castellan contemplated everything Leniste had reported, but something struck her as odd. "Ser, that seems like a lot of strategic planning for someone who has not served in the militia corps. Not to mention, Havington never came across as a psi of that mindset. Could there be someone else at the top?"

"Ser Enik Gannon." Greene looked around the room. "You've reported that he is Pon Havington's right hand. Has anyone figured out who he is yet? The name doesn't turn up anywhere in academy records."

Queen Olivara moved her gaze from Leniste to Renou, the two senior leaders of the militia corps. "Any clues? Reports have him at forty or fifty rotos which would put him near the time any of us would have been at academy. This is a psi who is clearly intelligent and talented to have evaded capture for so long. We've had criminal reports on him for more than a decaroto. You can't tell me that a person of his intellect and temperament just materialized from nothing!"

"Germaine," Leniste looked to his fellow general. "I heard rumors back when I was at academy, feels like a hundred rotos ago now." The group laughed. "Supposedly, there was scandal involving someone a few levels ahead of me and Olivara. You were a handful ahead of us, do you recall anything about that?"

"Hmm..." He rubbed his chin. "You know, I think I do remember that. It was so blasted long ago, and trying to pull a name out of my aether-addled brain from a time when I was but a boy..."

Olivara tilted her head in thought. "It started with an n, I'm certain of it."

Everyone jumped when Leniste slapped the table. "Nikone! His name was Nikone Gnan. I believe he got expelled for breaking into the academy head's office and attacking the instructor who found him. He was of age and supposed to be taken to Aetate for rehabilitation but disappeared before they could cart him off."

"That's him." Castellan's confidence on a matter that took place long before she was born caught them all by surprise.

Olivienne touched her future par's hand. "How can you be so sure?"

Castellan grinned. "Well, besides my channel jangling something fierce at the mention of that name, it's pretty obvious."

"How so, Tosh?" Olivara said.

"Ser, Enik Gannon is naught more than the rearranged spelling of Nikone Gnan."

"By the Makers, she's right!" Leniste exclaimed.

Olivara pointed to Greene. "I want everything you can find on this Gnan character when you get back to Instrucia. Family, other social ties at the time he disappeared, channels and testing results, everything!"

"Yes, my Queen."

Olivara took a deep breath and closed her eyes to see if the name would trigger a clairvoyant or prescient episode, a move that was familiar to everyone in the room. She sighed and shook her head. "I'm not getting anything, so here is what we need to do. Someone take this down, please."

"I've got it." Zane opened her vellum book and readied her stylus.

"The way I see it, we have four main priorities." Olivara ticked each one on her fingers as she spoke. "We need to defend the coast from both rebels and Atlanteens. We have to find a way to free any individuals being held on Ruina so we can neutralize those unwilling participants in Havington's uprising." She waited a meen for Zane to catch up scribing the notes before continuing. "And finally," Olivara shook her head. "The final two things will be difficult, if not impossible."

"What are you thinking, Maman?" Olivienne said.

"I don't like the idea of harming our citizens, especially if they're caught up in a war that is not of their making." Olivara frowned and Castellan suspected she thought of her own time fighting. "I want to find a way to immobilize the enemy combatants without killing them."

"My Queen—" Leniste stopped speaking when Olivara raised her hand.

"And my last wish is to find a way to negate psi channels, in an effort to take away the advantage they have with those poxing shards."

Leniste grumbled and Zane stopped writing.

"Is that even possible?" Keeley said. "We've not found anything in the research on Instrucia."

Zane added, "Neither have we read any accounts of such within the many velums left behind by the Makers."

"Not for as long as I can remember. Not even a hint of such a thing." Keshien tugged at his short, black beard in frustration. He'd been an adventurist for many rotos before consoring with the queen and becoming her chief advisor.

Olivienne shook her head. "Same here, despite the headway the interpretists have made the past few lunes with that new temple key. While I'm on board with both those final tasks, I just don't see how either can be done."

"My Queen," Castellan said. "This is not something I suggest lightly, but would it be possible to negotiate with the Atlanteens? The way I see it, they are a critical part of Havington's power structure. They control the waters and are one of the main instigators of attack along our major port cities. Is there a way we can discover what he promised them, and find an alternate solution?"

Leniste's gruff voice and expression carried a good amount of doubt. "And why would they negotiate? What advantage could we offer them that Pon hasn't already promised?"

Castellan frowned. "I know Pon Havington as well as any who has spent five long rotos in his frequent presence. He is a cunning liar and I think it's obvious by now that he doesn't have the support behind him in order to fulfill whatever promise he made. All the reports state that Psiere needs a certain percentage of their stock to come from the seas. We need it. You can't control the people if you take away their food. While he may not be a soldier, Havington knows how to lead and how to say things in such a way to get what he wants."

"I'm listening, Tosh. What could we promise the Atlanteens in return? What would you tell them?"

Castellan replied, "I'm not a negotiator but based on what I've heard, our war with the Atlanteens was escalated long ago because of the hubris of one psi. I've seen them from afar, I've witnessed some watching from deeper in the water. I don't think they are an ignorant race, they're just different. I respected that even as I performed my duties as a commander with Defense Corp suffering under their attacks. As most of us know, the biggest precursor to peace is simple understanding."

"Very well said, Tosh, and spot-on analysis," Olivara stated. "One of the main problems with this plan would be contacting someone in the middle of a war without getting the negotiator killed. We would also need a powerful telepath."

King Keshien spoke with his gaze fixed solely on that

of the queen. "They'd also need sovereign authority to properly negotiate." It was obvious to all at the table that the queen and her par were having a telepathic conversation on top of the one being spoke aloud to the rest of the room. Finally, he nodded. "I'm amenable if we can keep you safe."

General Renou abruptly stood, bumping the table in her haste. "No, absolutely not!"

Olivara looked to her long-time friend. "I'm sorry, Camen, but I'm the best choice for this. I possess all the skills and talents necessary for this endeavor. A powerful telepath wove a web of deceit with the Atlanteens and it will take another to unsnarl the mess."

General Leniste echoed his compatriot's sentiment. "My Queen, we cannot endanger our sovereigns at this time—"

"No! We cannot endanger our citizens, and each meen we spend in this foolish fighting puts everyone at risk."

"Maman?" Olivienne's face was a study of fear and horror, making it obvious how she felt about her mother risking life and limb to parlay with the historically violent ocean race.

Castellan alternated her gaze between Olivienne and Olivara. "My Queen, perhaps I should accompany you, in case—"

"I'm afraid you'll have your own duties to perform, Captain Tosh. We all have our parts to play here and each is critical in this fight with Pon Havington. My team will begin preparation for contact with the Atlanteens. Zane, I want your secure interpretists to scour the archives for any reference to those antoraestones, or for mention of some way to disable psi without harming them. Olivienne, it will be your team assigned if an adventurist mission comes from this. You'll run dark, understood?"

Zane and Olivienne both nodded.

Keshien added a comment for good measure. "Everything we say in this room stays within the circle of trust, which means, if you haven't done a truth reading, don't share. Even then, use caution because there are spies aplenty once you step off the sovereign estate."

Everyone around the table grimaced, understanding the utmost need for secrecy.

"We need more information if we are to save the citizens *and* win out with Havington." Olivara looked around the table, gaze stopping at the Defense Corp General. "Germaine, find out all you can from our lost bird when she arrives in Tesseron and reward her with a post here in the city where she can do the most amount of good. We don't let valuable resources slip away. Savvy?"

"Yes, my Queen."

Renou chimed in. "I've got a few Shield Corp openings, if she's amenable. Dedication like that..." She shook her head.

"I'll leave that decision between the two of you." She moved her gaze back to Instrae Keeley Greene. "Keeley, I need that information yesterdae." The head of the academy nodded to acknowledge her order. "Now, I think we can adjourn this meeting. Let's shoot for another two daes from now unless we have something new come up. Dismissed."

People shuffled out, but Olivienne hung back. "Maman..."

Olivara waited until the only ones left in the room were Keshien, Olivienne, and Castellan. "Do you trust your team?"

Caught off guard, Olivienne tilted her head and spared a glance for her future par, who also happened to be the head of her Shield Corp unit. "Of course, why?"

"Just as you trust your team, let me trust mine. They have a lot of varied experience, and I'll be sure to plan for any contingency. You know I wouldn't do this if there were another way, but negotiation is about trust and taking that first step. I want this to succeed, we *need* it to succeed. Please say you understand, my darling."

Olivienne took in a shaky breath before meeting her mother's identical, violet gaze. "I was undone when you were injured. I am not ready to sit upon the Divine Cathedra, nor am I willing to lose you for such a thing to happen."

"You are ready, whether you believe it or not. But you

won't have to."

"Have you had a vision?"

Olivara shook her head. "Not yet, it's gut instinct on this one only." She looked at Castellan. "What about you, Captain?"

Castellan frowned, knowing Olivienne wouldn't like her response. "Nothing but a vague sense of rightness to your plan. It's hard to say so far out though. But I know the Atlanteens and while it may seem strange to you three, they do have a sense of honor. My own instinct tells me that they wouldn't send their denizens to die so needlessly unless someone were forcing their hand. They've always come across as being more respectful of the ocean life than those of Psierians. Something that sounds strange given my career with Defense Corp. But I noticed a change happening before I left for the north."

"What are you trying to say?" Olivara appeared genuinely curious.

"It's just that, when I served down in Ostium, some of those attacks struck me as odd. Out of character, if you will. It makes me suspect that Havington has been planning this for a long time. Rotos, even."

"I'll keep that under consideration then. Thank you. Now, if neither of you have more questions, I'm off to retire for the evening. These late-night sessions are draining for an old queen."

Castellan snorted. "Begging your pardon, but you're not at all old. I'd wager you could give half the Defense Corp a run for their money."

Keshien's look was full of mischief. "Not the Shield Corp?"

"I would never disparage my *current* corp, ser! I'm afraid the rest are fair game." She winked to show she was joking. Olivienne was the only one who didn't laugh. Castellan could feel the vague emotion through their limited empathy channel and knew Olivienne's thoughts were heavy enough to weigh her tongue in a time of desperate joviality. She was about to suggest a late meal on the way out the door, but her tentative plans were unhitched by Olivienne's sudden request.

"Papan, do you have some time to speak with me?"

The elder royal couple stopped and met one another's gaze before Keshien smiled at his daughter. "Of course. Is something wrong?"

Olivienne looked from her mother to Castellan, and Castellan knew what it was about. "It's just, I have some questions for you. We can talk tomorrow if that's a better time."

Olivara patted her par's hand. "Go on, darling. Captain Tosh can walk me back to the royal residence. I'm not doing more than having a bit of scotch before bed anyway." They were currently in a separate building set off from the palace. Olivara had offices at the Imperium but none of their small counsel thought they'd be secure enough for their needs. Instead, they chose to meet on the grounds of the sovereign estate.

He nodded at Olivara, and as they embraced, Castellan gave her own love a telekinetic squeeze. She kept her conversation telepathic so it would remain private, or as private as one could get whilst sharing a room with the strongest telepath in Psiere. *Will you speak with him about your fears?*

Olivienne's fine, dark brows drew down with worry. *Is that okay?*

More than okay, I hope it helps. I'll let the team on duty know that you'll be a bit longer.

Thank you.

When Olivara was ready to go, Castellan stuck out her elbow to properly escort her future mamanar. As they were walking away, she overheard the king say, "Let's take a walk through the gardens. The paths are well-lit, but more importantly it's private."

Once they'd left the building, in the opposite direction that father and daughter had gone, Olivara spoke up. "Something troubles her, more than just fear for myself or our people."

Castellan sighed. It wasn't a matter of breaking confidence to tell Olivara, but she didn't want to burden the sovereign more than she already was. Unfortunately, Olivienne's tenaciousness was only eclipsed by one other psi, and that was Olivara herself. "She has not dealt well with the events over King's Marsh."

"How do you mean? Is she suffering some physical ailment?"

"No. This is something I've seen many times in soldiers who weren't ready for the rigors of vicious battle. It is mental trauma from which she suffers, not as easy to treat as a pain of the body. I, myself, have gone to a therapeutist but 'Vienne has spoken with no one. Until now, she's refused because she didn't want to burden anyone else with her trouble. Not even me."

Pain flashed across Olivara's face. "Oh. I hadn't realized she'd not gotten help. I knew she struggled after the loss of Lieutenant Savon but I had no idea how much."

"My Queen, if I may..." Castellan stopped walking and Olivara turned to look at her when their arms slipped apart.

"Go on."

"It's not merely Savon's death that torments her. It's the death of everyone aboard that dirigible she torched. She said the flaming bodies falling to their deaths would haunt her for the rest of her life. I know how she feels, perhaps on a stronger level than most. My own hands didn't come away from that battle unbloodied. I suspect the entire shield unit was affected similarly." Castellan swallowed and looked away from Olivara's penetrating stare. Even though it was too dark along the path between buildings, she could still imagine the disconcerting purple gaze that looked so much like her own love's.

"Very rarely do any of us make it through life unscathed in some fashion. And when it comes to speaking with someone who understands trauma, I think Keshien is an excellent choice. Don't despair or take it personally, Tosh. She's made the first step toward getting help. As for your team, you should address it sooner rather than later, I think."

They began walking again. "Thank you, and you're right. I know that Olivienne and I are different when it comes to the violence associated with battle. Of the lot of us that were there that dae, she was the lone civilian. I suspect that she fears I may not understand what is in her head. I hope you're right about the king. Maybe their similar adventurist backgrounds will allow her to confide in him in a way she couldn't do with anyone else."

"Perhaps. Because of your experience, I know that you of all people can see why I want this finished as quickly and with as little loss to both sides as possible. It's not just about saving citizens from death, it's about keeping all those psi out there from losing someone they love, children, parens, pars, and sibs."

Castellan's thoughts ran quiet for a meen as she took in Olivara's words. "I understand." She glanced to the woman walking on her left as they approached a small side entry into the palace. Olivara's shield team on duty ranged all around them, with one already ahead opening the door. Castellan spoke before Olivara could enter. "I pledge on everything I am and will be that I'll do my utmost to help make sure that happens."

Olivara patted her arm. "I know you will, Castellan."

Castellan watched for a few more secs before following another path that led off to her and Olivienne's residence.

Chapter Two

Castellan purposely chose the shift change for her shield team meeting so she wouldn't have specialists interrupting their sleep cycles to report. They'd either be coming off duty, starting duty, or waking for the dae. As they were currently experiencing a rare rain squall outside, they all met in the large sitting room of the connate's residence. Shields lounged around on various pieces of furniture, similar to what Olivienne herself was doing. Others remained standing, like Castellan. She tapped a rolled map against her thigh and waited as the final few stragglers came in and shed their rain gear in the entryway.

"Ser, are we heading out on another adventurist mission soon? I noticed a lot of interpretist traffic to and from the royal offices yesterdae." Specialist Ben Devin's deep voice belied his young age and relative inexperience compared to some of the others on the team. Both he and Specialist Tian Meza were two of the more hyperactive members who didn't idle well in their downtime, much like Olivienne. A fact that vexed many captains before Castellan.

Lieutenant Auda Madlin barked out a command before Castellan could answer. "Stay your questions until everyone is here."

Castellan watched her team, observing their interactions and the way they held themselves. The death of Lieutenant Gentry Savon had touched them all deeply and personally. Madlin had been the more serious and pragmatic of the two officers, but she'd become more so since her counterpart's death. Even in this time of relative calm, she stood off to the side of the room with arms crossed over her chest and exceptionally rigid posture, as if she held herself together by will alone.

Castellan realized right then that she'd failed her team in a major way. Every one of Olivienne's shields should have gone to mandatory therapeutist appointments following

Savon's death. One of the things she'd struggled with after switching to the Shield Corp was with how different the job of shield team leader was from her previous posts in the Defense Corp. Their shield team was small, tightly knit, and they spent all their time together. They'd been forged as sibs as well as any actual familial ties could bind. A fact especially true for the connate's unit because of the things they'd seen, and places they'd gone. Both unique from what anyone else in all of Psiere had faced.

The shield unit for Olivienne Dracore had a fantastical and traumatic shared experience. In the past six lunes they'd discovered a place of legend as well as lost a cherished teammate. Savon had been one of the longest serving members in the unit and his death left a gaping hole, much larger than rank and role alone could account for. Castellan put a figurative pin in her thoughts to request mental health sessions for her specialists, at least until they were required to head out again. She sighed and the sound was easily picked up by the woman sitting at her right hip.

What is it, darling?

I realize now that all your team should be speaking with a therapeutist after the events of King's Marsh. It's just that...things happened so fast and we've been doing our utmost to hold it all together when it comes to your safety. I forgot that, while extremely capable, my team has weak times just like the rest of us.

Olivienne peered up at her but continued with telepathic speech. *How do you mean? Nobody has said anything.*

They wouldn't. But look around, 'Vienne. Neither of us has empathy beyond our romantic bond, but you can read body language as well as I.

Olivienne discreetly glanced around the room and frowned. *You're right. All this is because of Savon?*

Not all. Some have sibs and other family down on Dromea, some were just rattled during that dirigible battle, never having been under fire like that before. I'm going to speak with Renou as soon as we're finished here. I want to get them talking to someone, or multiple people, as soon as possible.

"Ser, we're ready." Madlin said.

The telepathic conversation between the royal couple ended and Castellan gave Olivienne a telekinetic squeeze to her upper arm just to show that they'd speak more on the subject after the meeting.

Castellan acknowledged her lieutenant. "Thank you, Madlin." She looked around the room and met the gaze of all thirteen people under her command. "As you may have realized, the events down in Dromea have precipitated this holding pattern we've been under lately. Security is tighter than ever with the rebels doing their best every dae to bring down the rightful rulers of Psiere." Angry looks met her words as the entire team was aware the Dracona line had been engineered to be rulers by the Makers.

"What I'm going to tell you doesn't leave this room. I've had a trust reading with each of you but that's not why I'm making you privy to our plans. We are a team. We plan together, we solve problems together, and we count on one another to get it right."

Specialist Necole Lear interrupted. "Pardon my saying ser, but defense would have never trusted mere specialists with anything."

Lear was one of the ones brought to the team after Castellan took over, previously serving with the Defense Corp as Castellan herself had. Castellan acknowledged the notoriously cocky woman. "You're right. But we're definitely not in defense anymore. Because of the nature of Connate Dracore's duties, we're not even a regular shield unit. That's why I'm going to lay out Queen Olivara's goals and we'll go through the points one by one to see if we can come up with solutions."

Madlin spoke. "Ser, we don't usually leave the outside of the connate's residence unguarded for more than five meens, even if we are well within the secure sovereign estate."

"It's been taken care of. General Renou sent over a trusted temporary squad when I told her what I planned to do with my team. We're clear for a time." Castellan unrolled the map and gestured to Specialist Dante Lazaro and Specialist Branda Leggett to each hold a side. Then she glanced down to where Olivienne sat with a book of vellum and stylus. "Connate Dracore, would you care to read the queen's goals?"

Olivienne smirked at her. "Yes, ser." A few of the specialists snickered, but all settled quickly when Olivienne recounted the four main things Olivara wanted to accomplish. "The first is to defend the coast, which we all know is a given. My mother also wants us to immobilize the enemy combatants in a non-lethal manner. Then she wants to somehow negate the enemy's channels, and finally, lead a rescue mission to the Island of Ruina."

"Ruina? That's down off the coast of Dromea and naught more than a speck amid the sea. What could be so important to prompt such a fool's run?" Specialist Eliseo Calderon had been a pilot for Olivienne's team for a few rotos, nearly as long as Savon had been their lieutenant. But before academy, Castellan knew that he'd originally grown up in a small town halfway between Gomen and Soflin, down on the southern continent.

Castellan pointed out the island on the map as Olivienne went on to explain the hostage situation and why it was so critical for their side to resolve. Olivienne also stated that the queen was going to attempt to contact and negotiate with the Atlanteens, an idea that took most of the black-clad shields by surprise.

Specialist Ciera Penn asked a question. "Do we have anything to go on for channel blockers? Have the interpretists at the Temple of Archeos found anything to suggest that channels could be stymied or inhibited somehow?"

Olivienne shook her head. "Not to our knowledge. But we're still combing through hundreds of rotos of untranslated Antaeus documents. This project is under high security and we don't have enough trusted interpretists to get it done any faster."

"Captain Tosh, Connate Dracore..."

"Yes, Holling?"

"Ser, this may be a far shot when it comes to ideas, but I just thought of something that may help with immobilizing the enemy without harming them. It's been my experience with the wild creatures of Psiere that each has their own unique abilities that can aid beyond what we normally assume at first glance. As I said, it seems a bit of a reach, and well—"

"Spit it out already, Hol! The Makers will be come and gone again by the time you share your ideas." The interruption was by Meza, young and ever so impatient. Though Castellan knew she didn't say it with rancor as the two specialists had developed a mentorship of sorts from the beginning when Meza had been brought in and partnered with the senior medican of the unit.

"Fine. I'm referring to the sirens. Do you know if the scienteres and biologists had a chance to study the cave up on Instrucia to verify if their attack vector was channel, chemical, or aural-based?"

Castellan and Olivienne looked at one another in shock. Castellan pointed at the medican whom she knew to have a keen affinity with all the wild beasts of Psiere. "That's brilliant! I'll be sure to inquire when we're finished with this meeting." She glanced around the group, glad to see a few triumphant looks upon their faces. "What of the rest?"

"Ser," Castellan moved her gaze to Specialist Lear. "Before I transferred from defense, I spent the past couple rotos stationed over in Guin. The oceans and seas are vast and it's a fact that the Atlanteens don't concentrate in one spot for long. I'd wager even Ostium didn't see continuous action and from what I hear, they were by far the worst besieged."

"You are correct. What are you thinking?"

Lear moved toward the map and pointed at a spot just southeast of Ruina. "The bridges that span the islands between Annexus and Kemit are only about two hundred mahls away. What if an attack was focused on the bridge to draw any Atlanteen or dirigible support the island may have so that a stealth team could come in quietly to the island? It would require precise timing, of course. All parties would have to be in place and the rescue team would need to remain outside the detection range of their sonicas."

Castellan rubbed her chin in thought, putting her rotos

of defense leadership to work on Lear's idea. "Hmm, it could be possible with the right support and perfect timing. The nights are certainly dark enough to hide the black bladder dirigibles, and it's better than nothing. Well done, Lear!"

She looked around the rest of the group. "Anything more?"

Specialist Ciera Penn cautiously raised her hand. "Yes?"

"Ser, if we are locked down in Tesseron for the time being, I'd like to volunteer for interpretist duty during my off oors."

"Absolutely not."

Penn's eye's widened until Castellan went on to explain. "We have enough shields to cover for any that are interested in translating the texts as well as cover other team medican absences."

Madlin uncrossed her arms at that comment and gave Castellan a curious look. "Medican absences, ser?"

Castellan sighed and took a meen to put her thoughts in order. Soldiers were proud and no one wanted to admit to weakness of any kind. "The past six lunes have been…difficult." Someone snorted at the understatement but no one interrupted otherwise. Castellan glanced at her future par. *Do you mind if I use us as an example? After all, I can't expect them to do something that I'm not willing to do.*

Olivienne frowned but gave permission anyway. *Go ahead.*

"I've fought many battles as both a defense officer and shield. And I can tell you that no one comes away unscathed. Not mentally nor physically. We," she pointed back and forth between herself and Olivienne. "We have not been spared from the battle over King's Marsh and I suspect none of you have either."

"Ser?" Madlin asked.

"I've suffered night terrors since the loss of Savon, blaming myself for his death. When my mind doesn't take the blame, it will kill others in Savon's place so that I end the night staring into the unseeing eyes of someone close to me." She glanced up at Castellan before continuing. "I'd never been in such a battle as what we faced over that swamp, and certainly hadn't seen someone I care for die in front of me. But beyond that, I brought down that dirigible with the power of my channel alone. The...the screams of burning psi will forever haunt me."

Olivienne took a shaky breath and continued. "It has been extremely traumatizing and I've only just begun speaking with someone I trust about it."

If everyone in the room was surprised by the words of their fearless, and somewhat reckless, connate, they were gob smacked by Castellan's declaration. "I, too, have been speaking with a professional therapeutist since returning to Tesseron, under General Renou's orders. It was one of the stipulations for me continuing my duty as the leader of this shield unit."

"Ser! Why would they take away your command? You're the best leader we've ever had." Devin's voice was filled with the surety of youth and admiration, as expected for someone serving in their first assignment after academy.

Specialist Gar Soleng wasn't on his first assignment and he had a steady head upon his shoulders. He'd picked up much of the extra burden with Madlin since Savon's death. "I've been under a few captains, ser, and I'd have to agree with him. You did nothing wrong over that aether-forsaken swamp."

Castellan nodded to him. "Be that as it may, I was responsible for dozens of civilian casualties. I carry a guilt that will weigh on me for the rest of my daes. As will the death of Lieutenant Savon." She held up a hand to stay the words of protest that spilled from each shield's lips. "I'm aware that you don't all know the exact details of what went on above King's Marsh, nor is that something I can tell you, despite my trust in this team. I'm under sovereign oath."

Many nodded at those words, each knowing the harsh penalty of breaking the queen's word. "Just know that what I did to end that battle could have happened sooner but I put it off in an attempt to hold onto that secret."

"Sounds like you were banged either way. Whilst none of us know the details of how, we all know *what* you did up there. You saved our lives. More importantly, you saved the connate's life. And well, ser, as I learned a long time ago from my papan, better late than never."

Castellan observed her remaining lieutenant, instinct telling her that Madlin was going to open up. Sure enough, Madlin sighed and looked around to meet the faces of the rest of her team and admitted, "I was afraid to come forward before but the captain is right. I, too, have suffered since that dae but I haven't said anything. I thought I could get past it on my own." She met Castellan's gaze. "But I can't. I only get a few oors sleep a night and I'm constantly afraid I'll fail, afraid that I'll be seen as an imposter because I'm not half the lieutenant that Savon was."

Castellan put her hands on her hips and thought on her own sessions with the therapeutist. "How many of you have had flashbacks to that dae?" Every hand went up. "What about night terrors, or trouble sleeping?" All but a few of the hands stayed up.

Dozier shrugged at Castellan's questioning look. "I never remember my dreams, ser. Just." She snapped her fingers. "Out like a torch each night."

"What about mood swings, excessive guilt or emotional numbness, or even outbursts of anger?"

More than a few people nodded, others pointed at their other medican, Specialist Almeta Yazzie, then moved to one of the communications experts, Specialist Dante Lazaro.

Yazzie shrugged. "It's true. I've often felt angry and out of control since that dae." She looked around at her fellow shields. "While I know logically that there was nothing I could do for Savon, it still pains me that I couldn't save him."

Lazaro's eyes were shiny with emotion. "I still wonder if Doctore Shen could have saved him if she hadn't needed to patch me up." He gave a broken laugh. "I always joke about my bravery, that I've got guts enough for anyone. Yet when my guts were spilling out, another one of our own lost his life doing what all of us are trained to do. And after? I haven't even had the courage to talk about my struggle. To make matters worse, I have been growling and snapping at everyone like a wounded canid." He looked around the room. "I'm sorry."

Castellan drew in a steadying breath and became the leader they desperately needed at that oor. Not a soldier, not a captain, but a leader. "We are a team, but more than that, we're a family. We're also just people who will make mistakes on occasion. My next words are for everyone in this unit, and that includes myself and the connate." She pointed at Lazaro. "You are brave enough." Then Castellan moved her gaze to touch on each member of the unit.

"You are strong enough, you're talented, intelligent, compassionate, skilled, and none of you is alone. We will be here for one another in the coming lunes. And no matter what, I trust that every one of us will do the job we are here for, protecting our sovereign." She paused and glanced at Olivienne before turning back to her group. "I trust you with the safety of the most important person in my life."

"You all have my confidence, too." Olivienne stood and walked around the room, touching the hands, arms, or shoulders of each shield responsible for her protection. "Every one of us will heal from this and be better than we were before. Much like Tosh, I consider you all family of a sort. And I thank you for your continued service."

Once she'd made a full circuit, Olivienne moved back to stand by Castellan and saluted the entire team. As one, they saluted back. More than a few had tears in their eyes but no one was ashamed.

Two daes later, Castellan sat in General Renou's office with a velum sheet clutched in her hands. "You've had lunes to think this over, Tosh. Have you selected a candidate yet?"

Castellan leaned back in the chair and let the hand holding the list dangle to her side, as the other raked through her pale blonde hair. "To be honest, I haven't. Things are fragile right now. The team is only just beginning their therapeutist sessions, something that I regret not seeing the need for sooner."

Renou gave her a small smile. "Despite all you've done, Captain, you're not perfect nor invincible. Even I didn't see the necessity of it and I've been doing this a whole lot longer than you. The two shields we lost in the queen's unit during the attack on Tesseron were new replacements for ones that decided to transfer out after a number of rotos. The bond with the rest of the team simply wasn't there yet. Lieutenant Savon's death carved a hole in your group that none of us were prepared for."

"It certainly did."

"But Tosh," Renou waited for Castellan to meet her gaze before continuing. "It's time to move on and try to fill that void. Our connate's life depends on it. Your future *par's* life."

As if Castellan weren't under enough stress, Renou's words drove the need deeper. "I know, I *know*. Logically, I'm fully aware that Savon isn't irreplaceable. But for the first time in my life, logic isn't leading me here. I feel as though I'm capable of nothing but missteps. Do you have someone you'd suggest?"

Renou clasped her hands in front of her, leaving just the two pointer fingers point up to tap against her lips. "As it so happens, I've got dibs on Lieutenant Sinta Cando. She's not on the current recommendation list for transfer, but I think that based on previous notes in her record, as well as all she's been through the past few lunes, Cando would make an excellent shield." Castellan gave her a skeptical look and Renou added, "My instinct hasn't steered me wrong yet. After all, I tried to recruit you all those rotos ago, then again when the connate needed a shield lead."

"Great shield maybe, but I can't have her on my team."

Renou's mouth dropped open and fine gray eyebrows lifted with shock. "Whatever do you mean? Tosh, you yourself wrote the last glowing recommendation in her file!"

Castellan grimaced. It didn't seem that long ago when she was forced to admit to personal dalliance in front of her commanding officer, and yet it wasn't destined to be her final time doing so. "That was before I transferred out from Dromea. I'm sorry, ser, but it wouldn't be appropriate."

"I don't understand. Say it plain, Captain, because I've no time for riddles."

Castellan straightened in her chair. "Ser, Cando and I had relations."

Renou's face darkened at the news. "With a subordinate officer *and* direct report? I never thought you'd flout regulation like that."

"No, ser! It was right after I'd handed off my post to Lieutenant Commander Bello. The evening before I was set to head back to Tesseron. There was a celebration to see me off. It was that evening when relations occurred. Had a pounding good headache the next morn, too."

"Stone brew?"

Castellan laughed. "I see you've done your share of time down south."

Once the humore dissipated, both sat in silence, then Renou shook her head. "I swear you defense have certainly earned your reputation and put a right spanner in the cog of my plans. That old saying is as true as ever, *hmm*?"

Castellan grinned at her, well aware of the reputation that the hard-fighting Defense Corp soldiers had amongst the other corps. "To start, I'm no longer defense so I take offense at the implication that I'd be such a cad on the regular." Renou chuckled. "And I'm assuming that you're referring to the saying that defense lovers are like railers, in that there's one coming in and going out of every major city?"

"Obviously." She sighed. "I wanted Cando, Tosh. But we both know my heart daughter well enough to see that putting an old romantic liaison under your command, and partially in charge of her security, would vex Olivienne to no end."

"I'm sorry, ser. Perhaps the queen's detail if you've an opening?"

"Perhaps. Let's move on then, no sense dousing a spent stone. Look at the list in your hand and tell me if any of those names ticks your intuition."

Castellan lifted the rumpled velum and ran her gaze down the page. Not one of them twanged her channels. "Nothing."

"Close your eyes then."

"Come again?"

Renou rapped on her desk twice. "I said close your eyes." Castellan complied. "Now...tell me the first name you can think of that would honor Savon's post. Obviously, we'd move Madlin up to first lieutenant."

Castellan did as she was instructed. She considered her team and its specific needs in regard to Olivienne's adventurist career. One name stood out above the rest. The man she'd seen pick up extra work over and over. It was the specialist with a level head, calm demeanor, and proven track record. Despite being a roto younger than Savon, he'd been on the team a roto longer. Castellan assumed it had something to do with the fact that Savon transferred in from defense, much the way she'd done, whereas the unit's senior engineer went into Shield Corp straight out of academy.

She glanced up to meet the general's gray eyes. "Specialist Gar Soleng."

Renou looked contemplative. "Soleng...isn't he the one that reports say took command the dae you and Savon both fell on the dextra staging deck during the battle of King's Marsh?"

"Yes, ser."

"And you think he's ready?"

Castellan looked back at the list in her hand. It may as well have been a sheet of coded text with no cypher key for all it told her. She met her general's gaze again. "With some supplemental officer training, yes."

"And does he want it?"

"I brought it up to him when I first interviewed all the shields who chose to stay on Olivienne's team when I came aboard as their commander. I asked if he had aspirations of advancement. Soleng told me then that he'd accept what came to him, but that he was happy serving on the connate's unit. I think he'll take the promotion in stride. Even better, the team trusts him."

Renou placed both palms on her desk and stood. "I have confidence in your judgement on these things, Tosh. I'll take care of the velum work for his advancement to lieutenant. As for the opening on the team," she nodded toward the sheet still in Castellan's hand. "There are a handful of unassigned shields on that list that have tinker-ist or adventurist sub-degrees. That would be best to main-tain the working balance you've achieved the past few rotos." She patted a stack of pages on her desk. "Their files are here for you to peruse. Pick one so we can onboard them as quickly as possible. Submit the request by noon tomorrow. No more delays. Savvy?"

"Yes, ser." Understanding she was dismissed, Castel-lan saluted, then grabbed the stack of files and left Renou's office.

Knowing what she had to do, Castellan rode her cycle back around the bay to the shield residence at the edge of the sovereign estate. Lieutenant Madlin was off duty for the dae as she'd had her session with a corp therapeutist earlier that morning. The building was large enough to house all the shields assigned to the royal family, though admittedly it was more than half empty most of the time. Olivienne's younger sib, the sub-connate, remained in Scola up on the Island of Instrucia to continue his academy training, despite his protests. It was safer than Tesseron, given the current problems with the rebels.

When not traveling, or attending a high security func-tion, the royals typically only had a third of their team at any given time. Normal shield units ran at twenty-two psi, with one captain and up to two lieutenants. Olivienne's shield unit was even smaller with a captain, two lieuten-ants, and twelve specialists. The number was low due to the hybrid nature of the team, functioning in a dual secu-rity and adventurist capacity. Despite Renou telling her to simply pick a specialist with an engineering sub-degree, Castellan knew it wasn't going to be so easy.

The shield residence was a nice place to live. It was

one of the perks associated with a job that may require you to sacrifice your life to save a sovereign on any given dae. It had amenities often found at holidae destinations. Savon once told her that, while he liked the exercise and recreation areas, the food wasn't as great as what they found on some of their adventurist missions. The captain came across a few specialists during her trip to the upper level where Madlin's suite was located, each saluting until she was past.

Lieutenant Madlin answered her door on the third knock, looking rather surprised. "Captain! Is something the matter?"

Castellan returned her crisp salute with her right arm, holding the stack of unassigned shield files under her left. "I'm sorry to stop in unexpectedly on your dae off but I have something urgent to discuss with you."

Madlin stepped right and opened the door wider for Castellan to enter. On the other side was a sitting room, not quite as large as Castellan's old suite in Olivienne's residence. "Come in and have a seat anywhere. Would you like some water, or chava? I can put a kettle on—"

"Chava is fine, Lieutenant." Castellan understood Madlin's nerves. Not only was it the first time she'd ever visited her lieutenant's personal residence, but she imagined that Madlin was worried about all their places on Olivienne's team after realizing the extent of their collective mental anguish. "This isn't about anything critical. I just wanted to speak with you about my decision regarding Lieutenant Savon's replacement."

Madlin abruptly dropped the kettle in the small sink at the edge of the room and some of the water splashed out. She quickly picked it up again, then capped it and placed it on the hot plate. The plates were powered the same way as all the other buildings throughout the cities across Psiere. Wind and wave generators were one of the greatest adventurist finds from before even the current queen had been born. Energy traveled all around the continents via underground copere lines. Castellan stared at the kettle for a sec and tried to imagine what their nation would be like if they had the kind of portable power that the Makers used in their water vessel.

"Please, have a seat, ser."

Castellan was startled from her wandering thoughts but she quickly chose a chair a few yords from the door. She sensed that she would get steadier feedback from Madlin if she waited until they had their chava before bringing up Savon's replacement. A few meens later, Castellan took a sip of her cooling drink and observed Auda Madlin.

She was sturdy and strong, and a few inces short of Olivienne's height. Madlin had dark auburn hair and expressive eyebrows. Her skin was deeply tanned, as if she'd spent a lot of time in the hot sun of the southern continent. Though Castellan knew for a fact the woman had completed most of her corp career in the north. Her eyes were a deep reddish brown, striking with her auburn hair.

Despite her perusal of the nervous lieutenant, none of Madlin's physical appearance mattered one whit to Castellan. Because she knew that Madlin was Shield Corp through and through. The woman bled the black and silver of their corp every dae of her life. Castellan took another sip of her chava then gave Madlin the news.

"We are promoting you to first lieutenant and moving Specialist Gar Soleng to be your counterpart. Rather than replace Lieutenant Savon from outside the team, we'll only have to replace Soleng." Castellan saw Madlin's shoulders droop as they lost their rigidity, and heard her let out a deep sigh.

"Oh."

"Do you have any thoughts on the subject, on Soleng?"

Madlin wore a contemplative look but shook her head at Castellan's question. "Actually, ser, I think it's a good call. He's capable, qualified, we work well together, and the team respects him. What did the general say?"

"Truthfully, she wanted me to take Lieutenant Cando, one of my reports from my southern Defense Corp post, as a replacement for Savon. She, too, is highly qualified, loyal to a fault, and would be a good fit in the shields."

"So, why didn't you? Did you two not get along?"

Castellan shook her head and felt a wash of heat begin at her neck and continue up to the tips of her ears. "Erm, no. We got along quite well."

Madlin chuckled. "Let me guess, she served under you during your command, and over you after?" Castellan grinned in response. "I always knew you blasted defense had more fun than those of us unassigned shields. There were only so many places training can take you."

"Yes, well, stability and a home are nice too."

Madlin tilted her head at Castellan's words. "But, ser, you gave up on all that anyway when you took over the connate's Shield Corp unit."

Castellan smiled as she thought of all she'd gained since switching corps. "On the contrary, stability can be found in a variety of places. For me, home is where my heart is held fast. Which means, wherever Olivienne is."

The lieutenant snorted. "You two really are sweet like portea. I hope to find that somedae, you know. Love."

"Not now?"

Madlin laughed aloud. "No, ser! Right now, adventure is my mistress and I'm having too much fun serving with the connate's unit."

"Even though—" Castellan left her statement open, but the meaning was easy enough to figure out.

"Yes, this assignment has given me my greatest heartache, as I suspect it's done with many of our specialists. But it's also brought the most amazing things into my life and taken me places no one else has ever gone. So, it's been difficult but worth staying in. You've got at least a handful of rotos yet before I'm too old, jaded, and lonely to continue with such a high energy profession."

Castellan burst into laughter. "By the Makers, old? Spend five rotos fighting the Atlanteens on that sunbaked southern continent beneath Havington's thumb, then tell me how old you feel."

"If that were the case, by your own words, ser, I wouldn't lack for companionship to keep me young." Castellan shook her finger at Madlin but both women laughed heartily.

"Anyway, back to the business at hand. We need to

pick Soleng's replacement. Because of your rank, I want your input on the candidates. I think it would be smart to select another specialist with an adventurist sub, but beyond that, I'm open. Do you have some time now to look at their files?"

"Yes, ser. When do we need to decide, and will you be conducting interviews soon for the new specialist?"

"General Renou wants this decision made by tomorrow. And *we* will be conducting interviews as soon as we narrow down the list to two or three and contact their officer in charge." Castellan stood and was quickly followed by Madlin. "Are you ready?"

Madlin waved her toward the dining table in the corner of the room. "As a railer looking to make time."

Chapter Three

"Munitions?"

Castellan shrugged. "He's from defense, but due to be plucked black any time now, or so says Renou."

Olivienne's dark brows rose. "But how in the world did he achieve an adventurist sub-degree along with that?"

"You know, Madlin asked him the same thing. Specialist Mohdra Sehg claimed that it had always been a hobby of his. He even has some experience translating Maker texts. He used to help out at the Temple of Illeos when he was naught but a boy."

"I trust you to know what we need, I always do."

Castellan snorted, remembering how belligerent Olivienne was when she first began putting the new hybrid team together. She decided the past was best left that way for the sake of their eventual consorage and didn't mention the connate's obstructionist ways aloud. They were on their way to the next meeting with the queen's counsel, and Castellan had taken the opportunity to inform Olivienne of her choice for Soleng's replacement.

"Anyway, Sehg is due to arrive tomorrow for shield unit orientation, which I put Madlin in charge of. We plan to present Sehg officially in two wekes when Soleng returns from his officer training. At that time, we'll also have a brief ceremony for Soleng's promotion to lieutenant."

Olivienne slowed as they approached the door to the same building that they had met in two nights previous. "Just our group then?"

Castellan shook her head. "Renou will be there as well. She thought it would be nice since we can't have much of a ceremony. After that, Madlin has orders to get him up to speed as soon as possible."

One of the queen's shield guardians opened the door for them and they paused inside to acclimate to the interior that was significantly darker without the light of their two suns. "Things are moving so fast. It's hard to believe you put all this together since our last meeting with my maman."

"To be honest, I suspect we're going to see even more change when this dae is done."

They continued down the hall, heading for the room near the end. Olivienne glanced sideways. "What do you mean? Did Renou say something?"

Castellan sighed. "Gut feeling for this one, I'm afraid."

"Well, did your gut say if it will be something good or bad?"

"My stomach isn't that discerning." Castellan paused. "Unless we're talking about Druvvian Scotch."

They were still laughing as they pushed through the meeting room door that was flanked on each side by more of the queen's guardians. As soon as they cleared the doorway, a scruffy-haired woman in defense blue stood and saluted them with a big grin. "Commander Tosh!"

First Lieutenant Sinta Cando's mouth made a little o shape and she quickly amended her statement. "I mean, Captain. They said you'd been promoted." She finally moved her gaze from Castellan to Olivienne. "Oh, my apologies, Connate Dracore." Cando gave a low bow to Olivienne.

Castellan was already rounding the table to pull Lieutenant Cando into a quick embrace with plenty of back slapping. "By the Makers, I can't believe you crawled all the way across the Solis Sea, hanging beneath the bridges like a howler! It's good to see you, soldier." Once their greeting had ended, Castellan moved back to sit by Olivienne, curiously noting her lover's pursed lips and a faint undercurrent of negativity through their connection.

Olivara clasped her hands on the table and moved her gaze around the room. "If you can all be patient for a few more meens, we're still waiting on General Renou and Templar Aislyn."

Leniste grunted. "I'm assuming Greene sent a missive rather than come all the way back down for this?"

Olivara inclined her head. "She did. As did Engineer

Sendae."

As they chatted, Castellan looked closer at Olivienne, and grew concerned with her love's stiff and unyielding posture. *Is something the matter?*

Olivienne glanced sideways then turned her gaze forward. *Whatever could be wrong?*

You're angry with me but I have no idea why. That's not fair, 'Vienne.

A quiet sigh crept from between Olivienne's lips. *"You're right, and I apologize. It took me by surprise, too. What did?*

Olivienne turned to pierce Castellan with her violet gaze. *Jealousy.*

"What?" Castellan forgot discretion with her verbal exclamation. Everyone around the table looked at them, and the queen frowned. Castellan grew uncharacteristically nervous. "Uh, please disregard that. Olivienne just told me that, er—"

"I told her something unexpected but it has nothing to do with any of our efforts here todae so please, carry on. I apologize for scaring the captain so." Olivienne gave the rest of the table a sweet smile and Olivara narrowed her eyes suspiciously.

Keshien stifled a laugh behind his closed fist.

Castellan gave Olivienne a telepathic squeeze of appreciation. *Thank you. Now, can you tell me what has you so upset?*

It's just...I've never seen you greet a subordinate officer that way. I know you served together for a short time down in Ostium, but still.

Well, you see, Cando and I had become friends before I left.

Olivienne raised a single brow and it was then Castellan realized her future par's expressions could be more deadly than any pistol. She elaborated. *Just before?*

Castellan swallowed at the expression on Olivienne's face. *The night before.*

I see.

Castellan took a deep breath. She heard voices outside the door and knew their meeting would begin in a meen.

She didn't want the pall of jealousy hanging over their heads, so she had to reassure Olivienne fast. She gave Olivienne an earnest look and clasped their hands together beneath the table. *I consider Cando a friend and a good soldier, nothing more. You and I have had plenty of lovers in the past, but there is only one psi who has ever held my heart. The same who holds my future. For now, and always, 'Vienne. It's you.*

Olivienne lowered her gaze. *I'm sorry.*

Castellan gave her fingers another squeeze. *Don't be. I've held my own share of jealousy for your past lovers.* At Olivienne's inquiring gaze, she elaborated. *The pipeball player?*

Laughter spilled out just as loud and abruptly as Castellan's exclamation from meens before. At the same time Renou and Aislyn pushed into the room, Olivienne waved a hand as a show of apology. "Sorry, everyone. Just finishing up our discussion." Then she added for Castellan alone, *For now and always, you are the one for me, too. Thank you.*

The queen lay both hands flat on the table, taking a meen to glare at her daughter. "Now that everyone's here and focused." She moved her look of chastisement from Olivienne to Castellan. "I want reports. Let's start with Leniste todae."

General Leniste cleared his throat. "As you can see, Lieutenant Cando came rolling in with the morning railer. We let her rest for a dae or so down in Annexus before coming north. She hasn't been officially debriefed yet, just the highlights reported when she made it across the island bridges of Solis. I wanted the details to be for this counsel's ears only."

Olivara spoke to Cando directly. "How are you feeling? Are you well enough for this debrief?" She warned her. "It could go for oors."

"Yes, my Queen. I'm still a fair bit sore and a little on the lean side, but happy to do my part for sovereign and country." She shook her head and met Castellan's gaze. "That Havington, he's worse than any sea beast we ever faced down in Ostium."

Castellan nodded. "A fact I knew well and warned you of before I trekked north to Endara. Despite the position you were left in, I'm glad you were on the ground to bear witness. Your information could be what we need to win this fight quickly and decisively."

"I couldn't have said it better myself, Tosh." The queen turned back to Cando and the younger woman swallowed nervously. Castellan knew she'd never shared a room with a sovereign of Psiere before, let alone two of them. "Now, I want you to start at the beginning and tell us everything."

"Yes, ser…er, I mean, yes, my Queen. You want me to recount what happened after Havington declared independence from Endara?"

Castellan hid a smile behind her fist. Cando was only a handful of rotos younger but she lacked the worldly exposure that Castellan attained in the past few rotos. And Castellan knew from personal experience how disconcerting the queen's violet gaze could be.

Olivara shook her head. "No."

"No?" Both generals, Leniste and Renou, spoke at the same time. Templar Aislyn merely pulled a stack of vellum closer and readied her stylus. She had volunteered to record the dae's meeting so they didn't have to bring in an adminstre for the task. The fewer who knew of the details, the more secure they would be.

"I want to know everything that happened from the time Captain Tosh left that blasted continent. There are motivations and machinations that span longer than a few lunes. Some of these events had to have been conceived at least a roto in advance, in order to have transpired so smoothly. In that regard, anything you can tell us of his actions, friendships, and orders, could be helpful."

"Yes, my Queen."

They spent four oors listening to Cando recount two rotos of Havington's actions, as she was aware of them, only stopping a few oors in for a short break. Once the debrief was finished, Olivara sent for refreshments for the entire table. "Lieutenant Cando, I'd like you to lunch with us for your inconvenience. After, Leniste will see to it that you're allowed to clean up." She turned to the defense general. "Be sure that she is given proper quarters and a fresh set of uniforms. Give her a close assignment in case we have more questions."

Leniste nodded.

Castellan noticed that Cando looked drawn and certainly thinner, as she'd claimed. Not at all the robust soldier that Castellan had known down in Ostium. One could only imagine what lunes of sneaking about could do to a person, all sources of mass transportation guarded and rebels at every turn. She peered closer and wondered how Havington hadn't discerned her intentions, especially if he had the power of the antoraestone shards at his disposal.

Cando looked up at that sec and caught Castellan staring. "Is something the matter, Captain?"

"You mentioned many details of your time spent down in Dromea before you managed to cross the transcontinental bridges. But you never told us how you got out from under Havington's thumb, and away from Ostium."

"I didn't?"

Leniste and Renou both sat forward in their chairs and the scratching of Aislyn's stylus stopped. Olivara tilted her head, looking from Castellan to Cando. "No, you didn't. How did you get free?"

Cando sighed. "If you remember, Captain, I'm originally from up near Baen. My parens and sibs all settled around the area so I wasn't too worried about having someone I loved nabbed by Havington or his lackies. But that meant if I didn't cooperate, I'd be eliminated for sure. Once the announcement of Dromea's sovereignty was made, I knew I had to double-time out of the city." She paused to take a sip of water before continuing.

"Havington wasn't taking any chances. He and Gannon were personally verifying the loyalty of the upper officers. They'd call people into General Tenet's office on the Defense Corp base. Some came out escorted by the General's top lieutenants and I'd never see them again. Others came out with a shard of shiny stone hanging from a chain around their necks. That stone seemed to be a badge of some sort and that's how the rebels recognized one another."

Castellan gave her a curious look. "And? How did you get free?"

Cando laughed. "I stole a shard, of course. You remember Sergeant Beng? He's the one that had a droopy mustache and was terrible with maths?" Castellan nodded. "He verified quickly after the announcement. I simply ambushed him one evening on his way back to quarters and locked him in a supply closet. After that it was easy enough to pose as a railer guard and nobody asked any questions."

Olivara leaned forward. "Ambushed him, Lieutenant? Even with the shard around his neck?"

"Yes. His channel ratings were shite, not much good for anything."

Castellan interrupted with a snort. "With or without his channel."

"Anyway, there's a saying down in Dromea. You can't wick sweat from a dry stone. Twice a low rating is still a low rating. His two tee-kay couldn't budge me. Truthfully, I may have laughed before ripping it from his neck and knocking him unconscious. After that, it was merely a matter of getting to the railer that was set to depart that evening. I still had to be careful in case anyone else from the Ostium base recognized me and became aware of my duplicity."

General Leniste grunted. Castellan recognized it as a sign of approval.

Renou prodded the explanation further. "You say the shard was a symbol of the rebels yet by your own words you were found out. Tell us about that."

Cando rubbed the back of her neck. "Unfortunately, there was also a key word given at the time the shards were dispensed. Unaware of this key word, I was caught out a few lunes after escaping Ostium. I boarded a railer in Eous, which is a small town on the eastern end of the con-tinent heading up to Soflin. I'd heard that they took the dirigible production facility there and thought perhaps I could garner some good intel, or at least, throw a spanner in the works. After all, I didn't want them producing such ships to use against those loyal to the Divine Cathedra."

"And?"

"And I was a blasted fool!" Cando frowned. I didn't realize at the time, because I'd been crisscrossing along the southern line, never following farther north, but security was extremely tight entering and leaving Soflin. Probably because it was the heart of the rebels' greatest weapons against queen and country. A two-psi team of rebels came into my railer segment, demanding proof of entry from everyone. Those wearing shards, like me, were taken aside and asked for Havington's word, which I didn't know."

Cando took another sip of water. "I realized I'd been exposed and bolted out the back of the seg, then had no choice but to leap from the railer to avoid their pistols. Sprained my ankle, but I managed to find a safe place to hold up for a weke or so until it was well enough to walk. After that, it was a matter of sneaking into Soflin. The rest from there you know."

Olivara nodded, clearly satisfied with the lieutenant's expanded answer of her escape. "I'm sure I speak for all of us when I say that I'm glad you survived such a harrowing experience and even happier you made it back to Endara with your valuable intelligence." She looked at Leniste. "Germaine, I want you to assign a trusted taskforce to get a highly detailed account of everything Lieutenant Cando has told us todae. Names and descriptions of every rebel she can remember, rotation and assignments of Havington's security, and an estimate on how many rebels are loyal to that accursed man."

"Yes, my Queen."

She turned back to Cando. "For now, I thank you for your service. There is a shield officer waiting outside to take you to temporary quarters."

Leniste looked at her with surprise. "When did you—"

Olivara tapped her temple and everyone around the table laughed. Cando stood, saluted the room, then left. Once she was out of earshot, Olivara addressed the remaining people. "The first news I have to impart comes from Engineer Sendae. The production facility is finished and the initial ten dirigibles were completed a few daes ago. Not only that, but one of those dirigibles is a special one-off made just for Captain Velten's crew. The *Quaesitum* was stripped of all functioning gear, adventurist and other, and fitted within the new ship."

"Maman, what is the new ship's name?"

Olivara looked to her long-time friend. "What did you decide, Camen?"

"After speaking with Captain Velten via teleo, as she and her crew are all in Occasus, it was decided to officially retire the *Quaesitum* and choose a new one for her replacement. Velten and crew now sail the best ship in any fleet, the *Vestigo*. As before, they will aid in all future missions for the connate."

Castellan spoke up first. "Improved how?"

Olivienne asked a question immediately after. "One-off? You mean the new *Vestigo* will be different than the old ship, which was *also* a one-off?"

Renou shrugged. "I wasn't involved with the design. You'll have to ask the king."

The excitement over a new and improved dirigible was palpable in the room. Castellan knew most of it came from her and Olivienne. Keshien explained the changes. "I spoke at length with Engineer Sendae and a few trusted advisors here in Tesseron. I explained what I wanted for you and your team and they were able to come up with a reasonable design that incorporated some of the added stones you brought back from the Temple of Antaeus."

Olivienne's mouth dropped open but Castellan was more reserved. "You're referring to the archeostones, correct? Does this mean what I think it does?"

Keshien grinned. "It means less illeostones, so more storage space. It also guarantees more power and no limitations on distance other than essential restocking of supplies. But the added space and increased speed would cut those instances in half."

"By the Makers! When can we get some of those for defense?"

"Or for the non-militia corps?" Templar Greene was quick to jump in.

Olivara shook her head. "This is it for now. We've set

up additional stones in a temporary charging room in Occasus to aid in getting the newly produced dirigibles fueled and ready to go. Let's not get ahead of ourselves."

Keshien gave his par's hand a squeeze. "Another thing this dirigible and others will have, is a large tonal oscillator, an LTO. A device that can emit a sequence of sound frequencies capable of physically incapacitating any Psierian. It was thanks to your medican, 'Vienne, that our doctores, scienteres, and engineers were able to collaborate on this discovery."

"Papan, how is sound responsible for the paralysis we experienced in the cave on Instrucia? If I remember correctly, there was no sound at first, yet we all froze in place."

He grinned, clearly as excited as any about their new discoveries. Castellan assumed it was from his many rotos spent as an adventurist before becoming the chief advisor to Queen Olivara. "You're correct in that the sounds you heard in that cave were not responsible for the paralysis. The scienteres found that the debilitating sound was sub-tonal. It affected the nervous system, thus causing the paralysis. The three-tone remedy you discovered coded on the wall disrupts that sub-tonal barrage and frees the affected psi."

"How does one defend against the sub-tonal sounds their own ship is producing?"

Keshien inclined his head at Castellan's astute question. "Crews carrying the LTOs will be trained ahead of time to use special ear covers that hold tiny speakers they can plug into their voteos. When the LTO signal is given, every psi aboard ship will don the special gear. Counter tones will broadcast through the teleos as the LTO is in operation. We considered simply stopping up everyone's ears with a bit of wax, but this way they can still receive important messages via the teleo."

"Good call on that. And other ships will have this?" The king nodded and Leniste stroked his chin. "I think this solves one of your objectives, my Queen. If we put this on enough dirigibles, we can render at least some of those on rebel ships immobile, perhaps long enough to incapacitate and take them into custody."

"That it does. I'm still working on plans for contacting the Atlanteens and freeing those hostages on Ruina."

"You're still going through with that contact idea? Maman, the Atlanteens are dangerous."

"I know, darling. But I feel this is the right thing to do. If we can remove them from Havington's side, it will mean significantly less casualties for all our people. I have to try."

Renou gave the queen a piercing look. "Have you had any visions about this yet?"

Olivara shared a grim look with Keshien. "I have, though it wasn't long. Just this past night I dreamed of quite a few things that I'm still attempting to decipher. An island across the ocean—"

Olivienne placed her hand on the table and leaned toward her mother. "Magna?"

"No, it was clearly something different from all the stills your team brought back. There was an active volcano and a living tree. I also saw Atlanteens with two legs like a psi, walking across the water. They had made it to land where I stood when great tentacles rose from the depths and towered over us. I woke immediately after."

"Leviathan?" Castellan's voice was urgent. "My Queen, I should be the one with you when you attempt to make contact with the Atlanteens. For one, I know and respect them. Second, there is no one else who has my power that can protect you from creatures the Atlanteens could send up from the deep."

"No, Captain." Olivara's voice was firm. "Your place is leading my daughter's shield unit. You are to protect her at all cost."

"But, Maman, who will protect you?"

"That is for me and my team to worry about. Savvy?"

"Yes, Maman."

"Yes, my Queen."

None of the other four in the room spoke up. All carried obvious worry on their shoulders but the queen's word was law and no one would dissuade Olivara once set on her course. "Good. Next on the agenda is news from Keeley

Greene. Shortly before this meeting, we received a secured file on everything they have regarding Ser Enik Gannon, otherwise known as Nikone Gnan." She pointed toward a locked case leaning against one wall of the small meeting room. "I'm sending that with you, Germaine. I want you to pull every detail you can from those velums to see where this rogue may be hiding when he's not tugging at Havington's coattails."

She took a deep breath. "I also want to know if he has any known accomplices, friends, or family living on Endara. We need to be sure there are no more traitors in our midst." Leniste nodded and Olivara rapped the table twice with her knuckles, then moved her gaze to the lead templar. "Zane, tell us what your secure interpretists have found. You mentioned that it may relate to one part of my night's vision."

Templar Zane nodded. "Yes, my Queen." She bent down to retrieve a case sitting at her feet, then quickly unlocked it and removed a stack of velum from inside. "In an effort to keep the discoveries organized, I've parsed the documents brought back from Magna to two secure interpretists."

"May I ask their names?"

Zane smiled. "You know them well, Connate. It's Cadentia and Lyndee. Because they are trusted, highly ranked members of the Divinity Corp, we made the decision to pull them north from the southern temple a handful of lunes before the rebel uprising. They were amenable as neither had deep family ties down on Dromea." She waved her hand. "But that's neither here nor there. What is important, is that those two specifically have been tasked with the Magna documents, while Interpretist Solgin is heading the small, secure team translating the rest of the Antaeus coded velums we've compiled."

She fidgeted a bit, straightening her stack of sheets. It was a sure sign that the templar was excited about something. "Lyndee has those velums that were retrieved from the Temple of Antaeus, while Cadentia has been translating the ones collected from the two towers."

"And?" Olivara's tone of voice and quick prod was

indicative of her impatience.

"I think you should decide its potential importance for yourself."

Zane removed the top sheet of velum from her stack and slid it across the table in front of Keshien until Olivara could reach it. The queen scanned the page in silence. She pursed her lips and raised a single eyebrow. Castellan smirked at how similar mother and daughter were. She'd seen the same look on Olivienne's face many times.

"What does it say, Maman?"

Olivara's voice held a curious lilt, one of questioning and confusion. "It appears to be a weather report." She looked up to meet Zane's gaze. "Is this correct?"

"Yes. It's not the weather that makes it interesting but rather the location. We only have one known active volcano in Psiere explored territory and that is on the Island of Navis. The coordinates of the report are nowhere near Navis."

Castellan stood abruptly and walked over to the large map of Psiere that took up an entire wall of the room. "What are the coordinates?" Olivara read them off from the document and she quickly marked it out on the map with pins made for just such a purpose.

"Why, that's in the middle of nowhere!" Leniste squinted at the map and shook his head in disbelief.

Renou frowned. "As was Magna, before we discovered it." She turned to Olivara. "So, this ordinary weather report gifts us with the novel information of not just a new island, but the fact that it's an active volcano? How does that help us?"

Zane pulled a few more sheets off the top of her stack and passed them around the table, starting with the king, on her right. "We have velum after velum of weather reports like this. What makes this valuable information is that they aren't just *about* this new island, they were *sent* from the island. Specifically, someplace called Halcyon Station."

"The Makers..." Olivienne's comment was naught but a reverent whisper and the sentiment was easily shared by all in the quiet room.

Castellan prompted Zane. "When was the report received?"

"It appears as though the reports end around the same time as all the other documents' final dates. Shortly before the Tau Ceti left the Island of Magna if your Nessie is to be believed."

Excitement and thrill jangled along the bond Castellan shared with Olivienne. She glanced to her left just as Olivienne spoke to the queen. "When do we leave?"

Leniste grumbled an immediate protest. "I hardly think that would be the wisest course of action right now—"

"As soon as your team is properly prepped and supplied," Olivara said.

"My Queen, Soleng still has two wekes remaining on Instrucia, and we've got the same amount of time to prepare the new shield, Specialist Sehg, in his duties," Castellan said.

"How long do you need?"

"To properly prepare, we'd need a minimum of three wekes."

Everyone waited in silence. Castellan remained standing at the map and the queen closed her eyes, appearing to be deep in thought. Suddenly she froze in her seat and her eyes rolled back. The king was quick to stand and hold her steady as Castellan rushed to her other side and grabbed her shoulder.

As soon as they touched Olivara, she shook violently. Then all three froze in place, eyes wide and unseeing. Her voice came out strong and her words filled the small room at the same time as they pushed into everyone's heads via her telepathy.

"Two birds with their flock, shaped into a silver pistol shell shot after two times six daes. Follow the slow water west to fly free and find the fire. Knowledge is the salve gathered to treat the burn of treachery. Speak silently to those with no voice for balance to prevail. One must give to receive fair measure. Above all, remember the difference between shallow and deep."

As soon as she finished speaking her eyes flew open and both Castellan and Keshien released their grips. All three slumped and panted as if they'd run for oors.

"By the depths, what was that?" Leniste was the most reactionary of those seated around the table.

Renou looked on with narrowed eyes. "I've never seen one of your visions trigger a fit before, Oli. That seemed much stronger than normal. Are you well, now?" Olivara took a few calming breaths as Zane quietly scribed the queen's words onto a fresh sheet of velum.

Olivienne remembered a few instances that Castellan had told her about before. "Your countenance changed when Papan and Castellan touched you." She looked at her future par. "Is this like when you touched Savon on the railer down by Vesper? Or when you had Madlin and Meza clasp hands to figure out how to unlock the research station on Magna?"

Castellan straightened and took a calming breath. She glanced at the queen then retook her seat. "I think it's similar, but also enhanced by the fact that two of the three of us are holding antoraestones. That was—" She shook her head as if to clear the remaining fog from a vision that wasn't hers.

"It was the most powerful prescient vision I've ever had. Not only was it clear in my head, but the overwhelming feeling of *certainty* that accompanied it was something I've never experienced in all my rotos." Olivara gave Castellan a piercing look. "You've done similar in the past, combined channels?"

Castellan shrugged. "It's something we've done on occasion in the field. Not anything I was taught at the academy, but rather a skill I figured out when I was early on in my officer placements. I'll admit, it doesn't work with everyone. But we get a bit of accuracy sometimes."

"Fascinating," Renou said. "It may be commonplace to you and your younger compatriots, Tosh, but I assure you that it's not everydae knowledge. I think we should pass this information along to Instrae Greene."

Olivara pursed her lips. "Agreed. Keshien, can you take care of that after this meeting?" He nodded. "As for your earlier timeline, Captain Tosh, it needs to move up by a weke."

Leniste snorted. "You've sussed out the meaning of your vision already?"

She nodded. "The first half was easy enough, especially since I was so tuned into it."

Olivienne grinned. "Clearly the two birds with their flock would be myself and Tosh."

"Yes, and the rest of that bit is me sending you and your team out via railer, along the Mir Tardus, to Occasus. From there Captain Velten and crew will take you across the ocean to this Halcyon Station. There is no longer a concern regarding distance with the Archeostones chamber onboard, merely what you'll find there."

"My Queen, if your vision is as true as I suspect, whatever we find there will help us quell the rebellion. That part about knowledge being the salve that will treat the burn of treachery is as good an indicator as any. Sure as anything, we need to put out Havington's fire."

Leniste rapped on the table twice. "Well said, Tosh."

"As for the second half of my vision, that was a bit more convoluted. I highly suspect is has to do with the Atlanteens."

Castellan repeated what the queen had said at the end. "Speak to those who can't for balance. And someone must give something to receive in fair measure. Sounds a lot like common negotiation to me. But what was that bit about shallow and deep?"

The queen frowned. "I don't know but I hope to figure it out in the next few daes, or at the very least, before I parlay with our ocean neighbors. We need to set these plans in place as quickly as possible before more lives are lost on both sides of the Solis Sea."

"Are you sure my team should be leaving so soon?"

"What's this? Is my daughter balking at an adventurist mission?" Keshien smiled at Olivienne, who looked away briefly before turning back to meet her mother's gaze.

"It's just that once we're outside the long range voteo we'll be in the dark as to the outcome of your task. If something hap—happens to you as it did when I was on

Instrucia, I'll be too far away to help."

Olivara reached out to take her hand. "I have been planning for this, 'Vienne. While all the details aren't worked out yet, I will confide what my team has come up with should negotiations turn sour. You may not know, but Captain Torrin is a high five telekinetic. If things go poorly and I can't control the situation with my own telepathy and all the other skills at my disposal, he's to take the stone around my neck and get us all to safety."

Olivara tilted her head toward Captain Torrin, where he stood just inside the door. "While he's certainly not Tosh in channel strength, I think the stone will serve to level things sufficiently for our plan to work. The real issue with all of this will be getting my call out to a representative of the Atlanteens to let them know I'd like to parlay."

Torrin finally spoke for himself after the queen was finished. "Everyone in this room has had their loyalty personally verified by Queen Olivara. But I suspect that no one in this room needed it. I may not be family, but I have dedicated my life to keeping queen and country safe." He looked around the room and met Olivienne's gaze. "I'll dedicate my death, too, if that's what it takes."

Renou sighed into the silence. "Let's hope it doesn't come to that, hmm? But you know the old saying, if you plan for every eventuality at least you're narrowing down ways where things can go wrong. So, let's plan."

"Here, here!" Leniste shook his head ruefully. "If I had a cred for every time an engagement went sideways...well, I'd have a lot of cred!" Everyone around the table laughed and the mood lightened.

In the shuffle of topic change, Castellan gave Olivienne a telekinetic squeeze to her shoulder. When Olivienne looked up to meet her pale gaze, she made sure only her love could hear. *I know you fear for your maman, but everything within me screams that this is the correct path.*

Correct and safe are not the same thing.

True enough, but she'll have Torrin with her. There is no one more loyal or capable.

Olivienne sighed and moved her hand down so she

could clasp Castellan's beneath the table. *He's not you.*

No, he's not. Castellan paused and Olivienne waited for further explanation, hoping for reassurance. *You know you're worth the world twice over to me.*

Olivienne glanced toward Castellan and smirked. *So, you've said a few times, before and after a good tupping.*

Castellan's ears turned pink at that, much to Olivienne's delight. But she didn't lose her line of thought. *I'm telling you here and now that I'd trust Torrin with your safety as much as I trust myself. With or without an antoraestone.*

"Oh." The word quietly slipped out, causing only Olivara to glance her way as Leniste droned on about supplies headed for Occasus. Olivienne inhaled a steadying breath then turned her gaze to Castellan. *"You think she'll be safe?"*

Safe as any of us. Maybe more so, considering we're the ones heading out into the unknown looking for an active volcano in the middle of the sea that may or may not have living Tau Ceti still there.

Olivienne hadn't even considered such a notion. *You think they are?*

Castellan shrugged.

Your intuition?

Tells me bullocks about this, I'm afraid. But think about all we've found to this point. We know they left to someplace that was previously outside any of the seeded species' range, at least according to past reports. I think we'll either find someone there still monitoring, or the Makers will have been rescued and gone back home to wherever they've come from in the great stars above.

They were interrupted by Olivara's raised voice. "If that's everything, I think we can adjourn this meeting and begin preparations for the daes ahead. You've all got your assignments, let's get to them."

Olivienne looked up startled. "Assignments?"

Castellan hid a grin behind her hand as the queen sighed. "If you'd been paying attention, instead of gazing into your future par's eyes, you'd know what they are."

Stubborn temper rose to the surface and Olivienne felt

her face warm. Castellan must have sensed her imminent outburst and placed a hand on her thigh and spoke up in an effort to maintain the peace between the two women. "My Queen, we were discussing your safety in regard to your upcoming meeting with the Atlanteens." She paused and threw Olivienne a pointed look, "Olivienne had come to agree with me that Captain Torrin was about as safe a protector as one could get."

The room had cleared out other than Castellan and her parens. Olivara stared at them for a few secs before conceding. "Fine. Your assignment is simply to prepare for the upcoming trip. And Tosh, I'm aware the ranking ceremony won't happen as it normally would, given the circumstances. But know that both General Renou and myself will be in attendance to congratulate your new lieutenant."

"Yes, my Queen." Olivienne and Castellan stood to take their own leave, bidding goodbye to the older couple.

Chapter Four

What was originally supposed to be a small celebration, turned into a decent-sized gathering. Everyone in attendance stood in a small clearing within the sovereign estate gardens. The connate's entire shield team was present, as was every member of Queen Olivara and King Keshien's. Also in attendance were Gar Soleng's immediate family, General Renou, and General Leniste. The queen stood in front of the crowd of onlookers with Soleng kneeling at her feet, his back to the people watching.

"Lieutenant Gar Soleng, the weight of protection falls on you more than ever before with this rank. Not only for your sovereign, but hundreds of rotos of tradition and the Maker science that made Dracore the ruling family of Psiere. You will help lead your team in shielding your future cathedress. Do you understand the enormity of what you're being tasked?"

Castellan could hear the man swallow from where she stood a few foot away. "Yes, my Queen."

"And do you accept the weight of your new rank, understanding that greater service will be required of you?"

The big man bowed his head briefly then looked up to meet his queen's violet-eyed gaze. "My life for queen and country. I accept."

Olivara smiled and reached out to pin the new rank insignia to the collar of his crisp, black and silver uniform. "Congratulations, Lieutenant Gar Soleng. I entrust my daughter's safety to you and the rest of your team."

He stood, bowed, then saluted. "Thank you, my Queen." After he turned to give Olivienne a formal bow, he saluted the rest of the crowd. Castellan was proud to return that salute.

Most of the shields didn't stay long after the ceremony as many had to get back to their regular duties. Even Olivienne's guardians had a crew that returned to their assignments once congratulations were given to the newly promoted lieutenant.

Castellan left Olivienne talking to her papan and joined Soleng, waiting as he hugged his parens and sibs. It was a big family so she stood patiently by. A youngster no more than a decaroto in age stared up at Castellan with her mouth wide open. Castellan could see the child working up bravery enough to speak and gave a gentle nod of encouragement.

"You're Captain Tosh, aren't you?"

"I am. You must be Elidar. It's nice to meet you." Castellan was a good leader, not only because she knew everything there was to know about her team. But rather because she sought to learn about each guardian's history, their family, and their legacy. She genuinely cared about where each member of her team came from as much as where they were going.

While Castellan could name each of Soleng's sibs from memory, there was only one she could assign to a face and that was the youngest standing before her. Their interaction caught the attention of the entire Soleng clan and Elidar turned to them, whispering excitedly. "She knows my name!"

Lieutenant Soleng's ears flushed a darker shade as he tried to pull his youngest sib away. "Sorry about that, Captain. She's been a bit stars struck about the shields since I was recruited out of university."

The girl broke free from his grasp. "Gar's the best shield there ever was!"

Galot, Soleng's tall second father chuckled. "Elie, weren't you just saying that Captain Tosh was the best shield there ever was?"

The girl scuffed her feet on the grass. "I guess I did." She looked up to her first papan, then moved her gaze over to her other papan. "Can't I think both are best?"

"That's not usually how *best* works, my lovely girl. You can only have one best." Relizan's voice had the same deep rumble of his eldest son and their eyes were perfect copies of one another, both a burnished orange hue. But Castellan saw that her lieutenant's height and build were definitely from his papano.

Castellan squatted down so she could meet Elidar's gaze. "You know, there are other categories you can choose."

"What do you mean?"

"I don't have as many sibs as you, just two that are younger. Tessior is one of my sibs, and he's a lieutenant with Security Corp. Tellesen is between us, and he's the representative for Portorium, so is with the Politia Corp."

The girl's eyes widened. "Are they famous like you?"

Castellan laughed, as did the rest who looked on, including Olivienne who'd just joined the small group. "I wouldn't call myself famous, but they're certainly not as well known. What I'm trying to say is that I know a lot of good Security Corp people. I don't know if my sib is the best but he's definitely my favorite in that corp."

Using a child's logic, the girl's face lit up. "So is Tellesen your favorite Politia person?"

"No, he's just okay." She winked to show she was joking and the gathered psi around them laughed.

"So, Gar can be my favorite, and you can still be the best?"

Castellan nodded. "It's true, you can think that. But what makes you say I'm the best?"

Elidar's voice was young but strong with her certainty. "Because Papan said you've done amazing things, and Papano says you're the most powerful psi in history."

"Strongest? Yes, I am. But I'm not the most powerful."

"What's the difference?"

Castellan stood and gave the queen a mental nudge.

Yes, Captain?

May I put on a small demonstration for the youngest Soleng? I want to set an example for the next generation and Gar certainly has plenty within this gaggle of sibs.

What will you be doing?

Lifting everyone at once?

Castellan saw the queen stifle a laugh while speaking with General Leniste a few yords away. *By all means, put on your little demonstration. It will be an interesting dis-*

traction.

"Tosh, what are you planning?" Olivienne narrowed her eyes, following the direction of Castellan's gaze.

"You'll see." Castellan then raised her voice and arms to catch the attention of the remaining people gathered in the small garden clearing. There was a massive stele sculpture behind the small dais where the queen had presented Soleng with his new rank. "If I can have everyone's attention," People stopped their conversations and turned to watch Castellan. "I've just had a question from Lieutenant Soleng's youngest sib." She turned to Elidar. "Can you tell everyone what you asked?"

The girl hid behind her papan's legs. "Will I get in trouble?"

Castellan smiled. "Not at all."

She stepped forward, clearly bolstered by the large hand resting upon her shoulder. "I asked the difference between strength and power."

Castellan spoke to the entire group, not just the single curious girl. "Strength comes in many forms. For instance, Queen Olivara is one of the strongest telepaths Psiere has ever known. Connate Olivienne is one of the strongest pyrokinetics. I happen to be the strongest recorded telekinetic that the academy has ever seen. Most of you have heard rumors or read about it in the broadsheets but I can confirm that my tee-kay channel is a seven."

Murmuring followed her announcement.

She raised her hands to quiet the crowd. "With the queen's permission, I will give you a demonstration." Then with the power of thought alone, Castellan rose high into the air, higher than most would hope to go, but levitation wasn't her strongest asset. She lowered herself again.

Elidar spoke up to remind her of that fact. "You said telekinesis, that was levitation."

"So, it was. Is this what you want to see?" As one, every person watching rose into the air, as did the stele sculpture behind the dais. After a few secs, Castellan lowered everyone back to the ground, and took special effort to be sure the sculpture was as perfectly placed as before. Then she turned back to Elidar and the rest of her sibs.

"I've lifted many massive things during my time with the Shield Corp, but despite all that, I'm not the most powerful psi."

"What?" The comment didn't even come from Elidar, but rather one of her older sibs. "Bullocks!"

Castellan snickered when Soleng's papano, Galot, cuffed the sib's shoulder for his remark.

"No, I'm not. Because the difference between strength and power is this. Strength is the capacity with which you can do something. You can be physically or mentally strong. But power is having control or authority to influence others. So, you see, the most powerful psi in the land is none other than the queen herself. And after that, it will be Olivienne Dracore. Because they are our sovereigns. The most powerful people will control the strongest ones. Not through fear or intimidation but through the intelligence and wisdom of their actions."

She looked around to be sure the younger ones were listening. "Psiere needs such leadership to grow and be prosperous. And that." She turned her gaze back to the small girl among a sea of sibs and black-clad guardians. "That is why I'm a shield. It's why your sib is a shield, and all the rest of us here wearing the black and silver of our corp. Because we believe in our sovereigns and in Psiere. And the future doesn't need powerful people like me, it needs brave psi like you and your sib to carry this belief within your hearts."

Elidar was quiet, as were the rest. Then she smiled up at Castellan. "I believe in our queen and I want to be a shield like you and Gar when I grow up."

Castellan gave her shoulder a gentle squeeze. "Who knows, maybe *you* will be the best."

She spoke a little longer with Galot and Relizan before wandering away from the family toward where Olivara stood with Leniste, Renou, and Torrin.

Leniste chuckled and clapped her on the shoulder when she stood next to him. "I'll admit, you set my dingles a-dangling there for a meen, Tosh. Wasn't sure what you were playing at, but one look at the queen and I knew she was in on it. Seems like a lot of work just to impress a few younglings."

Castellan shrugged. "Maybe so, ser, but inspiration
starts small. I want them to understand that you don't have
to be the strongest in anything to matter, or to be powerful.
The best of us support a just cause not because we're
strong but because we believe."

Renou shook her head and laughed. "With a speech
like that, you sure made a believer out of me."

"Well, the truth is out there. I only wish more people
would see it and understand how much the sovereigns do
for all of Psiere."

Olivara smirked. "Good to know my daughter will
consor with her biggest proponent, Captain."

Castellan felt her skin flush from the top of her dress
collar to the tips of her ears. Olivienne walked up to witness
the sight and wasted no time commenting on it. "Oh ho,
what have I missed? You look just as you did when I—"

"I'm sure the queen and generals don't need to know
how you torment and vex me on the daely, 'Vienne."

The small circle laughed at Castellan's discomfort.

Olivienne and Castellan had a rare free evening back
at the royal residence. "Are you sure we don't have any
meetings tonight?"

Castellan picked up the tablet where she kept Olivienne's schedule. It was free as of that morning but sometimes items were added by Madlin when important
requests came in. "There is nothing at all and between the
both of us, I'm glad of it." She'd been counting on having
some time alone for the two of them and placed a few key
items upstairs just that morning. Castellan had every intention of getting Olivienne to relax after the stress of recent
events.

"Really? What makes you so happy to have a free evening with your sovereign, Captain?"

Seeing the familiar glint of flirtation in Olivienne's
eyes, Castellan played along. "I have it on good authority
that my connate hasn't been properly relaxed in wekes.
I'm sure she's due for a complete workout and rub down,

one that will have her sleeping the evening through like a canid after holidae meal."

Olivienne raised an inky black eyebrow. "Are you calling me a canid?"

Castellan used her telekinesis to deposit their meal dishes into the proper bin and moved closer to her lover. "Well...you *do* like to be stroked regularly."

"When you put it like that, I'm more intrigued than I am affronted."

"Should I keep going then?" Castellan pulled her into a tight embrace while maintaining eye contact with those purple Dracore eyes.

"Mayhaps."

Castellan bent to pick up Olivienne by the back of her thighs and the other woman wasted no time in wrapping her legs around Castellan's hips. She didn't need her levitation channel to carry them up to the connate's room on the second floor, but she used it anyway to save time.

"What would you say to a hot bath?" Castellan placed Olivienne onto a lounger near her large bathing tub, one they'd enjoyed on many occasions since becoming lovers. She quickly put a stopper into the drain and turned on the faucets, adjusting the tempyrature as she glanced back at Olivienne.

"I'd say it looks as though you've made up my mind for me."

Castellan wore a mock, innocent look and waved toward the tub. "Oh, this? This one is for me." She gave Olivienne a roguish grin and began unbuttoning her black uniform shirt.

Olivienne squirmed in her seat then impatiently stood and came closer. Olivienne stilled Castellan's fingers on the buttons near the bottom of the shirt and leaned in to speak close to her ear. "The water in the tub is deep. What if the heat overcomes you and you slip below the surface? It could be dangerous."

Castellan tilted her head in contemplation, attempting to calm her racing heart at Olivienne's nearness. It had been too long since their previous sexual contact and her breathing sped at the thought of it. "Hmm, it could. Are you a good swimmer then?"

"You know I am."

"And would you mind getting wet with me?"

Olivienne snorted. "My love."

"Yes?"

"I'm already there." Then Olivienne flexed her apportation channel and all their clothing disappeared, reappearing on the lounger Olivienne sat upon meens before. "I don't know about you, but I'm feeling particularly dirty, and I'd like that bath now."

Castellan grinned. "Yes, ser."

They carefully stepped into the deep tub, Castellan holding Olivienne's hand so she could enter the water first."

They wasted no time coming together in a passionate kiss. Olivienne's hands traced the muscles in Castellan's strong back, as Castellan buried her hands in Olivienne's hair. After a few meens, Castellan gasped and pulled away from those tantalizing lips, panting as though she'd been training back at academy. "'Vienne, it's been too long."

Olivienne clung to her, seemingly just as overwhelmed. "It has. I'm sorry."

Castellan pulled back to meet her gaze. "There is nothing to apologize for. The situation and events surrounding our lives right now make our personal time scarce. Not to mention the emotional toll all this has had on both of us."

"But you know me, Tosh. I've always been good at putting those emotional matters aside. The Makers know I've often used flirtation and sexual relations as a way to cope with a heavy heart."

Castellan shut off the water. She held Olivienne's hand and pulled down to indicate they should sit. "Let's get out of our heads right now and enjoy the moment."

Olivienne gave a long sigh once they were seated, facing one another in the steaming water. "I'd forgotten how amazing a hot soak feels."

Glasses and a bottle of vineo that Olivienne brought back from Dromea two rotos ago were already on the ledge near the tub thanks to Castellan's careful planning. She flexed her channel to remove the stopper in the bottle.

Olivienne's eyes opened at the sound and she watched Castellan pour them generous amounts of the fragrant, violet liquid.

"This seems incredibly well thought out. Is there a special occasion that I'm missing?"

Castellan smiled and handed over one glass. "The special occasion is a night to ourselves and I'd say neither one of us is missing it."

Olivienne raised her glass and winked at Castellan before taking a sip and humming with pleasure. "This vineo always reminds me of when we first met."

"Ah, yes. The volatile railer trip north from Ostium. How could I forget that? My sovereign vexed me, wooed me, and showed me an entirely new world."

"I must agree with you, the tupping was pretty phenomenal on that particular mission."

Castellan shrugged. "I was referring to helping translate the temple document, but the tupping was good, too." She laughed when Olivienne splashed her.

"You! I turned your head right quick, admit it."

Castellan took another swallow and placed her vineo off to the side. "The only thing I'll admit is that you were the first person I'd ever wanted to kiss and choke simultaneously."

Feeling heavy intent through their bond, Olivienne set her glass aside as well. "And now?"

Castellan rose in the water and moved so she was on her knees between Olivienne's legs. She leaned over her and Olivienne's gaze flitted from the water droplets running in rivulets down Castellan's toned body, to her breasts, then up to meet her eyes.

Castellan leaned closer. "Now, I only want to kiss you."

"Yes?"

Castellan nodded and moved closer yet. While their bodies weren't touching, Castellan's lips were near enough that every exhale moved wisps of Olivienne's hair around her face. "What's stopping you, Tosh?"

"As you know, I'm a creature of orders and rank. I wouldn't want to overstep any boundaries with a sovereign."

Olivienne's eyes grew darker as her pupils dilated in the low light of the bathing room. "Tosh?"

Castellan knew Olivienne loved it when they played with power dynamics during sex. "Yes, Connate?"

"Kiss me."

"As you decree, it shall be so—"

Impatient and breathing heavy, Olivienne didn't let her finish the sentence. She reached up and pulled Castellan down so the entire front of their bodies pressed together, slippery and sliding below the water. Olivienne moaned as Castellan's tongue found its way between her lips. The water sloshed around them when their hips rhythmically pressed together as each woman desperately sought release. With mouths and bodies otherwise occupied, that only left their minds to speak of thoughts and matters of the heart.

Too long...since I felt you like this.

Yes, but we're here now. Let me take care of you. Olivienne whined loudly and Castellan felt a tremor run through the woman below her.

Castellan...

Yes, love?

I...I won't last, cannot last.

Castellan used her telekinesis to caress down between them, causing Olivienne to shudder and let out a long moan. *You don't need to last. We have all night.* She used her channel to caress Olivienne's breasts while thrusting against the apex of her thighs. Castellan moved her lips away from Olivienne's mouth to suck along her jawline.

Olivienne stiffened and shook. She cried out as a wave of pleasure carried from her to Castellan, almost causing her own orgasm. It was a near thing and Castellan quivered on the verge. She held herself off Olivienne's torso as her lover came down from quickly earned bliss. "Are you okay?"

Olivienne laughed and met the eyes staring down at her. "Embarrassed at the speed of my release, but fine indeed. What of you?"

"I'll manage for a bit."

"Will you now?" There was mischief in Olivienne's eyes and before Castellan could answer, Olivienne moved her own hand down between them to caress Castellan's hard node of pleasure.

That was all it took for Castellan to shake apart above her. Less than a meen later, she collapsed into the water and they lay side by side, panting. Castellan caught her breath then chuckled. "I guess I should be embarrassed, too, then, hmm?"

"Not at all."

She gazed at Olivienne. "No?"

"As you said, we have all night. I'm not done with you in the slightest." She abruptly stood in the tub, letting the water cascade down her smooth skin. The lower half of her hair was dripping wet where it had been resting in the water but Olivienne didn't bother with a drying cloth. Instead, Castellan watched the water evaporate away with a gentle application of Olivienne's pyrokinetic channel.

Olivienne walked toward the door leading into their bedroom and Castellan's gaze followed. Before the sovereign could exit the chamber, she turned back and narrowed her eyes. "Best get your stamina in order, Captain. There is a lot more pleasure to be had tonight."

Castellan sucked in a breath and made short work of pulling the drain plug and scrambling out of the tub. She quickly dried herself, not having the benefit of a channel that could do such things. She paused before heading toward the other room. "Do you want me to bring the vineo?"

"If you wish. Though I have a smoother nectar on the menu tonight.

Their passion burned for a long time before the women grew too tired and sensitive to continue. Eventually they collapsed onto the coverlets, spent, and parched in a way that simple vineo or romance couldn't quench.

"Either I'm out of practice or I've been lax in my conditioning of late. I'm pretty sure my heart will beat out of my chest if we go again."

Olivienne laughed and rested her head right above the heart in question. "I like hearing your heartbeat, love. It's solid and reassuring, as if to remind me of your strength and place in my life."

Castellan drew Olivienne closer and used her telekinesis to pull a throw blanket over their cooling bodies to prevent a chill from setting in. She knew they'd have to get up to clean off but it felt nice to bask in the afterglow of their tupping. "It beats for you so it's only fair that you take comfort in the thumping."

"You're remarkably romantic this evening. One would think you were trying to woo me with the intention of eventual consorage."

Castellan laughed. "One would think." She was silent for a few secs before speaking again. "Despite the fact that it seems unlikely that we'll consor at the end of the traditional roto as planned, I would gladly wait a hundred more for you. The title doesn't matter. Neither does the ceremony. What *does* matter to me is that I can stand by your side for the rest of our daes, to face hardships and joys together as a pair united in love and future."

Olivienne rose enough to lay a soft kiss upon Castellan's lips. "We are on the same page love, because I share your passion in this. One way or another, we'll have our ceremony. Until then, we'll do what we can to protect one another and Psiere."

There were no words left after that. All Castellan could do was hug her future par even tighter until weariness drove them to sluice off and ready themselves for sleep. It had been a long dae and both knew the weke wasn't over yet. There was much prep to be done in a short amount of time for their trip to Occasus to meet up with Captain Velten and her crew.

Castellan was hard at work in her office at the Shield Corp headquarters. She'd been busy with filing, as well as filling out the supply requisitions they'd need for the next adventurist mission. She'd gotten a full list from her lieutenants just that morning. A rap on the door interrupted her quiet afternoon.

"Enter!" Castellan stood and saluted as soon as she

saw General Renou push through. "Ser, what can I do for you?"

"I came down to check on the status of your mission and team. I'm also delivering something that was dropped off this morning by Lieutenant Savon's sib."

Curiosity clawed at Castellan as she waved for Renou to take a seat and responded to the easiest questions first. "The mission is on track. I'm writing up the requisition slips now for our departure at the end of the weke. Soleng has returned and settled in well. I think having a counterpart is taking some of the stress off Madlin. She's relaxed a bit and everyone seems to be doing better now that they've been speaking with therapeutists. Specialist Sehg will take longer to get used to the unique nature of our team, but I've been getting good reports on him so far."

"Good to hear. Your team took a right beating over the past roto and I'm glad they're finding their way back to full charge." She held up a black, bound book of vellum. "Trylgen Savon came to headquarters to drop this off, stating that it appeared to be a private log of sorts. But rather than personal accounts, it's apparently full of dream or vision entries. He was prescient, right?"

"Prescience, telesthesia, and intuition. Together, the three were a potent combination and he had saved the team on multiple occasions, before and after I'd come along."

"I was going to have one of the shield's vision interpreters take a look at it but it seemed too personal. It's possible this booklet contains something relevant or vital to the future of our endeavors in this war, Tosh." She placed the velum book on the desk and slid it across to Castellan. "I have faith that between you and your team, you can put it to good use."

Pale brows rose. "Are you sure, ser? We may not be able to interpret as accurately as a professional."

"Captain, your team was as close-knit as any I've met in all my rotos heading the Shield Corp. I trust that you are the best ones to understand what Lieutenant Savon was trying to say within its pages. Report back to me when you've got solid intel."

Castellan picked up the book, feeling a weight greater

than a sum of pressed and inked velum. She swallowed back the guilt and grief that rose within her. It wasn't time to wallow in the past, but rather build the future. At least that was what her own therapeutist had been teaching her over the past few lunes. "Yes, ser."

Task accomplished, Renou stood. "You'll have a small group to see you off because as of right now the mission is to run black. That means your trip isn't in the official logs and your segs won't be hooked to the railer until a half oor before departure. Remember to put Engineer Sendae's name as the receiving party on your requisitions. She's been briefed to verify and hold anything we send with a shield stamp."

"I've already added her."

"Well, then, I'll leave you to it. See you in a few daes, Tosh." Renou was through the door but she leaned back in. "And let me know what you find out about Savon's log."

Castellan saluted. "You'll be the first I report to, ser."

Oors later, Castellan was seated in the lounge area outside Olivienne's residence. She hadn't seen Olivienne all dae, with her own time spent at headquarters and Olivienne sitting in meetings at the Temple of Archeos. Rather than wait for her return, Castellan assuaged her grim curiosity by cracking open the book she'd been gifted earlier. She had a glass of scotch in hand as she leafed through Savon's logbook.

Because of the nature of Savon's gifts, as well as his untimely demise, she thought it best to start near the end to see if anything had come to him in the final daes of the mission. One passage in particular caught her attention as she took a sip of her drink and she nearly spat the liquid across the flagstones of the courtyard. "By the Makers!"

"What is it that you're reading that's caused such a reaction?"

Castellan jerked her head up at the sound of her lover's voice. She was gob smacked as she blurted out what she'd just discovered. "Savon knew of his own death!"

Olivienne paused in her walk toward the sideboard

where drinks were kept and she spun to look at Castellan. "What? How would he know such a thing?"

Castellan drained the rest of her drink and held the glass up. "I'll tell you in exchange for a refill. I suspect I'm going to need it."

As soon as she said the words, her glass disappeared from her hand and reappeared in Olivienne's, courtesy of the sovereign's apportation channel. Olivienne filled two glasses and took a seat on the long lounger next to Castellan. She handed off the glass then tapped the book. "I'm assuming this has something to do with your declaration?"

"Thanks, love. And yes." Castellan took a few fortifying swallows, enjoying the burn of the liquor as it went down. "Just this morning, Lieutenant Savon's sib brought in a log that was tucked away in his personal effects. She mentioned that it seemed to be a record of his deepest thoughts and was concerned that it may hold Shield Corp secrets so she brought it to headquarters and turned it over to General Renou, who in turn gave it to me."

"Did she say why?"

"Renou said that we knew Savon best and would have the most luck at translating potential prescient episodes he may have written down."

Olivienne nodded. "That tracks. We'd spent many oors going over his visions, trying to discern what could help a mission, or hinder it."

"Yes, well, I started near the end because I was curious to see what I'd find." Castellan opened the book to where her finger was placed between two pages of velum near the end. Then she held it out so Olivienne could read it. "This entry was made the night we spent in the Magna tower before heading across the island to seek the Temple of Antaeus."

Olivienne read the passage aloud. "This morn I woke from a recurring dream. I am recording it now because I don't trust such dreams unless I've had the same one at least six times. This past night made the sixth in a row for this particular vision. I was with my entire team on a mission, only instead of floating upon a dirigible in the air, we sailed the Latus much like the past few daes. Sharcs circled us, five great ones in total. One Atlanteen wearing the garb of a Psierian intoned from a distance that the land would be cut in half. I don't know what that means but I'll ponder it later. Then he pointed at the connate, looking as though he were sending the sharcs to attack her. The sea beasts grew wings and flew straight for our sovereign charge and I had no choice but to throw myself in front of her and take their teeth into my own body. I wake at the same meen of pain and darkness each time I've had the dream."

Olivienne paused before continuing onto the next page. Castellan saw she was visibly upset but knew that she'd finish the passage so continued to hold the book. Olivienne swallowed and spoke aloud again. "There is something dark coming for us all and I suspect I will not survive this trip. But I mustn't worry the team so I'll keep the dream vision to myself until I can better understand it's meaning." She stopped reading and lifted her own glass with a shaking hand.

Castellan rubbed Olivienne's back. "Are you okay?"

The only sound in the courtyard for the next few meens was that of birdsong, a strange dichotomy to the dark passage they'd just read. After a few more swallows of her own scotch, Olivienne turned watery eyes toward Castellan. "He never said a word. Even when we'd completed the mission to the temple and were headed back to Tesseron. Why didn't he tell us?"

"I don't know. I didn't start at the end, he has at least a dozen more pages between that entry and the last. But the strength and accuracy of this one causes me to wonder if he predicted even more in his final daes. Perhaps there will be something that can help us navigate the uncertain future before us."

Olivienne's voice was quiet. Clearly what she'd read weighed on her as much as Savon's death. "Perhaps."

"Either way, I promised I'd look through it and report back to Renou with any relevant information. It's early enough. We can teleo for meals to be brought over from the palace and work together on this tonight." She paused, considering the fact that Olivienne may not want to read more of Savon's thoughts given that it was more of a reminder of their loss. "Or, I can read it on my own if it pains you."

Castellan made to pull the book away but Olivienne stilled her with gentle fingers against her wrist.

"No. I'd like to read more of his thoughts and emotions. It makes me feel a bit," she searched for the words. "Closer to him. Does that make sense?"

Castellan gave her a tender smile. "It does. Together then." She pulled the voteo from her belt and made good on her promise of a hot meal with little effort on their part. Then she contacted the guardians on duty just outside the entrance to their courtyard and let them know to expect someone from the palace kitchens. That done, Castellan lifted her arm in invitation and Olivienne snuggled closer. Then Castellan read aloud, picking up where Olivienne had left off. Her quiet voice didn't carry to those outside their little sanctuary but it was comforting to the woman whose life was purchased with the cred of Gentry Savon's sacrifice.

Chapter Five

Olivara requested one more meeting the dae of Olivienne's departure to Occasus. It wasn't an official one in the usual location. Instead, it was an intimate affair in the queen's private study within the palace. Castellan and Olivienne filed in to see the queen and king, General Renou, and General Leniste seated on comfortable loungers with glasses of scotch.

Olivienne smiled and waved to the decanter in the middle of the low table. "I see we're the last to arrive and that you've all started without us." She and Castellan took seats on a free lounger and poured their own glasses.

"Actually," Olivara paused, as if speaking with someone telepathically. "There are two more on their way."

"Who—"

Captain Torrin pushed into the room followed closely by Gemeda. The doctore bowed to Olivara. "My Queen, I apologize for being late. There was an emergency case that came in tonight and no one else with the telesana channel was available. I couldn't leave them to suffer."

Olivara stood and clasped Gemeda's hand, giving it a squeeze. "Completely understandable, Doctore Shen. If you will have a seat?" She waved toward one of the remaining chairs and Del Torrin took the other.

"Please, call me Gemeda, or Gem."

The queen nodded and smiled.

Olivara spoke once everyone was settled with drinks in hand. "I'm sure you're wondering why I called this last meen meeting. I'm well aware everything is handled for Olivienne's trip west." She glanced their way. "Security is set and your gear should have gone out on the morning railer. This isn't about your trip to Occasus, nor the farther mission to the Halcyon Station."

Castellan narrowed her eyes with speculation. "Does Gem need to travel with us again?"

"Not with *you*, no."

"Maman, what is it?"

Castellan took note of the way Keshien moved his hand over to rest atop Olivara's. He squeezed gently and Castellan scrutinized the action. "Something has happened."

"Nothing has happened yet, Captain. The reason we are all here is because of an event that *could* happen. I had a clairvoyant episode just last night and wrote everything out as soon as I woke, but I'll admit that even I can't make sense of most of it."

"And Gem? What has she to do with all of this?" Olivienne almost spilled her drink as she carelessly waved it in Gem's direction.

Gemeda's eyes widened. "Should I be worried that I feature regularly in your dreams of danger and destruction?"

Olivara gave her a kind smile. "On the contrary, you should be proud that your talent and loyalty has marked you as someone capable of great power and change." She took a deep breath as the rest waited. "In my vision, we were enacting my plan to contact the Atlanteens, exactly as Keshien, Torrin, and I had settled on. We make contact in the vision and all goes well, until it doesn't. Something happens as we are clasping hands in a show of trust, and the Atlanteen emissary dies within my arms a meen later."

Olivienne looked at her in shock. "You're having visions about yourself? How is this possible?"

The queen shrugged. "It's exceedingly rare but not unheard of. In this instance, I suspect is has something to do with the stone. Anyway, their death while we are mentally entwined does me ill and I'm unable to communicate to the rest that we have no harmful intent. A ferocious battle ensues as we are all still reeling in shock and many lives are lost."

Castellan had a sense where the queen's request was going, but she needed to clarify. "And why will you need Gem? Skilled though she is, even Gemeda can't heal everyone injured in a great battle."

The gathered psi in the room no doubt thought back to the lives lost over King's Marsh.

Olivara didn't meet Castellan's gaze when she

answered. Instead, she turned those piercing purple eyes to the doctore. "No, I would never expect such a miracle. I only need you to heal a single person."

One didn't become a medican of high regard on channel talent alone. Gemeda easily guessed her role in the upcoming negotiation and was taken aback. "But, my Queen...you're asking me to heal something, someone, that is of a biology completely foreign to me."

Castellan added, "I know you've already said no, but perhaps Olivienne and I should stay in Tesseron while you make contact in case your vision comes to pass. I may be able to prevent catastrophe before it happens—"

"No, Captain. Your place is to ensure my daughter's safety. We need whatever information or technology you can find on that blasted island, this Halcyon Station."

Gemeda took a fortifying swallow of her scotch before speaking again. "My Queen, I don't know if I can do what you need."

"If anyone can, it's you."

Gemeda smiled at Castellan's words of support. "Well, then, I don't know if anyone can do it."

"Doctore Gemeda Shen." The entire room froze as a wave of mental fortitude washed through them.

"Yes?"

"I have faith in you."

Castellan knew the queen was breaking a few laws by pushing her will with the use of her stone, but in that instance, with such a positive wave bolstering her own emotions, she couldn't bring herself to care.

Olivara looked around the small group. "I have faith in all of you."

Captain Torrin faced Gemeda full on. "If you are worried for your own safety, Doctore Shen—"

"It's Gemeda, please." Gemeda smiled up at Torrin. Castellan knew the look on her friend's face well and she rolled her eyes.

Torrin gave a little bow. "Very well, Gemeda. If you are worried for your safety, rest assured I will be in the water with both of you. Your life will be guarded just as closely as Queen Olivara's."

Olivara smiled at their interaction. Castellan saw Olivienne's eyes narrow with suspicion before she addressed Castellan privately. *She's up to something.*

Who, Gemeda?

No, Maman.

Castellan gazed from the queen to Torrin, then Gemeda. *Seems like meddling to me. Look at them, half besotted after only a few meens.*

Hasn't Gem collected enough captains already?

Castellan startled at Olivienne's words. *Come again?*

Eyes front, darling. Wouldn't want Maman to catch on to the fact that we've caught on to her. And we both know Gem captured you a long time ago. The good doctore simply elected to throw you back.

Castellan scowled. *I threw myself back.*

Olivienne laughed aloud, startling the rest of the group. *Now you just sound ridiculous.*

Perhaps. Castellan conceded.

Rather than continue their conversation, Olivienne pressed her mother on her plan one more time. "Tell me again why you need to be in the bay for this to work instead of safely on land and surrounded by plenty of strong guardians?"

"You know from the last official briefing that we can only communicate with the Atlanteens while touching their medium. It's the only way, 'Vienne. I'll be as safe as I can."

Olivienne sighed. "I know, but I'll worry the entire time we're away. Promise you'll send word of whatever happens so that we can receive it when we return to Occasus?"

"Of course, darling. And you do the same. I want a full briefing as soon as possible. And by the Makers, let's all hope you bring home something that can help."

Leniste gave a loud bray of laughter. "If they do bring something that can help, it can only be by the Makers." The rest quickly caught on and laughed with him.

Olivara raised her glass. "From your lips to their ears, erm, whatever it is these Tau Ceti have. Either way, let's all plan for the worst, but hope for the best."

The secrecy surrounding Olivienne's newest adventurist mission meant that the team left quietly. Olivienne,
Castellan, and the shield team left on the overnight railer
that departed at twenty-two hundred oors. They didn't use
the royal railer segs as they'd done when traveling on
Olivienne and Castellan's oathing holidae to Instrucia. The
only segments available for the overnight trip were standard passenger berths and one deluxe, much like the one
the sovereign and captain first met upon.

The group of sixteen filed onto the railer carrying
weapons and basic gear packs and naught much else, with
the exception of Castellan. She decided to bring her old
Defense Corp saber to supplement her normal weapons
after their previous island adventurist mission.

Madlin and Soleng were flipping a coin to see who
would get the other suite on the deluxe seg, as Castellan
slid open the door to their room.

"This brings back memories."

Olivienne followed her in and smirked as she took
note of the trundle bed pinned up against the wall. "The
bed looks the same at any rate. Care to ruin your reputation
again amongst my shield team?"

Castellan grimaced and shook her head. "It's *my*
shield team and I'd rather not. Only a few of our current
guardians were there on that fateful trip to remember the
way we carried on. I rather like it that way."

"You're such a spoilsport, Captain. Whatever shall I
do with myself then, hmm?" She trailed her index finger
down the side of Castellan's face, then skimmed it along
her neck and into the opening where the two fasteners
were unclasped on her uniform shirt.

Castellan caught her hand in a firm grip and she used
it to pull Olivienne closer. "You could try sleep. I've heard
it's quite handy when one is embarking on a perilous journey. As we won't arrive until near eight hundred tomorrow, it's probably best to keep our sleep rhythms as
normal as possible."

"Darling," Olivienne pulled the timepiece from her

pocket, then looked at Castellan with a raised brow. "Since when have I ever gone to sleep so early when I have an attractive bedmate?"

"Or *any* bedmate if the old broadsheets were to be believed."

Olivienne laughed, "Not that I'd give credence to some of those printed rags. But to set the record straight, I only chose attractive ones in body, mind, or spirit. Lucky for me, you hit all three marks in a dead shot." She maneuvered Castellan closer to the trundle wall and a sec later the trundle pin appeared in her hand. Olivienne grinned as the bed unfolded behind Castellan.

"According to your maman, you mostly chose for the first—"

"Oh, you!" A well-placed leg and strong push sent Castellan sprawling backward onto the soft coverlets. The women devolved into laughter as Olivienne collapsed on top of her. "I've got you where I want you now. Whatever shall I do?"

"I think it's the other way around, love. Nothing you've got can hold me, while on the other hand..." Castellan trailed off as Olivienne became immobilized. "Seeing as how you've gone to all this effort to get us into bed, it would be a shame not to use it. Be a dear and take care of our gear, won't you?"

Olivienne didn't need to be able to move to use her apportation channel and within secs both women lay pressed together completely nude. Castellan craned her head to check the location of their clothing and pistol belts and was quickly assured of both their weapons' safety by Olivienne.

"Our pistol belts are hanging from the hook on the wall. After all, I wouldn't want anything to discharge prematurely."

"I suspect you are remembering an old conquest. Perhaps that pipeball player? None of my weapons would go off without proper handling ahead of time," Castellan said.

Castellan released her telekinetic hold and Olivienne laughed and gave her a poke to the chest with her right first finger. "Even after all this time together, you're still jealous! Admit it."

"I am."

Olivienne's mouth opened with surprise at Castellan's answer.

"I'm jealous of every breath that caresses your lips, of the clothing that touches your skin on the daely, and of each person that knew all the different versions of you before I came along. I'm not jealous of a past lover's emotion with you, but rather of all the experiences I haven't gotten to share with you yet."

Olivienne's features softened at the uncharacteristic slew of romantic words that poured from Castellan's mouth. Her answer was a balm to sooth any amount of jealousy, faux or otherwise. "Darling, we'll have the next hundred rotos to make memories together. I can assure you that nothing that has come before could ever compare to what it's been like after you entered my life."

Castellan sighed and cupped Olivienne's cheeks between the palms of her hands. "I can't wait to consor with you properly. It's as the queen said, we need to end this conflict as soon as possible. I quite enjoy spending my time traveling the length and breadth of Psiere with you, solving mysteries and discovering new riddles."

"Speaking of mysteries," Olivienne leaned closer. "I believe I've found a clue to one right here in this seg."

"Where? A clue to—" The kiss was on the sweet side rather than passionate. But seeing as the trip brought back a lot of nostalgia for the two women, it suited both just fine.

The railer rolled into the brand-new transportation hub located on the outskirts of Occasus at eight hundred oors on the dot. The city was naught more than a fishing port before Olivara ordered the new dirigible production facility to be built. Now it housed numerous manufacturing processes. Their sole purpose was in defending against Atlanteen and Pon Havington's attacks.

Both suns rose over the horizon directly behind the railer, so the shield team and their precious charge didn't see the changing colors until they exited the segs and stood upon the platform.

Olivienne took a deep breath of salt-tinged air and smiled. "It's a new dae, we're beginning a fresh adventure, and I feel surprisingly well-rested."

Lieutenant Madlin snorted and quickly hid a laugh behind her closed fist. Never one to shy away from a humorous topic, Specialist Qent added his thoughts on the subject. "That's good to hear, Connate. I'd wager at least as well rested as you were on that railer trip back to Tesseron a few rotos ago. We all heard how well rested you were."

Soleng, Devin, and Holling laughed at their fellow shield's observation, each one having been on the trip north when Olivienne met Castellan, who was at the time naught more than a lieutenant commander. After a few secs, the rest of the unit began laughing as well. Presumably due to someone telling the tale telepathically.

Castellan flushed with embarrassment but she refused to reprimand the team and chance dampening spirits that were low for too long. But good humore or not, they still had a job to do. "If you're all finished, I'd like to make our way to the dirigible section and get aboard the *Vestigo* before the psi figure out the connate is in Occasus."

Madlin smirked. "Yes, ser." With that, they picked up their packs and began walking in formation with Olivienne in the middle of the group. Anyone who hadn't been born the dae before would suspect that a sovereign was in the area due to the group's uniforms alone. But they didn't have to know *which* sovereign nor have their suspicions confirmed. It took no more than ten meens to traverse the outskirts of the transportation hub until they came to the dirigible shipyard. Numerous completed black dirigibles floated in the sky. They saw even more gondolas constructed on the ground farther out, still requiring bladders to reach the heights they were meant for.

Someone whistled when they mounted the steps of one tall platform bearing the number that Castellan had been given the previous evening. The entire group paused to appreciate the dirigible that was larger than any they'd seen before, including the previous iteration of Velten's ship.

"By the Makers, they weren't kidding when they said this would be even better than the past one." Specialist Lear's awe-filled voice broke them from their shock.

Specialist Calderon, the other pilot of the group, followed her sentiment. "She's beautiful!"

Castellan gave the unit a mental push. *Beauty or not, let's get aboard. We're not meant to stay in port long so we need to check in with Velten and her crew. March it forward, guardians.*

Captain Seema Velten herself came out to greet Olivienne and Castellan before they trekked the full distance to where the *Vestigo* was winched low to the platform. "Connate, Captain Tosh, good to have you aboard again."

Castellan smiled and held out her hand to clasp Velten's. "You say that like we didn't break your last ship."

Velten's expression grew solemn. After all, Castellan wasn't the only one who lost soldiers that dae. "We won't discuss the past when embarking on the future. I'd like to think each new mission carries the souls of previous ones at its heart."

Olivienne tilted her head curiously. "Even those no longer living?"

"Especially those who were lost." They all paused for a few secs in deference to the souls referenced, then Velten waved them aboard. "Come. We've got your supplies already inventoried and stowed aboard. First Officer Vex will show your team to their berths while I take you to your quarters. I think you'll appreciate some of the upgrades. Unfortunately, I have a negative report regarding our departure."

"Will we be delayed?"

"Has there been malfeasance?"

Olivienne and Castellan looked at one another and smiled to acknowledge their similar train of thought, even though the words were colored by the women's disparate disciplines. All three had paused on the side deck at the captain's announcement, and Castellan waved the rest of the team around them to follow Vex into the massive ship.

"Always a soldier, eh, Tosh?"

Castellan laughed and clapped her fellow captain on the shoulder. "That's like one canid saying another borks too much."

Olivienne rolled her eyes. "She's right. You're both the most—" She paused when Castellan and Seema turned their intense gazes upon her.

"Most what, exactly?"

"Dedicated soldiers I've ever met."

Castellan grinned at Velten. "She was going to say infuriating."

Velten laughed and shook her head. "I suspect you're right. Now, if you'll follow me, we can go by your quarters to drop your gear packs. Then we'll retire to the captain's room after and I'll fill you in over a few fingers of scotch." She held up her hand to pause them. "But rest assured, we are safe. As far as I'm aware, no one knows of our purpose nor the connate's presence here in Occasus."

A few meens later, they all sat on low loungers in the captain's room, glasses of Velten's favorite distillation of scotch in hand. "Let's get to the hull of our situation. Engineer Davine found a crack in the drive rod of the aft dextra engine when he performed final checks at six hundred oors this morning. He said it didn't look tampered with but occasionally the casting process will turn out a bad one."

"Are there no quality checks in that new manufacturing facility?"

Velten took a sip. "Oh, there are. The problem is that everything about the *Vestigo* is custom built. Somehow this slipped through. It's lucky that Davine found it before we left port. That part would have been impossible to replace or repair to the correct tolerance once we were across the ocean."

Ever the impatient one, Olivienne pressed for answers. "How long will it take to get a new part?"

"Davine contacted the foundry first thing and it looks like the brunt of time to repair is due to how long it will take to switch out the molds and smelt the metal used for our drive rods. They gave us a two to three dae estimate for repairs. They have to complete the current run of rods first, before they can change over the equipment for the new ones."

Olivienne leaned forward. "Can't we interrupt the current run? This mission is high priority."

Castellan rested her hand upon Olivienne's wrist. "High priority, yes. But it's under an even higher order of secrecy. We can't pull rank on this without letting people know of our plans and your location."

"Shite. So, what? We're forced to sit and wait as the greatest discovery we've ever made lies just beyond our fingertips?"

"I'm afraid so, Connate."

"Fear not, love. I'm positive we can find plenty to do aboard ship to pass our time."

Velten leaned forward and placed her drink tumbler in the special divot built into the low table that was bolted to the floor. "Oh no you don't! I remember the last trip, and I know how warmed up the randy royal gets when on a mission. There are plenty of stories throughout the corps to back me up. I don't want you in my head when I'm trying to get my manual oors each night. Savvy?"

Castellan's ears warmed and Olivienne smirked as she took another sip. "You didn't mind it before, Captain. Perhaps if a certain doctore were here to keep you company, hmm?"

Velten waved off the suggestion. "Bah, Gemeda is an absolute dear but we all know that she's as consored to her duties as a doctore as I am to this ship. It was naught more between us than a bit of fun, and we both knew it well."

"Even so..."

"Even so. There are plenty of willing bed mates to be had when one steps from the sky for an evening."

Castellan laughed and finished her drink in a few swallows. "If you're looking for bed sport with someone who has plenty of stamina, 'Vienne knows a pipeball player she can introduce you to—"

In a pique, Olivienne apported the top clasp clean off Castellan's uniform, then threw it at her. The action only served to make her laugh harder. "Oh, you! But in that regard," she looked at Velten. "Benicia's head would certainly be turned by such a handsome and commanding figure as you make, Captain."

Sudden humore gone, Castellan glowered at Olivienne. "I expect you to put that clasp back on before we depart Occasus."

Olivienne stifled a giggle and Velten gathered their empty tumblers to place in the collection bin for the porters. Velten smiled at both of them. "Rest easy, Tosh. Just leave the uniform in your cleaning bin as normal. Whomever collects them will check for damage and be sure it's repaired before returning the garment. As for your pipeball player," she shrugged. "Perhaps I'll take you up on your offer when I next have downtime in Tesseron."

Velten checked her pocket chrono. "They're serving middae meal in the canteen. Can I interest you both in a bite?"

Castellan stood as well. "Absolutely. I didn't eat much on the railer north."

Olivienne gave her lover's bicep a squeeze. "I could argue that, Tosh. But I'll let you keep your honor in front of the captain a wee bit longer."

Laughter burst forth from Velten's lips as she led them through the portal into the passageway. "Too late for that, I'm afraid."

"Drat."

Castellan contacted Madlin and Soleng telepathically and relayed the news of their delay. She instructed them to brief the team over their own lunch. After that, they were to find an open space within the dirigible that was large enough to hold the entire unit and practice some of the group therapeutist exercises they'd learned during their downtime in Tesseron.

Once they parted ways with Velten, Castellan and Olivienne returned to their cabin to go over what information they had on the Halcyon Station.

Castellan watched as Olivienne pulled multiple books of vellum from her satchel. "All of those have been translated and verified by Templar Aislyn?"

"Actually, no." Olivienne made two separate stacks

with the files on their private table, and they each pulled out a chair to sit. "This," She gestured to the larger stack. "Is the pile of Magna documents that have been translated and appear to be reports to or from Halcyon Station. The other stack are the pages that have yet to be translated but hold the same distinctive stamp of symbols as the verified Halcyon ones."

"And our job is?"

Olivienne grimaced and pulled out blank translation sheets as well as a few styli. "To figure out if there is anything else here that could be useful to the mission."

"We could have delegated some of this to Penn but I think their group exercises assigned by the therapeutist are more important. I suppose we'll just have to lift our chins and accept the hit on this. And by we, I mean you since we both know which of us enjoys maths more."

"Tosh!"

Castellan laughed and her side warmed from Olivienne's pyrokinesis channel. She held up her hands in a show of surrender. "I'm only joking with you, love."

"Your jokes hit the mark as accurately as maman's pistols. Fine." She glanced at the table and hard chairs, then shook her head. "Let's at least grab lapboards and get comfortable on the lounger for this. Perhaps the captain will entertain us with a bit of gaming in her room later."

Castellan grinned. "Cubes?"

"By the Makers, no! None of us like losing so blasted smartly. We'll pick something that is more about chance and luck than prediction and counting. Otherwise..."

"Otherwise?"

Olivienne leaned over and gave Castellan a sweet kiss. "Otherwise Velten may dump you over the observation deck somewhere between here and our new mystery island."

Castellan snorted and returned her kiss with a much slower and deeper one before they both settled in to begin translating. It would take daes to convert the rest of the stack to something they could read. It was a perfect use of their unforeseen delay.

Chapter Six

Olivara stood on the black sands of a popular beach ten mahls to the southwest of Tesseron, around Bindle Bay and away from the city. The park was spacious so they were able to set up rail guns and armaments powerful enough to fend off some of the larger creatures from the deep, not that she hoped they'd need such. The water was shallow for a good forty yords before the sand dropped off into the bay proper. The generals were certain the layout of the smaller bay would deter a strong offensive should her attempts at contact fail.

"My Queen, are you positive this is the wisest course of action?"

Olivara moved her gaze from the horizon to look upon the worried face of her longtime friend. "Camen, dear, you're starting to sound like my daughter."

General Renou inclined her head to acknowledge Olivara's truth. "It's merely an abundance of love and worry. You know I'd follow you to the top of Zha Endain and back but I don't like entering any engagement at a disadvantage. And this," She waved a hand at the expanse of indefensible water around them. "Is nothing but."

Another voice spoke from somewhere behind the queen. "Not that I don't have plenty of worry for our venerable sovereign, but I have concerns about my own skin in this, too. How can you guarantee the Atlanteens won't attack first and, well, attack again later? I suspect they're not much for questions based on the stories I've heard from Tosh."

Gemeda stumbled a bit where her boot sank into a particularly soft spot in the sand and Captain Torrin reached out to steady her. "Careful, Doctore Shen. The beach is loose with the tide recently receded."

Gem shot a disdainful look at the dark hand that held her elbow then moved her gaze up to Torrin. "I'm quite capable of looking after myself, Captain. Strangely enough, I've tramped across the width and breadth of

Psiere with no help at all. So, if you'd please?" She gave the hand upon her elbow another pointed look and Torrin quickly let go. "Thank you. It's nothing personal but past training dictates I be ready for action at any time and I can't draw a pistol or grab onto someone for a healing if I'm being restrained. I hope you understand."

The captain flushed red enough that it could be seen despite his darker skin. "Apologies, Doctore. I forgot that you've had a fair amount of training yourself. It's good to know there is another psi of action nearby to assist with the queen's defense."

That earned the large, well-built shield a smile. Castellan would say the quickest way to Gemeda's heart was to acknowledge her capability, but then the same could be said for most people. Especially those often overlooked. Gem gave Torrin a wink. "That being said, if you witness one of those blasted tentacles questing for us, you're free to come to my aid as you see fit."

Olivara and Renou chuckled at the exchange. "Don't be too hard on Torrin, Doctore Shen. It's in a shield's nature to be protective. He's only doing his job."

Gem snorted. "The last I checked, the seat of my trousers had yet to grace something as fine as the Divine Cathedra."

"Fine and hard, don't forget to add hard. I've never sat in a seat so blasted uncomfortable in my life."

Renou smiled. "I remember your maman saying much the same thing when she was queen, back when we were younglings at academy together."

They stood for a few meens in silence until Torrin's voteo crackled to life. He pulled it from his belt clip to acknowledge the report. "Everything is ready, my Queen."

Olivara pursed her lips and sighed. She looked at Renou. "We can begin as soon as you take your place."

"I should stay here with you—"

"You'll do no such thing. It wouldn't go well for us if half the key members of our trusted circle are taken by the Atlanteens should things twist awry here todae. No. You'll return to the heavily shielded observation point with Keshien and Germaine. I need level heads up there managing this engagement. She held up a finger and met the gaze of the other three people on the beach with her. "And remember, no one fires without my say so. Savvy?"

Torrin, Gemeda, and Renou all nodded. "Yes, my Queen."

"Give me your voteo. I want to make sure the rest know as well."

Torrin handed the communication device to Olivara and she pressed the alert button, then repeated the exact same words to everyone within range, as Renou mounted on a fat-tired cycle and took off for the observation point.

It would have to do. The success of their endeavor depended heavily upon level heads and steady hands. She glanced off in the distance to where she knew her par waited and sent an antoraestone-boosted wash of love to him. They'd said their goodbyes earlier. As much as she took strength from his presence, she had to do this alone rather than risk another from the sovereign family. Even if he was a Vincender by blood. He was still Olivienne and Kesharan's papan.

As they'd previously discussed when plotting out their mission, Olivara, Torrin, and Gemeda waded into the water together. While she could send out a mental request for contact by simply touching the water with her fingertips, Olivara wanted to be close to the drop off so an Atlanteen emissary would feel safe enough to come near their group.

"This is the spot, my Queen." She knew Torrin's spatial sense to be top notch and he stopped them about ten yords from the swim buoys bobbing in the water that marked the end of the shallows.

Olivara dropped her hands beneath the surface and pushed her thoughts out through the only medium that Atlanteens could communicate. *Peace. As queen of the two-leggers, I wish to conference with your leader. I am standing within your element as a show of trust.* She also sent images with the same intent, hoping that someone with high enough importance would respond to her request. She had no doubts that her mental call could be heard. After all, she was the most powerful telepathic psi in generations and she had the full strength of an antorae-stone at her command.

"What now?" Torrin's voice was a quiet rumble and his hand rested upon the grip of his pistol, ready for any action.

"Now, we wait. I suspect it won't take long for them to respond. Whether or not we get someone of high enough rank to negotiate with, that's another story."

No voices carried to them across the bay, despite all the shields and defense soldiers ranging around the beach. The only thing that could be heard was the water lapping greedily at their clothes, the wind whistling through the buoys, and birds calling out for their dinner where they circled in the breeze above.

They waited five meens—then another five. After fifteen meens in the water, long enough to begin feeling chill, a low sound came to them on the blowing wind. It was so low that it was as though it rumbled up through their feet in the water. Gemeda tilted her head curiously. "It sounds like whal song."

Olivara closed her eyes and cast her senses out over the water, as well as down into it. "They're coming."

Secs later, a blast of sea water shot into the air as a massive whal greater in size than a standard dirigible rose from the deepest depths of Bindle Bay far out in front of them. Fins of sharcs broke the surface near the whal but none swam closer to the trio. Olivara sent her telepathic voice and emotional purpose again. *I come to you with peaceful intent and seek only to communicate. In return I promise safety as long as I am not attacked.*

A much smaller tale flipped in the water closer to them and Olivara knew it was an Atlanteen. The sharc fins gathered in formation and approached the three Psierians. Olivara glanced briefly at Torrin and Gemeda and could see and feel that they weren't pleased. "Keep steady. I suspect they are for protection much the way the two of you are."

Torrin's displeasure was obvious in the tone of his voice. "Yes, my Queen."

Olivara counted the secs as the fins approached and

she let out a breath of relief when they stopped near the buoys. A head popped up from the water and all three recognized the smooth, genderless features of an Atlanteen, though none had seen one in person. With skin a mottled mix of blues, greens, and grays, they had strong arms that ended in strange web-fingered hands. The Atlanteen had a fin ridge that bisected the top of their skull, and another larger fin on their back. Both fins were finer than the large, scaled swimmer tail that was located where a Psi's legs would normally be.

Gemeda whispered in awe. "Tosh was right. They are beautiful."

"But foreign, like naught I've ever seen or encountered before. Perhaps I should have started in defense like Captain Tosh," Torrin said.

Olivara trailed her fingers in the water and spoke again. *Are you here to parlay?*

At first, she worried she wouldn't be able to understand the Atlanteen. The ocean-dweller opened their mouth and all that came out was a series of squeaks and clicks, much like the dolpheens that occasionally ventured into Bindle Bay. When she held up her hands in a sign that she didn't understand, the Atlanteen's words came through as telepathic speech instead. There was a strange accent to their mental voice and she attributed it to the make-up of their disparate races.

You show much bravery coming into our world, two-legger.

Some would call me brave, others foolish. I'm here in an attempt to better the lives of both our peoples.

And who are you that aspires to such lofty goals as only Posidee could grant?

Olivara wondered who Posidee was but her attention was caught as more Atlanteens arrived in the water between their group and where the whal sat like a sentinel. They were only recognized by the occasional flip of their tails because none surfaced like the one she was speaking with. *I am the queen of Psiere, which is all the land above, just as your people rule the water below.*

The Atlanteen's sharp-toothed mouth gaped open in

what appeared to be shock. *You acknowledge our claim to the depths? None of your race has ever said as such. We have feuded with your kind for hundreds of rotations because of the assertion made by one of your leaders.*

That was no leader, merely a man with nothing more than a closeminded view of the world. As a matter of fact, that man is the descendent of the one whose wills and whims you currently carry out. Olivara lifted one hand from the water and held it palm up in a show of openness. *Please, we have learned a great deal about our race and this planet since that long ago time in history. I would like to learn about your race and put an end to the senseless violence that stains the seas with the blood of our peoples.*

The Atlanteen remained silent, as if in thought. Two more heads rose out of the water next to him and the three of them spoke verbally with one another in their strange language. Finally, a different Atlanteen came forward. While their face and shoulders were slightly narrower, there was no difference in gender that Olivara could see.

All the Atlanteens' skin were of similar coloring. They had little gills at the edges of their jaws and she briefly wondered if they could breathe water and air equally or if they'd need to drop below the waves to replenish after too much time. It was possible they were truly like the dolpheens and it was the other way around.

I will parlay with you.

Other than a necklace of woven kemp and shells, Olivara saw no discernable difference in status between the first Atlanteen and the one that spoke now. Though if one were a stranger to Psierian ways, she wouldn't appear any higher status than Torrin or Gemeda either. *Do you have authority to negotiate on behalf of your entire race?*

I have as much authority as you, Tau-chosen. I am the Keeper of the Trident, Queen of the Atlantee in this region. You may call me Eurynome. The ocean queen lifted one of her hands from the water and the three Psierians watched in shock as sand trickled upward from below the water's surface to form a column, then the column lit brightly causing everyone but Eurynome to cover their eyes. When they opened them again, the Atlantee queen was left holding a beautiful trident of glass.

Olivara glanced toward Torrin and Gemeda, taking note of the doctore's single raised brow. She spoke to them privately, not wanting their counterparts to hear. *What was that? Telekinesis and pyrokinesis working in tandem? I had no idea they possessed more than communicatory channels!*

My Queen, Olivara's attention focused on Gemeda. *Perhaps it's much like the sovereigns in that regard. The queen has more power than the rest of her people. It could be why she's referred to as the Keeper of the Trident.*

Do you have any thoughts on this new bit of information? The queen spoke to Torrin who shook his head.

What Doctore Shen says makes as much sense as anything, standing waist deep in the bay, surrounded by swimmers of all types and a strange race of swimmer-folk.

Finally, Olivara moved her attention back to Eurynome. There were more questions to be answered than that of channels. Her mind latched onto something else the Atlanteen had said. *Of this region? Do you not speak for the area around our northern and southern continents?*

You misunderstand. There is more to this planet than what you are familiar with. Your Psiere, as you call it, is nothing more than the collection of continentus on this side of the planet. I rule Hespiris, while my brother, Vulci, rules Erus.

It was a struggle for Olivara not to show her immense surprise at all the new information Eurynome was sharing with her. She briefly wondered if Pon also knew such things. *I had no idea. Please forgive me and my kind for our ignorance and lack of initiative in regard to learning about your people. I fear that we have all been living under the weight of past mistakes, something I'd like to rectify going forward.*

You spoke of peace in your initial contact with my emissary. What can you offer that the other two-legger has not?

Olivara took a deep breath and met the mesmerizing eyes of the other sovereign. *I can offer truth, trust, and fair negotiation. All things you won't find from Pon Hav-*

ington. I can hypothesize what he may have promised to garner your aid, but he is a powerful telepath and is known for his ability to lie convincingly. There is no way he could follow through with his promises without the full cooperation of all our people.

I can sense that you, too, are powerful, more so than even he. How do I know that you are not lying to garner favor from the Atlantee?

To prove my intention, I'll offer telepathic vulnerability in the form of a trust reading. You will be able to see my thoughts and intentions, as I will see yours. We need but touch for the reading to begin.

Eurynome didn't speak for a few secs, then she turned to address the other Atlanteens. After a few meens, the clicks and squeaks grew louder and more intense, then shoulders drooped on all but Eurynome. A much larger Atlanteen swam near and she handed them her trident. Eurynome turned back to Olivara. *Murroh is in charge of my safety whenever we are away from the sacred city. He will hold the trident to your heart to deter any nefarious acts on the part of you or your guards. I will not participate in your trust reading without this failsafe in place.*

Torrin voiced his displeasure. "My Queen, putting yourself in peril like that is absolutely out of the question! General Renou—"

Olivara raised her hand to stay the forthcoming rant. "Peace, Captain. This is the only way. If you recall, I foresaw it in my vision."

"But the rest..." He didn't finish speaking, all three of them knew what the rest of Olivara's vision entailed.

"That is why Doctore Shen is here." She nodded to Gemeda.

Torrin and Gemeda sighed in unison, indicating acquiescence to Olivara's wish. She turned back to the Atlanteens. *I agree to your condition, if you agree to mine. I wish for my compatriot,* Olivara pointed toward Gemeda, *to stand next to us while we are vulnerable.*

Eurynome narrowed her eyes and peered closer at Gemeda. *Your two-legger female is no guard, what is her purpose?*

She is a doctore, someone who is capable of healing with their hands—

Do you think Murrow will leave any part of you alive should harm befall me?

Olivara shook her head and smiled kindly upon her fellow queen. *She's not here for me, but rather for you. I had a vision of this time and saw danger to your person, but not from me or mine. I suspect that Havington has spies and they'd not hesitate to do either one of us harm. A potential alliance between us would do much to impede Pon's plans for his future greatness.*

Eurynome's eyes darted around with worry at Olivara's words. *I'm suddenly less certain of this current we swim. Perhaps we should meet at a later time when you haven't had such visions of death and ambush.*

Olivara took two steps closer and lifted her left hand from the water. She stared into the sea-green eyes of the Atlantee queen, who floated less than two foot from her. *I, too, am afraid, but I'm still here standing in the sea with you.* Olivara paused then held her hand out. *Eurynome, the time for peace is now. Of that, I'm certain.*

Eurynome's eyes narrowed with determination as she lifted her own hand. *Have your doctore stand ready then.*

Gemeda and Murroh both moved closer to the powerful women just as two hands, one of which had sharp nails and webbed fingers, met above calm blue water. She stiffened and the gleaming, lethal glass trident moved to within an ince of her chest. Meanwhile, her conversation with Eurynome continued on a much deeper level, one that those around them couldn't hear.

I promise you that I only seek peace between our people.

Eurynome spoke back, deep within their minds. *Tell me why I shouldn't trust this two-legger, Havington. Show me with your thoughts.*

It took only secs for Olivara to impart hundreds of rotos of history, and the details of Pon Havington's rise to power and his machinations to rule all of Psiere. She also told of his ancestor's actions on that fateful dae in the Solis Sea, when countless lives were lost due to the hubris and ignorance of one foolish man. It was a brutal history lesson and both could see ways toward a calmer future between their races, if only they were willing to take the first step and put trust in one another.

The others, Atlantee and Psierians alike, looked on as the queens were frozen in the water, deeply locked into the other's mind. A strange splash formed in the water just beyond Eurynome, then she jerked as a wound opened in her chest.

Torrin yelled out. "Ambush!"

He waded forward but was unable to prevent Olivara from being struck in the shoulder. Moving as fast as possible in waist deep water, he forged toward the queens that were only being held up by Gemeda and the Atlanteen who still gripped the trident in his free hand. Sharcs swam closer and the Atlanteens visibly bristled farther out in the water. Blue blood leaked from Eurynome's chest.

"What do I do?" Gemeda yelled.

"Heal them both if you can." Torrin folded himself around Olivara and turned to block Eurynome and Gemeda with his own body. Understanding that he was putting himself in harm's way to protect everyone, including the Atlanteen queen, Murroh swam around so he could do the same.

It was obvious that Eurynome's wound was the more serious of the two. Gem grabbed the woman's strangely textured arm and closed her eyes in concentration. Three tense meens later, the Atlanteen queen roused into consciousness. Murroh spoke with her as Gemeda began working on their own queen.

Torrin adjusted his grip on Olivara and looked back at the beach. There were countless soldiers in black standing with rifles at the ready, many of which pointed at their parlay group. Unfortunately, he'd ruined his voteo when he dropped lower into the water to grasp Olivara. Thinking fast, he pulled the thong holding the stone around Olivara's neck and touched it, then contacted General Renou with his boosted telepathy channel.

General, the Atlanteens are not the aggressors. Gemeda healed their queen and is in the process of healing our own. But we are still in danger and you need to catch that shooter. The trajectory of the shells mean they must be somewhere east or northeast from us.

He didn't try to listen for a response. Instead, he tucked the stone back into Olivara's shirt as delicately as possible. Torrin glanced at Gemeda, whose eyes were closed with concentration. He was vaguely aware that more Atlanteens had gathered, forming a protective circle around their group. Based on the rapid chattering of Queen Eurynome, it was on her direction.

Olivara gave a gasp and came awake. It was her turn to catch Gemeda as the Doctore's eyes rolled back with unconsciousness. "Help me, she's used all she had between us."

Torrin released the queen and lifted Gemeda into his arms. He looked at Olivara with surprise. "How—?"

"She warned me when I was healed that the shell in my shoulder had deflected toward my heart. She'll need to be carried out to replenish her reserves. Can you hold her for a bit like that?"

"As long as necessary. She's naught but a tiny psi."

Olivara quickly took in the scene around them then moved her gaze back to Eurynome. *Thank you for having your people shield us.*

We could do no less with honor at stake. If not for your Doctore, I would have gone back to the sea as naught more than a sacrifice to the currents. I owe you thanks on two levels.

Two?

For saving my life, and for showing me the truth of our former ally. Those under my command grow restless and fear another attack but I wish to form an alliance with you, here and now. Your two-legger, Havington, promised that no Psierian would set foot in the oceans once he was ruler. I suspect that would be an impossible promise to keep.

Olivara spoke to Torrin. "Captain, were you able to

contact General Renou?"

"Yes, my Queen. I had to use your stone so I don't know of a response. I just informed them that the Atlanteens were aiding us and gave them the general direction of the shooter."

She nodded. "Thank you."

Olivara turned back to Eurynome. *It's true that my people need the bounty of the sea to supplement our food stocks for survival. However, I'm willing to negotiate boundaries with you if it helps.*

The large Atlanteen that appeared to be Eurynome's main guard, spoke with her and the queen nodded. Eurynome smiled toward Olivara. *Murroh has suggested that we use the shelves of each continentus as boundary lines. If your people stay out of the deep seas, I think we can work out an arrangement. But you should know that if you misuse your resources in the shallows, they will disappear. You will not be allowed access to the deeper bounty if you're foolish enough to waste what you have.*

Olivara looked back and forth between Eurynome and her guard. She raised a single dark brow. *Your guard has opinions on political negotiations?*

He is also my mate.

Fascinating.

Do you not do as such? Is he, Eurynome waved toward Torrin, *not your mate?* Olivara shook her head. *Who protects you if not the one who loves you most?*

It has never been done before... Olivara paused. *Actually, my daughter's mate is her lead guardian so perhaps it is a method that could work well.*

Olivara had studied every imaginable map of Psiere that had been created when she was still just a connate. She'd learned the topography of their land, as well as the shallow and deeper seas around Endara and Dromea. It wasn't a detailed map, but she knew that at a certain point all the way around each continent, the ocean floor dropped significantly. Intuition told her that Eurynome's offer would work, with careful resource conservation. *I agree to the terms of your offer. We may require aid in mapping out the boundaries between the regions of our peoples but I think it will work well for us. Is there anything else you'd like to add?*

Eurynome thought for a few secs then nodded. *Yes. While we have many cities beneath the sea, we have one that is sacred to us and has often been disturbed by your fishing vessels. Though not so much in recent rotations. There are two islands on the eastern end of your southern continent. A large one and a smaller one. Gaiana lies between the two. We would like that entire region to remain off-limits to your kind.*

Olivara pictured the map of Psiere in her head. She knew there were no large cities along that particular stretch of Dromea. It was an inhospitable region, good only for a railer recharging station. Fishing was also poor there because of aggressive Atlanteen activity, and now she knew the reason why.

The islands you mention, Magnise and Parvise, are both uninhabited. It will take some organization on our part, which will have to wait until after we've quelled this blasted rebellion, but that is another item we can guarantee. What is the timeline for this pact? Is it something that should be revisited at a future date? What are your laws and traditions for such?

Eurynome nodded. *We have a tradition in the Atlantee nation and contracts bring stability. Aggression from one ruler or another will invalidate it. We should revisit the contract with each leadership change. If there is no meeting, we shall assume the contract remains valid as-is. We will also provide an ambassador and other emissaries as necessary to further the education of our race and wish for you to do the same. What say you?*

I would ask one boon of you?

You may ask.

I would like to be allowed sea travel outside the shallows until the rebellion is quelled.

Eurynome looked at her with surprise, leaning back a bit where she floated in the water. *You do not wish for aid in your fight the way Havington did?*

I've no want, nor will, to put your people at risk for our war.

The other queen smiled with a mouth full of sharp teeth, clearly pleased by Olivara's words. *You have much honor. I think we will have a marvelous alliance going forward and I will enjoy learning about your people in the rotations to come. Your wish is granted. Send word via another emissary to arrange our next meeting when your battle for supremacy is finished. I will meet with you again at that time.*

Olivara nodded. *I'd say we are in agreement. Here is to prosperity and peace between both our people's.* She held out her hand, palm facing Eurynome. The other queen raised her own hand to press their palms together.

When they finished, Eurynome swam farther away, past the buoys. The other Atlanteen guards moved with her. She gave one final look toward the trio. Then, as an afterthought, she broke the kelp bindings of two shells on her necklace and tossed them one at a time to Olivara. *One is for you, and the other is for your doctore who saved my life. Should you ever need anything, the back of each is inscribed with the symbol of my trident and will guarantee you safety in deep waters.*

Olivara glanced to where Gemeda remained unconscious in Torrin's arms. *She saved both of our lives. I will be sure she receives your gift when I explain all she missed. Thank you again and I look forward to a conversation in calmer waters.*

May Posidee shine down upon you, Psierian queen. Then Eurynome dove backward into the sea. Olivara and Torrin watched as the rest also dropped beneath the surface. Secs later the sharc fins and the great whal sank and disappeared as quickly as a dream.

Chapter Seven

"By the depths, I'll go mad if I have to stay on this bloody dead-air ship any longer. Are you sure we can't pop out for a brief stroll around the city in the dark? No one will know I'm here."

"Better dead air than dead sovereign. You know we can't do that, 'Vienne. All it takes is one precog, or even a spotter on the top of one of the new buildings to see you and we're finished. Secrecy is our main priority."

Olivienne paused in her pacing to tap her lip. "What if we go out in disguise?"

"A full team of shields? It's highly unlikely we'd find clothing enough let alone have it fit the stature of our guardians."

Olivienne tried one more avenue. "Just us then? No one can touch us as long as you hold that stone."

Castellan tensed at the suggestion and quickly denied the request. "Out of the question! I can feel the acid roiling within my gut at the thought of taking you out there by myself. And no one has to touch you to put you in danger. All it takes is one long range voteo call to do us in. For all we know, the beasts in the ocean below are spies for Havington as well."

"Fine." Olivienne threw herself backward onto the bed in their cabin. "I'm still bored. The captain won't throw cubes with us anymore because of your blasted skill—"

"It's luck I tell you."

"And she's already given me a sound talking to about our romantic foolery aboard the *Vestigo*, no matter how big a ship it is. Apparently, my mental voice is too loud."

Castellan chuckled. "It's not just your mental voice, love."

"Oh, you!" Olivienne pitched the nearby pillow toward Castellan's head. She caught it and let it drop onto a nearby lounger without lifting a hand.

Castellan sat upon the edge of their bed and winced as the wood frame pressed into the back of her thighs in a most uncomfortable manner. "Perhaps you need to take up a hobby when on your missions. Or at least for tonight, try to sleep. It's twenty-four hundred oors, after all."

"I'm not tired, and I've got a hobby." She grinned. "It's one I quite love."

"You do?"

Olivienne narrowed her eyes and sat up to lean closer. "Yes." she grabbed Castellan by the front of her black shirt and pulled until their lips were inces away from one another. "You."

Castellan sighed and felt her cheeks grow warm. "But the captain's orders—"

"Fie on Velten. You're the only captain I listen to." Castellan snorted at the sometimes-true statement and Olivienne grinned. "Well...when I *wish* to listen to a captain, that is. Now, where were we?" She leaned in for a kiss when the alert tone sounded on Castellan's voteo.

Castellan gave Olivienne a quick peck on the lips before pulling away and grabbing the device from her belt. "Yes?"

Olivienne rolled her eyes and threw herself backward onto the bed again.

"Ser, Soleng sending."

"Go ahead, Lieutenant."

Gar Soleng didn't answer for a few secs, then his voice came through the small speaker. "Sorry, ser. I'm still not used to the title."

"Give it time. Do you have something to report?"

"Yes, ser. Madlin is off shift for the night and I'm standing on the side deck watching them load the replacement part onto the ship. Engineer Davine says they'll work through the evening to install the shaft. It should be tested and ready to go by first light."

Olivienne sat up. "At first light? Finally!"

Castellan smiled at her. "That is great news and you've just made the connate happy. Make sure your night guardians stay alert. It wouldn't do to be so close to departure and have a saboteur find us."

"You can count on us, ser."

"I know I can. Tosh, out." Castellan placed the voteo

in a nearby bin then removed her pistol and belt and did the same with them.

Olivienne grinned mischievously when she began unbuttoning her trousers. "Are you finally coming around to my way of thinking?"

"On the contrary," Castellan slipped the fabric down her legs, folding the garment once it was removed. Her slow pace continued as she methodically worked through the clasps of her uniform shirt. "I'm going to get sleep while I'm able. I want to be ready if we're to leave at first light."

"Ready for what?" Olivienne extended her leg and hooked one foot seductively around Castellan's thigh to pull her closer to the bed.

"Anything. Which means I'll need sleep tonight."

Olivienne clucked her tongue and Castellan continued on, knowing how the other woman would react. There was only one way to wear out her sovereign when she was on the brink of adventure and in one of her moods. "The Shield Corp manual clearly states that—"

Olivienne gave a hard pull with her leg at the same time she used her apportation channel to remove Castellan's uniform. The black fabric settled into a heap atop the carefully folded trousers. "You're not consoring with that blasted Shield Corp manual!"

Laughter rang through the small cabin. Castellan allowed herself to be pulled down but used her levitation to control how and where she landed to avoid hurting herself or Olivienne. Bare skin slid together and she was surprised to find that Olivienne had removed her own clothing as well. She leaned closer until she could whisper into Olivienne's ear. "I'm certainly not. I'm consoring with the most beautiful psi in all the land."

"I'm not so fair as that." Olivienne's eyes gave away the vulnerability that lay beneath the bravado gifted to her by strength of channel and her status as the future ruler of their people. Just like anyone else, Olivienne had her own fears of inadequacy that were exacerbated by Savon's sacrifice. It was a fact that Castellan knew well after countless oors of late-night conversation.

Castellan didn't want her in that particular headspace. Her goal was to distract and tire out her lover so she could start their mission with a fresh mind in the morning. "You are to me. Now, I believe you mentioned something about listening to me as your captain?"

"I—by the Makers!" She gasped as Castellan gently thrust her hips where they lay at the juncture between Olivienne's thighs.

The firm but persistent movement never stopped. "I like the sound of your pleasure. If you're willing and able, your captain has a few demands."

Olivienne moaned and gasped her acquiescence. "Yes, ser!"

Everyone was well-rested the next morning, with the exception of a certain connate and her Shield Corp captain. Olivienne rubbed the space between her eyes when they stepped through the portal onto the brightly-lit bridge.

Captain Velten greeted them as soon as she turned their way. "Good dae, Connate Dracore, Captain Tosh." She peered closer at Olivienne. "Are you feeling well, Connate?"

Olivienne blew out a breath. "Just an aching head from lack of sleep. I could do with a brew or a stim."

Velten removed a small tin from a front pocket in her uniform shirt. She opened it and offered the container of stim-roots to Olivienne, who gratefully took one and began chewing on it. Velten then offered the tin to Castellan, who shook her head. "No, thank you. Too bitter for me. I'll be fine."

"Well enough." She closed the tin and returned it to her pocket. "I trust that your lieutenant informed you of our imminent departure."

"Madlin is on now and she did. How long did you estimate it would take for us to arrive at the coordinates found on Magna? The way it was spoken of in prep meetings, this ship is faster than your old one."

Velten wobbled her hand in front of her. "Yes and no. Faster than the average ship, sure. But it's only slightly faster than the *Quaesitum*. Not enough to make a difference unless we're flying into a headwind. We have more power but are still limited by the physics of a dirigible." She led them to a worktable that displayed a map of Psiere with their destination clearly marked far to the northwest of Occasus. "All in total, we're looking at about twenty oors to the Halcyon Station."

Olivienne reached out to touch the small dot. "It's hard to believe that it's been so relatively close this whole time. What will we see there? What further marvels of Maker technology will we find?"

Castellan scowled. "Or what trouble? I'm pretty sure we were on the same missions with many of those close calls. Their traps are lethal."

"They're ingenious!"

"Ingenious and lethal. That's not even considering trouble from Havington that may yet appear."

Velten shook her head at the pair of them but focused her attention on Castellan. "Do you know something I don't?"

"No official intel. What I do know is that the queen was supposed to attempt contact with the Atlanteens any time but there's no way to learn how well their plans play out due to the communication blackout we're all under."

"Are you afraid she won't be successful?"

Olivienne sucked in a breath and her voice held the fine tremble of fright. "What is it, Castellan? Do you think she'll fail and place herself in danger?"

"On the contrary, I have a feeling she'll succeed." She caught the surprised lift to Olivienne's brows. "It's a gut feeling only, a twinge of my channel. My worry is that if Havington realizes his Atlanteen allies have turned against him, he'll send dirigibles our way."

Velten scowled. "But he doesn't know where we are."

Castellan shrugged. "It's never stopped him from finding us before."

"So, what are you saying?"

"Be wary and watch for any suspicious ships."

"Ser, we have an incoming transmission from General Renou!" Both captains and the connate turned to look toward Specialist Tohda, the operator of the communications array.

Velten led the way to and aimed her question at Castellan. "Why in the deep-sea depths are we being contacted? We're supposed to be running black as far as the capital is concerned!"

"I have no idea. Something must have happened."

"Maman," Olivienne whispered.

Castellan attempted to reassure her. "We don't know anything yet."

She turned back to the communications specialist. "What does the message say?"

The woman gave her a look of confusion. "I don't know, ser."

"Explain yourself," Velten demanded.

Tohda swallowed and glanced nervously back and forth between the two intense captains. "I mean that it's written in code. Looks like what's on those temple sheets we used to study back at academy. I was never any good at ciphers though."

Velten looked at Castellan, and Castellan looked to Olivienne. "Surely, they wouldn't use something as easy to crack as one of the temple keys, right?"

Olivienne tapped her lower lip. "They would if it were an emergency. They'd most likely use Antaeus as the key."

She gestured to Tohda. "Let me see it."

Once the sheet was in hand, Olivienne took it to the worktable they'd been standing at meens before. She placed it flat on the surface then withdrew a translation velum and greased stylus from the ever-present satchel at her hip. When she was finished, Velten and Castellan both leaned closer to read what was on the sheet.

Velten's brows lifted with surprise. "Well, this is the best possible outcome."

Olivienne's mouth dropped open as she glared at the dirigible captain. "Best possi—she was shot! I'd say there were other, safer outcomes than that."

Castellan caressed her arm in an attempt to sooth her fiery temper. "Peace, 'Vienne. I'm sure Velten was merely speaking of the end result, not the way it came about."

Velten looked chastised. "Of course. I would never wish ill on our queen, or another."

"So, what does this mean for us?"

Castellan moved her gaze between the other two. "A treaty between Queen Olivara and this Atlantee queen, Eurynome, means that we no longer need to be wary of the Atlanteens or their sea beasts. However, we need to watch even closer for spies or Havington's ships. They're certain to be on the move now."

"Ser!"

Captain Velten abruptly threw up her arms and turned back toward Tohda. "What now?"

"I've got three ships approaching from the south on the sonica."

They strode back to the communications console. "Sheddech!" Velten hit the ship-wide intercom. "Engineer Davine, report. What's the status on that aft dextra engine?"

Davine's voice came back, sounding as though he were straining at something. "Nearly finished, Captain. I'm readjusting the torque on these clamps. I don't want them coming loose once we get going."

"Work faster, we've got enemies approaching."

"Here?"

"Now, Davine!"

"Aye-aye, Captain."

Velten peered closer at the sonica. "How long until they hit Occasus?"

Tohda grabbed a straight rule and held it to the grid on the sonica display, looked at her chrono and marked time, then repeated the action a meen later. She frowned. "They're going fast, ten meens out, maybe more."

"Shite! The new kevlan bladders certainly even the scales for those blackhearts when it comes to facing off against them."

"Better question, Captain, is how were they able to make it this far north? Their stones should be spent without a steady supply line to swap out for charged ones. And we'd have heard if they hit any of our outposts."

Castellan listened to the voices drone around her but

Olivienne's words prompted deeper introspection. Her intuition jangled as she contemplated all the possible ways the rebels could arrive so far north within the distance limit that carrying stones placed on every ship. Suddenly she blurted out the solution. "Except for ours!"

Velten looked at her as if she'd gone mad, an expression that Olivienne somewhat copied. "Except for ours what, Tosh?"

"Every ship is limited in distance because they can only carry so many stones, which have to be recharged. Every ship except for ours. Which means if they've come this far north, they must have archeostones aboard those ships."

Olivienne furrowed her brows and her mouth twisted. "You think they have someone on the inside that what, stole the stones that we brought back from the Temple of Antaeus?"

"Impossible." Olivienne and Castellan looked at Velten and she elaborated. "Those stones are under the tightest security. As a matter of fact, only Renou, Leniste, and the queen know where they are. I was given my stone for *Vestigo's* charge room personally before setting out for Occasus."

"There is only one other source of archeostones left to Havington."

"They wouldn't!" If Castellan thought Olivienne had been furious on previous occasions, nothing compared to the look that drew down the connate's dark brows at her suggestion.

Velten rubbed her chin. "They'd need only one. A charging room on one ship could keep the other two going as long as they had a way to pass spent and charged illeostones back and forth."

"It sickens me to know they'd desecrate the temple of Illeos in such a manner but it seems like something that Havington would do to further his cause."

"Either way, we need to hasten our departure. You may want to find a seat and strap in." Velten called to the rest. "Spool all but the aft dextra engine, we need to be ready to go as soon as Davine gives us clearance. Savvy?"

Pilot Seben nodded and began flipping switches. "Aye, Captain."

Castellan called out to her own team in the quickest manner available to her. *All available shields, we have enemies rapidly approaching our location. Head to the nearest rail guns and prepare for imminent departure.*

Lieutenant Madlin responded. *I'd ask how they discovered our coordinates but the better question is: how did they make it this far north?*

We suspect they've taken an archeostone from the Temple of Illeos. That means not only have they come all this way, but they'll be able to follow us when we leave. Castellan and Olivienne each took a seat out of the way and strapped in. Castellan elaborated on her explanation to Madlin. *We don't know much yet, but I'm guessing they won't be able to match this new ship's speed. Even so, there is nothing to prevent them trailing us like canids after a bone.*

Should I rouse the off-duty shields, ser?

No, leave them to sleep if they can. I highly doubt the rebels will face off with us at this time but post those on duty at each external deck until we're clear. I want everyone as well-rested as possible when we reach Halcyon, just like when we went to Magna.

Yes, ser.

Velten spoke above the ship wide com. "Prepare for departure. Davine, spool up the engine as soon as it's ready. We can't outrun those ships without it."

The *Vestigo* lurched as the mooring cables were released. Despite only having three engines, Castellan was glad to see them rapidly pick up speed, heading vaguely northwest.

Olivienne unclasped her safety harness along with Castellan and they both stood to make their way back to the main observation window where they could see the ships in the distance. It wouldn't be long before they realized the *Vestigo* was on the move and they were forced to correct their course. Not one person on the bridge thought they were after anything other than the connate.

Olivienne jumped when Davine's voice came across

the bridge speaker. "The aft dextra engine is spooling now, Captain. All looks shiny on this end. We should be at full speed within three meens."

Velten answered. "Steady as she goes. Let me know if anything changes."

"Aye-aye, Captain."

Velten then turned to Castellan and Olivienne with a grim look. "They won't catch us now. At least not until we reach our destination or something untoward happens between here and there. What do you say we retire to the captain's room and plan for what to do against our new friends?"

Castellan sighed and ran a hand through her hair. "I'd say that's as sound of an idea as any."

Meens later they were across the ship and seated around the table in Velten's personal meeting room. She snagged glasses and a pitcher of water before they sat down. "I don't think it's likely we'll see any attacks before we get to your new island. While our speed is only about five mahls per oor above theirs, we're too far ahead of the rebels for them to bring their rail guns to bear."

Olivienne gave Castellan a concerned look. "I have to admit, I'm not particularly pleased to have Havington's ships following so close on our heels. How am I to do my job on this adventurist mission if we're going to be attacked as soon as we try looking for that blasted Halcyon Station? I'm not a soldier, Tosh."

The look on Olivienne's face was easy enough to read for someone who knew her intimately. Castellan grasped her hand in an attempt to give comfort. She knew that Olivienne was afraid to be in another situation like the one above King's Marsh. "I know you're not. And if it comes down to fighting like that once more, rest assured, I will never put you in such a position again."

"Will you use your stone then?" Both of them looked at Velten with surprise. "What? I was briefed on the two stones, as well as your continued possession of one of them by Renou. While the situation above King's Marsh wasn't ideal, doing what you did before shouldn't be off the table, Tosh—"

"No!" Castellan thumped her fist against the table, causing water in their glasses to slosh. She took a deep breath and spared a glance toward Olivienne before answering Velten. "The cost was simply too high for what I did. However, there are other ways we can mediate some of the risk those ships present, without dashing them from the sky in such a callous and cold-hearted manner." She turned to look at Olivienne and hoped her promise would reassure her. "I won't risk innocent lives again in such a way, nor will I expect anyone else to. We are better than that."

"Innocent, Tosh?"

"Per the intel we received from Lieutenant Cando, some of the people serving Havington are being coerced under threat to their family members."

Velten must have sensed deeper strife associated with her words because when Castellan looked back at her, Velten's lips were pursed together with displeasure, but she didn't argue the point. "What can we do?"

"What if the *Vestigo* drops us off under the cover of night then leads them farther out?" Olivienne looked between the two captains.

Castellan shrugged. "It seems like a solid plan. I think it's reasonable to assume that we will get there at least a few oors before the ships trailing behind us."

Velten agreed. "More actually, because the trip there is our old max range. They'll have to stop and exchange spent illeostones for charged ones from whichever ship is holding the archeostone. A twenty oor travel time to Halcyon Station puts our estimated arrival around four hundred oors so it will be plenty dark. We can circle the island from above to search for a clearing using that modified sonal ocilloscope you showed me from a previous mission. I believe it's in your gear room. We just need someplace where your team can safely rappel down."

"Yes, probably best not to winch down to the ground and give away our presence. Let them think we are merely waiting above."

Olivienne looked back to Castellan. "What does your intuition tell you on this one?"

"Bog all, I'm afraid."

"Well, that's unfortunate. What about you, Captain?"

Velten's eyes widened at Olivienne's question. "What about me, what?"

"You've never once mentioned your channels in all our past conversations. Do you have anything that could help with this decision?"

Castellan pursed her lips as Velten let out a long sigh and responded. "Tosh hasn't mentioned my ratings to you then?"

"No, I haven't. Renou explicitly stated that officially the Shield Corp doesn't make exceptions for their members so I've kept the knowledge safely under my collar."

Olivienne shot them both a confused look. "What knowledge?"

Velten gave her a wry smile. "I'm practically a null. At least compared to you two overpowered behemoths."

"Really? But don't you need to have a minimum overall channel rating of a three and a half, and a minimum telepathy of four to be a shield?

Castellan answered. "Yes. However, some exceptions needed to be made to get Velten and her entire crew to join the Shield Corp as your personal transportation team."

"It's true, Connate. I am but a lowly three in tee-kay, and a two-point-three overall. My highest rating is enhanced awareness and even that is only a four."

Olivienne's mouth dropped open with surprise. "But you're so, so, successful!"

That drew an actual laugh from the oft-time serious captain. "Contrary to popular belief, you don't have to be powered to be capable. I've learned to rely on naught more than my wits and wisdom when it comes to getting by in life."

Castellan rapped her knuckles on the table. "Great philosophy. I'd say it's served you well enough so far and we're luckier for it. However, in this particular instance with the rebels on our trail, we're all equally in the dark."

"My advice to you, Connate, is that we wait and see what this blasted island with the Maker's station has to offer before we make solid plans. We don't know if there is a transportation hub, like on Magna, or if there will be traps and such in store for us. I can't imagine such a place wouldn't be well-guarded if it is so relatively easy to find."

Castellan groaned. "That's what I'm afraid of."

"So, our tentative plan is to stay ahead of the rebels, scout the island from afar, and send my team down under the cover of darkness if the opportunity presents itself?" Olivienne said.

"Yes."

"As it always seems to be, it's naught but a waiting game then." She looked at Castellan. "I suppose, in the meantime, we can read some more from Savon's log to see if there are any other prophetic words of enlightenment contained within."

"Savon, your previous first lieutenant?"

"Yes, the one. He kept a log that was suspected to hold visions and other corp secrets so his sib gave it to General Renou who in turn gave it to me to decipher," Castellan said.

"Have you learned much so far?"

"Only that he dreamed of his own death and that the land would be split by civil war."

"Was he so powerful then?"

"Powerful enough. He was a four in prescience and a three in telesthesia. But something about his foresight channel combined in a strangely efficient way with his ability to see in the distance and he was accurate more often than not."

Velten rubbed the first finger of her right hand across her upper lip. "Foresight and far sight, that is a strange melding of channels indeed. There is much about our makeup that we still don't know. Even the academy with all its focus on research and testing makes new discoveries every roto."

"It's true. There are things we are only just learning in the field, abilities that some of us who have spent time in the trenches battling Atlanteens and other organized ne'er-do-wells knew but that our officers and the instrae had never even considered. I feel as though every question we answer in the quest for knowledge about the Makers only serves to open up three more about the past and makeup of Psiere's people."

Olivienne smiled. "Maybe now you both can understand why I love my job as a historical adventurist so much. There are questions out there that still need answers and I'm doing my level best to find them."

"A curious mind is rarely idle. I read that somewhere but cannot for the life of me remember the tome." Velten paused, then placed her palms flat on the table in front of her. "Either way, it looks like we all know our duty for the coming oors."

Chapter Eight

The *Vestigo* arrived at the island containing the Halcyon Station early in the morning. Velten's crew kept a close eye on their pursuers during the course of their twenty oor trip. As predicted, they gained even more air when the three ships stopped and grouped closer together. It was probably the only way to exchange spent for charged stones when so high above the ocean. That left their ship with some time to explore before the rebels arrived.

Olivienne and Castellan were on the bridge with Velten, despite the late...or early... oor. Both Madlin and Soleng joined them a few meens later. "Ser, the team is fully assembled with all our gear and rappelling lines are set up on the dextra staging deck. We're ready to head down as soon as a suitable landing location is found."

Castellan returned their salutes. "Thanks, Madlin. We're just beginning our approach now."

"I'm not going to lie, Tosh, the glow from that volcano has me nervous."

Olivienne looked at Velten with surprise. "But you piloted us to another island with a volcano just a few rotos ago with no issue. And unlike that ship, this one has an impenetrable bladder."

Velten shook her head. "The pyroclastic displays from Mount Ignis have been well-studied and documented. Winds are predictable and steady and rarely change course. Approaching the cliffs on the opposite end of the island away from any potential volcanic eruptions was a sure thing. We don't know anything about this one, or the wind currents here. Given the way it glows and sparks, it could be on the verge of eruption any meen. The only good thing right now is that it's dark enough we'd be able to see any ejecta heading our way."

"Captain, what are your orders?"

Velten glanced at her on-duty pilot, then back to Castellan and Olivienne. "I'm not comfortable with it but the call is yours, Connate Dracore."

Olivienne chewed her lip for a few secs. "Perhaps take us forward slowly."

"You heard the connate, Neela. Take us forward at one-sixth speed."

"Aye, Captain. Forward we go."

The dirigible slowly drew closer to the dark mass with its glowing, mountainous center. Olivienne was the first to speak. "You have to admit, dangerous or not, the radiance is certainly beautiful."

"You may want to stay your opinions on that. I wouldn't wish to draw the eye of bad luck onto our backs—"

"Captain, we have ejecta coming straight for us!"

"Bollux!" Velten yelled to the specialist seated to the pilot's right. "Gadol, open reserve canister one on my mark." She slammed her hand on ship wide coms. "All hands, prepare for evasive maneuvers! Gadol, now."

Castellan knew what was coming and used her teleki-nesis to steady Olivienne, Madlin, Soleng, and herself. A great hissing sound echoed through the bridge and the diri-gible abruptly shot straight up from their previous posi-tion. The fireball that had inexplicably been heading toward their exact location flew harmlessly beneath the *Vestigo*.

Velten released the cross bar she'd grabbed to hold herself steady. "Well, that was blasted poor luck that we just happen to be in its path."

Castellan kept her gaze fixed on the volcano in the dis-tance as her intuition channel jangled ferociously. "Was it though?"

"Tosh? What are you going on about?"

"Captain, we have another incoming fireball."

Velten certainly wasn't slow and caught on immedi-ately to what Castellan implied. "Gadol, canister two. Neela, spin us around and get us away from that island, full speed."

Twin voices responded. "Aye-Aye, Captain." Hissing filled the bridge for a second time and the *Vestigo* shot up yet again.

Castellan had a feeling they weren't going to move

fast enough for whatever was controlling the fireballs. "Velten, how many of those canisters do you have left?"

The ship captain gave her a worried look. "Just the two. They take time to recharge."

"Sheddech." Castellan strode toward the windows where she could view the volcano as the dirigible turned slowly toward its dextra side. Another fireball was headed their way. Rather than call a warning, she reached into her uniform shirt and tightly grasped the antoraestone. She was able to turn it away with a flex of her expanded telekinesis.

The captain wouldn't be worth her rank if she wasn't aware enough to have eyes on the threat at all times. "Thanks, Tosh."

Castellan nodded. "I'll stand here until we're certain no more are coming our way. The three we've seen so far have been ten secs apart."

Velten grunted, and it was obvious by her expression that she'd not thought to count the timing of the shots. What are you at now?"

"Seventeen."

"Good enough then. Neela, full stop and spin us around to face the island again."

"Yes, ser."

Madlin was no fool either. "Ser, you think that was some sort of defense mechanism? How can the Makers harness such energy as that from a volcano? It's unbelievable."

Olivienne tapped her bottom lip. "Tosh, you remember what I told you about caches I've found that are made to look like the natural surroundings?"

"Things like the stalagmite in the sirens' cave?"

"Yes, the hollow one that looked like all the rest until I broke it free. What if this were something similar? What if the Makers wanted to scare people away without letting on that there was anything unnatural about the place?"

Soleng's deep voice cut through the quiet hum of the idled engines. "It would either scare the curious from the island or kill them. Either way, they'd be rid of anyone wishing to land."

Olivienne threw up her hands with exasperation. "Great! How do *we* land then? It's too blasted early to deal with Tau machinations."

Castellan snorted. "But 'Vienne, I thought you loved your job as a historical adventurist and all the challenges involved with it?"

Olivienne scowled back at her. "I usually have a little more control concerning the when and how of things. By the depths, this is as out of control as any worst-case circumstance I could have imagined."

"Captain, the attacks appear to have stopped. Orders?"

Velten pulled out her chrono to check the time and frowned. She turned to Castellan and Olivienne. "We have blasted little time before those rebels catch up with us, but I suppose we don't have a lot of options here. Tosh, can you do what you just did again?"

"Of course, but my concern is this. The nearer we get to the island, the more force I'll need to turn it away enough to miss the ship. And what happens if the fireballs come faster when we don't heed the initial warning?"

"That's a good point. Even a poor shot knows that the closer you are to something the easier it is to hit. What's left for us to do then? Sit like fish in a pond waiting for the three gulls that follow?"

Velten took another look at the glowing volcano in the distance. "We may not be able to approach yet but that doesn't mean we have to put ourselves between the rebels and the island. Perhaps the volcano will remove the threat for us."

"Excellent plan, Captain."

"Neela, plot an arc around the island without taking us too close. Keep us at half speed." She turned to Olivienne and Castellan. "Shift change happens in a few oors, probably around the same time we'll see our friends on the sonica. Maybe the light of our two suns will shine down on a fresh idea because I'm all out."

"Do you have a direction preference, ser?"

"Keep the island to the laeva side."

Neither Castellan nor Olivienne cared which way they circled and keeping the volcano to their left seemed as safe as any other direction. Castellan glanced around the bridge. "I'd say there's naught much to do now but wait for Havington's men to arrive. We'll head back to our cabins until then. Call me as soon as you pick up the rebels' approach."

"Ser, want us to let the rest of the team know what is going on?"

Castellan waved off Madlin's suggestion. "I can do it, Lieutenant." She pulled the voteo from where it was secured on her thick, black belt. "Attention all shields. Secure the gear on the staging deck then take some down time. Our mission has been delayed by a defensive mechanism on the part of the island. Stay wary. The *Vestigo* will head partway around the island and we'll most likely see action again when the rebels catch up with us."

Olivienne grumbled as the four of them left Velten and her crew behind and made their way off the bridge. "I hate waiting."

Castellan took her hand in a rare show of public affection and gave it a squeeze. "I know, love. Nothing that can be helped, I'm afraid. I just hope the rebels aren't as fast thinking as we are. Or at the least they decide the prize of our flesh isn't worth the risk."

They had first meal in their cabin as they reviewed more entries in Savon's journal. Castellan went to fetch some water as Olivienne flipped to a new page in the book. She quickly called out upon seeing a too-familiar style of poetic phrasing. "Tosh, look!"

Castellan returned and placed the glasses in a recessed stand near their lounger. The additional space within the ship also gave them more room in the connate's personal cabin. It was a luxury both women enjoyed. "What is that, another prophesy?"

"This entry is written the same way as many of the convoluted texts found within the temples. Not the schematics, mind you, but rather the ones that are clues to hidden caches. Look here at the pattern of the lines."

She skimmed her finger down the page to highlight the

passage, not that Castellan needed any aid in seeing what Olivienne was referring to. Castellan read aloud, careful of the individual lines and pacing. "Beware swimming sharcs three, who pursue the gem of Psiere. O'er the waves through air, to the volcano across the sea." She paused in acknowledgement of the on-the-nose reference to their current situation. "Fire and ash rain down, in the space between threats. One visitor who never forgets, three enemies who would de-crown."

Olivienne read the final stanza aloud. "In the darkness you see, the dangers that wait, as focused fires glow. Two of the three, will meet their fate, one high and one low."

"It seems to define our situation. But who is the visitor that never forgets?" Castellan shrugged at her question. "Read the part below the poem."

Castellan skipped down to a passage that Savon had underlined. "There is only one way in, but every way out. The island leads to the island." She looked up and raised a pale brow. "I have no idea what that means."

Olivienne's pondering broke the silence a few meens later. "Perhaps there is a direction we can approach the island from, that will not garner the attention of those blasted fireballs."

"Unfortunately, it is too dark to see if there are any other islands nearby. I'm afraid the answer to this may have to wait until suns rise."

Olivienne groaned and picked up her stylus and book of blank velum to begin copying Savon's two passages, the sonnet and the added comment below.

It was still dark outside when the ship wide alert sounded. A meen later, Velten's voice came across Castellan's voteo. "Connate Dracore, Captain Tosh, the rebels have reached the area. They are a quarter way around the island from us."

Castellan responded as Olivienne quickly stowed their supplies and stuffed Savon's journal into the satchel at her hip. "We're on our way." She mentally contacted the rest of the shield team. *All shields, be ready. The rebels are approaching from the southeast.*

Madlin responded for the group. *We'll head to the external decks in case we need to lend aid to the ship's defense.*

Good thinking, Lieutenant.

When the pair arrived at the bridge, there was a sense of anticipation and dread from all the specialists manning their posts. Velten stared resolutely out the plexi windows at the front of the dirigible with chin in hand and fingers worrying at her upper lip. Castellan interrupted her deep thoughts.

"I'm assuming if we can see them, they can see us." She peered into the twilight sky, only marginally brighter with the imminent rise of Archeos. "Though I'm not sure how you saw anything this far out."

Velten waved toward the sonica array. "They showed up on the screen a few meens ago. But you're right, if we can see them on the sonica, they can see us, too. Our ship is bigger but the equipment is still the same. Sadly. The real question is, will they come for us or head to the island?"

"Aren't they after me? Why ever would they head toward an unfamiliar island if they followed me here?"

Castellan shook her head. "They followed an adventurist as much as they followed a connate. I think Havington must know that wherever you go, things are found that can aid Psierians. My guess is that he's interested in whatever you're interested in and most likely gave instructions to his rebels to take both if possible. And we, for good or ill, are a known quantity. We've taken down his ships before. My instinct is telling me they'll try the island first."

Velten gave her a grim look. "Little do they know the island may be the more dangerous choice. Either way, let's see what happens."

"Ser, one of the ships has broken off and is heading toward the island."

The sky was significantly brighter, with a blueish-white glow off to their left, as they were facing due south. Velten peered through her spyglass then handed it to Castellan, who was standing at her left. Once Castellan was finished, she passed it to Olivienne.

"The volcano is still glowing and sparking the way it did when we first arrived. How certain are we that those fireballs weren't random?"

"Certain."

"Pretty certain."

Both captains answered together and turned toward one another with a grin. Castellan pointed out the obvious evidence. "There were only three flaming projectiles and they all came right for us."

"Will they be able to evade in the same manner?"

Velten shrugged. "Sure, they can expend their gas canisters just as we did. But if they keep going..." She glanced toward Castellan before meeting Olivienne's eyes again. "I'm afraid they don't have someone aboard any of their ships with your captain's power. I don't think they'll have a problem if they turn back now."

"They won't turn back."

Olivienne gave Castellan a curious look. "What makes you say that?"

Castellan had her intuition, but she also had a lifetime of service in one corp or another. "They have their orders and there are three ships to carry them out. I can imagine retrieving whatever is on the island is secondary to retrieving you. But barring all else, this could be a fact-finding mission. They'll risk one or two ships. But mark my words, they won't risk the third. Not to mention, the strange poem that Savon wrote within his journal has described this scene perfectly."

"Look!" Olivienne extended a finger toward the distant dirigible. Sure enough, there was a fireball on a collision course for the approaching vessel. Before it could strike, the ship shot upward about the height of a full-size vessel. The ship stopped its forward advance and the volcano simply glowed and sparked like before. They saw the occasional small bit of pyroclastic material fly out, but nothing that would endanger anyone hovering around the island. Olivienne smirked at Castellan. "Perhaps you were wrong on this one."

Velten sighed. "Or not. It's moving again."

"Well, nobody said the rebels were smart."

Sure enough, the dirigible moved again and ten secs later another flaming ball arced in its direction. Once again, the ship shot upward and missed sure destruction. "Captain, the rebel dirigible isn't stopping." The specialist monitoring the sonica was accurate and they all watched with dreaded anticipation as another ball of fire tracked toward them.

Castellan grimaced. "They won't evade that one. What are they thinking?"

"Well, the black bladders are inflammable so maybe they think that will protect them," Velten said matter-of-factly.

Castellan felt a swell of sorrow through her empathy channel with Olivienne and the connate's words confirmed her thoughts on the topic. "Not completely inflammable."

Whatever the makeup of the volcanic projectile, it didn't strike the black bladder and burst into flames as everyone expected. Rather, it blasted a hole through the sturdy material and out the other side, sending the gondola plummeting into the ocean below. A gasp sounded through the bridge. Castellan's eyes darted toward Velten, taking in the captain's clenched jaw, then flitted to her left to see Olivienne with a hand over her mouth.

Olivienne addressed no one in particular. "Do you think there are any survivors?"

Velten shook her head. "They were hundreds of yords up after that final canister. Hitting the water below at their speed and distance would have been like hitting solid stone. No one could have survived that."

"Captain, another ship is approaching the island."

Sure enough, Illeos broke the horizon to highlight the next dirigible that foolishly sought to approach a place that was obviously protected by Maker artifacts and science. "Wait, is that dirigible dropping?"

Velten lifted her spyglass again and confirmed Olivienne's keen observation. "It is. Looks like they're going to approach from near water level in an effort to avoid the projectiles."

"But will it work?"

Velten shrugged. "I guess we'll find out."

Tense secs passed by with no fire coming out to lay waste to the rebel ship. As it drew within a few hundred yords of the black sand beach, Castellan grew concerned that they may make it. "If they land safely, I'd say we found our way in but also found a whole host of other trouble in that we'd have to deal with whomever comes off that ship."

Suddenly, massive tentacles rose from the water all around the slowly approaching rebel dirigible and enveloped the bladder and gondola alike. Before anyone could say a word, the ship was pulled beneath the waves leaving a plethora of bubbles foaming the surface to mark its disappearance. "By the Makers, what was that?"

Castellan's intuition jangled and she grabbed the voteo from her belt. "Madlin, Holling, is there any greater beast activity in the area?"

"I'm not sensing any, ser."

Holling responded after. "Nor am I."

"Would you both be able to sense something like a massive leviathan from a half mahl out?"

Holling came back. "I would, ser. I've sensed them before. It's not like a warm-blooded animal, to be sure. They're strange but I'd certainly know the feel of one, especially if it were large enough like what we just saw rise out of the water."

Madlin's statement confirmed Castellan's theory. "If you remember, ser, I sensed the rocs from farther away than that. Though to be fair, they were in distress."

"Thank you, Lieutenant and Specialist. Everyone else continue to stand ready. We don't know what else this blasted island has to offer or what that other ship is going to do. Tosh out." She clipped the voteo back to her belt. "It wasn't real."

"By the depths, what do you mean it wasn't real? We all saw it plain as the suns' shine, Tosh."

"It must have been a mechanical construct!" Olivienne's obvious excitement was at odds with the fear and apprehension no doubt felt by the rest of the crew. "This is an amazing find."

"Amazing find or no, how do we get past that bloody thing?"

Olivienne pursed her lips and met Velten's gaze. "Of that I'm not so certain."

"What about that journal you keep mentioning? You said this was all described within the pages?" Velton asked.

Olivienne pulled it from her waist pouch and turned to the page she'd marked with a scrap of velum. "Yes, right here. It also said there was only one way in but every way out, and that the island leads to the island."

Velten grunted. "Convoluted. My guess is that there is more than one land mass in the vicinity of this island. Perhaps now that it's lighter, we can continue around and see if there is another island. Though I'm unsure how to use one in order to get to the other."

"Castellan, remember our quest for the third temple key within Dir Sanguis?"

"Yes."

"Perhaps there will be a passage below the water."

Castellan rubbed her chin. "A passage could be possible with Maker technology. Though it wasn't a passage in that instance, but rather their ship from the stars."

Velten gave them both a wide-eyed look. "What is this? What do you mean from the stars?"

Olivienne lowered her voice to avoid nearby ears. "If you recall from your briefing the past roto, the Tau are not originally from Psiere. They crashed here on Psiere with their menagerie of species. The adventurist mission that led to the third temple key took place below a small lake that was on an island in the middle of Dir Nubila. We thought it was merely a strange sunken sea vessel at the time but it was the ship the Maker's came down to Psiere in."

"What happened to it?"

Castellan shook her head. "I'm afraid it was lost to the water. Probably flooded by now with that Maker forsaken acidic pool."

"Pity. I would have paid good cred to see a ship that

could fly so high or so far. Fascinating."

Olivienne smiled at her. "Once a captain always a captain I suppose."

"It's true, I confess." Velton spoke to the pilot. "Continue the original course around the island. I want to see the size and shape of this blasted place."

"Aye-aye, Captain."

Next, Velten pulled the voteo from her own belt. "Vex."

The first officer's voice came back. "Yes, Captain?"

"Assign a team of watchers to make sure that final rebel ship doesn't get within rail gun distance, then take control of the bridge. Savvy?"

"Yes, ser. Vex out." She spoke to Olivienne and Castellan. "What's next?"

"Food. You soldiers may be able to ignore your yowling stomachs but I'm afraid I cannot. It's been a long night."

"Well, if you—" Castellan's teasing comment was cut off by the sound of her own stomach grumbling at its emptiness. "Fair point, Connate Dracore. I suggest we move any further discussion on this matter to the mess. We'll all think better on a full charge."

The trio stayed in the mess hall for oors, socializing after their meal. Olivienne was recounting a funny story from one of her past missions when Velten's voteo sounded with familiar alert tones. She grabbed it from her belt and answered immediately. "Velten here."

"Captain, Vex sending. The sonica is picking up another land mass farther ahead. Based on the size and shape we've already mapped of—uh, what are we calling this island, ser?"

Velten turned to Olivienne. "It's your mission, Connate. Ideas?"

Olivienne tilted her head and Castellan smiled to see the familiar indication of intense thought. "As we're here to explore this Halcyon Station, let's just refer to the island as Halcyon."

Velten made a face. "We'll have to spell it out for the ship cartographer since that's not a standard Psierian name." She addressed her voteo again. "The connate says to call it Halcyon. We'll spell it out for Zenta later. Anyway, what was your point before you lost track on the lack of name?"

"Sorry, ser. But we suspect this smaller land mass was closer to our starting point when we initially discovered Halcyon. If only we'd gone the other way."

"It is what it is, Vex. Keep the same amount of distance from the smaller mass than we've kept from that blasted volcano. We don't know what other surprises are in store for us here. We'll be on the bridge soon. Velten out."

Castellan had already returned their meal trays to the bins. Olivienne caressed her hand on the way by. Then the three made their way across the ship back to the bridge.

Ten meens later they all stared toward the lush green island that sat just west of the much larger one. "That can't be more than forty mahls around. It doesn't seem likely your station will be located there, especially since the other island is so well defended." Velten called out to the pilot. "Take us around so the smaller island is between us and the big one."

"Yes, ser."

The remaining rebel ship trailed them from afar like a canid looking for scraps. The bridge had a three-hundred-and-sixty-degree view and Velten frowned when she caught sight of the dirigible out of the corner of her eye. Castellan had been keeping track of it since they arrived back on the bridge. Velten lowered her voice and leaned in, though there were no other crew near enough to hear. "What do you want us to do about them, Tosh? We're out of range of their rail guns but that means they're out of range for ours as well. I suspect the only way to bring them down would be for you to take action."

Memories of the last time she ripped a dirigible from the sky with sheer thought alone assailed Castellan and she felt a wash of shame and anger. "That's not going to happen. As long as they don't attack us, we're to leave them alone."

"And if they make a move on your team, should you

find a way to shore?"

"You know your job, Captain. Just as I know mine. We're both tasked to protect the connate with everything we have."

"Ser, we're in the area you wanted us. Orders?"

Velten turned to Olivienne. "Yes, Connate, do you have orders for us? What does your book say again?"

Olivienne recited the words she'd memorized. "The island leads to the island. Could it be a heading?"

"Only one way to find out. Seben, plot a course line that leads from the center of the smaller island to the center of Halcyon then hold."

"Aye, captain."

Velten turned to Castellan. "You think you could be ready to deflect a few of those stones if this doesn't work? Our canisters aren't finished charging yet which means we'll need time to reverse course if that volcano starts spitting again."

She grimaced. "I can. Lend me your spyglass and I'll move to the front plexi where I can see best."

Once everyone was in place, Velten made a forward motion with her hand and the dirigible began moving above the top of the smaller island on a direct course toward the volcano in the center of Halcyon. "See anything yet, Tosh?"

"Nothing. Let's give it a few more meens."

Sure enough, they made it to the beach with no signs of attack. "I think it's safe to say we found the way in." Velten turned to look behind them and pointed toward the rebel ship. "They didn't follow. I'd bet a roto's cred they don't have any idea why we were allowed to pass and don't want to risk themselves."

"Even so, Captain. I suggest you keep a watch on that ship the entire time we're dirtside."

Olivienne motioned for Castellan to give her the spyglass. She trained it on the island, scanning the beach below them then lifted it to see farther out. "The trees look too thick to anchor anyplace other than the shore. We'll have to walk in from there."

"In where though? I think that is the greater question.

We've found our way here, but we have no idea what we're looking for," Castellan said.

"It will be just like our trip to Magna. We don't know what to expect, only to look for anything out of the ordinary. Perhaps we should tell the team."

"The gear is still lined up on the staging deck. We just need an anchor line to make our way down. We're ready when you are, Connate Dracore." Castellan saluted for good measure and grinned knowing that Olivienne clearly saw through her sassy attempt at command obedience.

Olivienne swatted her arm and spoke to Velten. "Anchor anywhere along this stretch. Tosh will voteo when we're ready to head down. I'd wager less than thirty meens though. I only need to grab a few things from our cabin before we go."

"Yes, Connate."

Chapter Nine

Olivienne and her Shield Corp unit stood upon the black sand beach less than a half oor later. They removed their rappelling harnesses and stowed them in the packs each person wore. Much like their trip on the island of Mater rotos before, the team was equipped for a long hike with all-weather sleep cubes, a long-range voteo carried by Lazaro, an expanded medican kit slung across Holling's back, a water purifier, weapons, and anything else they'd need for both an adventurist mission and Shield Corp trek into the wild unknown with a sovereign in their midst.

The only difference between this mission and Mater was that Castellan had the entire strength of a full team at her disposal. "Connate Dracore, what is our heading?" She grabbed a cloth from a pouch on her belt and wiped a small trickle of sweat from her brow. "Gah! This place is strangely warm and reminds me of Dromea."

"It does, doesn't it? Perhaps it's due to the location of the volcano. As for a heading, I'm uncertain. Does your intuition tell you anything?" Olivienne said.

Castellan shrugged. "Any of you?"

One hand lifted slowly and the rest turned to gaze upon their newest member, Specialist Mohdra Sehg. Castellan gave him a welcoming smile. "Don't be afraid to speak up, Sehg. What are you thinking?"

Sehg glanced nervously from Castellan to Olivienne. "Uh, Connate, and uh, ser, every good gunner knows that you can't shoot without a shooter."

Castellan prompted. "And? Say it plain for those of us who didn't spend half a career neck deep in munitions. I don't bite, I promise. Though I can't say the same about the connate." There was a snicker from somewhere in the group and Sehg appeared to relax at the joke.

"Ser, you said that the volcano was a weapon of sorts and don't you need someone to fire a weapon?"

"Hmm, astute observation. However, the Makers also had many automated devices." The team watched as Olivienne thought it over, waiting for her decision. "You're right though. Even if it's automated there must be Maker technology near or in that mountain."

Castellan smiled proudly at their newest member. "Well done, Specialist."

Olivienne followed suit with the praise. "We'll make a blasted adventurist out of you yet!"

Specialist Qent, always quick with wit and jokes, pointed toward the spitting volcano in the distance. "I don't think you should talk about blasted anything in range of that Maker forsaken volcano."

Devin gave his shoulder a light punch. "I think the entire point of this mission indicates that it's not so forsaken after all. What if we find one?"

"One what?" Lear piped up.

"One of the Makers. The Tau," Meza whispered.

"Oh."

All the specialists clamored at Olivienne in the relative safety of the beach with the *Vestigo* keeping watch above them. She held up her hands to still their questions. "I don't know what we'll find on this island that was referenced in texts from so long ago. But I do know one thing for certain," She paused to look around the group. "No discoveries will be made if we don't get moving. Let's set a course for the center where the volcano is located. Hopefully we'll discover something near the base."

Castellan circled her finger in the air. "You heard the connate, move out."

"Yes, ser!" The entire group saluted and made their way toward the thick trees and brush that surrounded the beach.

Olivienne and Castellan watched them head into the flora. Some had half-length blades made just for cutting through thick foliage. Others used their channels or just pushed the leaves out of the way to make it through. Castellan grimaced. "I'm not looking forward to that mess."

Violet eyes twinkled at her exclamation. "But you brought your trusty sword with you." Olivienne bumped against her shoulder. "And I must say, you look particularly dashing with it strapped to your waist."

Castellan narrowed her eyes playfully. "You just want me to cut a path for you so you don't have to tire yourself out using your apportation channel."

"I would never say as such."

One of the nearby guardians snorted.

"Oh, you wouldn't. However, you're much like your maman in that regard. You have a way of getting psi to do your bidding without asking," Castellan said.

"There is only one psi I want to do my bidding, Captain." Olivienne leaned in and was inces from kissing her when Madlin interrupted them.

"Connate Dracore, you should probably see this."

She huffed out a breath and stole a quick kiss. "What is it, Madlin?"

Castellan and Olivienne followed Madlin a few dozen yords into the thick trees and stopped when they saw the group gathered in front of a twelve-foot-tall wall that went off to the left and right as far as they could see. Curving, most likely to encompass the region around the volcano. "Well, this is certainly unexpected. Tosh?" Olivienne questioned.

"Do any of you have sense beyond this wall? Yazzie and Sehg, you've got psi empathy." Both shook their head. "Madlin and Holling, what about you?"

They closed their eyes and Madlin made a face. "There is something, but it feels slippery in my head. Tired, slow—"

"Foreign. It is like nothing I've felt from any land or water beast. I'm sorry, ser, but other than a vague sense of anticipation and strangeness, I've got nothing else."

Castellan asked the obvious question. "Can you tell if it's dangerous?"

"Yes."

"No."

Both shields looked at one another, then spoke in tandem. "I don't know."

That made all but Castellan chuckle. "This certainly poses a problem. We cannot proceed toward our goal unless we cross this wall. But if we cross the wall, we'll be faced with some sort of foreign danger the likes we've never seen before. Connate Dracore, what say you?"

"Sounds like most of our adventures of late, doesn't it? Let's proceed—"

"Cautiously!"

Olivienne nodded toward Castellan. "Cautiously. Just like the mission up on Instrucia, look for anything strange or out of the ordinary. If a tree, stone, or any other part of the natural surroundings looks like it doesn't fit, tell me immediately. Savvy?"

Castellan looked at the wall and called out to the team. "Let's not waste time on ropes for this. I'll boost to the top of the wall so I have a good vantage point then I'll lift you across in pairs." It only took a few secs for Castellan to levitate herself and stand tall on the three-foot-wide stone surface. Her back brushed against thick vines dangling from the massive trees on the other side of the wall.

Olivienne called out to her. "What do you see?"

Castellan looked around then faced down to the team. "Trees. Even more blasted trees. If anything, it's worse on this side, thick as illeostones in a charging room here."

Suddenly two voices called out.

"Captain!"

"Beware!"

Then before anyone could react, those same hanging vines and more wrapped around Castellan from ankles to face. "Wha—" Her eyes rolled back and a sec later she was ripped from her perch on the wall before anyone else could react.

"Tosh!" Olivienne's piercing scream prompted the rest of the shield team into action and everyone grabbed pistols and rifles.

Madlin's firm voice yelled orders to the rest. "Shields, fall back! The connate is our first priority."

It was an order that the connate in question wanted no part of. "What are you doing? We have to go after her."

"Connate, please. We can't go in there unprepared. If it was fast and powerful enough to take the captain, we wouldn't stand a chance."

With a worried look toward the wall Olivienne followed where the rest of the shields attempted to lead her. "Fine. But someone better come up with something fast or, by the Makers, I'll go there by myself with my pyro channel blazing if I have to."

Madlin called them into a circle once the team had regrouped closer to the beach. "We need to see where the captain is." Madlin looked around the group, trying to problem solve in the way she'd been taught since coming to the connate's shield team. Despite their therapeutist sessions, Madlin remained afraid of letting them all down. She remembered a time on Magna when two of them combined powers. "Hmm."

"What are you thinking, Lieutenant?"

Madlin mentally catalogued the teams' channels. "Holling, Sehg, to the front and take off your gloves."

Both complied and Sehg gave her a curious look as she removed her own gloves. "Ser?"

Madlin fixed Sehg with an intense look, then grabbed Holling and Sehg's hands in her own. "Tell me what you see."

"She's combining their channels," Olivienne said.

All three stiffened and Holling spoke first. "It's protective, defending."

Olivienne asked, "Is it one of the island's defenses then?"

Sehg's light tenor spoke next. "I see a cave and a tree. Captain Tosh is between the two wrapped in vines all the way up to her neck and face."

"Is it choking her?"

His eyes were shut and his brows furrowed. "No. She lives. But something is keeping her unconscious."

Madlin saw and heard what was going on but she remained gripped in the triad like the other two. She was grateful when Lieutenant Soleng pressed on. "Tell us about the cave."

"It's glowing inside, lit by phosphorescent bulbs around the ceiling and walls." Sehg winced. "Ugh, my head hurts."

Soleng encouraged him, "You can do this, just a little

more. Pull back out of the cave and tell us what you see."

"A tranquil lake. There is a large tree outside with strangely shaped fruits. A stone monolith with a carving—arhg, I'm sorry." Sehg's eyes blinked open and he dropped Holling and Madlin's hands. Then he rubbed the space on his forehead right between his brows. "I'm sorry, Lieutenant."

Madlin took a deep breath. "It's quite all right." She nodded toward Soleng. "Thanks for guiding him. I was focused on keeping the connection between us."

"What do we know?" Olivienne asked.

Madlin's mind was already whirling with a plan. "Qent, can you differentiate between fresh and salt water?"

"Yes, ser."

"Good. I want you to see if you can point in the direction of the nearest body of fresh water. That has to be the lake that Sehg saw."

Qent closed his eyes and slowly turned in a circle. He wavered, then stopped and raised his arm to point. It was toward the wall, but not directly in front of them. It was more to the left, indicating that the cave with the captain was farther around from their position. He opened his eyes. "I can find the lake easily, but how will we defend ourselves against something that even the captain couldn't handle?"

Holling answered him. "Many plant species have a defensive secretion that can cause adverse reactions to psi when it touches their skin. Perhaps there is something on this vine that renders a person unconscious."

"And how do we counteract that?"

Yazzie stepped forward. "Holling makes sense. First, we'd have to make sure we have as much skin as possible covered. Hoods up, gloves on. That should leave all but our faces."

Olivienne frowned, most likely because she didn't have a Shield Corp uniform. "And for those of us without such accessories?"

Madlin shook her hand. "I'm sorry, Connate. Without the coverings I don't know if you will be able to accompany us on this rescue mission."

"I will not stay here!"

"Connate—"

"No. Find another way, Madlin."

"Ser," Madlin turned toward Leggett. "I think we could pool our gear and come up with something to finish covering the connate. I've got an extra hood in my supplies. Perhaps we wrap her hands in something to protect them."

"There is no need. I do have gloves. What about the rest of our skin?"

Lazaro, their specialist with sub-degrees in communications and chemistre, snapped his fingers. "If we can find suitable mud and the right tree, I could probably come up with a coating for our skin made with sap. One that will protect us from the touch of the vine."

"Preferably without giving us a rash, eh, Laz? Devin snarked. "The last time you tried something new I itched for a weke!"

Madlin nodded at him. "Done. Let's get going, shields! We don't know the long-term effects that vine will have on our captain, so we need to get her out as soon as possible. Not to mention we need to get back on track with our mission."

"Bollux on the mission! Our first priority is saving Tosh."

"Yes, Connate," Madlin said. "Lazaro, take whomever you need to start making the coating."

"Yes, ser."

Less than an oor later, everyone sported a foul smelling greenish-brown goo on every ince of exposed skin on their faces and neck, much to the team's displeasure.

"Ugh, this concoction of yours smells intensely foul, Laz."

Lazaro snapped back at Meza, "Just be glad I was able to find a streambed within walking distance to get the needed mud. Not to mention, we're lucky the trees on this island were conducive to mixing without giving us skin reactions."

"Enough! We've got plenty to worry about without snarling at one another." Madlin said.

"Are we finished here? Because reactive or no, this muck is starting to make me itch and I want to get my future par back as soon as possible."

"Apologies, Connate." Madlin let her gaze roam around the group. "This is as good a place as any to make a temporary camp. We should probably split the team, half staying with Connate Dracore and the other half—"

"Think of another plan, Lieutenant, because there is no way I'm staying behind."

Madlin sighed. "Fine. Penn, voteo the *Vestigo* one final time to let them know that we're ready to go in for extraction." They'd already sent word to Captain Velten to inform her of their situation and plan. Castellan had been explicit in her orders that none of Velten's crew set foot on the island. The Shield Corp captain wanted to make sure the ship was at full fighting strength to prevent any aggression on the part of the rogue dirigible.

Once communications were complete, Madlin had the team stow any surplus. They took the long range voteo, their weapons, and big medican kit, hoping none would be needed.

"Any last thoughts before we attempt to track down the captain?" Madlin asked Soleng.

"My only idea is that we should circle this wall as far as we can until we hit the nearest point to where Qent indicated the cave was located."

"And how are we to do that?" Madlin asked.

"I knew that my engineering sub-degree would continue to be useful, despite my new officer rank." He pulled out a folded sheet of velum to show a crude drawing of the wall that seemed to circle the mountain in the middle of the island. "I was able to walk a good portion of the wall and mark the arc of it using my compass and foot strides. I took that and the angle of orientation from our starting location to find the approximate point where we need to cross the wall that will bring us closest to the cave."

"Large scale area and spatial relations definitely aren't

within my bailiwick." She lowered her voice, not realizing
Olivienne could hear her. "I'll concede to you here and
now that your competence in the role as second lieutenant
takes a weight off my shoulders that I was getting tired of
bearing. I'm glad it was you that took his place instead of
anyone else, Gar. You take the lead on this one."

Soleng called out to the group at the same time he circled his finger in the air. "Shields, form up. We're going to
pace the wall a bit before going over so follow my lead as
I'll be counting steps around. I want two to either side of
the connate at all times. The rest of you range out from our
position."

"Yes, ser!"

Within a half oor they'd covered a considerable distance in the jungle-like expanse of trees and underbrush.
Soleng stopped and pointed toward the wall. "This is the
spot that I estimate is closest to the cave. "Qent, can you
do another dowsing for that lake just to confirm?"

Qent closed his eyes and pointed directly across the
wall toward the mountain. Soleng's calculations proved
accurate.

"Excellent." Madlin looked around the group. "Of
course, all the preparation will probably be for naught as I
suspect the vine beast will simply snatch us up as soon as
we cross."

Devin asked, "Weapons, ser?"

She frowned. "Only if you can guarantee a clean shot
that won't endanger anyone else in the group. Savvy?"

"Yes, ser."

Madlin turned to Olivienne. "My main concern now is
that we've yet to see a part of this Maker-forsaken wall
that didn't have vines hanging out above it,"

"I think I can help with getting past the wall. I can
apport chunks of it from the bottom to make an opening
large enough for us to crawl through. Unless you'd rather
use ropes to get to the top?"

Madlin snapped her fingers. "That's right, you've a
four rating in apportation. Dozier and Lazaro can give you
a hand."

"You know my rating?"

Soleng spoke up. "Of course, Connate. It's a requirement for all officers to memorize the channel makeup of the entire team. Luckily, I've always had a good memory so it was no great effort."

Dozier snorted. "Good thing I'll never be an officer then because my memory is shite. I'll stick with apporting brick walls for sport."

Lazaro laughed and held up a gloved hand. "Same here." The two gloves slapping together made a muffled clap sound.

Madlin shook her head. "Fine. Connate, begin whenever you're ready."

Ten meens later, Olivienne and two specialists were sweating from their mental exertions but there was a three-foot-by-three-foot hole near the bottom of the wall. Once they were rested, Madlin ordered, "Line up and crawl through in the order I call out. Be as silent as possible on the other side and try not to touch any of the surrounding vegetation. And stay away from those poxing vines!" She looked around to be sure everyone had eyes on her, then continued.

"Soleng, Qent, Lazaro, Meza, Devin, Penn, Connate Dracore, Lear, Yazzie, Sehg, myself, Holling, Dozier, Calderon, and Leggett."

The way was slow going because they had to field crawl through the opening as quietly as possible, then reform on the other side without touching any hanging vines. Despite the difficulty, they all made it without being attacked by strange plants.

Madlin gave orders that everyone was to remain silent once they crossed the wall. The team relied on telepathy and special Shield Corp hand signals that Castellan regularly tested Olivienne on. She was glad that both lieutenants were living up to Castellan's faith and certainty because Olivienne herself had been a wreck of nerves and panic the meen her love was ripped from their sight. Her thoughts were interrupted as the black-clad body in front of her came to an abrupt stop.

Even though Specialist Penn was stockier than Olivienne, she was still shorter. Olivienne grabbed

Penn's shoulders to prevent them from both going over. It was a move that earned a stern look from Soleng, who stood at the front of the line. He made the sign for danger and waved them back ten paces. As one, the entire group did an about face and walked the distance instructed. Once there, they regrouped and Soleng stepped out of the way and pointed in the direction they'd been going. *Look.*

The game trail they were following was crisscrossed with vines of all sizes farther ahead. Olivienne was dismayed. *How are we to get through all that?*

Madlin sighed. *As much as I hate to say it, perhaps one of us should attempt to cross.*

To what end, Lieutenant?

Soleng answered. *At the least, we'll be able to see if the vines will react to people on the ground.*

Olivienne asked, *And if they do?*

Then I guess we'll see if our clothing and Lazaro's skin muck works.

Madlin looked around the huddled circle of mud-caked faces. *Any volunteers?*

You mean to meet a new species of flora that behaves a bit like one of the greater beasts? Absolutely! Holling was already removing the main medican pack as he spoke. *I just need Yazzie to swap with me.*

Done. Yazzie, take the big kit and give Holling yours. Then proceed forward as you see fit, Holling. If you're grabbed, keep us updated as long as you're conscious.

Yes, ser.

In no time at all, Holling made his way back down the trail they'd been following, doing his level best to avoid the vines that grew thicker around him with each step. The entire team watched as he made it through to a small clearing. He turned and gave a smile. *I think we'll be okay—bollux!*

Quick as a thought, everyone watched as Holling was caught and wrapped in vines just like Castellan had been. Madlin called out telepathically as he disappeared from sight. *Holling?*

It's got me wrapped blasted tight but I can still see

and hear everything around me. Oh, and I can breathe, too, an important fact. I'm only about thirty foot farther than where I started.

Olivienne asked the most important question. *Can you see Tosh?*

I'm sorry, Connate but—no, wait. The vine just turned me and I can see both her and a massive tree. I saw the cave when it was dragging me closer. She appears to be unconscious still and hanging like overripe fruit about five yords from me. The tree by the lake that Sehg described is fascinating, I've never seen the like. It appears to be the central locus for all the vines. Though many run along the ground into the cave.

Holling, focus. Can you see Tosh's necklace? Olivienne remembered Castellan opening the top two buttons on her uniform after the comment about the heat of the island. She had an idea but it wouldn't work unless she could see the antoraestone necklace.

There is something around her neck that is dangling from her uniform shirt but it's too far away to say for certain if it's a necklace or just a loose vine.

Madlin's voice followed quickly in the wake of their captured medican. *Do you have a plan, Connate?*

Mayhap.

While you've got a decent apportation channel, it won't work on living bodies and you'll only tire yourself out trying to carve out those vines.

Olivienne knew she had a point but her plan involved a little more than straightforward apportation. *That's why my idea hinges on being able to get close enough to Tosh in order to apport something small into my hand. The only way to do that is to offer myself up to the vine.*

What?

Out of the question.

Soleng and Madlin's voices conveyed their displeasure at the logistics of Olivienne's plan but she wasn't to be deterred. *No one else on the team has a combination of apportation and teleportation. This is the only way.*

Madlin tried to reason with her. *Meaning no disparagement, Connate, but your teleportation is rated low enough to be useless. What could you possibly do with your teleportation that you can't do with apportation?*

Olivienne made eye contact with Madlin and spoke only to her. *If I get that stone in my hand, nothing I have is useless. Savvy?* Madlin was no fool. Castellan wouldn't trust such to lead the team. The lieutenant was debriefed after the events concerning King's Marsh and knew about the antoraestones but she was the only one because the information was still protected under sovereign oath.

Sheddech! Indecision and duty flickered across Madlin's facial expressions. Her shoulders drooped after a meen of thought and she sighed before addressing the entire shield unit. *Let the connate through.*

But, ser!

Yazzie was the one who protested but Madlin addressed the entire team. *There are things the rest of you don't know, things I wish I didn't. She can do as she says as long as she's not rendered unconscious by those vines and Holling has proven against that worry. Unfortunately, we must let the connate put herself in some danger in order to save all of us and complete this mission. We learned that such actions may be necessary while training in a hybrid adventurist and shield capacity. Let her have point.*

Olivienne carefully maneuvered to the front of the line and looked back to meet the lieutenant's gaze. *Thank you, Madlin. Holling, do you think I could make contact with this vine creature if I could get to the tree?*

I'm not sure. It's too bad you don't have animal empathy.

She thought about his comment as the rest of the team stood nervously behind her. *I don't have it but you do.*

Madlin asked, *What is your plan?*

Olivienne sent a message to Holling. *What's your weight?*

The past medican check was one hundred and seventy-five punds.

She turned to meet Madlin's gaze. *Let the vine take me. Once I'm close enough to* Castellan, *I'll grab the neck-*

lace and teleport to Holling. He's light enough that I can port him to the tree, though I may have to leave his pack behind. I'll follow immediately after, then we'll clasp hands and attempt to make contact.

And you can't just teleport everyone out, including Captain Tosh?

She shook her head. *We need to neutralize that tree. Tosh would say the same.*

Madlin made eye contact with Soleng, who in turn looked to Olivienne. Soleng made the sign for weapons ready and Olivienne set off down the game trail. She made it to the edge of the clearing as Holling had before the vines took her. She found herself trussed up within an instant and the vines moved to bring her near Holling and Castellan.

Connate Dracore, are you well?

The plan worked. I'm currently hanging like a crunchy red in sight of both Tosh and Holling. Give me a few meens to get myself and Holling loose.

Yes, ser.

Olivienne focused on the pendant she saw hanging from Castellan's neck. Anticipating getting caught up by the vine and having her arms immobilized, she'd purposely kept her right hand near her neck so she could use it to hold the antoraestone once she apported it into her hand. Secs later she held the blasted thing and wasted no time shoving the stone into her mouth in order to get the skin contact needed to use it.

Olivienne was smart enough to clench the thong between her teeth so she wouldn't accidentally swallow it. Then she teleported to Holling. Once her hands were on him, she apported him away so he was right next to the trunk of the massive tree and quickly followed before the vines could react. *Glove off now!*

Holling removed the glove from one hand and clasped it with Olivienne's. They pressed their skin against the rough bark of the alien tree and attempted to make contact. She spat the necklace into her free hand and draped the thong over her head, then tucked it securely beneath her shirt to rest between her breasts.

Olivienne called out to whatever was listening. *Can you hear me?*

The response was as strange as the tree itself.

??

Pushing her voice to whatever consciousness the tree held was like wading through sweet sap. *Do you understand us?*

A strange sound came from Castellan and they both looked to see the vines twisting and twining around her throat and chest. The vines weren't hurting her but what they were doing was more horrifying to the two people watching.

"Doo noooot beelooooong!"

Holling made to jerk his hand away, but Olivienne clasped it tight against the tree trunk. His voice held fear rarely displayed by the curious shield. "Is that thing making the captain speak?" He squinted toward Castellan. "Is she awake?"

"That's not Tosh." She tried to project her thoughts again. *Please! I am one of the sovereigns of Psiere, created by the Tau Ceti to rule this land. We seek aid.*

Tau?

At last, a response that was easier to understand and less frightening than the Castellan/not Castellan wheezing voice. "Can you understand me if I speak aloud?"

Waking. The tree shuddered beneath their palms.

"You've been asleep?"

Tau guardian. Duty. Protect cave.

Holling's voice was an awed whisper. "Fascinating."

"We need to seek help in the cave."

Protect cave.

Olivienne gave a frustrated growl. "This is going nowhere! How are we to get access when this tree barely understands us?"

Access?

Finally, something Olivienne could work with. "Yes, access. I am Olivienne Dracore and I seek access to the cave."

??

"Bah, this isn't working!"

"Connate, is there another phrase the creature may know based on interactions with Nessie or from the texts you've studied?"

She considered Holling's question and thought back to the vellum she'd read with Tosh concerning the creation of her family line. "That's it! The Tau Ceti created the sovereign line from which I'm descended and I seek access to the cave."

Proof.

Olivienne looked at Holling. "What sort of proof?"

Sample.

He tilted his head. "Could the creature want a blood sample?"

Blood.

"Okay, that was a dead shot guess. Thanks, Holling. How do I give it a blood sample?"

A vine startled them as it slithered out of the foliage above. The tip of the vine stopped in front of Olivienne and her gaze honed in on the wicked sharp thorn attached to the end. She sighed. "It's just a prick, I suppose." With a grimace, then immediate wince, Olivienne pressed the pad of her first finger against the thorn until blood dripped free.

Patience.

Olivienne contacted Madlin as they waited on the strange guardian. *We are safe and have made contact with the sentient tree. It keeps watch for the Tau much like Nessie.*

Like Nessie, Connate?

Okay, not at all like Nessie, but a guardian nonetheless. I believe it will let us pass as soon as I've proven that I'm a sovereign. I will contact you again when I know more.

Yes, Connate.

Meens went by as they waited for the tree to give some indication that Olivienne had provided the necessary proof. She glanced at Castellan and wanted nothing more than to go retrieve her future par but knew she had to be patient. It was as she watched her love that the vines around Castellan lowered and placed her on the ground before retracting again.

Access granted

"What about her?" Olivienne waved toward Castellan. "When will she wake?"

Soon.

"Is there anything else we should know about the cave?"

Keys. Monolith.

Olivienne groaned and Holling asked his own question. "Is the lake water safe for us?"

Safe water. Protect seeds.

He looked at Olivienne. "Seeds?"

"Perhaps it refers to the pods hanging in the cave."

"Ah, yes. That makes sense."

She sent one more question toward the tree. "I have others with me. Passage for all?"

All welcome with sovereign. Obey.

Holling shrugged. "The rules, probably."

Olivienne rushed to Castellan's prone body as she mentally called out to Madlin. *Bring the team. Safe passage for the lot of you.*

Give us a few meens, Connate.

She saw Holling make his way to the lake in order to wash the dried mud from his face. Olivienne didn't follow his lead. Her first priority was to wake Castellan. She shook her shoulder. "Darling, it's time to join the rest of us."

Castellan moaned but otherwise didn't respond.

Olivienne saw a bit of ichor on her love's neck and used a cloth from her pouch to wipe it off. "Come on, love, let's see those pretty blues, hmm?"

"Ugh, 'Vienne?" Castellan's eyes fluttered open then they widened in shock. "By the Makers, what happened to your face?"

Olivienne put her hand up to check for injury, then remembered Lazaro's muck. "It's a funny story, actually. Now that you're awake I can tell you."

She heard the rest of the shield team trooping into the small clearing near the giant tree and lake. Madlin called out to them as they came into sight. "Captain, it's good to see you again!"

"I wish I could say the same about the lot of you. It's as though bog monsters took the place of my shields." She gave a sniff and her nose wrinkled with disgust. "Whatever happened?"

Olivienne stood and pulled Castellan with her. "We'll brief you as we clean up."

Chapter Ten

The shield team took time to clean up and refresh themselves with water and rations while Castellan, Olivienne, Madlin, and Soleng made a plan for their next steps.

"First, we'll need to examine the monolith outside the cave."

Castellan looked at Olivienne. "Do you think it could be another controller to unlock a door, like the one for the research station near Dir Lacrimise on Magna?"

"It seems overly large if that's the purpose." Madlin looked around the small circle.

Olivienne shrugged. "We won't know much of anything until we have a look, whether it's a controller or something more decorative." She stood from where she'd been sitting on a large stone near the water's edge and brushed off the back of her trousers. "We certainly can't make any determinations from here."

Castellan gave a whistle and circled her finger in the air and the rest of the shield unit formed up around them. "We're heading to the monolith then most likely into the cave. As you've already been told, be wary of the vines crisscrossing the ground." She held up a hand to forestall any potential comments. "I'm well aware that the tree says we're cleared to pass but it's better to be safe than sorry. And regarding what the tree said, don't touch a single glowing ova in that cave. Savvy?"

As one, the entire group turned their gaze on Holling who raised his hands. "Ser, I would never! I may be curious but it's not worth our lives."

The landscape around the lake wasn't flat. The ground dropped, then rose again the closer they got to the cave. The pillar was about ten yords from the entrance and significantly taller than Castellan initially guessed. Perhaps it was due to its proximity to the side of the volcanic mountain.

"Sheddech! This thing has got to be at least fifteen yords tall but it looks to be one single slab of stone. How?"

Olivienne scratched her temple in thought and most of the team stayed a few foot away from the Maker construct, except for Dozier.

Castellan watched the guardian move closer with her hand outstretched. "'ware, Specialist."

"Ser, I think," Dozier put her hand down but leaned even closer. "As I suspected. This isn't stone at all. I think it's metallic."

"Bah, why didn't I check for that?" Castellan closed her eyes and felt with her channel. She shook her head. "Definitely metal but not a high iron content. My ferrokinesis won't touch it." She opened her eyes and turned to Olivienne. "What could this be?"

Olivienne circled it again and frowned. The object had four sides and appeared to taper to a point at the top. "There are no markings, grooves, or other indications that we should interact with it in any way. I'll admit that I've never seen the like and I'm at a loss here."

"Connate, if I may make a suggestion?"

"Go ahead, Penn."

"There is only one use I could think of for a tall, slim metal object."

Lazaro thumped a fist against his free hand. "Communications. Brilliant!"

Specialist Leggett stepped closer as well. "Can I touch it?"

Castellan addressed Olivienne. "Well, can she?"

"I'm not sure. Until we know what it is, there is always potential risk involved with Maker artifacts. What are you thinking, Branda?"

"Perhaps it's a sensor of sorts? After all, whatever is inside that mountain knew when ships were approaching. Its color and texture are such that it can't be seen from the air, despite the fact that it's taller than all the trees around it."

Olivienne shrugged. "Both ideas have a lot of merit."

Castellan addressed the group as a whole. "Yazzie, Dozier, Lear, Penn, or Holling, what is your intuition channel telling you? Dangerous?" They all shook their heads. "Meza, clairvoyance?"

"I'm getting nothing from it, ser."

"Tosh?"

She shook her head. "Not even a tingle of warning for me either. Go ahead, Leggett."

The specialist walked the final few steps to the monolith and placed her hand on the surface. "It's warm, which isn't surprising given the climate. It also has a slight mechanical vibration or hum."

Curious, Castellan strode forward and did the same. "She's right. While I'm unsure if this is antenna or sensor, I suspect that it's full of machinery of some sort."

Olivienne gave the monolith one more look then glanced up at the sky. "Whatever it is, we're not going to solve the mystery out here. Let's explore the cave and see if there is an entrance somewhere within." She led the way past the large cave mouth and the entire group stopped in shock once they'd made it a few yords inside.

The large, glowing ova they saw hanging from the outside of the cave extended all the way to a wall at the back. Despite the dangers of touching the objects, there was no denying their usefulness as they kept the cave well-lit. The team picked their way through until they stood ten feet from a metal door set in what had to be the wall of the mountain. Olivienne made to touch it but Castellan held everyone back with her telekinesis.

"Wait. Before we begin, we should ascertain the danger potential."

"How do you mean?"

Castellan waved toward the door. "We watched fire and flame spitting from the top of this volcano from the meen we arrived in the area. I'm not sure if it is an active volcano or if all the theatrics were solely due to the Makers. But I hesitate to enter such a structure if there is heat danger to our team."

"Anything from your channel?" Olivienne asked.

"Mild jangling so I'm guessing there is something inside that can do us harm. Perhaps it is more of the Tau security in the form of greater beasts or mechanical constructs. Either way, let's be logical about our next steps."

"I'll concede to that, but we need to get closer in order

to see if it's even possible to open that door."

Castellan reached out with her ferrokinesis channel once again. "At least I can work with this one, if I need to. I'm afraid that a brute force approach may not be the way to go where the Makers are concerned."

Olivienne smirked at her. "Oh, just now figuring that out, hmm? We'll make an adventurist out of you yet." All the shields snickered at her comment and Castellan took it in stride.

"Fine, fine. Let's go investigate." She glanced at Madlin and Soleng. "I want half the team watching the other way to be sure nothing else wanders into this cave as we're trying to sus out an entry."

"Yes, ser."

Satisfied that the lieutenants would sort the team into front and rear guard, she joined Olivienne at the door. "What do you think?"

"Here." Olivienne pointed at a rectangular shape set into the stone wall. "This doesn't look like any other control panel we've come across in previous missions."

"Why would it be," Castellan muttered beneath her breath.

The comment earned her a gentle smile from Olivienne.

"Perhaps if I try," she said as she reached out to press the panel. There was a click and hiss before the entire metal plate popped up and slid down to reveal familiar looking indentations in a black surface. There were glowing symbols next to each, but representative of no language either woman had ever seen.

"That's easy enough that even I can figure out it's meant for the temple keys. But that language isn't Psierian, cipher or no."

"Do you think this is the Makers, uh, the language of the Tau Ceti themselves?"

Castellan shrugged. "We've no way to know for sure but it's as good a guess as any."

Olivienne squinted and leaned closer, but the black obsidae panel made seeing detail difficult in the low light. She called to the rest of the group. "Who has an illeostone-powered torch? We need more light here."

"I've got one, Connate." Dozier stepped forward and held the light where indicated.

"Tosh, look! There are images at the bottom of each indentation."

"Fascinating," Castellan said to Olivienne, who had already removed the thong holding the three temple keys from around her neck. She pulled out a knife and cut the knot from the tie so she could free them.

Olivienne held the three in the palm of her hand and looked from Castellan to the panel. "There doesn't appear to be a particular order to insertion and the placeholders are in the shape of a triangle rather than a straight line."

"I see no vials around, so my thinking is either there is no order, or there is no consequence to incorrect order."

Olivienne shrugged at her observation and picked up the first pendant with her free hand and reached toward the indention with a tree carved into the bottom. The blue gemstone in the center of the temple symbol reflected the light of the torch. They heard a chime and the gem lit from behind with a pulsing glow. Olivienne looked back at Castellan and grinned. "So far so good."

She picked up the next temple key and placed it into the space with a carved cliff inside. As with the first, another chime sounded and the green stone glowed. One of the guardians watching behind them gave a little whoop of joy. Castellan thought it sounded like Specialist Qent, one of the most boisterous of the group.

"One to go." Olivienne held the pendant out to Castellan. "Would you care to do the honors?"

Castellan sucked in a breath, surprised by the move. "Are you sure? This is your mission, Connate Dracore."

Olivienne swatted her on the arm. "Stop being so infuriatingly formal, we sleep beneath the same coverlets every night." More laughter followed her words and she waggled the last pendant. "Go ahead. You've earned this as much as I have."

Rather than argue with her, Castellan picked up the pendant and inserted it into the space carved with a riveted portal. The red gem in the middle glowed like the rest as the third chime sounded. Then all the stones flashed three times and deep thumping and clanging echoed through the cave. Castellan gestured everyone back but they needn't have worried. It was anticlimactic when the door swung open with the screech of long unused metal to reveal an innocuous corridor beyond.

The temple keys stopped glowing and Olivienne took that as her sign to remove them. She quickly threaded them back on the thong and tied a new knot.

"Captain, what are your orders? Do you wish for the entire unit to enter or should we leave a small team here as a guard?"

Quite a few people frowned at Madlin's suggestion and Castellan considered the area they were in. She blew out a breath. "I don't think a few shields could make this location any safer than it already is. The only way anyone can get through the vine defense is if they are a proven sovereign. Those attempting to come in after us would fail."

Olivienne agreed. "This mission belongs to the entire team and we're all going to enter."

"Yes, Connate." Madlin grinned at the declaration.

Castellan raised her voice to address the entire unit, though it was unnecessary due to the acoustics of the cave. "All right, listen up. I'll enter with the connate and I want you to follow in pairs behind us. Madlin and Soleng are going to split you up by ability, soft and hard channel strengths paired. Let's all take ten to prepare ourselves for what could be a long exploration inside the mountain."

Calderon snorted. "I don't know about anyone else, but I could certainly use a free bush outside."

Groans echoed around the group and Devin spoke up as they began heading for the cave opening, "Going to play find the snake, huh?"

Lear added her two stones of fun regarding her fellow pilot. "Most likely going to wiggle his rudder."

"At least my rudder doesn't flap in the wind."

"That's because it's too small."

Castellan shook her head at their antics and Olivienne covered her mouth to stifle a giggle. "Well, my team has certainly loosened up during the past few rotos."

Castellan smirked. "You mean *my* team and yes, they have. I'm glad because that means they've come together as a unit. They're family and families are built on trust and respect."

"It's nice seeing them smile again."

Castellan took Olivienne's hand and led her toward the sunlight as well. "It's good to see you happy, too. I know things are tough right now but something is telling me that we'll prevail."

"Your intuition channel?"

She shook her head as they stepped outside the cave. "No. My belief in the people of Psiere, especially those around me. We've got good minds and better hearts leading and I'm certain that will mean success in the end."

Olivienne gave her a kiss on the cheek. "From your lips to the Maker's ears—" She glanced around and gave a little chuckle. "For all I know we are being watched and listened to right now so maybe my words will prove prophetic."

"Maybe. Now, if you don't mind, I think I need to find a bush myself."

Olivienne laughed at her statement and slapped the back of Castellan's trousers as she strode away.

Castellan and Olivienne were the first to step through the doorway into the mountain corridor. As with most Maker constructs, lights came on immediately. Unfortunately, the passage spanned left and right, causing a dilemma as to which direction they should head.

"Could this circle the entire mountain? Perhaps it must because it's built above or around an actual volcano." Olivienne tapped her top lip in thought.

Dozier spoke up from near the back of the group. "Ser, I believe that even if the Makers found a way to stabilize or use the actual volcano, they'd need to build around the perimeter due to the amount of heat. I'm sure they could shield it with their science and such, but it would make the most sense. The cave outside this passage was pretty solid blue rock from what I could see. It's especially difficult to break so I'm curious how this was all made."

"That supplemental cave training is coming in handy, eh? We appreciate the info, Specialist."

The younger woman's cheeks pinked at the praise. "Yes, ser."

Castellan looked back at Olivienne. "The possibility that this facility is nothing more than a ring seems more and more likely. Would you prefer all going one way or splitting the team?"

"Bullocks! I hesitate to split us up in case there are more access points requiring the three temple keys, or more tests requiring a sovereign's blood. But I suppose we'll have to do what makes the most sense. We're inside now and perhaps that's well enough."

"Ser," Qent called out. "I sense water a little farther down the passage."

"Why don't we check that out first and make a determination after?" Castellan kept her gaze fixed on Olivienne until she gave a short nod. The group made their way along the corridor, noting the gentle curve to their right.

Olivienne stopped short when they came upon a door to their left, on the outer wall. "Well, this looks familiar."

"That's like the doors in the Magna towers and the research station!"

Olivienne smiled at Penn. "Yes, it is. Only one way to find out what's inside." Without warning, Olivienne raised her palm and touched the pad next to the door. They all stepped back as it slid open displaying darkness beyond.

Castellan could feel the shield guardians crowding at her back and sent a call to all of them. *Wait. Be alert.* She focused her senses forward but felt nothing untoward so raised a hand to wave Olivienne into the room. "After you, Connate Dracore."

As soon as Olivienne stepped inside, overhead lights came on to highlight plain gray walls that matched the corridor outside. The room was large in area, though it was no taller than the passageway they'd come from.

Specialist Devin pointed to the right of the door. "Sers, those are like the storage cubes from the research station." He looked at Olivienne. "May I open one?"

"Go ahead." Olivienne waved him toward it.

Devin walked a few paces to the right and placed his hand against the pad on the nearest cube, which gave a hiss as the top popped up. He lifted it farther and grinned back at the group. "As I thought! Looks like dry goods, foodstuffs and the like." He closed the cube again and peered at the top. "There is writing, but not anything I've ever seen before. Perhaps it's their home language?"

Everyone filed into the room as Olivienne and Castellan went over to look at the top of the storage cube. Olivienne shook her head. "Nothing I've seen before either."

Castellan called over her shoulder. "Leggett, can you take a few stills of this?"

"Yes, ser." The specialist rushed to comply.

Olivienne placed her hands on her hips and looked around the large space before she sighed. "No water in this room but perhaps we'll find a lavatory farther down the way. I think that, much like the research station, we should probably break up the team for this. It's a large area if we're trooping our way around this entire Maker-forsaken mountain. It will save the most time. How do you want to split?"

Castellan looked around her unit. "I'm not sensing any danger yet. I suspect we're safe inside the main protection for the facility. Why don't you lead one group and I'll lead the other?"

Olivienne's lips parted with surprise. "You'd let me go off on my own?"

"You wouldn't be alone." Castellan smirked. "I think that's the point of having a shield team. Madlin, I want you and Soleng to split talent, just as we did below the Temple of Antaeus. I want Madlin's team with the connate and the rest with me. Split medics and adventurists specialties. We should have enough overlap to have well rounded groups. Connate Dracore will pick one direction and we'll take whichever she doesn't prefer. Savvy?"

Madlin saluted. "Yes, ser."

Soleng gestured to the first lieutenant. "I'll let you split the unit as you've had previous experience with such." She nodded and gave a loud whistle, gesturing everyone off to the side as she called out who was to go where.

Olivienne raised her eyebrow. "Is there a reason you chose to take a separate team from me?"

"It's as I said, we're splitting channel strengths to give each team the best combination. I know how powerful you are, stone or no stone. And after a few rotos together, I also know how you think and what things you'd be most interested in. The teams will stay in constant contact as well as we can with a blasted mountain between us."

"And when we can't?"

"If the worst happens and we lose voteos and the long-range, there is always the stone. I'll listen for you. If you call, I'm certain I can hear."

Violet eyes widened at her statement. Olivienne put her hand on Castellan's forearm. "Darling, if you're listening that intently for so long, you'll go mad."

Castellan grinned. "Perhaps I'm already there."

"Tosh." She warned.

"I know. I've never promised something I wasn't capable of. Trust me. I'll only start listening if we lose normal communication."

After a long meen of silence, Olivienne nodded and stepped close to wrap Castellan in an embrace. She kissed the corner of Castellan's mouth when she pulled back. Heat infused Castellan's face at such an intimate action in front of the watching guardians. "Be safe, Captain."

"The same to you, love." Castellan spoke to Madlin. "Long range will go with your group and I want check-ins every fifteen meens. Catalogue all the doors you come across, have someone make a crude map we can follow later if the need arises. We'll do the same."

"Yes, ser. We won't let you down."

Castellan clapped her on the shoulder. "I know you won't, Lieutenant." She circled her hand in the air. "You lot that's coming with me, let's go. We've got a mission to complete."

The two groups exited the room and started off in opposite directions. Olivienne's team continuing the way they'd originally gone as Castellan's half of the shield unit backtracked toward the entrance they'd come from.

"Tosh."

Castellan stopped at the call of her name. She turned to see Olivienne staring at her.

"Be safe."

"Of course. See you on the other side of the mountain, Connate Dracore." Olivienne grinned and spun in place to jog back toward the front of her group.

"Ser,"

"Yes, Sehg?"

"I've heard the stories and it seems quite odd the way the connate worries about your safety. You're her shield captain, not the other way around. She's a sovereign and you've taken on armicrustes, leviathans, and entire dirigibles of rebels. You're the greatest captain that Psiere has ever seen!"

Castellan laughed at the man's outrageous statement as much as his enthusiasm. "Who said that? What a load of sea wash."

Soleng, Qent, and Lear all laughed, but the rest were silent. Sehg answered her question as though it were serious. "Everyone, ser. I was on the southern continent for a bit after you took over the connate's shield team. There was much talk about a lieutenant commander being offered such a post since it was unheard of. Then the broadsheets began publishing all your past accomplishments."

"What?" Castellan didn't stop walking but was startled by his words.

"After the announcement of your oathing, there were even more. I'll admit to following your career for the past roto, not to mention the briefing I had once I was made part of the connate's shield unit." He shook his head. "The things you've done, it's…amazing! I only hope to be half the shield as you somedae."

Meza gave Sehg a light punch to the shoulder. "Someone is a bit stars struck."

"What, and you lot aren't?" Sehg looked around the group and Castellan grew uncomfortable.

Leggett shrugged. "I mean, we are. We've talked

about it plenty. But we also know the captain doesn't like a fuss made so we just, uh, take it in stride." She looked at Castellan. "Sorry, Captain. But it's true. And no matter what, this is the best assignment I've ever had. I'm proud to have you as my senior officer."

"Same, ser." Meza's sentiment was echoed through their small group and Castellan felt her face heat for the second time in less than ten meens.

Soleng's voice was a welcome distraction. "Ser, we've got another door."

Castellan muttered beneath her breath, "Glad to be away from that blasted topic."

"You say something, ser?"

"No." Castellan touched the plate next to the door and waved them forward after it opened. "Let's get on with our mission, yeah?"

Qent grinned at her as he pushed through. "Yes, Captain Amazing."

"Don't chance your stones, Specialist."

"No, ser!" He was still laughing as he went to investigate with his fellow guardians.

Castellan sighed and rubbed a hand down her face, to either hide or cool the blush. She hoped that Olivienne's team gave her lover as much grief.

After traveling a little less than half an oor around the corridor, Olivienne thought it necessary to break the silence to alleviate some of the boredom of documenting storage room after storage room. "How is Specialist Sehg settling in with the team?"

"He's doing just fine, Connate. I partnered him with Qent to be his immediate trainer in all things relating to this unit."

Olivienne laughed. "Knowing the humorous Zed Qent, poor Sehg is probably getting a colorful education along with it. Castellan was worried any new guardians brought in would struggle with the dual priorities of my team."

Lazaro replied, "I don't think you have to worry about how Sehg feels about the adventurist side or the captain."

Others laughed with him and Olivienne narrowed her eyes.

"Is there something I should know, Specialist?"

"Uh," Lazaro swallowed and looked around the group as they walked along at a steady pace. "No, Connate. On the contrary, our psi, Sehg, is a bit taken with the captain and her career."

Another door appeared and Olivienne was grateful for the brief stop. "Taken?"

Calderon snorted. "He means stars struck."

"It's true, Connate." Dozier nodded. "All he ever talks about in the downtime is Captain Tosh this and Captain Tosh that. He thinks she's simply amaaaazing." The group laughed.

"I suppose stars struck is better than sun blind, eh?"

"Not to worry, Connate Dracore. I'm sure he'll acclimate soon. He would never do or say anything improper so please don't be angry with him. It's certainly not worth mentioning to the captain." Madlin glared around the group.

Olivienne tried her hardest not to smile but broke into a mad grin after only a few secs. She touched the pad to open the door and waved the group inside. "Oh no, I'm going to use this knowledge for ages to come."

"Use it?"

"I'm sure you've noticed how, uh...staid the good captain is in front of you lot."

Specialist Devin barked out a laugh. "She's more serious about you, ser. Like a canid guarding a bone."

"Yes, well, she can be infuriating about that, sure. But I'm talking about the way she gets when praised for her talents or looks. There are blood blossoms with less color. I can't wait to see how she reacts to this news."

Holling grinned at her. "I've worked alongside him enough to guess that if the captain didn't know about Sehg's fascination before, I'd bet good cred she does now. He won't be able to hold his tongue with such a long bout of silence and mahls to travel."

"Ser, it's time for the fifteen meen check-in." Lazaro swung the large pack from his back. The long-range voteo took up most of his gear capability due to its weight.

Olivienne speculated again on what other wonders could be accomplished if Psierians had access to the portable power found in the Maker's boat on Magna. Making a decision, she pushed closer to the communications specialist as the rest investigated the chamber. "Bring up the other group and I'll make the check-in."

He gave her a quizzical look but nodded and flipped the proper switches to activate stone power for the device. "Yes, ser." He lifted the receiver and spoke into it. "Sovereign unit to Tosh, over."

"Tosh receiving." Castellan's voice crackled a bit but was easy enough to hear.

Olivienne made a motion with her hand indicating she wanted the receiver. Lazaro made sure the cord wasn't tangled and held it out to her. "Just checking in with you, my love."

"Oh, 'Vienne. I didn't expect to hear you. Things are fine, nothing but storage so far. I wonder if the Maker ship we found was cleared to this area."

"Mayhaps. We've discovered much of the same in our direction. Say, I've been meaning to ask you if you'd like a name change once this business with the rebels is finished."

"Name change?"

"Perhaps something like," Olivienne paused for dramatic effect. "Captain Amazing?"

"Bollux!"

The group of guardians in Olivienne's team had paused what they were doing to listen and broke into laughter at Tosh's exclamation.

Rather than answer on the voteo for everyone to hear, Olivienne heard Castellan's voice in her head. *Who told you?*

Olivienne smiled. *Question is, who told you?*

Nobody had to. He's very...vocal with his appreciation.

Do tell?

Mental laughter echoed through Olivienne's head. *I'm pretty sure Specialist Mohdra Sehg has followed my career better than I have.*

Darling, you deserve every bit of the praise that comes your way. You don't have to like it, but at least accept the fact that you've done amazing things for Psiere and for me.

Perhaps when we get back to our private room aboard the Vestigo *I'll perform a few more feats to get your attention.*

Olivienne felt the warmth on her cheeks and shook her head. *My love, you've always got my attention but I certainly wouldn't turn down a few...demonstrations when we return.*

Noted.

Over the voteo Castellan added. "As much as I love speaking with you, we're wasting precious time and we've got not one, but two dirigibles waiting in our shadow outside. We best be on."

Olivienne responded with a cheeky, "Yes, ser. Connate out."

"Feeling a bit warm, Connate?"

She looked up to see Madlin watching her. "Erm, yes. It's warm in here, don't you think?"

Madlin's eyes twinkled and Olivienne knew she was in for a bit more teasing. "Oh, we're quite comfortable, right guardians?" The rest of the team nodded. "But then, we weren't speaking with our oath mate. Based on your expression during the silence, I can imagine what she was saying to you."

Olivienne brushed a speck of dust from her sleeve and straightened the adventurist pouch slung across her chest before giving a sniff. "Yes well, *that* particular conversation was above your rank, Lieutenant. Now, as Tosh asserted, we should get on with this mission." Snickering followed her from the storage room and Olivienne muttered beneath her breath, "Loosened up indeed."

Soleng had estimated the full circumference of the lower level to be eight mahls based on the arc of the corridor and the measurement of his own footsteps. Even half that per team meant it would take close to four oors each due to searching and cataloguing the rooms found. Olivienne's team had walked three quarters of their half when the contents finally changed from that of preserved foodstuffs and other stored goods necessary for a long stay or journey.

Madlin was the first to the hand lock but paused when Dozier called out a warning. "Lieutenant, wait!"

Everyone gathered around the door and Olivienne looked at her with concern. "What is it?"

"I'm not sure, Connate. My intuition is jangling something fierce."

Devin laughed. "You sound like the captain."

Madlin placed her palm against the door itself and closed her eyes. "Danger—no, wait, not danger but potential danger. It's hard to explain."

Olivienne looked around her shield team. "Does anyone have an idea what could be potentially dangerous inside?"

"An animal?"

Holling shook his head. "I'm not sensing anything alive. My intuition rating is the same as Dozier and I agree with the warning, but nothing I'm picking up with my animal empathy."

Madlin pulled her hand away from the stele surface. "I'm not getting anything either, Connate."

"Okay. Madlin, you take lead on this since you're in charge of my safety."

Devin chuckled. "That's a nice change of pace." Olivienne swung her gaze to the specialist. He held up his hands and grinned at her. "No offense, Connate, but you have a bit of a reputation for action above caution." Heads nodded around the group and Olivienne rolled her eyes.

"I promised Tosh I'd be careful so go on with you and do your jobs." She moved off to the side, farther down the corridor.

Madlin motioned for all of them to draw pistols and range around the door. She stepped just to the right of the entrance as well and slapped her palm to the locking pad. It slid open to the left just like all the rest. Familiar lights came on overhead and the room looked like most of the others they'd already searched. Large storage containers were stacked around the walls, little to indicate special danger detected by Dozier's intuition or Madlin's psychometry.

"I don't understand. What is so unique about this room?" Calderon scratched his temple looking thoroughly confused.

Olivienne waved at one of the containers. "Only one way to find out."

Madlin moved toward the nearest crate and placed her hand on the top. "I'm not sensing anything other than what I got from the door. Even so, stand ready in case this goes poorly for me, Holling."

"Yes, ser."

She turned sideways and carefully reached to open the container. Nothing seemed out of the ordinary, barring Madlin's gasp.

Olivienne stepped closer. "What is it, Lieutenant? Are you well?"

Madlin met her gaze. "I think you need to see this, ser."

Indeed, the crate held the potential for danger and much more. "By the Makers! These look like weapons."

Calderon called out from one of the containers farther into the room. "Looks like they all contain the same type of rifles, Connate. These are like nothing I've seen before. Should we take a sample?"

Olivienne's heart raced at what the Maker-made weapons could mean to their war against the rebels. The notion didn't instill confidence. Instead, the powerful weapons roiled the acid in her stomach. "No."

"Ser?"

Olivienne cut her hand through the air. "I said no! Our task here is not to find a way to slaughter our fellow psi, no matter what side of this conflict they're on. These rifles would be neither fair nor moral and I refuse to bring them back to Tesseron. No. We'll leave the blasted things here where they are hidden and protected from those who would seek to do harm with them."

'Vienne, is everything okay? I can feel your worry and

anger.

We've found a storage room full of something that appears to be Maker weapons.

There was a pause before Castellan responded. *And?*

And they will stay here. I know how Maman feels about the cost of war and I won't be the one who introduces such horrors upon my people.

I agree with you. Soleng says we're about three quarters of the way around. He estimates another oor of travel time before we meet up again provided your team is on track.

We are. See you soon, love.

"Ser, what are your orders?" Clearly, Madlin had been waiting for Olivienne to finish her silent conversation with Tosh.

"Close it all up and note the contents of this room as classified w so we'll know what it is but the information can't fall into the wrong hands."

"Yes, ser." Penn had been in charge of noting the contents of each room on a map she'd drawn up. She nodded and wrote as directed onto the velum.

Once everything was returned the way they found it, the entire team left the storage room and continued down the corridor. Olivienne worried whether she'd done the right thing but was bolstered by her conversation with Castellan. She knew her role to play when it came to the future of Psiere and she was also aware of how her mother felt about their responsibility to the people.

The moral dilemma wasn't about whether or not they should use dangerous futuristic weapons. The decision that had her heart racing involved weighing the benefits of shortening the conflict with such weapons to save lives, or not using them and hoping to save lives in other ways. Olivienne stopped walking as the memory of that dae above King's Marsh hit her in full. She sucked in a breath.

Madlin stopped and looked back at her. "Connate?"

Olivienne took a few calming breaths and held up her hand. "I'm fine, just contemplating my decision."

"What did you discover?"

"If those weapons can do anything as amazing and terrible as what we saw above King's Marsh then I made the right choice." She narrowed her eyes to discern any minute expressions on Madlin's face as they continued walking. "What about you?"

Madlin frowned. "I wouldn't have been comfortable taking anything from that room."

Olivienne smiled and clapped her on the shoulder. "Let's not dwell on it then."

Chapter Eleven

Castellan found herself distracted by Olivienne's distress. Once she'd confirmed that her lover was well, she focused on the door her team approached. Soleng was closest and slapped a palm to the touch pad. The door slid open like all the ones before it, only Soleng didn't enter. "Sheddech!"

"What is it?"

Castellan thought perhaps the room would hold weapons, much like the one discovered by Olivienne's team. "What is it, Soleng?"

"By the Makers!" Half the guardians stood near the lieutenant and they all stared slack-jawed at something through the open doorway.

She pushed past them until she could see for herself what was so fascinating. A massive chamber full of strange machines spread out for hundreds of yords, illuminated from high above in the two-story space. They looked like open air haulers with no wheels.

Specialist Lear moved toward the nearest one, running a hand along the sleek side, before vaulting over the edge and staring at the control console. Castellan called out to her. "Report."

Lear flipped a few switches. Two things happened at once. Lights came on all around the base, and the entire machine rose into the air three foot. Lear grabbed the top of the console to maintain her balance then turned to Castellan with a grin. "Ser, this is a moto."

"Where are the wheels?"

"How does it float?"

Castellan held up her hand for quiet as the specialists bombarded Lear with questions. "How easy is it to use?"

Lear shrugged. "The control console looks similar to the boat on Magna, which is how I realized it was intended for transport." Lear looked around the inside before folding something down and taking a seat. A few of the specialists snickered as her knees came up to hit the console. "It's certainly not built for someone my size, ser."

Castellan contemplated all the uses the Makers could have for such fantastical machines. Something about the motos tickled her intuition and she closed her eyes to think about all the information they'd discovered during the course of the past few rotos. Sehg jumped when she snapped her fingers. "They're transport shuttles from the Terra Halcyon!"

"The what now?" Qent scratched his chin.

"One of the documents we found stated that many of the species around Psiere were originally from the great Maker ship we found below Dir Sanguis. They used something called transport shuttles to take them around the planet, to *seed* it. This must be where they stored them. These don't seem practical, large though they are. What would you do during inclement weather?"

Lear pressed a button on the panel in front of her and a clear barrier shimmered in place above the entire top of the floating conveyance. They could still see Lear on the other side but the image was rippled and hazy.

Leggett reached out to touch it and pulled back with surprise. "It's solid. Amazing!"

"Lear, can you drive it?"

She flipped a few more switches and clasped what could only be a steerage stick and the shuttle crept forward. Her moves weren't entirely visible through the barrier but she did something else and the shuttle spun in place. Specialists stepped back but more than a few looked on with delight. "How is that?"

Castellan grinned. "You've answered my questions sufficiently. Shut it down and come out of there. I want to know how many transports are here as well as whether or not there is a variety of sizes and shapes. I also want everyone to look around the outside perimeter to find the exit. If they got these things in here, there must be a way to get them out."

"Will we take any back to Tesseron and the queen, ser?"

"We'll take the news of them only. Psiere isn't ready for advanced mechanical constructs of this nature. Perhaps somedae, but not todae."

"But ser! These could help bring an end to the rebellion if we weren't limited by wheels and stones."

She nodded to acknowledge Qent's words. "They could, certainly. But one thing I've learned since joining the connate's shield team is that there are some things that hold too much power." Castellan gestured toward the large sled type moto that had once again settled on the ground. "Something like this is too fantastical, and I can say with certainty that we're not ready yet. There are mysteries to be discovered and, more importantly, *understood.*"

"Pardon my saying, ser, but if we're to just leave the floating beasts to rot on this island, why bother finding an exit?" Meza gazed at her curiously.

"Three reasons. One, never discount an advantage. Two, it would be nice to have an exit closer than the one that we entered. Three, to know of something is to be prepared. Queen Olivara prides herself on being prepared and I intend to give her as much information as possible."

Cataloguing and finding an exit took some time but Castellan thought the duty well worth it. They resumed exploration along the massive corridor a half oor after they discovered the transport chamber. The tones of a voteo alert echoed around the group shortly after. Castellan held up her hand for the team to stop and she answered the alert. "Tosh here."

"Madlin sending. We've reached the opposite side of our arc and found a lift door. What is your ay-tee ser?"

"Arrival time," she glanced up at Soleng, who signaled four fives. "Twenty meens. I want you to wait for our arrival. Savvy?"

There was a brief pause, then Madlin's voice came across the small speaker. "Ser, the connate has already gone ahead."

Castellan's heart clenched. Surely Olivienne wouldn't have— "Come again?"

Another pause then Olivienne spoke. "We're only teasing, darling. I'm right here under the safe protection of my shields, as promised."

A few of the guardians chuckled on Castellan's end but she merely blew out a relieved breath. "Well enough.

We'll double time to catch up with you, then we'll take
five meens to confer and decide how we should proceed."

"That sounds like the best plan. I'll see you soon,
love."

Castellan grimaced and tried to insert a little more
professionalism into the conversation. Just because they
were oathed to consor didn't mean they needed to be
sloppy in front of the unit. "Yes, Connate." She ignored
the second round of snickers from her half of the guardians.

All in all, a short time later, Olivienne and Castellan
stood in front of the familiar looking Maker-designed lift
doors. They'd selected Madlin, Holling, Leggett, and
Lazaro for the initial trip to the next level. That was
enough to cover a variety of specialties.

Olivienne looked at Castellan from her position next
to the lift palm pad. "Ready, Captain?"

"When you are, Connate."

Olivienne raised her hand as Holling and Madlin
simultaneously called out, "Wait!"

Madlin elaborated. "Something comes." Sure enough,
the indicator light near the lift doors began moving down
toward their level.

Rather than waste precious secs in communication,
Castellan sent her command telepathically. *Fall back.
Defend the connate.*

Shields drew pistols and ranged around the corridor in
a practiced formation as Olivienne scrambled away. Castellan herself stepped back from the doors but stayed near
the front, being the best person to confront whatever threat
may be coming. She worried it could be a defensive measure, though the idea seemed strange after being left
unmolested throughout the entire lower level.

Holling spoke into the tense quiet. "Ser, it's not psi,
nor is it any animal I'm familiar with."

"Be steady, shields. Do not fire unless danger presents
itself."

"Yes, ser."

"Tosh," Olivienne called out. "Could this be..." She
trailed off, as if afraid to finish the question.

Castellan spared her a glance. "I suspect as much as you but we'll know for sure soon."

Secs later, the lift door slid to the side and a small-statured gray humanoid with large eyes stepped out into the corridor. Castellan nodded and relaxed her posture. Her intuition had been right. She holstered her pistol and signed to the rest of the team. "Stand down."

"Sheddech!"

She wasn't sure who said it but it was only then that Castellan realized few members of the team had seen the skeleton retrieved from the cave on Navis. None of the group save herself and Olivienne were privy to the images provided by Greene's forensic sculptistes. Olivienne pushed through her guardians to stand near Castellan's side as the Tau Ceti held up one four-digit hand with the palm facing them.

"Greetings, humans. Welcome to Halcyon."

Tosh?

Castellan answered the panicked query. *'Vienne, I'm here if you need me but this is your history to make. As a sovereign, you are the best of us. It's time the Tau was introduced to the fruits of their meddling.*

You're right, though I may disagree with you on the best of part. For good or ill, we've come full circle.

Though their conversation took mere secs, being mind-to-mind, the Tau spoke before Olivienne could. "You need not fear, the sovereign line is well regarded among my people."

"My apologies," She paused and glanced at Castellan, who shrugged. "How should I address you?"

The Tau gave a short bow. "I am Scientere Extremus T'kinsaa Flx'n. I am the watcher assigned to this planet. To spare you difficulty with the pronunciation, you may refer to me as Kinsa."

Olivienne tilted her head. "Watcher?"

Something in the Tau's words made Castellan's intu-ition channel buzz and she stared at them intently. "T'kin-saa Flx'n…"

"Yes?"

"I recognize your name. Olivienne, I believe it was on

one of the documents we've retrieved in the past roto."

"Hmm, you're right. Kinsa's name is familiar." Olivienne snapped her fingers. "The document we retrieved on Instrucia!" Her mouth dropped open as she stared at Kinsa. "That document was written hundreds of rotos ago. How?"

Kinsa gave them something that vaguely resembled a smile. "Ah, yes. You've probably found one of my logs that were cached away." They looked around the large group. "Perhaps you should all come up to the habitation ring. Your security force can rest as we speak."

Madlin spoke up for the first time since the lift door opened. "Ser, are we safe?"

Castellan turned to address the rest of the shield unit. Their expressions ranged the gamut of awe, curiosity, fear, and stern regard. "This is what we were hoping to discover on Halcyon, or at least the outcome we'd hoped for. Fear not, guardians. I know none of this makes sense now, but all will be revealed soon. Savvy?"

"Yes, ser."

Castellan glanced around the rest of the group and they all nodded.

"Connate Dracore," Olivienne glanced at her. "We will follow your instruction. Once we're upstairs, I'll personally contact Captain Velten and give her an update. I'm afraid the long range voteos won't penetrate the rock above us."

Olivienne smiled. "Perhaps we should properly introduce ourselves before we head up. I think it will do much to assuage the concerns of my companions."

Kinsa tilted their head down. "As you wish."

"You already assumed correctly that I am of the sovereign line. My mother is Queen of Psiere and I am her heir, Royal Connate Olivienne Dracore." She gestured toward Castellan. "Captain Castellan Tosh is in charge of my immediate security but is also my oath mate. We are promised to consor at a later date. My shield unit consists of two lieutenants and twelve specialists," She gestured toward the team and introduced them individually.

Kinsa bowed again toward Castellan, then the rest of the team. "It is an honor to meet you all. Now, I believe refreshments and conversation are necessary. We have much to discuss."

It didn't take long for the large group to make the needed trips up to the next level. Kinsa explained that it was a smaller ring than the previous. There were multiple rooms for habitation and enjoyment, though the furnishings would be a little short-statured for the much taller Psierians. The team, with the exception of Sehg, was already familiar with the facilities since the ones on Halcyon mirrored those found on Magna at the research station.

"Ser, do you wish for us to stay here with the team?"

"Yes, enjoy some down time. The conversation ahead will best be had in small numbers. I'll contact Velten now to let her know what the situation is."

"Yes, ser." Madlin saluted and turned away.

Castellan wasted no time in doing what she promised. *Captain Velten.*

I'm here. Have you returned from your exploration?

We are inside the mountain and have made contact with the Tau Ceti residing within.

Bollux, you say!

I assure you that it's the truth.

It's hard to believe one of the Makers has been living this close for so long.

Yes, well, Olivienne and I are heading into a private meeting with Scientere Extremus T'kinsaa Flx'n...gah, but that's a mouthful. Kinsa has given the team a space to relax, similar to what we found in the research station by Nessie. I'm aware of our remaining sharc, so we won't take any more time than necessary to explain our current predicament. I just wanted to let you know the status of the mission.

Thank you, Captain. We'll remain ready for extraction on your word.

Well and good. Tosh out.

Olivienne waited as Castellan summed up her conversation. "I've informed Velten of our current state. The *Vestigo* stands ready."

That settled, Olivienne spoke to Kinsa. "I'd like to

have that discussion now."

"The *Vestigo* is one of your airships, yes? My system tracked four initially. I apologize for the destruction of two, they are automated defenses."

"The two that were destroyed, and one of the remaining, are not our ships and therein lies part of our problem as well as the reason we are here."

"If you'll follow me, Connate Dracore." Kinsa led the way down the corridor of what they referred to as the residential ring. Eventually the trio came to a door that opened automatically when they neared. There were low couches around the perimeter of the room with a strange metallic round table in the middle. "Please, sit. Do you have a beverage preference? My selections are safe for human consumption."

Castellan and Olivienne exchanged a glance. "Perhaps some water."

The table had a strange black panel with a grid marked into it filled with various symbols similar to what they'd seen since entering the mountain. Castellan was no scholar but assumed it must be in the language of Kinsa's people. Each press of a gray finger elicited a beep until the center of the table irised open and a tray of pouches lifted into place.

"I'm afraid we do not use the same appurtenances as humans."

"Appurtenances?" Olivienne wore a look that Castellan recognized well, that of insatiable curiosity.

"Perhaps a different word would better suit you. I forgot that the humans didn't get the recent Terran update like the species seeded elsewhere. The Tau Ceti, though similar in humanoid requirement and physical process, are still innately different. Our...equipment, for lack of a more appropriate word, has been developed to suit our needs during the course of many millennia." Kinsa picked up a pouch and twisted a button on the top, then aimed toward their strange mouth slit and squeezed.

"Fascinating." They grabbed their own pouches and followed Kinsa's instructions. Thirst quenched, Olivienne wasted no time in starting the discussion. "On the topic of language, you speak excellent Psierian. Or would it be Humanese? If we are originally from this other race of people."

"Humans had hundreds of languages on Terra and the one we chose for you to speak on Psiere happens to be English, altered by your people through the centuries."

Olivienne shook her head and Castellan marveled at the complexities involved with their existence on Psiere. "There is much of what you've said and few words that leave me with more questions than I have time to ask. However, I feel it is my duty to tell you why we've sought you out. Before I do that, may I ask why you are still here when the rest of your people have clearly left?"

Kinsa rested their hands in their lap, loosely holding the half empty pouch between their clasped fingers. They sighed and Castellan thought it sounded especially Psierian...or human as her own people apparently were. "This is my punishment. Yet at the same time, it is also my reward."

"That makes no sense."

"Patience, Captain. I will explain. When I introduced myself as a scientere extremus, it was more than a simple title. I was the leader of the entire collection expedition."

Castellan's intuition rang with concern caused by something in Kinsa's words, but Olivienne asked the question first.

"What do you mean collection? We've read the documents and spoken with Nessie. Did something happen to all the, uh, places where you collected the species you kept on the ship? Why else would you be collecting them?"

Expression was impossible to read on Kinsa's face. With a largeish oblong head, overly large black eyes, and no nose to speak of, the touchstones that Castellan had been trained to decipher were missing. Even so, there was something in the way Kinsa slumped that indicated regret. Perhaps the Makers weren't the saviors that everyone believed. Castellan spoke her mind. "You didn't do it for a purpose, did you? Are the Makers nothing more than collectors of civilizations? Did the people and creatures on that ship originally have families and homes?"

Kinsa straightened. "I assure you that it's not like that." They sucked in a breath and thin, bony shoulders shuddered with the exhale. "The Tau Ceti pride themselves on being the oldest and most advanced race in the history of our universe, but we are not so arrogant to miss the significance of other developing peoples. We are thinkers, explorers, and also protectors to an extent."

"To an extent?"

"Yes, well, we are forbidden from interfering with the genetic makeup and social development of an established species. What we *are* allowed to do is collect samples of species who are on the brink of extinction."

Olivienne frowned. "To save?"

"It is my shame to admit that is only part of the purpose."

"Whatever do you mean?"

"I'd wager they mean to save and study. Is that correct, Kinsa?"

Olivienne straightened. "What?"

Kinsa held up a hand in supplication. "Please, you have to understand that our race is far flung and more powerful than anything you could imagine. We are long-lived and it is exceedingly important that we followed the regulations set forth by the ruling council, else it would all fall to chaos. All Tau Ceti have roles within society and I played mine as expected."

Castellan tilted her head and narrowed her eyes. "Until you didn't. Why were you left behind?"

Kinsa finished their pouch and placed it back on the tray. Then with the press of a few more of the strange obsidae buttons, the image of a faintly glowing globe appeared above the table. Castellan recognized the familiar shapes of Endara and Dromea. "That's Psiere."

"Yes, or as we referred to the previously unexplored planet, Tin'glk 32456 quadrant 43, star xtv-42. The name Psiere originated from your people much later."

The globe rotated slowly and Olivienne gasped. "We aren't alone." She looked at Castellan. "Tosh, there are other lands out there for us to explore."

Castellan moved her hand a short distance to clasp

Olivienne's. "I think we need to finish learning about our own before we get into all that."

Olivienne smiled ruefully. "True enough, darling."

"You can see the planet was large enough to seed most of our collected species. As I mentioned, some were on the verge of extinction, quite a few coming from your originating planet, Terra." They paused. "Though from the update I received, I believe many of the locals refer to it as Earth. Nessie herself is the last of her kind. Very long lived, telepathic, and incredibly fascinating. We made sure she had a safe place and a purpose before leaving her on Magna."

"She's lonely. One of our people spoke with her at length and she revealed that she's been lonely since the Tau left the island. I believe that my mother plans to send scienteres and more to Magna to stay for a time, once our people are safe and society is stable again."

That knowledge appeared to sooth Kinsa. "Thank you, it means a lot to me. Nessie and I used to speak quite frequently after the initial seeding. As you surmised, not all of the species are from extinct worlds. Terra was a regular stop in our travels because my people were fascinated by the planet's sheer determination to spawn and sustain life. There was originally an entire race of giant lizards until a cataclysmic event sent the planet into an ice age. Sadly, we weren't able to save any of the specimens before this happened."

"Why were we taken? I mean, uh, humans? Were they going extinct?"

"Not exactly. Hominins were particularly hardy and resourceful. When multiple evolutions split and kept going, some dying out and others continuing...well, we scienteres were utterly fascinated by the process. A few even based their entire research on which tracks would fail and which would succeed. This one instance—"

Castellan held up a hand when she sensed Kinsa was meandering in the conversation. "Please, despite our relaxed nature, time is a bit of the essence and I'm afraid we don't have the luxury of a full explanation. Though I'm sure Olivienne would gladly come back to speak with you again."

"Very sorry, Captain. It's been so long since I was able to sit and converse that I got carried away. *Verlnk stux'm.*" Kinsa touched their large forehead, then the center of their chest. Castellan gathered that it was a formal apology.

"All is well."

"What happened to the humans, our Psierian ancestors, that deemed them necessary for collection?"

"There was a great plague that spread across multiple continents. One of the more advanced societies had yet to find their way around the world in large numbers. Other civilizations were a lot less enlightened. Given the severity of the sickness and rapidity of its spread, we thought that it would be wise to collect some samples on our pass at the time. We also collected Nessie on the same trip."

Castellan tilted her head. "How did you preserve proper diversity?"

"Genetic diversity, yes. We collected from around the world. Your race here on Psiere is made up of a panoply of Terran peoples. We traveled for a time after that past trip with no plans for further acquisitions because the *Terra Halcyon* two-four-seven-nine collection chambers were at capacity. We were taking all specimens back to our home sector when we were caught in a meteor shower."

"What is a meteor?"

Kinsa paused and Castellan wondered if they struggled with the apparent differences between their current Psierian language and things that were missed in whatever update they'd received.

"Meteors are fragments of rock traveling through space at high velocity. Sometimes there is an explosion or great impact that will hurl debris along the trajectory. Most Tau ships are advanced enough to track such things but the explosion must have happened on the other side of a large gas giant in your system. The captain had plotted a course around the planet and brought us straight into the asteroid field."

"How did you end up here?"

Kinsa rubbed their forehead with two fingers, a movement that Castellan had observed a few times already. She endeavored to assign the action to an emotion once she figured it out.

"Long range scans discovered this previously unexplored planet. It was ideal that we found no native life advanced enough to worry about breaking the tenets of our people. The captain plotted a course down to the surface. Not only was the Terra Halcyon damaged but an interstellar cruiser isn't meant for such atmospheric gravity and pressure. Even still, the navigation team, under the direction of the captain, brought us down with less damage than originally feared. We lost some specimens and crew but, for the most part, we fared well."

Olivienne shook her head in wonder. "It seems unbelievable that something the size of which we discovered could fall from the stars and remain relatively unscathed."

"Once we took stock of surviving Tau as well as collected samples, we explored the world to best map out where each species should be seeded. Staying on the ship wasn't tenable and we were off course and unlikely to be found for some time. I ordered the most adaptable to be transplanted, and we put the more dangerous or volatile species into a deep sleep before giving them a safe and needed death."

Olivienne gazed at Castellan. "Those were the bones we found on the ship below Dir Sanguis."

"I thought as much too." Castellan looked back at Kinsa. "And the rest? If you weren't allowed to interfere in a species development or evolution, why the temples, or caches of valuable information?"

"It may help to explain the timeline of your existence. Your ancestors were collected around—" Kinsa paused in thought before continuing. "I believe somewhere near thirteen hundred and fifty Earth rotos according to their Gregorian calendar."

At Olivienne and Castellan's confused look, Kinsa elaborated. "It is the current date method in use, which follows a solar dating system. We traveled for two decades—"

"Decades...deca, is that ten?" Castellan interrupted as

she attempted to puzzle out some of the unfamiliar words. "Decaroto?"

Kinsa inclined their head. "Yes, exactly that. Your Psierian revolution around the suns is a few wekes less than an Earth roto. The humans prospered for three generations, or a hundred rotos. By that point the seeded species displayed the same psionic powers as the native ones."

Olivienne nodded. "You wrote about that, too. I remember the document that first mentioned the in vitro chambers to facilitate non-sexual reproduction."

"Exactly."

Castellan considered what they knew of Psi history from the documents discovered. "Three generations, that would put you near the time of the destruction of Antaeus, yes?"

Confirmation didn't come immediately. Rather, Kinsa sat in silent contemplation for some meens before they finally spoke. "Just as humans amazed us with their ability to adapt and prosper in a variety of environments, one thing that threatens their existence even now is their propensity toward war and aggression. We'd already begun work on the temples when Antorae struck to forever darken the night skies." Kinsa sighed and their shoulders slumped. "We had no idea that increasing the humans' powerful psionics would trigger a war across both the continents you call Endara and Dromea."

Olivienne leveled her purple eyed gaze upon Kinsa. "We've never found any mentions of war in all the velums collected to date."

"That is because it doesn't exist in any of the standard documents placed within the temples. That information can only be found within personal logs scattered in specially coded hidden caches. The more your current society learns about your true past, the more you'll be able to discover. I anticipated a...maturation of your species to the point where you would be receptive to the history of Psiere and the power such knowledge brings."

"Unfortunately, we've certainly gained the knowledge, though I'm unconvinced we are capable or worthy of the self-restraint you hoped for."

"It is as we feared then. Our humans prospered for a long time considering their newly gained abilities and the strange environment. But the power discovered within the antoraestones decimated them by the end of the next Psierian century."

Castellan did the maths in her head. "If Antaeus was destroyed in the roto one hundred and six, that puts us past two hundred our time. That document you left behind said there were only a few of the original seedling lines left when the Tau Ceti interfered. That's when you engineered our genetics?"

Kinsa nodded and shifted in their seat. "It is. At the time we had no idea if our collection was truly the last of the humans and we didn't want to lose them. After discussion with my fellow scienteres, as well as the ship officers, we decided to intervene and genetically engineer the race. Leadership was a critical need but since we were already working on improvement, we made a few other changes as well to make the species hardier. Longer lived, less prone to abnormalities like cancer and disease."

"I'm guessing you didn't temper the human inclination toward power or aggression."

"While the physical condition is easy enough to adjust genetically, the changes needed to alter emotions and thoughts are much more difficult to enact on a larger, species-wide scale. As it was, we did much more than wise."

"How do you mean?"

Kinsa rubbed their head. "Besides providing the humans with genetically superior leaders, we rebuilt society, established laws, and left coded texts to aid in human advancement. It seemed dishonest to guide you to such an extent, but we'd been cut off from the greater expanse and we had become invested in your survival. Being unable to have our own progeny while on Psiere, many looked upon humans as surrogates."

Kinsa drew in a deep breath. "We thought it safe enough once we'd gathered and locked away the antoraestones, much the way you pull something dangerous from a small child's grasp. We agreed to help the remaining humans provided they didn't speak of their history. We even implanted false memories on the first re-seeds before retreating from their lands seventy rotos after breaking the Tau covenant of non-interference. That meant the altered generation knew nothing of your origins, which continued until now."

"I thought you said you had reason for breaking your laws and interfering? Extinction of species and all that." Olivienne waved a hand through the air.

"Yes, despite the logical reasoning behind it, we still went against our laws. A fact which incurred proper punishment once we were discovered by the greater mind."

Castellan shook her head. "A span of five hundred rotos is a long time to savor success. Unfortunately, right at this time we are at the brink of civil war due to the machinations of a man who seeks power more than peace. We discovered the antoraestones you'd hidden away."

Kinsa tensed and leaned closer to Castellan. "Is that the reason behind this civil war?"

She shook her head. "No. I personally locked away the stones the Tau Ceti had placed within the Temple of Antaeus for safekeeping, by request of our queen. But the man leading the rebellion has discovered many shards of the same material on Dromea and is using the power they provide to usurp the sovereign line."

Kinsa sat back and their eyes dilated with what Castellan could only determine to be alarm. "Truly? This is not a good turn of events."

Olivienne held out her hand with the palm up. "Please, this is why we're here. My mother still sees the rebels as her people, even though they fight against us. Some of them are being coerced, some fight willingly. But because of her belief in Psiere, she wants a way to neutralize their powers without harming them. In all your time on this planet, have you discovered anything of the like?"

The room grew silent as they awaited Kinsa's answer. Castellan reasoned that if anyone would know of such a thing, it would be the one who began and led it all.

Unfortunately, Kinsa's answer left them equal parts elated and disheartened. "There are only two ways that I know of. One is a scalar field disruptor and is centuries beyond your technical capability."

"And the other?" Castellan was impatient to move forward with their quest. Every dae they were away meant more possible deaths from rebel action.

"We call the second items power sinks. They are not as efficient but it's something that your people could create with the right equipment." They held up their hand, palm out. "I must warn you, their unique abilities cannot be fully controlled and thusly, could be dangerous."

Olivienne frowned. "I don't know if we have much choice."

"In that case, there is a small cache of them near the southwestern coast of Endara."

"What are power sinks?"

Kinsa paused for a few meens before inquiring, "How much do you know about the origination of your psionic abilities?"

Olivienne answered. "We found documents that explained the properties of the illeostone mineral. We know that every Psierian carries it within their bodies, much like we have iron and calcium. And apparently a person's channels will be strongest with prolonged fetal exposure to archeostones."

Kinsa nodded. "Quite a lot, actually. You know the basic workings of magnetism?"

"Of course."

"The illeostone within your cells is attracted to what Psierians call aether in the atmosphere. Archeostones are natural producers of that particular element, which is how you charge your stones and bodies. Illeo mineral draws aether in and stores it as energy, which is then controlled and utilized by your pineal gland. Outside the body, the aether is released into the atmosphere when in contact with water. A most fascinating process."

Castellan held up a hand. "While fascinating, that doesn't explain how power sinks work."

"Ah, yes. A power sink is naught more than highly compressed illeostone mineral in the shape of oval disks. Not only will they draw all the aether from the surrounding area, but when pressed against the skin, they'll also drain absorbed energy from any Psierian. The greater the body mass, the more sinks needed."

"Don't we charge illeostones with archeostones? They can't simply charge on their own."

"The temple chambers are set up specifically to charge many stones at once, in a relatively short amount of time, by saturating the space. But we discovered that when compressed, the illeostone mineral property changes and will draw from anything nearby with much greater strength," Kinsa said.

Olivienne's face brightened for the first time since arriving. "That sounds like what we need!"

"You must use caution though because there is no way to control the absorption of the power sink. That's the reason we hid them away in a cave filled with water. Once in use, they'll need to be changed out once a day and discharged in water or they stop working."

Castellan had a feeling they'd need to heed Kinsa's warnings carefully. "How do we transport such stones if they would drain the power from our cells, or even our own illeostone-fueled conveyances?"

Kinsa held up his hands in a gesture that Castellan recognized. They had no clue.

Chapter Twelve

"What if we coated them in a thin layer of oil or wax?"

"It would depend on how porous your materials are. Do your people have anything that is airtight?"

Castellan answered, "No, but you do. I believe the storage containers we've found here and on Magna were all sealed. If the seals work with regular air, they should work for aether. With your permission, we could use the ones below."

Kinsa tilted their head toward Castellan. "It would seem you've found the solution. I have no problem gifting you a few containers."

They paused, making little motions in the air with a single finger while mouthing silent words. To Castellan it looked as though they were counting.

"If my calculations are correct, you shouldn't need more than three of the large crates but I'll send you with three smaller ones in addition in case you wish to split them up for transport. You shouldn't need to build the machines to compress illeostone dust if you collect the entire stored quantity from the cave."

"How did you create the sinks?" Castellan smiled as Olivienne's curious nature took over.

"We used technology aboard our space vessel before it became unsafe to visit."

"I wish we'd had more time to explore before it submerged."

"'Vienne, we just barely made it out with our lives. I think we should count ourselves lucky we got what we did out of it."

Kinsa's thin lips shaped into what Castellan had come to realize was their version of a smile. "The frequency key and map for the Temple of Antaeus?"

"Yes." Olivienne was silent for a few secs. "Kinsa, you don't have to answer if the question is intrusive, but who was the Tau Ceti that we found on the Island of Navis with the second temple key?"

Kinsa placed a palm on their chest and glanced down briefly before answering. "That was my mate, N'tovi Flx'nde. They were damaged in the initial asteroid incident and suffered cellular decay from the solar radiation leak in the hull before it crashed. While our shipboard technology could repair a basic injury, once cellular decay has set in, life span is significantly decreased. They elected to stay on Psiere with me during my exile rather than seek treatment on a home world."

"Why? Couldn't your mate have come back?"

"They were never given the choice. Once Tau leave a site, the exploration and collection team leave as well. Unless you elect to become a watcher. That is the only circumstance that we are allowed to remain on a developing planet after initial exploration."

They looked away and sighed. Kinsa didn't display sorrow the way Castellan was familiar with, even so, she could tell it was an ever-present weight. "So, they stayed."

Kinsa nodded. "They stayed with me. We promised one another five thousand revolutions and we made it to five thousand and twenty-six."

Olivienne covered her mouth. "Oh. That's a long time."

"On the contrary, it wasn't long enough."

"I understand." Castellan took a deep breath and stood from the low couch. "As much as I've enjoyed learning more about the Tau Ceti and where we come from as a people, we have the information we need to complete the mission for the queen. Lives depend on us returning as soon as possible."

Both Kinsa and Olivienne stood as well. Kinsa responded to Castellan's declaration. "That's logical. You must curb this violence quickly to prevent the disaster perpetrated by your ancestors."

Olivienne held out her hand to their host. "I have enjoyed our visit immensely. Do you think it would be possible to meet again? I'm not sure what the laws are regarding your duties here as a Watcher."

"A select few know of my existence now, but I'd like to keep that number as small as possible. That being said, I would love to speak with you again and meet your queen."

Olivienne smiled. "I think my mother would love to sit down with you and discuss our histories, but my father would probably enjoy it more. He was an adventurist, the same as I. I'll be sure to remind them that a visit is due once we've quelled this rebellion. Maybe you could even return to Magna and spend time with Nessie now that we know of your existence. I'm certain she would be delighted by your company."

"I can't be away from Halcyon for long because of my duties here, and being a Watcher, the knowledge of my existence should remain with as few individuals as possible. But now that I know your people don't have the capabilities to detect one of my transport shuttles, I'll be sure to pay her a visit." Kinsa slapped their small hands together twice and turned to make their way around the couch they'd occupied for well more than an oor. "It is time we retrieved your empty storage crates so you can make your way back to the mainland. I'll lead you and your team to the lower level and provide you with coordinates for the power sink cave."

"Thank you."

"You should be wary during the retrieval because you'll be stripped of your channel abilities when you approach the cavern. The sinks are powerful, especially as they are gathered into one place."

Olivienne tapped her bottom lip. "Are there traps or other challenges in the cave where they're located?"

Kinsa shook their head. "No. We thought the natural location and fauna would guard them well enough."

She looked at Castellan, who shrugged. "Our team is highly trained. I think we'll be fine even without powers. Especially now that your mother has negotiated peace with the Atlantee."

"It sounds as though you have the issue resolved. I wish you best of luck with your travels. Let's get you back to your team and ship."

Kinsa was able to make their return much easier with the use of smaller versions of the floating sleds Castellan's team had found during their exploration. There was a hidden door near the lift that Kinsa revealed once they'd all traveled below. Each sled held twelve standing psi, plenty of room for the sixteen-member team plus one small gray being. They could also steer themselves, making it safe for them to travel at high speed along the corridor back to where they entered the volcano. The pilots were disappointed they wouldn't have hands on the controls but Castellan was glad the return would take a fraction of the time it took to make their way around.

Castellan and Olivienne rode in the same sled as Kinsa, who planned to help them find the empty crates, then would program the sleds, and return with them to the other side.

Once everything was set, the shields milled around behind the royal couple as they made to take their leave. Olivienne bowed to Kinsa. "There is so much more I wish to know but time is of the essence. Is there a way we can communicate with you here at Halcyon?"

"Sadly, no. I'm afraid you lack the proper technology to work with my station. However, should you send people to Magna, perhaps we can open up a line of communication using the towers and research facility. Provided, as I said, it remains with only a select few of you to maintain the secret of my existence." They did that strange motion with their lips indicating pleasure. "This is not goodbye."

"I hope not. It would be wonderful to see you again."

Castellan joined them. "I would like to promise you that we will return in short order and all our troubles will be resolved, but I can't predict the future. I also fear that you will get more curious visitors sent by Pon Havington if things go poorly for us. Tell me, do you happen to know our light flash code communication?"

"I do since I was the one who made sure it got added to the human education kit when we helped to re-build your people after the antoraestone catastrophe."

She shook her head, incredulous that the being in front of her was so long lived. "I will be sure that only our people know to send a coded transmission to you. I'm assuming your equipment will let you observe such things in your nearby airspace? You said yourself that you saw the fate of the other two ships."

"I did and I can. What code will you use."

"We'll keep it simple with your abbreviated name only. K-I-N-S-A."

Kinsa nodded then bowed and made a complicated gesture that involved touching each arm, their head, and their chest. "I shall look forward to the return of the sovereign and loyalists. Until then, safe journey, Captain." They turned to Olivienne. "Connate Dracore."

"Thank you."

Castellan instructed Lazaro to contact Velten and request a pickup as they were saying their goodbyes. Kinsa made sure the tree would not accost them as they made the trek back to the beach where they'd left their gear.

Castellan carried all the cubes with her telekinesis, a feat of concentration more than strength since they were empty. That wasn't the case during their short ride up the ropes using Illeostone-powered drivers clipped to their harnesses. It was well known that the farther from the ground you were, the heavier the mental load. Castellan instructed her team to stow away all the gear as she and Olivienne made their way to the bridge to speak with Captain Velten.

Once on the bridge, Velten met them looking equal parts concerned and impatient. "What are your orders, Connate Dracore?"

Olivienne pulled the slip of velum from her pouch and handed it to her. "These are the coordinates for a cave south of Pentole. We'll find something we can use to...absorb a Psierian's power."

"Not just a psi's power, 'Vienne."

Velten handed it off to her navigator. "Plot the course and give me a time estimate."

"Aye, Captain."

She called out to another psi working at the pilot station. "Spool the engines and prepare the *Vestigo* for departure."

"Yes, ser."

"Your description of the solution is vague and doesn't seem as though it would be fast acting. What about the cubes you brought up?"

"Those are to safely transport the power sinks."

The captain remained quiet for a few secs, then grimaced. "The blasted rebel ship is still floating around. I was hoping they'd make another attempt to land on the island while you were down there and solve at least one of our problems."

"Ser," the navigator called out. "Straight course would be fifty-seven oors."

Velten frowned. "That's too long. We'll need to stop in Occasus and replenish supplies. Plot the course there and I'll contact Sendae once we're within range."

Olivienne shifted impatiently. "And after Occasus?"

"We're probably looking at another thirty-seven oors from Occasus to the coordinates on that velum."

"Ser, we're ready for departure," the pilot called out.

"Orders?" Velten asked Olivienne and Castellan.

"My gut says they won't shoot us if we go. Let's head top speed back to Occasus. We'll deal with the other ship if they try to interfere."

"That we will." Velten circled her finger in the air. "Sound the alarm for full speed in two meens. I want all power returning to the shipyard. We'll outrun the bloody rebels."

Olivienne groaned and ran a hand through her hair, forgetting that she'd braided it back out of the way before they went into the trees to rescue Castellan. "It's been a long dae. How about a tumbler of scotch while we debrief?"

Velten gave her a suspicious look. "I suspect you want my liquor more than you want to tell me what you found."

Castellan laughed heartily. "I suspect you'll want your liquor, too, after you hear what we've found."

"I was afraid you'd say that."

The alert tone sounded in the captain's quarters and Velten quickly made her way to the com panel. "Velten." They'd been traveling southeast for a few oors, plenty of time to put sufficient distance between the rebel dirigible and the *Vestigo*. Even so, Olivienne worried about what the alert could mean.

"Ser, the enemy has turned away and is no longer following our ship."

Velten pursed her lips and glanced toward the table where the other two sat. "When? And turned away how?"

"About five meens ago, ser. We wanted to be sure of a heading in order to report."

"Direction?"

"East-northeast."

"Thank you, ensign. Velten out." She asked Olivienne, "Any idea what they could be after?"

Olivienne rubbed her bottom lip. "Do you have a map of Psiere?"

Velten moved to a cabinet and withdrew a rolled-up map from one of the cubbies. She pinned it to the table with the scotch glasses then pointed to a spot in the middle of the water. "We're here."

Olivienne traced her finger east to see if there was anything of importance along the way. "Could they be heading to Baen?"

Castellan tapped the map above the northern city. "Or maybe here. Iuvenis or Aetate."

"The prison islands? What would they want there?"

Velten growled. "Not what, who. Perhaps they have intentions of removing someone who has been previously sentenced."

Olivienne looked to her right. "What do we do, Tosh? There's no way to warn Maman of a possible escape attempt."

Velten shook her head. "True. The only option would be to alter our own course to follow them."

Castellan stared hard at the map before shaking her head. "I don't know if that's where they're going but we have to trust in the system they've got in place at the islands to prevent such a thing. My gut is telling me that we need to get these power sinks."

The ship captain was skeptical. "You're sure?"

"As sure as I can be so far out. My intuition is vaguely telling me we need to carry on."

"We trust Tosh on this. Don't alter course. You can inform Sendae about the rogue rebel ship heading east when we reach Occasus."

"Yes, ser."

Olivienne rolled her eyes. "Don't be troublesome, Captain. I get that enough from Tosh."

Velten freshened all their glasses then resumed her seat. "Me troublesome? You lot make my stomach burn on the regular."

Castellan tapped the side of her glass with a blunt fingernail. "It's never dull with the connate aboard, is it?"

Velten grinned. "At least you haven't quit or retired before your time. That's quite a feat from what I hear of the corp gossip."

Olivienne snorted. "Yes, well...Tosh is uniquely hardy."

Castellan's ears grew warm as Velten remarked on it. "So I've heard."

"If you two are finished poking holes in my reputation, I think I'm going to head back to the room." She looked at Olivienne. "Stay and gossip longer with the captain. I'll be sure the shields on duty know to escort you back to our berth."

"Are you tired, love? You feel all right after the tree mishap?"

Castellan gave her a gentle smile. "On my word, I feel fine. But I missed my normal morning exercise routine and you know I like to keep up, 'Vienne."

Olivienne rolled her eyes and blew out a frustrated breath. "Bah! You're so...dedicated, Tosh. You should stay and throw the cubes with us."

"You know what, you do look a little less muscled than normal. You should *not* stay and throw cubes if you feel as though you've neglected your proper training, Tosh."

Castellan pointed at Velten and chuckled. "You just don't want to lose."

"True enough." Velten lifted her glass of scotch and moved to take a sip, pausing when her hand was tilted the tiniest amount from Castellan's telekinesis. Velten *tsked* and took a steady sip after. "We don't waste good liquor here. I'll have you thrown in the stock room if you do that again."

That earned another laugh and casual wave of Castellan's hand. "I shall mind my manners then. I wouldn't want to be locked away in a dark closet with no way out."

All three laughed at the ridiculousness of such a task. Olivienne held up her own tumbler. "I'll be along in a bit. I want to finish this first. Maybe later we can do a little light reading."

Velten scowled. "That better not be a euphemism."

Olivienne snickered before her expression grew serious. "I meant reading a little more of Savon's journal. He recorded some good insight. I can only imagine there may be more to guide us."

"Well enough." Castellan hesitated then leaned down to kiss Olivienne's cheek, knowing what the out of character display of affection would mean to her future par. "Until then."

They stayed in Occasus long enough to get a secure message out to the capital and replenish supplies, then they were off again heading south. They traveled another twenty-one oors after they left the dirigible shipyard before they had to make another stop. It was longer than anticipated because they needed to detour around the roc territory above Mater Island, then a storm front forced them to winch down just on the other side of Bindle Bay. They sheltered in a remote location for another six oors. Everyone aboard was surprised when they made it to the coordinates safely with no rebel interference on their fourth dae of travel.

The *Vestigo* floated offshore near a cliff face along a barren stretch of the peninsula south of Pentole. Caves similar to the ones located on Navis dotted the expanse of rock. Castellan's stomach had been cramping with intuition channel anxiety since waking that morning. She scowled. "This was too easy."

"What do you mean easy? Maman's truce with the

Atlanteens all but guaranteed us smooth sailing when still in Endara territory. And the three rogues would have taken one of the three archeostones from the Temple of Illeos. They'd need the others to maintain the charging rooms so I doubt we'll see any more long-ranging ships so far north."

Velten cleared her throat. "We still have one ship out there prepared to cause trouble. I wish I knew where it went after turning east."

Castellan shook her head. "Not likely we'll find out barring some sort of emergency. With us running black, the queen won't have anyone contact us, despite the secure message we sent with Sendae."

"Even so, something's had you twisted since we woke this morning. What is it, darling?"

Castellan ran a hand through her hair. "I don't know. Just a sense of wrongness that feels connected to the rogue that got away."

"Nothing else, Tosh?"

"This entire thing has me a bit twisted. I sense danger ahead as well as what we left behind."

Velten and Olivienne gave her a concerned look but it was the ship captain who answered. "Nothing we can do about it now, I'm afraid. We are well past the point of decision regret and into the planning stage of decision worry. Were you given any other information about the location of these power sinks? There are dozens on that cliff face."

"Kinsa didn't tell us much. We know it's the largest cave—"

Castellan scowled. "Which looks to be half under water."

"But the opening is big enough to fit those inflatable rafts we've got in the adventurist staging room."

"True," Castellan said.

Velten raised her hand. "Didn't you say you'll have no channel ability when in close proximity to the cave?"

"Yes, why?"

"I hope you're planning on rowing yourselves inside because you won't be able to use the small illeostone powered propellers."

"Shite!"

Castellan grinned at Olivienne. "The shields can handle a little physical labor. And on that thought, I believe we should limit the retrieval to a small team."

"Who are you thinking?"

She ticked off guardians on her fingers. "Us, of course, Madlin, Dozier, Qent, Holling, Meza, Devin, and Sehg. The rafts easily hold ten plus supplies, plenty of room for the nine of us and the three large cubes."

"You've listed all with adventurist sub-specialties. I like the way you think, love."

Her cheeks warmed with the endearment. "Yes, we won't need a pilot, nor communications. But a medic is non-negotiable where a sovereign is concerned, and the rest will come in handy. I chose Madlin because she's senior with tinkerist training in case there are Maker technologies inside."

"Ser, you intend to go into those caves?"

They turned to the communications officer on duty. The woman's face was pale and her eyes wide with fear. "Yes, they are, Velten answered. "Is there something we should know, Folnir?"

Specialist Folnir's voice shook. "I grew up in the back country near these cliffs. There were always rumors of animals going missing if they wandered into the forest at the cliff edge. When we reported the disappearances, experts were sent out but could find nothing in the greater woods. They told us it was probably Atlanteen activity carrying our stock into the sea."

Castellan examined the tall cliff face. "That seems a bit far to be the Atlantee."

"We thought so too, ser. But what could we do? At least the instances only happened at night," Folnir said.

Olivienne's voice held a fair amount of trepidation. "What do we do, Tosh?"

"If those responsible were Atlantee creatures of the deep, we won't have any problems with the truce in place."

Velten frowned. "And if it wasn't of the sea?"

"Then we have something possibly living in the caves

that is large or strong enough to make away with livestock from the forest above. But it appears as though whatever it is could be nocturnal so we should be safe enough during the dae." She asked Folnir. "Does the forest have a name?"

"Aranea." Her one-word answer was whispered and Castellan saw her fear clearly despite lacking a general empathy channel to feel it.

"That word is familiar..." Olivienne rubbed her lip then held her finger in the air. "I believe it's, uh, related to spiders. Spider web or something of the sort. I've seen it in Maker texts and the context led us to believe that was the meaning."

Chill bumps raced down Castellan's forearms and she shivered. "Spiders?"

"Yes, I'm certain."

She sighed as multiple pairs of curious eyes stared back at her. "I hate spiders."

Olivienne grinned. "You can always stay behind if you're afraid."

The mere notion of it rankled Castellan. "I will not!" She grabbed her voteo from her belt rather than entertain the idea that Olivienne had purposely goaded her with. "Madlin, prepare cave gear for nine and an inflatable raft. We leave to retrieve the stones in twenty meens." She named the seven shields who would undertake the retrieval with them and signed off.

Velten looked at her with surprise. "You're not going to warn them about possible cave spiders?"

"I will before we depart. No sense getting them worked up now."

"You mean the way you are?" Olivienne's grin was infuriating.

"I'm not worked up!" When every person on the bridge turned in their direction, Castellan conceded that she was unsettled. "I'll be fine. But we should probably make sure our own gear is in order before we depart."

Olivienne's expression turned softer. "Sorry, love. I'll stop. Let's go check our satchels." She turned to Velten. "Our channel strength should return once we have the power sinks sealed away in the cubes but we won't be able to contact you until then."

"And if something should go wrong?"

"Give us," She looked at Castellan, who shrugged. "Let's be generous and say an oor and a half once we enter the cave. Kinsa didn't indicate it was a long trek to the sinks. But I'll concede that I don't know how difficult the terrain will be to traverse inside. That should allow us time to get there, pack them away, and get back out."

"Well enough, Connate. My crew will await your return."

Fifteen meens later, the inflatable raft dropped into the water from the staging deck of the *Vestigo*. It was connected to the dirigible via a long line that the team used to rappel down. The cubes were airtight so it was no issue dropping them into the water and fishing them out again once the partial team was safely aboard the boat.

Castellan and the seven guardians all retrieved the paddles from where they were tied and took their positions along each side. "Connate, if you would take a seat at the bow, we'll be on our way."

"I'm fully capable of paddling, you know."

"We are all aware of your imminent capability but we only have eight paddles, therefore you are in charge of navigation. Make sure there are no sharp outcroppings that can damage the raft once we enter the cave. Waves are coming up, which will make our jobs a touch tricky."

As if to prove Castellan's point, a wave hit their boat sideways and Olivienne slipped and fell upon her rear into the seat indicated. She sighed and the rest of the team stifled chuckles.

Olivienne called out a rhythm until the group got the hang of rowing in unison, then she focused on the way forward. The water grew rough nearer the cliff face. It seemed plenty deep to Castellan's untrained eyes though. "Qent, Dozier, you two are the ones with water and cave training. You think we'll be safe enough rowing in?"

"Water will speed up once we enter the cave proper, pushing and pulling outward with the waves," Dozier said. "We'll have to see if we can anchor once we're inside and hope for dry space wherever the sinks are located. The stone looks solid and not likely to crumble."

Qent nodded. "Obviously one of our biggest worries will be whether or not there are any sharp outcroppings beneath the boat once inside. Our lanterns will only reflect off the water and we'll lose all visibility to what's below. It'll look like naught more than a black mirror."

"Great."

Olivienne called out from the front of the boat. "Ten foot to go. I've lost my channels already. What about the lot of you?"

"Nothing here."

"Mine are gone too, Connate."

"Same."

Castellan reached out with her strongest channel and felt nothing, even boosted by the antoraestone. The power within her cells had already been depleted. It was disconcerting and she didn't like the vulnerable feeling, not that she'd ever admit it to her team. "I've got nothing." A few looked worried so Castellan reassured them, "I picked this team for their skill, not their channel strength. We don't need our powers to retrieve a few cubes of compressed illeostones."

"Tosh, did you tell them about the spiders?"

"What?" Sehg's tan face paled noticeably as he moved his gaze from Olivienne to Castellan.

"Eyes front, Guardian. No, I haven't."

"Spiders are completely normal. Caves are usually dry and a good place to shelter. There may or may not be spiders in this one because of the proximity to the ocean."

Holling added to Dozier's explanation as they paddled that final couple yords. "They don't typically like the humidity."

Castellan grimaced as the chill bumps raced down her arms. "Does the same hold true for spiders of unusual size?"

"Unusual size, ser?"

The boat rocked with another wave but slipped inside the large cave easily enough. Knowing they couldn't use illeostone lanterns in proximity, Olivienne pulled out antiquated torches and a striker as she answered Madlin's question. "There have been reports for rotos that something is taking game and livestock from the forest above the cliffs. Many speculated they could be Atlantee creatures responsible. But the name of the forest is a word we've seen in adventurist texts that relates to spiders."

"Maker's take me!" Sehg's comment caused a few more snickers.

"Steady. I'm not a fan of the infernal creatures either but let's focus on the mission."

Lucky enough for the team, the water went in a dozen yords before ending along a wide ledge of rock. A small stream originated from farther in the cave but nothing large enough for the raft. Dozier clambered out of the boat and secured an anchor stake using a hammer and piton.

Long shadows shone upon the walls closest to the boat from the one torch Olivienne had lit and Castellan scanned the space intently. It was too large for the torch to do more than light the immediate vicinity, meaning the ceilings and path farther along the ledge remained black. She was certain her intuition channel would be jangling if there was a wit of strength left within her. She kept her face clear of fear because she knew her team was unnerved by the news of potential threat.

"All secure, ser."

Dozier pitched her voice above the sound of the crashing waves outside and the slurping sucking sound of the water in the cavern. Castellan gave a small jerk and quickly stowed her oar. One thing she'd learned during the rotos she'd been an officer was to never let her soldiers see her as less than confident. Her job was to bolster, to lead, and to support should the team falter. She called out as they exited the boat one at a time.

"As you've already been briefed, your pistols won't work until the power sinks have been sealed away. That's why you're leaving them on the boat with illeostones sealed in wax to protect their charge. Everyone should have a torch in one hand and their blade in the other, with the exception of Olivienne."

Olivienne's single raised brow looked sinister in the flickering torch light. "And what will I have to protect myself?"

Qent grinned and puffed out his chest. "You'll have us, Connate!"

She laughed. "So, I will."

Castellan shook her head but appreciated Qent's perpetual good humore. "All right you lot, the cave appears to be quite large as it heads away from the opening. We'll keep to the right so we have a solid wall on one side. Dozier will watch the front with the connate and I. The rest I want paired off for guard and cube transport. Qent and Madlin left, Devin and Holling above, leaving Meza and Sehg for the rear."

"Um—"

She turned to look at Madlin, who was strangely reserved. "Yes?"

"Above?"

Holling spoke up but didn't make eye contact as he was busy peering all around them with fascination. "If there are large spiders, they could come from any direction. Normal spiders have small hairs on their feet. Each of those hairs has even smaller ones with triangular tips. That allows them to climb just about anywhere. We studied them at academy as part of our arthropodis education." His roaming gaze finally returned to the group of wide-eyed, black clad guardians. "And strength, whew! If you account for proportions, the strongest spiders are two hundred and fifty times that of a psi."

Castellan gave a shudder. "Holling."

"Yes, ser?"

"You're not helping."

He looked repentant. "Oh. Sorry, ser."

Castellan sighed. "We're wasting torchlight. Let's move. Madlin, Devin, and Meza picked up the three cubes and the team set off deeper into the cave.

Occasionally they'd hear skittering, but nothing could be seen on the far side or high ceiling of the cave because their torches simply weren't bright enough. Castellan was uneasy and she gripped her sword tighter.

Dozier's voice broke the tension after a thankfully short walk. "Ser, I see something ahead."

Castellan lifted her torch higher and moved to the front so her night sight would be a little better. They'd found the origination point of the small stream. Water cascaded from an opening high on the far wall. Below it sat a large bin full of what could only be the power sinks. Water filled the bin then poured over the sides to form the stream. Mist rose into the air before dissipating. It was ingenious, really.

Chapter Thirteen

The group moved forward, still wary of the large cave. Meza stepped closer and placed her cube on a raised bit of ground, near the bin. "Why would they store them like this?"

Olivienne stood next to the misting container, heedless of the water that splashed around her boots. "It's brilliant." She turned to look at the rest of the group. "Think on it. Illeostones absorb aether from the air around, just as our cells do."

"Cells, Connate?"

"Yes, much like any other mineral, our bodies contain illeostone which fuels our channels." Some looked unsurprised by the information, others nodded with sudden understanding. "So, if you have created something with an extreme ability to absorb aether, more powerful than anything else, and you want to store them for a long time..." She paused and Madlin continued the thought.

"If these are naught more than compressed illeostone material, then the water would continuously release the aether as the power sinks absorb it."

Castellan strode forward and gestured to Devin and Meza to bring their cubes. "Which makes them more dangerous to us until we get them sealed away. And once they are, we'll still need to wait for our channels to replenish. At least the cave is saturated with aether so the process should start immediately."

"Ser, what is that?" Everyone turned to look where Sehg pointed. A vague white shape was attached to the far wall, twenty yords from the group.

Castellan frowned. "Madlin, Meza, and Devin, get those cubes filled now! Holling with me and the rest of you guard the connate."

"Tosh, I'm coming with you."

Castellan held up her hand to stay her headstrong lover. "I beg of you, not this time."

There was a standoff of sorts as she met Olivienne's

dark gaze. Finally, Olivienne nodded and moved back toward the power sinks. Castellan and Holling made their way through the stream and across the cavern. They saw even more white masses stuck to the wall once they were closer. Castellan poked the nearest with the tip of her sword. It was about half the size of a psi. "It's strangely springy. What are we looking at?"

"If I had to guess, I'd say they look a lot like web wrapped prey, but these are immense."

Castellan held her torch higher to look above them. There were at least two large round white objects suspended from the ceiling, only noticeable because of their color. Other vague pale shapes were lost in the darkness. "And those? More of the same?"

For the first time since she'd known him, Holling appeared nervous when he followed her gaze. "No, ser. Those look like ova sacs."

Something caught her eye and she squinted but the sacs were too far away. She turned to her medican. "Stand behind me and hold both our torches up." He complied and Castellan pulled out a small spyglass from her hip pouch. It was dark but she could easily make out the magnified white ova sac. The sides rippled and a small split appeared. She looked around and thousands of little reflected eyes appeared in the torchlight as larger shadows moved above them. "Bollux!"

"Ser?"

Castellan took her torch back and bellowed to the group. "Beware! Get those cubes filled and double time to the boat!"

"Tosh?"

She sprinted back to the team with Holling fast on her heals. "The spider ova sacs are hatching."

"Sheddech!" Qent's curse was felt by everyone. Once the cubes were sealed, the unit beat a rapid retreat toward the cave mouth. Unfortunately, the full cubes were a lot heavier and required teams of two to carry them.

Their jog back was slower than Castellan would have liked. She took the rear guard and left Dozier at the front with Olivienne. Movement caught Castellan's eye and she watched in horror as hundreds of creatures swarmed toward them. From farther behind came larger shapes and she knew their time was up. "Faster, you lot!"

Despite her abundant channel strength, it was still too soon for her powers to replenish. All Castellan could do was keep her blade and torch at the ready. One large spider surged forward. It brought its abdomen around and a stream of webbing shot out to hit Devin in the back, jerking the man off his feet. He yelled in terror and his abrupt stop caused the cube to fall to the ground as it was ripped from Holling's grip.

The rest of the team paused and she urged them forward. "Don't stop, don't look back. Get to the boat!" With a few slashes of her trusty blade, Castellan severed the web. Another spider took aim at Castellan and she threw herself forward into a roll as the web hit where she'd been. Smaller spiders caught up and one dropped down onto her shoulder. She brushed it off with the flame of the torch and hissed as the heat singed her face. The smaller spider shrieked and Castellan felt a wave of cold dread. Another fell and she batted it away like a professional pipeball player.

Castellan stumbled onto the ledge where the boat was anchored, relieved to see the cubes already stowed and the team getting themselves situated.

"Tosh, come on!" Olivienne yelled and Castellan heard the brittle sound of fear in her voice.

Two more small spiders dropped and she pierced one that landed on the floor and burned the other. A larger spider skittered down the wall nearby and she swung her blade at its leg, severing it at the second joint. Castellan swallowed the bile that rose at the sight of the massive beast. Each leg was longer than she was tall. She tested her channels and felt the smallest trickle of power. It was enough to shove the off-balance spider into the water.

With a burst of speed, she sliced the anchor line and yelled, "Get us out of here!" Olivienne had taken Castellan's previous position with an oar and rowed along with the rest of the shields. Castellan balanced near the back of the boat with torch and sword at the ready.

Another web shot and connected with Qent's shoulder, pulling the man up out of his seat. His oar fell into the boat as he rose. Only his quick thinking with a hip blade prevented the shield from becoming a meal. He dropped down and quickly picked up his oar again, paddling with fear-fueled strength. Small spiders fell into the boat from above and the guardians did their best to stomp them while rowing. The opening loomed ahead as a large spider lowered to block their way, hanging upside down from its silk line.

"Tosh!"

Olivienne's cry struck fear into Castellan's heart. She stumbled toward the front of the boat while maneuvering around the storage cubes and swung her sword as the massive abdomen took aim. The blade cut through the spinnerets and the creature shrieked. Another descended and she sliced open its abdomen as the boat moved beneath it. Ichor poured from above, coating her and the cubes in the middle of the boat but leaving Olivienne and her guardians untouched. Despite the waves pushing them back toward the cave, the boat moved out of the darkness and into the light of the late afternoon suns.

"Captain!" Madlin yelled as Castellan did her best to wipe her eyes clear of the viscous fluid. She turned to see where her lieutenant pointed. Spiders large and small poured out of the opening and skittered up the side of the cliff. They were still too close and another string of silk hit Sehg. Castellan severed that one as well and stood ready.

Tosh, give me your stone.

Olivienne sat near Castellan so she threw her torch into the water and used her free hand to pull the pendant out of her shirt just enough for Olivienne to apport it into her own hand. Then she watched in fascination as fire raced across the face of the cliff.

Castellan gritted her teeth as flaming spiders shrieked and fell into the water all around them. She swung her blade to keep one small flaming projectile from landing in the inflatable raft. It wouldn't do to survive the beasts only to lose the cubes in the ocean because their boat sank.

Castellan guarded them diligently. She used her sword and returned channel strength to prevent anything else from endangering them. "Get us far enough away from this cliff for the *Vestigo* to drop us a line."

As one, the shields chorused back their agreement. "Yes, ser!"

Castellan accepted the pendant Olivienne discreetly slipped back into her hand. "Well done, 'Vienne." She looked toward Holling, who kept glancing back at the cliff with wide eyes. "No comments about article twenty of the Psiere Legibus, Holling?"

He swallowed. "No, ser. I felt them when my animal empathy channel returned." The man shuddered in a rare show of distaste.

Madlin spoke up from the front of the boat. "He's right, Captain. I felt them too. It wasn't good. Makers take all of those vile creatures!"

Castellan grimaced and took a sec to contact the dirigible. *Velten, Tosh here. Mission success with no casualties.*

Casualties, Tosh?

I'll explain once we're safely away. We'll need the medican basket dropped down to get these cubes aboard. I'm not at full power yet so it's probably the most secure way to get them up to the ship. We can't afford to lose these power sinks.

Will do, Tosh. I'll send Vex out to organize your retrieval.

Thank you. Castellan released their telepathic connection and focused on her crew. A line dropped from above and Qent quickly tied it to a cleat to keep the boat in place. She watched as the familiar outline of their team's medican basket lowered from the staging deck using an illeostone powered driver. Now that they were safe, the team nervously joked and laughed with one another. She found Olivienne's purple gaze focused on her, eyes crinkled at the corners with mirth.

"What is it?"

Olivienne grinned. "You look a wreck, Tosh."

As if her lover's words opened her senses, Castellan grew aware of the ichor staining her black uniform. Her skin was itchy and uncomfortable where it touched and she thought perhaps she should try to clean herself before they were pulled up to the dirigible. She looked at her blade and frowned. There was no way she'd re-sheath it while covered in the viscous liquid. It would have to be cleaned and sharpened once aboard. Castellan carefully placed it atop the nearest cube and stripped her belt and devices.

"Tosh?"

"I need to get this stuff off me."

Holling nodded. "Probably a good idea, Captain. It could cause a reaction."

"That's what I was thinking." Castellan didn't bother removing her boots since they'd already gotten wet in the cave stream. She dove over the side of the boat and into the water and did her best to scrub her skin while staying afloat.

By the time she was finished, the cubes were well on their way back up to the staging deck as the shields began pulling their climbing harnesses on from where they'd been stowed in compartments on the boat. Castellan took stock of her channels and sighed with relief to find them replenished enough to lift them all to the staging deck in one go with assistance from the antoraestone. It would wipe her out again for a bit, but at least they'd be safely aboard.

"Don't bother with all that."

"Ser?"

Castellan lifted herself back into the boat, water streaming from her clothes. "I'm going to take us all up at once. Hold on to the ropes and cleats and don't move around."

"Are you sure?" Olivienne looked up at the dirigible that hovered at least twenty yords above them. "That's a long way for your levitation channel."

"That's why I waited until the cubes were aboard, so the weight would be lighter."

Meza gripped the side of the boat. "Thank the Makers, ser. I'm ready to be done with this entire poxing mission."

Qent guffawed. "No, thank the captain!" He sobered abruptly. "But yeah, I'm glad to be done too. That was—" he shuddered.

"That was a lot of no thank you. I hate spiders." Heads nodded in agreement with Madlin's declaration.

"I've been an adventurist for more than a decaroto and it was certainly a first for me."

"What, no other encounters with psi-eating giant spiders, Connate?"

Olivienne shook her head and made a face. "This one is going to give me night terrors for lunes to come."

That was something they could all agree upon.

Velten met them on the staging deck. Castellan was grateful that the space was significantly larger than the one they'd had on the *Quaesitum*. There was plenty of room for personnel and the raft. Dirigible crew members began their job of cleaning, deflating, and stowing the raft while Castellan sent her own team off for sluicing and downtime.

"I had the cubes moved to your storage room. I figured that was the safest place until we can deliver them to defense. At least I assume that's where they're going. We won't know until we contact the capital." Castellan nodded in agreement with Velten.

"Ser, what do we do with these?" One of the *Vestigo* crew picked up a crushed baby spider by its long leg. The dead creature was larger than her hand.

Velten's pale brows lifted and she turned to look at Olivienne and Castellan with shock. "That's what you lot faced in there?"

Olivienne shook her head. "No, those were the babies that hatched when we were inside filling the cubes."

"Sheddech!" Velten turned to the crew members. "Toss them overboard and scrub the surface good before stowing the raft and equipment away."

"Ay-ay, Captain."

"I'd suggest a debrief but you're looking a little less put together than normal, Tosh."

Castellan glanced down at her dripping, stained uniform. She knew she looked a sight. "That's an understatement if ever there was one. Perhaps we could meet for evening meal once we've cleaned up and I get my gear in order." Her fouled sword sat off to the side where one of the crewmembers had placed it on the staging deck.

"I'm guessing you two could use a drink as well. There will be a fresh bottle waiting for you in the mess."

Olivienne snorted. "Oh, I'm not waiting that long. I'll be into the decanter in our cabin before Tosh takes first crack for a sluicing off in the head. I may not even use a tumbler."

"That good of a dae, eh?"

"And it's just barely gone on one hundred oors! Others of a sort have been few and far between, thank the Makers."

Castellan peered at the bright suns. "The dae is moving along and I'm not getting any cleaner." She looked at Olivienne. "Are you coming with me, or will you stay out here for a bit?"

"Oh, I'm coming. Despite the disgusting nature of our mission and my joke about needing a drink, I'm ravenous and could use a bite or two to tide me until evening meal."

Lazaro chuckled where he stood guard nearby. The team that had come into the cave with them had been replaced by four fresh guardians. Lazaro and Calderon stood to each side of the port leading into the ship from the staging deck. Soleng and Yazzie were closer. The medican gave Castellan a concerned look. "Are you well, ser?"

She shrugged. "Well enough. I'll be even better when I can finish washing the guts of the roc-sized spiders from my person." All the shields wore looks of horror and disgust. Castellan nodded then strode toward the portal with Olivienne and her black clad guardians following quickly behind. The morning had been particularly nasty but the afternoon was still salvageable.

Olivienne and Castellan recounted their adventure to Velten oors later during evening meal as the *Vestigo* made its way toward Annexus. When they broke communication silence in Occasus by sending a long-range coded message to the capital daes before, they were instructed by Renou to proceed directly to their main base of defense once they'd completed the adventurist mission to retrieve the power sinks. Annexus was the final city before the railer line continued across the islands to Dromea, and where many of their forces were staging against Havington and the rebels.

Velten shook her head as she placed her eating utensils on the empty tray and wiped the corners of her lips. "You make me glad I'm merely a ship captain and not an adventurist. The only creature I deal with on the regular is our ship felid, Mully."

"You know, I've yet to see that blasted cat. Not on any of our missions." Olivienne appeared more than a little put out. Castellan knew how much she loved small felidae and was well aware that Olivienne never got one because of how much she traveled in her job as an adventurist. Castellan herself preferred canids but had never gotten one for the same reason. Not enough time in one place to properly care for an animal companion.

"Mully mostly earns her keep at night, keeping the *Vestigo* clear of vermin and the like. Go by the bosun's office on the way back to your cabin if you want to meet her. She'll probably be asleep in her basket."

"Oh, Tosh. Can we?" Olivienne pleaded.

Castellan laughed. "Why are you asking me? I'm certainly not your keeper."

"From what I hear, our dear connate isn't one to be kept."

"If anyone could, it would be Castellan. And the reason I asked is because I assumed you'd be tired from our ordeal. After all, you were the one primarily fighting off the spiders as we rowed."

"Tired?" Castellan saw humore shining in Olivienne's eyes but rose to the challenge anyway. "I'll have you know my stamina isn't so poor as all that. I could have a go at ten more of those creatures and still be fighting fit."

"But you won't."

In a rare dip into vulgarity, Castellan laughed. "You bet your arse I won't. Ugh, those things were like something out of the worst night terror I could imagine."

Velten laughed. "I'm sure."

"Captain, how long until we reach Annexus?"

Velten pulled the time piece from her pocket. "Probably

another fifteen oors, provided we are not accosted by more of those blasted rebels."

Olivienne smirked. "Perfect. That gives me plenty of time to test Tosh's stamina and rest after."

Both captains groaned but Velten was the one who pushed away from the table. "Just be sure you have a care with your stray thoughts, Connate. I don't need the rest of my crew worked up by your antics. Savvy?"

"I'll do my best." Olivienne winked at her.

Castellan sighed and scrubbed her face with the hand not holding her drink tumbler. She knew how Olivienne got after a successful mission. It was sure to be a long and satisfying night.

'Vienne, stop torturing the poor captain.

They watched as Velten dropped her used tray into the bin bolted to a counter near the exit. *But why? It's so much fun. Not my fault she has no outlet aboard the ship.*

On the contrary, she's probably one of the few who do have an outlet with the privilege of privacy.

She stood with her empty tray as well, and Olivienne followed.

How do you mean?

Only a few officers aboard get their own cabin. Crew-mates are often assigned to communal bunk rooms.

Oh.

I'm sure some, uh, share a rack on occasion. At least Defense Corp do in the barracks. But it's not the same with your fellow psi all around you.

Olivienne made a face as they wandered down the cor-ridor toward the bosun's cabin with two guardians follow-ing in their footsteps. *I imagine not. But how does that help the captain?*

Castellan glanced to her left and smiled. *The captain can take care of herself and probably has the tools and utensils to get the job done right.* Castellan laughed at the look of intrigue on Olivienne's face. Her jealousy didn't flare because she knew it had more to do with the idea and not the person involved.

"Oh, you!" Olivienne gave Castellan a little shove. She looked back at her shields. "We're going to visit

Mully in the bosun's cabin, then back to our own. After that you can be excused for the evening."

Lazaro moved his gaze from Olivienne to Castellan. "Ser?"

She shook her head. "Unfortunately, you're on until shift change. But you only need to remain in the corridor near our cabin as we won't be leaving until morning."

Olivienne sighed.

"You know the rules, 'Vienne. No less than two at all times."

"But I have you!"

Castellan frowned at the statement. "I'm not perfect. Even I need to sleep. This is best for everyone."

"Fine, but they may get an earful because I have plans for you." With those words, Olivienne stalked farther ahead.

Castellan saw Lazaro and Calderon share a look before they grinned and rushed to catch up with their sovereign.

A short time later, Olivienne pushed into their cabin and Castellan followed, carefully bolting the hatch once they were inside. She turned to see Olivienne wearing a mischievous grin. "You've been full of sprite and spit all evening. Has your success gotten you so worked up as all that?"

"*Our* success and you know me well. Are you telling me you're not feeling a bit energized from our experience?"

Castellan grinned and moved closer. "I certainly wouldn't mind a little distraction this evening."

"Distraction? Is that what we're calling it now? If that's the case, I may as well do a little solo exploration and save the trouble of connecting with someone of such lackluster passions."

Instinctively, Castellan knew that Olivienne was toying with her in order to instigate a reaction. Even so, she sputtered, "Lackluster! I'll show you how hot my passions run." Secs later she embraced her lover, pinning Olivienne's arms to her sides. "And I'll need no tools or devices to do it."

"But I like tools and devices."

"Perhaps once we're home again, as I've brought nothing on this trip but my sword, which is as sharp as your wit." Castellan conceded.

Olivienne squirmed her arms free and draped them around Castellan's neck so she could play with the fine pale hair she found at the nape. It was a move that sent shivers down Castellan's spine. "What shall we do now that we're here?"

"I've got a few ideas." Castellan loved having her hair pulled and nails scraped along her scalp. Her arousal grew as she leaned ever closer. She used her telekinesis to dim the light and Olivienne's irises looked dark purple as her pupils grew larger. Warm breath caressed her lips, smelling of the scotch they'd been drinking at dinner. It overpowered the salty tang of the air they'd breathed since leaving Tesseron. Castellan's hands wandered downward along Olivienne's curves until she could take her backside firmly in each palm.

She squeezed and Olivienne gasped. "Aren't you going to at least kiss me before getting yourself a feel?"

Castellan grinned at her impatience. "My love, you don't immediately pour and drink when you open a new bottle of vineo. Rather, you let it rest for a number of meens to soften the flavors. All parts of the process should be savored to get the best experience."

Olivienne moved her mouth closer until her full lips barely grazed across Castellan's. "Are you saying you plan to drink of me?"

"Only if I'm lucky." Castellan surged into the kiss, opening her mouth greedily to taste every bit of essence from Olivienne's tongue. The flesh was firm and she explored Olivienne's parted lips.

The kiss grew heated in a short period of time and Olivienne's haste returned. *Let me remove our clothing so you can enjoy me properly.*

Just the thought of tasting one another drew a groan from low in Castellan's throat but she didn't relent. *Better yet, why don't we do this the slower way and take our time. We have all evening.*

Olivienne broke the kiss and pulled back. "You're punishing me."

With a smirk, Castellan responded, "No, but I certainly could. It would take no power at all to hold you steady enough to deliver a few solid smacks to your bottom."

"You wouldn't dare."

Despite her words of warning, Castellan saw how stimulated Olivienne was. She began unbuttoning Olivienne's shirt while maintaining eye contact. "Won't I?"

Not wanting to be outdone, Olivienne unclasped the fastener on Castellan's belt and removed it along with her pistol and pouch. She did cheat a bit by apporting the gear to a nearby hook on the wall. Castellan was nearly finished with the shirt by the time Olivienne started on her trousers. The notion that they were undressing one another's opposite halves made her chuckle.

"What's so funny?"

She finished with the last button and gestured between them. "This."

"You find our imminent tupping humorous?"

"No, just the circumstances of our preparation."

Olivienne scowled and Castellan knew they were finished with the undressing part. 'Vienne had finally hit her limit. Their clothing disappeared and reappeared a few foot away on a chair. "Fic on you and your preparation. I'm ready for the good bits now."

Castellan kissed her again and without breaking the connection between their lips, she bent her knees just so she could move her hands down to the juncture between Olivienne's upper thighs and her buttocks. She lifted smoothly and Olivienne wrapped her legs around Castellan's waist. Her excitement left obvious evidence where she rubbed against Castellan's stomach as she walked them toward the bed. *You'll kill me 'Vienne.*

But what a way to go, no? Now about that savoring...

You're impatient.

Tosh, there were giant spiders in that cave. I think I deserve a little love and tenderness right now, not judgement.

Castellan broke the kiss as she deposited Olivienne

onto the bed. "Oh ho, love and tenderness? I thought you were to be punished.?"

Eyes narrowed and Olivienne pursed her lips before saying, "I'm warning you, Tosh."

"I believe that is my cue to begin." Castellan quickly lifted Olivienne with her telekinetic channel and spun her midair until her backside was displayed in all its naked glory.

Olivienne yelped with surprise, "Tosh!"

Castellan didn't fully immobilize her because she wanted Olivienne to be able to turn her head and move her arms and legs. Then with a swift swing of her arm, she delivered a resounding crack to the skin of her lover's firm cheek. Olivienne gasped and the flesh turned just the slightest bit pink.

As expected, Olivienne squirmed in the air whilst she panted with mock outrage, "What do you think you're doing?" Her words did not at all match with her telepathic thoughts. *Yes!*

Gauging Olivienne's breathing, expression, and continued arousal level through their bond, Castellan delivered another smack to her backside. "I'm only taking revenge for all the captains before me, 'Vienne." Seeing the skin redden further prompted Castellan to gently massage the warm flesh. During the firm caress, she let her fingers wander toward Olivienne's treasure and felt the wetness seeping out.

Olivienne moaned. "Yes, more of that."

The hand moved away. "More of what? This?" Another crack sounded in the room, this time on the other cheek. Olivienne was definitely panting now and Castellan gave her another slap before caressing that side in the same way. They'd never played in such a fashion before but Olivienne seemed keen on it.

Once she was certain of Olivienne's stimulation level, she lowered her lover to the bed on her stomach then floated herself upward and gently settled along the full length of her. Her pubis rubbed against Olivienne's warmed backside and Castellan's small breasts pressed into her back. Castellan held Olivienne's hands pinned next to her head with the sheer strength in her body alone. No channel was needed.

She rubbed herself against Olivienne's entire body, thrusting into her backside and knew that it would only frustrate the prone woman.

"Tosh,"

"Yes, love?"

"More tasting and less teasing or I swear I'll get even."

Castellan chuckled and released Olivienne's hands and slowly pulled her fingers down to trace along Olivienne's arms and shoulders. Chill bumps followed in the wake of her fingertips. "How do you plan to get even? Will I like it?"

"I'll warm *your* backside with my channel."

She laughed. "That's decidedly less fun."

Castellan moved toward the foot of the bed and sat on her haunches, allowing Olivienne to turn over. Once she was on her back, Castellan pulled her legs apart, taking a meen to admire the abundant wetness at the juncture of her thighs. She slid her hands up each leg and shifted forward onto her knees.

"Finally."

Movement caught Castellan's eye and she watched Olivienne caress her own breasts, pinching nipples between thumb and first finger. Her chest rose and fell rapidly in anticipation. Castellan swiftly closed the remaining distance and caressed both sides of Olivienne's labia with her thumbs. She massaged the entire region, avoiding that small node of pleasure until Olivienne whined. "Please!" Her clitoris was hard.

Castellan moved closer until her face was inces from Olivienne's folds. Warmth radiated from her glistening flesh and the scent made Castellan's mouth water. Unwilling to wait longer, Castellan tasted her from bottom to top, swirling as she moved across her clitoral nub. When Olivienne jumped at the contact, she used her telekinesis to hold her in place, then repeated the caress with her tongue. After the fifth of such swipes, Castellan pulled back and ran two fingers through Olivienne's wetness.

"Please…"

"Patience, love."

She entered with the first two fingers on her right hand and thrust slowly for a few meens before adding a third finger and licking the hot flesh above. Olivienne's keening grew louder until Castellan finally curled her tongue and swirled it at the same time she sucked rhythmically on Olivienne's clitoris. She continued thrusting and curling her fingers upward.

Olivienne threw her arm across her mouth, stifling her cry in the joint of her elbow. Castellan continued her motions until the tension left Olivienne's body and she lay boneless upon the bed. Olivienne's arm flopped back to the side as she tried to catch her breath. "By the Makers."

"I'm pretty sure the Makers had nothing to do with that one, love."

"Smart arse."

Castellan waited until Olivienne opened her eyes to remove her fingers and lick them clean. "You were delicious, and I was right."

"Right?"

"Yes. Savoring you was worth the wait."

Olivienne wrapped her legs around Castellan's waist and pulled her off balance until she landed so their bodies were once again pressed together. "What about you? I'd love to have you in return."

Despite efforts to remain in control, Olivienne's release only served to excite Castellan more. Her own clitoris throbbed and it took all her willpower not to simply press herself against Olivienne's firm thigh and find relief. Instead, she smiled and acted nonchalantly. "I could certainly stand a little attention. A long drink, if you'd be so kind."

As an answer, Olivienne pushed Castellan to the side, then shifted so she sat upon her pelvis. "Maybe I should make you wait as you did to me."

Castellan groaned and thrust upward hoping to find contact where she needed it most. There was a saying that what was given is often returned two-fold and she feared Olivienne would tease and incite the way she herself had done. "Perhaps you could punish me next time and take a long draught now."

Delicate laughter was muffled when Olivienne pressed her face between Castellan's breasts. Once she'd calmed down, Olivienne moved up to kiss Castellan. When Olivienne pulled back again, she smirked. "I suppose I'll give in just this once. But I'm not doing it for you."

Castellan sucked in a ragged breath as Olivienne crawled backward on her hands and knees until her face was even with Castellan's mons. "No?"

"I'm getting right to business because I'm terribly thirsty and I want to see how much I can tap you for."

Castellan's groan quickly morphed into a stuttering whine when Olivienne attacked her wet folds with passionate ferocity. Thirsty indeed.

Chapter Fourteen

The total trip between the spider cave, as the team had taken to calling it, and Annexus was estimated to be seventeen oors. Long enough for Olivienne to feel a bit crazy from inactivity. Not only was she ready to reach their destination, but Tosh's behavior had become worrisome.

"Darling, you've been troubled since we returned from the cave yesterdae. What's wrong?" It was near twenty-four hundred oors and she had been pacing and agitated since evening meal.

She ran a hand through her pale hair, mussing it thoroughly. Her uniform shirt was partially unbuttoned but she'd yet to remove her belt and service pistol. "I don't know, 'Vienne. There is something I'm missing."

"Why do you say that?"

"My intuition has been jangling and getting steadily worse. It started when we sheltered during the storm on the south side of Bindle Bay. It calmed when our channels were drained in the cave and seemed settled that evening, so I assumed it had to do with the mission."

Olivienne patted the small lounger seat next to her. She'd already changed into a sleep shift for the evening. They were slated to arrive around mid-morning at Annexus but were hoping for a restful night. "But something else is causing it?"

Castellan slumped into the cushion as if she were a puppet with her strings cut. "Obviously." Her sarcasm was biting and it was more than a little out of character. Olivienne frowned and Castellan looked up to see it. She grimaced. "Sorry, love. I'm clearly out of sorts this evening. I tried everything to dispel the sense of…bollux, but I don't even have a word for it."

"Wrongness, anxiety, fear?" she added helpfully.

"Yes. All those and more. Perhaps I should get some sleep and I'll feel better in the morning."

Olivienne rubbed her bottom lip as she stared across the cabin. Her eyes fixed upon Savon's journal and she moved to retrieve it. "Maybe we'll find something in here."

"It's fairly picked over from our other sessions. The next unread section is marked."

Olivienne found the place that Castellan pointed out and began reading Savon's precise script. It looked to be another stanza like many of his other prophetic passages. "Beware the lone sharc, circling the swimmer school, stealing the second from rule, they flee in the dark." Olivienne raised her eyebrow and Castellan shrugged so she continued. "Their way will be swift, across the northern land, forcing the queen's hand, and suns to suffer a rift."

"Well, that sounds decidedly ominous. Is that sons as in sibs?"

"No, Illeos and Archeos. But in what way I know not. Shall I continue?"

"May as well get it all out."

Olivienne read the final three short stanzas of the poem aloud. "Nothing to be done, to stop the black fall, in captive desolation. Two will become one, spreading fire to all, and freedom for a nation." She looked up to see an expression on Castellan's face that appeared to mirror the way she felt. "I certainly don't like the sound of that."

Castellan leaned closer so she could look at the book and she pointed to the first section. "Based on his other passages, I'd say the lone sharc is easy enough to guess."

Having spent half her life deciphering Maker's text, she found Savon's not too dissimilar. The answer hit Olivienne as sudden as a gut punch. "Tosh, this is talking about the academy. The rebels weren't heading for the prison islands, they're going for Kesharan!" She stood to inform Velten and was held back by Castellan. Anger rose swiftly when she looked upon the hand holding her wrist. "What are you doing?"

Castellan stood as well. "Whatever was to happen has already passed and the captain is long abed. I'm sorry, 'Vienne, but if they took your sib hostage, there is naught we can do about it at this point."

"No!"

Castellan persisted and refused to let go of her arm.

"Think on it, love. We left Halcyon and parted company with the rebel dirigible daes ago. They'd already be to Scola and gone again if that were their intent. All we can do is consult with the capital when we reach Annexus."

Fear for her sib seized her chest and Olivienne found it hard to breathe. "They can't have him, they can't."

"Breathe, 'Vienne. A level head is all we've got left to us now. We'll get him back."

Olivienne couldn't imagine what she'd do if something happened to Kesh. She couldn't fathom what her parens would do. Once she was able to steady herself, Olivienne pulled back from Castellan's embrace. "How could this happen? He was supposed to be safe there."

"We don't know that anything has happened yet—"

"What does your precious intuition tell you?"

Castellan paused. "This feels right. Defense Corp had most people from the academy pulled south to aid the effort against Havington. All he'd have there would be his shield team to face off against an enemy dirigible with an unknown number of rebels aboard."

Olivienne lashed out as an uncontrollable amount of fear and fury swelled inside her. "Nothing about this feels right. You told us they would go to Aetate or Iuvenis, Tosh. We should have followed them. This is your fault!"

Castellan staggered back as though she'd been struck and Olivienne realized what she'd said. She swallowed at the look on her lover's face. Guilt pulled Castellan's shoulders down and her eyes held shadowed depths of sorrow Olivienne had only seen after the battle of King's Marsh.

Olivienne held out a hand, wanting the reassurance of Castellan's touch. "I'm sorry, I didn't mean—"

Castellan didn't reach for her in return. Instead, she grabbed the crown of her head in both hands and sank back into the cushion of the lounger. "No, you're right. I did say we should continue south to retrieve the power sinks and I'll live with that for the rest of my daes if something happens to your sib." She took a few deep breaths before she pulled her hands away and turned a haunted gaze toward Olivienne.

"Darling, no. I should never have said that. I was just—you know how I am, Tosh." Castellan's pain and anguish radiated through their bond and Olivienne's stomach cramped with worry.

"'Vienne—" Castellan shook her head. "I'm not perfect. I make mistakes like anyone else but you've put me on a pedestal again and again. I can't protect you on my own, and I don't always know the right way to go. I'm not one of the bloody Tau with their advanced knowledge. I'm just a lone psi trying to do her job."

Olivienne sat beside her and clasped Castellan's right hand between both of her own. "I...I guess it's because you've always seemed larger than life to me. You're strong, capable, and decisive, all things I wish I could be sometimes. I'm well aware of my own failings. After all, I've had them listed to me for rotos by previous shield captains."

"You don't have failings, 'Vienne. You just have a job that previous captains failed to understand. That's on them."

"Even so, you're right. I did hold you to high standards and it wasn't fair."

Castellan kissed Olivienne's temple. "I think that under the circumstances, I understand where you were coming from. But we need to be better going forward. We've suffered in the past from poor communication. I don't want to be in that place again."

Olivienne looked into her pale eyes and knew what wasn't being said. She'd caused a rift with her words of accusation, pouring pain on top of a heart that was still healing from the deaths of Savon and the civilians. "You're being remarkably mature about this when I know how much I hurt you with my words."

The muscles along Castellan's jaw tensed and she looked away. "Your words did hurt. Some daes my guilt feels...immeasurable. I carry on because that's all I've ever known. I'm a soldier, 'Vienne. We keep marching forward no matter what."

"That can't be healthy, at least from what my papan has been teaching me."

"So says you and Gem. But who will carry the weight if I don't?"

Olivienne frowned and looked down at their joined hands. Regret was a burden upon her shoulders and she wished she'd never said anything. But Olivienne was self-aware enough to know that she'd been ruled by her passions her entire life. The stronger her feelings, the more explosive they made themselves known. "I'm doubly sorry then. Forgive me?"

"I do." While the words were reassuring, Castellan didn't meet her eyes.

She didn't want to let it go. "You're still angry with me though. I can feel it through our bond."

Castellan pulled her hands away and stood again to pace in the limited space afforded to them. "Of course, I am. Angry, hurt, afraid, and more. By the Makers, I'm capable of more than one fecking emotion!"

The outburst was uncharacteristic and Olivienne wondered if she'd damaged their relationship too much. If her beloved captain had finally reached her breaking point. While her own anger was significantly less than when Castellan had locked the stones away on Magna, the tension between them was all too familiar. "I know you are, Tosh. This entire thing has me out of sorts, just like you. I wish I'd never said anything but I can't take it back now any more than I can place a shell back in the pistol once it's been fired."

"I know. We should sleep. Once we dock in Annexus and debrief, we'll probably be stuck in never-ending meetings. It's hard to say when good rest will come next. We can figure out what to do once we have all the information."

She made to walk toward the facility and Olivienne stopped her with a hand to the wrist, as Castellan had done meens before. "Hey."

"Yes?"

"I love you and I just realized that I don't tell you enough, considering how I feel."

That earned her a smile. "I love you, too."

"Will we be all right?"

There was a pause that felt too long considering Olivienne's frayed nerves. "Yes. I think I'll be less sensitive once we make sure your sib is safe. That will be one less guilt upon my shoulders."

She turned away to begin removing her belt and holster. Olivienne took a meen to hug her from behind before walking to the bed and sliding beneath the coverlets. There was nothing more to say. The next dae would bring plans and truth aplenty, and hopefully a little more forgiveness for her hurtful and careless words.

The *Vestigo* docked a half oor earlier than predicted due to a beneficial tailwind. The time of arrival wouldn't have mattered because the transportation hub was a frenzy of activity. Railers were leaving along the east and west lines as the massive dirigible winched down to the platform. Castellan expected security to be tight but nothing like what they saw waiting on the ground. It looked much like what they faced after the queen was injured, the dae Olivienne landed in Tesseron to take her place on the Divine Cathedra.

Velten joined them on the staging deck and sighed at the fifty Defense Corp soldiers below. "Well, this certainly tracks."

"Come again?" Castellan looked at her in surprise.

"I just got word from Leniste himself that we're to report directly to his office for debriefing. Connate Dracore is also requested to be there. I've no clue why it needs this level of urgency and secrecy."

Castellan met Olivienne's worried gaze. "We have a guess."

"It has to be about Kesharan." She nodded in agreement.

Velten burst out in surprise. "The sub-connate?"

"We think that's where the rebel ship went after we lost it just south of Halcyon."

"Bollux! And we let them slip away. They probably put him on Ruina with the rest of the prisoners."

Castellan sighed but wanted to assuage Velten's

worry. "It was on my orders, Captain. If blame needs to be taken, I'll do it for all of us. After all, I'm the one who stated we should pursue the power sinks."

"Nonsense."

Olivienne looked at Velten with wide eyes, appearing as shocked as Castellan felt. "What do you mean?"

"I mean that if I fundamentally disagreed with your call, I would have certainly said something, Tosh. I may not have your fancy channels but I understand tactical strategy, logic, and risk well enough. You made the right choice. It would be a tragedy if he were taken, but it doesn't mean he was lost. And looking at the other side of the decision, how many Psierians would for sure die if we didn't have a way to negate their channels and make prisoners safe for transport? These power sinks will help us achieve the queen's objectives."

"But what is she willing to sacrifice for success? Surely not her son, my sib?"

Velten gave Olivienne a piercing look. "Connate, I'm sure she doesn't want to sacrifice anyone. Especially either of her children. But if we don't win this conflict and preserve our citizens, none of the Dracore line will be safe from Havington and his rebels."

"'Vienne, let's see what we learn in the debriefing, and plan from there."

Olivienne's eyes swam with worry and unshed tears. She looked away and answered, "Fine."

"Hey," When Olivienne met her gaze again, Castellan made a promise. "I'll get him back. I swear on Archeos and Illeos that I'll find your sib, even if I have to cross the Cunis Sea on the back of a great whal to reach that blasted island."

The dirigible lurched when it reached the platform. Ship crew scurried about attaching more anchor lines and the soldiers below saluted the connate and two captains. A Defense Corp lieutenant marched up the steps toward them as they walked down the gang plank. The members of Olivienne's shield team were all behind her, armed, wary, and watchful.

"Connate Dracore, Captain Tosh, and Captain Velten,

I've been instructed to take you three straight-a-way to General Leniste's office. There is grim news from the capital that couldn't be transmitted to you due to the possibility of spies listening in on our voteo frequencies."

Olivienne straightened and tilted her chin up. Castellan knew it was one of her tricks to maintain control of her emotions. "We're pretty sure we know already."

"You do?"

"You mean, you don't?"

He looked around worriedly. "No, ser. I suspect only the general does. How could you lot know?"

Castellan stepped forward. "The how isn't important. Do you have transport large enough to carry us and my unit?" She gestured toward the fourteen hardened soldiers behind her.

"We have a moto for you three and a hauler for your—"

"I'm not riding without my guardians."

The lieutenant appeared taken aback. "But Connate Dracore, surely—"

"Lieutenant!" The man jerked to attention and turned wide eyes to Castellan. "Yes, Captain Tosh?"

Her voice was a menacing growl. "You heard the connate. The two of us will ride with our guardians."

Velten smirked. "Three, Tosh. I'll just stick with you lot if you don't mind."

Castellan nodded. "Great, that's settled then. We should be off."

"But ser, what about the moto?"

Olivienne put her hands on her hips, a little too close to her pistols for the lieutenant's comfort based on his worried glance downward. "You can take your moto and stuff it up—"

"What the connate is trying to say is that perhaps someone else has use of the moto in this busy hub."

He swallowed, then looked from Castellan to Olivienne, his gaze touched on Velten, and moved back to Castellan. "Yes, ser. If you'll all follow me, the hauler is waiting in the lot nearby."

Someone snorted behind Castellan and she turned to see Qent roll his eyes as a thought came through to the entire group, captains and connate included. *Defense. Worthless as a spent stone.*

Castellan chided, *Best you watch your words, Specialist. Captain Velten and I used to be defense.*

He remained unrepentant, grinning around the group of guardians. *Clearly there are exceptions to every corp.* The rest chuckled at his mental remark.

Fifteen meens later, the trio was seated in Leniste's office as the shield team remained on guard outside. The grizzled general wore a grim look upon his bewhiskered face. "We've had disturbing news since your past contact with the capital."

"We assume the rebel ship that headed east wasn't after the prison islands, but rather they sought out the sub-connate instead?"

Leniste gave Castellan a calculating look. "How the Makers did you know that, Tosh? I'm the only one in Annexus who knows and I just arrived on the railer first thing this morning. Even in the capital, word has been kept within the trusted circle. We've not told a soul, hoping to keep the citizens from panicking."

"We made a guess based on something from Savon's journal." Castellan shook her head. "I'm sorry ser. We had to make the decision whether or not to follow the rebel dirigible when it veered east, or continue on with our mission to retrieve the power sinks."

"You got them, then?"

"Yes, ser."

He sat back and put both hands flat on the desktop. "That's one weight from our shoulders at least. You made the right call, Captain."

Velten jogged Castellan's arm with her elbow. "I told you so."

"But, the sub-connate…"

"We think he was taken to the island of Ruina where the rest of Havington's hostages currently reside. And rest assured, we have a plan to get them all back."

Olivienne leaned forward in her seat. "Soon?"

"As soon as you tell me how to use those blasted power sinks. Your brief description in the coded message to Tesseron left a lot to be desired."

"They're not ideal, ser. They pose a risk to anyone nearby. However, from what Kinsa told us, if they have skin contact with a psi, they will drain the channel of that person first before pulling aether from the surrounding area."

"Kinsa?"

"Uh—" Castellan looked from Velten to Olivienne. She forgot how jarring it would be to hear that one of the Makers was still alive and living so relatively close. Olivienne explained for her.

"Kinsa is their nickname. The real name is difficult to pronounce if I do say so myself. They are the remaining Tau Ceti still here on Psiere, left from the original crash that brought our people to this planet."

Leniste's mouth dropped open and he abruptly held up both hands, palms facing the three guests. "Halt that line of thought. You can debrief with the queen and Renou when they arrive on the next railer."

"What? My mother is coming here? But it's not safe!"

He frowned. "The queen is not one to be coddled as you should well know, Connate. She does what she wills and no one, save your father, can dissuade her from something once her mind is set."

Castellan snorted and Olivienne scowled her way. "Rather than go off on another tangent, Let's get the important information out now. The power sinks are naught more than highly compressed illeostone material. We've stored them in three airtight containers taken from Halcyon Station, Maker technology. There are three more empty, smaller, containers you can use to transport them around. The amount of power sinks per psi depends on their size and channel rating. If we could have shackles or something similar made that will hold the sinks against their skin, that will drain power."

"And they work continuously like that?"

"No, much like a charged illeostone, they can only hold so much. The sinks will need to be replaced with fresh every twelve oors or so."

Leniste looked thoughtful. "And what do we do with

the full sinks?"

"If I may, General." Velten lifted a hand. "I think that if we have enough, you can perhaps use some to power larger devices for longer. They dissipate much like any other illeostone, they just draw and hold a lot more power. If you need any immediately, it's easy enough to dowse them to release the accumulated aether."

He rubbed his chin. "Hmm, I wonder if we could create a smaller charging chamber here on the base. Seal it off and drop a few of those full power sinks into a tub of water to charge illeostones."

Castellan shrugged. "It certainly couldn't hurt to try. I think there are enough to use as channel absorbers for any rebel prisoners and to give a few to the scienteres for study."

"Excellent idea, Tosh."

"Now that we've settled our bit of news, what are we going to do about the sub-connate?"

Olivienne leaned forward at Castellan's words, even as Leniste sat back in his chair. "That's a little more difficult to say. We've been planning a rescue mission but the queen wants to move up the timeline which is making it tricky to put together the right team."

She had a feeling Olivara would want to enact a swift rescue and remembered something said in one of their brainstorming sessions with the team. "Will you create a disturbance along the bridge then, to pull Havington's focus there? Perhaps you could make it look like we'll do a full-on attack to give breathing space for a dirigible to come in across the water toward Ruina."

"That's what we've got. But we ran into a snag."

"What's that, ser?"

He scratched his jaw and sighed. "Two things. Reports of a heavy battery of railguns along Ruina's northwest side, and an estimate of more than fifty prisoners. It would require multiple dirigibles to bring everyone back making the chance of success lower than we like."

"Multiple dirigibles, or one large one with speed and storage to match...especially if we dump all that poxing adventurist gear."

Both Castellan and Olivienne turned to Velten wearing matching looks of shock. "You're a genius!"

"Hardly that, Connate Dracore. I've always had a head for strategy and common sense. It's the most logical option, especially since there are no other missions for us to perform."

Leniste looked interested in the idea. The three women waited in silence, each one wanting to go on the mission for different reasons. He groaned. "Renou will surely skin me if we break her favorite new airship. I like the idea. Captain Velten, I want you to work with Lieutenant Bondle to help with the preparation for operation."

"What about us?"

"I'm sorry, Connate, but we can't let one heir to the Divine Cathedra go haring off into danger to rescue another of the Dracore line."

"On the contrary, General, that is my sib we're talking about. I'm one of the most powerful psi around and you won't keep me from this mission."

Leniste's mouth twisted with displeasure and he turned to Castellan. "Tosh, talk some sense into her, will you? Surely you understand why the connate must stay on this side of the Cunis Sea."

Castellan tilted her head and smiled grimly. "On the contrary, ser, we are the team that needs to go to Ruina." She paused and closed her eyes briefly, then met his gaze again. "I know it in my gut."

"Your intuition?"

"Yes, ser. But it's more than that."

He was clearly disgruntled. "You're not always right, Tosh, even your blasted intuition."

His words twisted within Castellan's heart. "I know quite well how wrong I can be." She chanced a look at Olivienne, who pressed her lips tightly together. "But we also read a passage in Savon's journal that can only refer to us."

Olivienne put her hand on Castellan's forearm. "You figured out the riddle then?"

Castellan shrugged. "It's the part about the sharcs traveling across the northern land, forcing the queen's hand. It also says the suns will suffer a rift. I think it was talking about us, we are the suns."

Velten looked skeptical. "It could simply be talking about Archeos and Illeos in general and the rift between the continents holding their two temple namesakes."

Olivienne caught on. "But that rift already exists. This is a new one, such as—" She froze and met Castellan's gaze, who nodded her permission. "Such as the one we suffered just last night when I realized the first part of the passage referred to them taking my sib. I won't go into our disagreement, but there was a rift."

"Not only that," Castellan continued with her explanation. "But it talks about two becoming one after mentioning Ruina. "Some of his notes have referred to us as two before and I think this is the same."

Leniste held up his hand. "Alright, Tosh. You've convinced me. Now you need to convince the queen when she arrives."

"But that's too late! My sib could be…there is no telling what Havington will do with him. He hates the Dracores and will surely make an example out of him."

"Connate, we can't just take off on a whim. This requires planning and procedure—"

"Which you said yourself you've already done. You merely lacked the means to get there."

"But the queen," Leniste paused and leaned his elbows on his desk to scrub his face. "You lot make my acid rise and hair white."

"Olivienne, do you have Savon's book with you now?"

"Yes, in my pouch. Why?" She pulled it out and handed it to Castellan, who opened the book to where they'd left off the night before. She scanned the next few pages until she came to a sentence that repeated again and again down the velum.

"Look at this. It says two at one for two to come. And there are twos around the border. Tell me, what time did your plans say would be best for arrival at Ruina?"

"Two hundred oors, when most would be sleeping and the sky darkest."

Velten shifted in her seat. "How many mahls is it between Annexus and the island?"

"A little more than seven hundred. We estimated a ship would need to leave here around middae to arrive at the optimal time."

"Or thirteen hundred if you have a faster ship." Velten grinned.

Castellan pulled out her timepiece. "Let's adjust our departure forward an oor. That gives us roughly an oor and a half to strip the *Vestigo* down to make room, and for us to prepare our team." She met Leniste's pained gaze. "All we require is your say so, ser."

"And your crew can do this, Tosh?" He looked to the left. "Captain Velten, what do you think?"

"You'll find no better crew than mine, no better unit than those guardians. They're more versatile than any small force I've ever seen, in shield or defense. If Tosh says it can be done, by the Makers, they'll do it."

"What will you tell Maman?"

He grimaced. "Nothing until she arrives and you're safely on your way, of that I'm certain." He picked up the teleo on his desk. "Now, let's get Captain Vinz in here. She's the one who has been leading the rescue plan. I want you all on the same page, with some allowances made for your...different team."

"Yes, ser."

Leniste punched a few numbers and spoke, "Send Vinz to my office as soon as possible. How long? Fine." He turned to the trio. "Five meens. After confirming the plan with her, I want you to speak with Bondle about fresh supplies and a small crew to help you unload the adventurist gear. There's a building near the dirigible yard where you can store it safely away. I've got a few things to discuss with my captains in charge of the bridge offensive but I'll meet you at the docking platform at quarter to the oor of departure to see you off."

Olivienne's expression was a mix of relief and worry. "Thank you. You have no idea what it means to me."

He gestured with his finger at all three of them. "Just make sure this mission is a success and we won't speak of it again."

Nothing would make Castellan happier. After all, she had a promise to keep.

Chapter Fifteen

"Do you find it strange how often we watch the setting suns from the stern observation deck of a dirigible?" Olivienne asked.

Castellan smiled at her. "Not when you consider how much time we spend flying around Psiere. Some lunes I feel as much like a ship captain as Velten."

"You've often stated that you like the adventure and I know you're accustomed to life ever-changing, but do you enjoy how we're living, Tosh?" She held up a hand to forestall Castellan's initial reaction. "I'm well aware that you served in defense most of your life, but even in the military corps you were in place for rotos at a time. The way I live as an adventurist...it's different."

Castellan faced Olivienne and leaned an elbow on the rail of the deck. "I knew what your life was like before I oathed to you."

The words weren't an answer and Olivienne feared that she hadn't fully thought it through, or worse yet, would come to regret all their travel. "Aren't you afraid you'll get sick of it though? At what point do you say you want to settle in and enjoy the rest of our lives together?"

Castellan's laughter was unexpected and she pulled Olivienne into a loving embrace. Her answer was spoken directly into her ear in the windy deck, but Olivienne knew it was more for intimacy than privacy, since they could speak mind to mind if Castellan didn't want the on-duty shields to hear.

"My love, isn't that what we're doing now? Enjoying the rest of our lives together?" Castellan leaned back so they could gaze into one another's eyes. "I thought you'd know by now that my home has never been a place. Perhaps it began with my rotos of service in the Defense Corp but meeting you has definitely solidified it."

"If not a place, then how do you define a home?"

"'Vienne, it's always been you. You are the place my heart lives and the only one I want to return to. The fact that my heart, head, and corp are all on the same course is nothing but the best of luck. I can assure you that I'm where I need to be and I love our life together."

Castellan's admission lit a ball of warmth in her belly and Olivienne thanked the Makers that she'd gotten everything she never knew she wanted. Neither one of them were perfect but they acknowledged that fact and learned from their mistakes. She looked up to see Castellan watching expectantly, as if she were waiting for Olivienne to say whatever was going through her head. Olivienne didn't oblige her, instead she drew Castellan into a passionate kiss.

They pulled apart in time to witness Illeos follow Archeos over the horizon. The water turned black as shadows rose from the sea below. Somewhere down there was an entire race of people they were now bound to by pact. One of the updates they'd gotten from Leniste was the full description of her mother's interaction with the queen of the Atlantee. It was an exciting new chapter for their people. Unfortunately, before Psierians could move forward, they needed to end the rebel uprising. And get her sib back.

"What are you thinking about?"

She shook her head at Castellan's question. "Everything and nothing at once. I'm worried for Kesharan."

"On my life, we'll get him back. I promised you, didn't I?"

The words prompted a wave of panic and Olivienne clutched the sleeves of Castellan's uniform shirt. "I don't think I could choose between the two of you, Tosh."

"I don't understand."

"Please don't say on your life. We'll both do our best but I can't lose you! Promise me that."

"'Vienne—"

"Please."

A sigh echoed between them in the darkness. "You know there are no promises when we face off against an enemy. But I'll vow my honor before my life. Will that suit you?"

Olivienne knew her love, and how much it cost her to

pledge that. "I'll do the same. I know that the events over King's Marsh left me in a poor way but I'd do it again to get Kesh back." She shivered.

Castellan rubbed her arms. "I know it did and let's hope it doesn't come to that, yeah? We'll all do what we're trained to do. And if the worst should happen, I'll take responsibility. You're not a soldier and I'm only going to call on your channels under dire need. Savvy?"

It was a fair concession and Olivienne nodded. "Okay. And speaking with my rational mind, I give permission ahead of time. I know what's at stake here." She changed the topic to draw them away from the heavy time and harder memories. "Did Velten comment on our progress at your update?"

Castellan pulled the chrono from her pocket. "Nothing other than assuring me we were on schedule. We're set to arrive at Ruina in about six oors. The current plan is for us to come in low near the water on the north side of the island, to avoid creating a shadow on the night sky by blocking the brightest stars. It also keeps us out of the way should they mount a dirigible defense to go help the bridge road. Once we're near enough, I'll take the team down with my channels. It's quickest and quietest and with the antoraestone it will mean a minimal power drain."

"Velten has a landing team picked as well, correct?"

"Six psi only. They'll make landfall and disable the railguns to keep us from being fired on when we try to leave."

Olivienne thought about the rest of the plan. They were making landfall at two because Leniste's defense forces plus a dozen dirigibles would make a run at taking control of the line between Annexus and Kemit. The hope was that a consolidated attack in that region would bring any dirigible stationed near Ruina to the rebel's aid. "What are the odds of success with this?"

Castellan was silent for a meen. "You can never truly predict such a thing, and in defense it was widely believed that doing so would bring ill results to the mission." She groaned. "There are a lot of factors here that need to go right. We can't be seen by anyone on the island or by rebel ships in the air. Velten's team needs to disable those rail-guns, and we have to find the prisoners, preferably without raising an alarm."

"It's too bad we couldn't disable those rail guns from a distance."

"Agreed. But there is no point in wishing for—wait a meen! You're brilliant, love."

"What?"

"Maybe we can disable those rail guns from a distance utilizing yours and Sehg's channels along with the anto-raestone." Castellan turned to the shields on duty at the door. It was Dozier and Penn. "Where is Sehg now?"

Dozier spoke. "We're on short shifts until we make it to Ruina, ser. He's probably catching some rack time while he can."

"Well enough. Soleng is on duty now so I'll have him do the legwork." Castellan grabbed the voteo from her belt and spoke into it. "Soleng."

"Yes, Captain?"

"I need you and Specialist Sehg on the bridge in ten."

"I believe he's asleep right now. You want me to wake him, and should I get Madlin, too, ser?"

"No, just Sehg. If this is successful, we may save ourselves and Velten's team a lot of work. Castellan out." She clipped the voteo back on her belt then grinned at Olivienne. She looked a little mad in the darkness.

Olivienne returned the crazed grin. "Are you going to tell me what this plan is?"

"Not yet. I just sent a telepathic message to Velten and she'll meet us on the bridge as well."

It didn't take long to get there yet Olivienne still chafed at being left in the dark. Even knowing this, Castellan insisted they wait for everyone to arrive. Velten was the first through the portal. "What is this plan you've put together, Tosh?"

Sehg and Soleng walked through a few secs later and Castellan answered. "Olivienne, you can apport with incredible accuracy, and at a few hundred yords distance. Even under poor visibility, such as when we saved those children in Vesper."

She conceded, "Sure, I'm a fair hand at it provided I can see the object. But, Tosh, if you think I can do anything with those blasted stele rail guns, I can assure you they're well beyond my weight limit."

Castellan shook her head. "No, no, we don't want to take the entire gun anyway. That is too obvious. We need to disable them so the rebels have no clue they won't fire until they're needed. Sehg, what would be the best way to disable a rail gun that, one—makes it impossible to fire, two—isn't obvious, and three—would be difficult to fix?"

He scratched at the curly hairs on his chin. "Well, there are a few critical pieces that are not obvious. The best one, in my opinion, would be the firing pin. That actuates the aether release, which in turn fires the shell out the barrel. They rarely fail and are difficult to manufacture, so supply is pretty limited. Especially since they're produced in just one location."

Soleng looked at him curiously. "And that is?"

"The facility is in Ancra. My sib works there. I'm guessing if the rebels have a supply of such things, they'd probably be given to the dirigibles first since they're most often on the offensive." He paused and shrugged. "At least that's what I'd do."

Velten was already nodding. "That would be my prediction as well. But what does that do for us, Tosh? The last time I checked, firing pins were located *inside* the rail gun, and not visible. That eliminates Connate Dracore's channel as an option. I can have my team try to disable the pin, but it may be easier just to damage the blasted things."

Castellan held up a finger. "Yes, but Sehg here is a four rating in telesthesia."

"Far sight? Even Savon was only a three." She'd done a bang-up job at memorizing her shield team's information, but Olivienne still didn't know much about her newest guardian.

"Yes. So, now we're going to perform a little test to see if you can combine your channel with Sehg's to apport something from the captain's cabin here."

"Why my cabin?"

"Because neither of them is familiar with the space.

You just need to choose what you want them to find. After, we'll try something harder that isn't out in the open."

"Fair enough."

"But ser, the connate and I are only fours in the needed ratings. We're not like you with your inspiring channel strength."

Castellan smiled and clapped the man on the shoulder. "Don't sell yourself short, Specialist."

Olivienne glanced to the right when she heard Castellan's voice in her head.

Can you discreetly apport my antoraestone into your hand? I'm aware that most of the shield team has figured it out by now but I'd rather not call attention to it on a bridge half full of psi.

Yes, ser.

Castellan winked and Olivienne did as requested with the pendant that was just visible through the open top two buttons of her shirt. The weight in her palm was light enough, but her stomach twisted as she remembered the previous time that she held the stone aboard a dirigible. Hopefully this would save lives before they could be lost. She looped the chain around her neck and tucked the necklace down the front of her shirt for skin contact.

"Now what?" Olivienne looked to Velten. "Do you have an item in mind?"

"I've got a novel sitting on the stand next to my bed. The cover is green."

Olivienne nodded and held out her left hand to Sehg. "Just like you did with Madlin and Holling. I want you to try to find what the captain is referring to. You know the direction of her cabin, let's start there."

"Yes, Connate."

As soon as their hands touched, Sehg closed his eyes and Olivienne followed suit. Castellan prompted quietly. "Tell us what you see."

"I recognize the captain's room door. I'm going through." He paused. "There are two other doors inside."

"One is for my head, the other is my private sleeping quarters."

He was quiet for a few secs. "The right one is your

personal room."

"Correct."

Castellan asked, "Are you seeing this too, Olivienne?"

"Yes. I don't know if it's the telesthesia, but he's able to push images just like Savon did."

"Good. Do you both see the book Velten spoke of?"

They answered in unison. "Yes."

"'Vienne, apport it here."

Olivienne flexed her apportation channel and it was one of the easiest things she'd ever done. The power of the antoraestone was exhilarating. When she opened her eyes, she held a book with a green cover in her right hand.

"Sheddech!"

Olivienne offered it back to Velten and Tosh praised them both. "Excellent. Now, Sehg, what is the easiest way to reach the firing pin?"

"From a section that flips open in the back."

"And do you think you can find and show the pin for each railer gun along the coast so Olivienne can apport it away?" He nodded. "Good. Your test is to find the firing pin from the fore dextra rail gun on this ship." She paused and met Sehg's gaze. "That's front right if you're not familiar with dirigible terminology."

Olivienne snickered at Sehg's affronted look. "Ser, I've served on a dirigible before."

"Very well then. Begin."

It took less than a meen for Sehg and Olivienne to locate the nearest railgun and for Sehg's telesthesia to show them the inner workings. She apported the pin into her hand then grinned at Tosh. "It worked!"

"Of course, it did. Do you two think you can do that at a greater distance? Say, half a mahl out?"

"Sure, as long as it doesn't strain my channel. But to be honest, I felt no drain whatsoever just now."

"I think you'll be fine." Castellan took the pin that Olivienne held out to her and handed it off to Sehg. "Specialist, I trust you to put this back and leave that rail gun in working order. Then go get some more rack time. We'll call everyone to duty when we arrive at the island."

She looked at Soleng. "Have him report to me directly

on the bridge. I'm not sure what the best deck to do this will be so we'll decide then. Dismissed."

Both men saluted the three higher ranking members on the bridge. "Yes, ser."

Olivienne reached into her shirt for the antoraestone chain as she met Tosh's gaze. "Here."

"Keep it. You'll need it again soon enough."

She knew it made the most sense but Olivienne didn't like holding such power any longer than necessary. But she accepted the necessity and let the pendant drop back into her shirt.

Castellan addressed her and Velten. "So, an obvious change of plans. It seems safest to disable the rail guns in this manner. Velten, that will free up your team to take one direction on the island to look for prisoners while we go the other. It seems to be the best use of our resources."

"How about my team works at disabling the rebels instead, as yours perform the search and rescue?"

"Quietly, right?"

Velten scoffed, looking much the way Sehg had meens before. "We were all defense once, too, Tosh. We know how to do our job. My crew may not be as diverse as you lot, but we can certainly get the task done."

"Well enough." Castellan spoke to Olivienne. "Is this plan satisfactory?"

"I like it a lot better than the last one." She glanced at Velten. "No offense, Captain."

"None taken. I like this one better, too, because it means less risk from those blasted coastal weapons." Velten glanced at her pocket chrono. "Should we reconvene here in five oors?"

Olivienne looked at Castellan and neither needed words nor telepathy to know what the other was thinking. "We'll see you then."

Plan in place, Olivienne and Castellan left Velten on the bridge, heading back to their cabin for a few oors of sleep.

"It's too blasted early."

Castellan smiled at Olivienne's grumble. "Or late. I suppose it depends on which way you're holding the chrono."

"More like how much sleep you've gotten before. I'm out of stims, too. I'll have to get some from Velten."

That earned a laugh. "Love, you'll be hard pressed to find a soldier who doesn't have a tin of stims somewhere on their person. Natural, healthy, and gives just the right amount of boost. Whomever discovered that herb has been the real hero of the corps for at least a generation."

"True enough. Yet you still don't use them."

Castellan shrugged and Olivienne turned toward the nearest guardian, who happened to be Lazaro. "Well, can you spare some wakefulness for your tired sovereign?"

He snickered. "I've actually got two tins. You can have my spare."

Castellan smiled at him. "Always be prepared, right Specialist?"

Lear shook her head and started laughing. "He's not the least bit noble or prepared. Laz makes cred by selling them to the rest of us when we run out on missions."

"I guess that does make me prepared because I've always got them to sell," Lazaro fired back.

The laughter cut off and Lear looked as though she swallowed something unsavory. "Bollux, but he's right."

The mood sobered once they reached the bridge. Velten met them as soon as they stepped through the portal. The plexi windows gave them three hundred sixty degrees of blackness in view, with the exception of faint lights far in the distance, off their dextra side.

"I'd say the connate and your specialist will do best near the aft dextra engine. I've ordered the pilot to hold us steady here. It seems the best place to avoid detection by rebel dirigibles and island guards alike. My only concern is that it's a long stretch between Endara and Dromea, and we don't know when Havington will take the bait."

Castellan closed her eyes and pondered the question with her channels. Her intuition had saved her more often than not. She knew Leniste and how the man operated. "I feel as though the general would have thought of this problem."

"And?"

"My gut instinct is saying he would have started the offensive early, anticipating a delayed reaction on the part of the rebels."

Olivienne looked from Velten to her. "Now what?"

"Continue with the plan. We can attempt to disable those guns whether or not the dirigibles are still in the area."

Velten growled. "Oh, they are. One of my spotters with keen sight noticed two moored on the far side of Ruina. But there could be more in the sky that we can't see, hidden from the sonica near the waves and rocky out-croppings the same as us. I'll say this, at least this blasted island is a little smaller than Iuvenis and less settled. It should help with the search efforts."

Castellan looked around the bridge at the assembled members. Both her lieutenants were there, as well as Sehg. Lieutenant Wern was the head of ship security for the *Vestigo* and he had a team of five others hand-picked from those with the most active combat experience. It was true that most fighting in defense happened against the Atlantee and their monsters from the deep, but some attacks were quite stealthy, with more intelligent creatures making land than the simple armicrustes. Not to mention, there had been rebels and other ne'er-do-wells around for generations, always trying to disrupt polite society. Castellan shook her head and knew it was as good as they'd get. She circled a finger in the air. "What are we all waiting for? Starlight is wasting."

Once they arrived at the staging deck on the side of the ship facing the island, Olivienne and Sehg settled into the decking and held hands. Olivienne still wore the antorae-stone necklace from earlier. Castellan had given her a kiss for luck before exiting the cabin to find Soleng, Madlin, and their newest specialist waiting.

"Ser," Sehg spoke up. "How will I know if we've got them all?"

"Well, I'd suggest you start with one end of the rail gun line and follow it as far as it goes. We'll just hold our breath and hope there aren't any more set up away from the immediate perimeter."

He nodded and closed his eyes. Olivienne gave Castellan a wink then did the same. Castellan called out encouragement from where she stood nearby. She didn't dare touch Olivienne. It wouldn't do to interfere with their channel share.

Five meens went by before the duo found their first success. The sound of a small brass pin hitting the decking seemed loud, despite the gusting wind and crashing waves below. Soleng was quick to step on it to prevent loss over the deck edge. He picked it up and put it in his pocket, then stood waiting for another. The next dropped closer to Madlin and she did the same. It was working, but it took nearly five meens between each.

Conscious of the passing time, and after they'd accumulated two full hands of pins, Castellan spoke quietly, "Sehg, can you tell how many are left?" Both he and Olivienne were sweating, despite the moderate breeze.

"I think no more than two. Blast but this is giving me head pains."

"Keep at it, Specialist. You're doing a great job."

Not wanting to bother the two sitting on the deck, or put more pressure on them, she spoke directly into Madlin and Soleng's minds.

I want Madlin to get the rest of the team ready. Have them join Velten's team on the laeva deck. Minimal equipment, blacked out if it isn't already. Soleng, check in with the bridge to see if they have any updates, then join the rest of the shield team.

What of med?"

Castellan paused as she met Madlin's gaze. Her eyes flickered to Olivienne, then back to Madlin. It was her call to make. Stealth was essential, yet they were taking a sovereign into a hostile situation and there were regulations to follow. She sighed. *Field kits only, not sovereign, and full weapons for everyone.*

Yes, ser. Both saluted before heading off to their tasks.

She hoped her decision wouldn't come back to bite her in the boots later.

Time was of the essence but Castellan directed Olivienne and Sehg to take a twenty meen break to recoup their energy. The Antoraestone gave them the boost of power necessary to do the job but it was precision work and mentally draining in an entirely different way.

Castellan tried one more time to dissuade Olivienne from coming with them. "Are you sure you wouldn't rather stay on the *Vestigo*? Your pyrokinetic channel could be valuable from a distance." She wanted to bring up the fact that Olivienne wasn't a trained soldier but didn't dare.

Olivienne scowled. "Tosh—"

"I know." Castellan held up her hands. "I had to try."

"If you're worried about my skill, you'll find my eye keen and hand steadier than most, as you're well aware."

"It's not those things I'm worried about. It's your head and heart, love."

"We'll get through this together. As long as we have one another's backs we'll be fine." She paused and looked around the rest of the assembled team. "Now, let's go get my sib and all the rest of the innocent people subject to Havington's machinations."

The unit wore their usual uniforms plus hoods and gloves. Even their faces were blacked out to help hide them in the shadows. Anyone they encounter on Ruina would be hard pressed to spot one of their guardians, and no one would guess there was a sovereign in the mix. Olivienne looked like the rest of them with hood up, gloves on, and every bit of skin darkened.

"We look like we did on Halcyon Station, bog monsters the lot! Except we smell significantly better." Qent leaned closer to Devin and gave a sniff. "At least *I* do."

Quiet chuckles moved through the group as Castellan checked her side arm and shells one more time. She looked up and panned her gaze around the group, meeting fifteen pairs of blinking eyes in the darkness. All external lamps had been switched off before they made their final approach to Ruina low across the water.

"Are you lot ready?"

"Yes, ser."

"Good, we're just waiting for Lieutenant Wern and his team to join us from their briefing with Captain Velten." As soon as the words left her mouth, a short, stocky psi pushed through the door to the staging deck, followed by five others. Some faces were familiar, but others Castellan had only seen in passing when traveling aboard the dirigible. All were dressed and blacked out, just like Olivienne's team. "Ready, Lieutenant?"

Wern peered around at their group, then looked over the rail. "You're not lifting us down to a boat?"

"I'm taking us all to the island. It's quicker and quieter that way."

"Can you do that? Pardon my skepticism, ser, but I don't want to end up in the drink tonight."

"Who do you think saved our stones over King's Marsh? Of course, she can do it!"

Castellan appreciated the defense but it was unnecessary. "At ease, Madlin. It was a legitimate concern." She looked at Wern. "I assure you I can take us to the island and not be worse for wear. Now, if we're all ready?"

Lieutenant Wern nodded.

"Make sure all your gear is strapped securely. I'll not be responsible for items lost in the Cunis Sea." She watched as everyone did one final check. When finished, she lifted the entire lot, including herself.

It was a real test of Castellan's power, not just for the strength required to carry something above the waves, but to lift so many people at once for such a distance. She was also using her telekinesis and levitation channels simultaneously, a feat few, if any, could match as effectively. It was less than what she lifted at Soleng's ranking ceremony, but they were easily twenty yords above the water and a good half mahl out from shore. Despite her words of reassurance, Castellan breathed a sigh of relief when they made it to a stretch of secluded sandy shore ten foot below the rail gun line with nary a stone dropped.

She addressed the entire group telepathically. *Just like we planned with Velten. Wern, you'll take your team to start disabling the rebel guards. Knock them out, tie them up, and steal any of those shards you find. Savvy?*

A chorus of agreements sounded in her head. She wished they could have brought some of those power sinks but they didn't have shackles ready, nor was there a good way to transport them, so they were best left with Leniste.

The group waited for the nearest guard to walk farther down the line on her patrol, then Castellan lifted them in twos. She figured that was less conspicuous than everyone together. Once above, Wern's group melted into the shadows, following the rail gun line. Castellan's unit split into three teams. The buildings on Ruina didn't follow a grid pattern like most cities or towns. Instead, roads meandered around trees and rock outcroppings, with the buildings interspersed along three main paths.

Madlin, take right with Devin, Lazaro, Leggett, and Calderon. Soleng, take left with Qent, Yazzie, Dozier, and Sehg. I'll take center with the connate, Lear, Meza, Penn, and Holling. Check the buildings and use your channels as much as possible. Stealth is of the highest priority. And keep in mind, they could have a prescient in the ranks, though the channel is quite rare.

Orders given, the three groups left in their separate directions, sticking to the shadows. Castellan's team worked for half an oor checking buildings with no success in finding any prisoners. They took a few rebels by surprise and dealt with them swiftly before they could give their presence away. Everyone froze when alarms sounded in the distance. They took cover in the trees and waited to see what would happen.

Boosted by the antoraestone and familiar with their minds, Castellan checked in with her lieutenants. *Madlin, Soleng, report.*

Ser, we've made it to where enemy ships are winched down. It looks like the dirigibles are scrambling to leave. At least one has been loosed from its mooring and appears to be heading northwest.

My team doesn't have eyes on any of the ships but the rebel guards are definitely awake and active now. We've retreated to an empty storage building to wait for things to calm down.

No sign of prisoners?

No, ser.

Nothing by the docks, ser.

Castellan made to run a hand through her hair with frustration, then remembered the hood. She sighed and clenched her fist. *Okay, keep looking but we wary of the guards. At least until those blasted dirigibles are well and away.*

Yes, ser!

Her own group was secluded in a small stand of trees near the center of Ruina at Castellan's best guess. She felt a hand on her forearm as Olivienne whispered. "Tosh?"

Castellan addressed her group. *Stay quiet. Timing is critical right now. Madlin says they're scrambling the dirigibles. My guess is to go aid in the bridge defense. We need to be careful not to give ourselves away until they're all gone. Neither of the other two groups have found the prisoners.*

Ser, what about Soflin? Won't ships from there go right overtop our location?

Penn made an excellent point. *I guess we'll deal with them should they come our way.*

Once things sounded as though they'd calmed down on the far side of the island, Castellan's team resumed their search. Ten meens later they came across a cluster of large buildings. The sheer size made them unique from others they'd found, as well as the guards on duty at each entrance.

Ser, how do we get by the guards? They've got full sight of one another so it will be hard to take them by surprise. You said earlier you didn't want to do anything that would alert the other rebels.

True. Let me call the rest of the team to our location. My intuition is telling me this is the place.

It didn't take long for the other units to arrive. Madlin and Soleng said they turned inland once they realized no prisoners were kept near the coast.

Madlin pulled out a spyglass and peered through to the four buildings. *I don't see how we can take them by surprise all at once. Someone is bound to get a warning out no matter what we do.* She put the implement away. *Blast, but it's a dark night.*

Mads is right. I'd recommend we split up and come around from behind the buildings. From what I've seen so far tonight, the rebels are spread pretty thin. Our number is great enough that we can incapacitate the lot of them but we'll be found out no matter what.

Madlin followed Soleng's observation. *They've less here guarding than common sense would dictate for the size of the buildings. Either there are more guards inside, or the prisoners are incapacitated somehow.*

If those buildings are full of prisoners, will we even have room for them all on the Vestigo? Soleng said.

Castellan frowned into the dark. *I certainly hope so. As for the rebel guards calling for reinforcements, we'll just have to hope that Wern and his team have done their jobs by cutting down the number of rebels that can respond to the alert. Now, let's take care of the task in front of us. Teams of four, split two and two around each side of the buildings. I want this quick and quiet as possible. Savvy?*

Yes, ser.

Good, let's go.

The group fell into natural splits as they'd done it often enough on adventurist missions. Once they were in place, Castellan readied herself to give the signal. Their surprise was ruined by one of the rebels, who must have sensed something was off and sounded the alarm. "Beware!"

It didn't take much to subdue the ten rebel guards, even though more than a few had shards of antoraestone. Unfortunately, the damage was already done. Another siren sounded through the woods and Castellan yelled to her team. "Get in those buildings now! We need to extract the prisoners from the island as soon as possible."

A group of six black clad soldiers burst through the trees as a number of Castellan's team swung weapons around.

"Friendly!" Wern called out.

Castellan gave Olivienne a telekinetic nudge, knowing

she would want to search for her sib. "Go, I'll get Wern's status." She turned to the man in question. The rest of his team ranged out and assumed guard positions. They were crouched low, wary, and with weapons ready. "Report."

"We got rid of all the rebels stationed along the rail gun line."

"What did you do with them?"

He smiled, the only part of it visible in the dark was his teeth. "The island is well defended with a tall rock wall along the water. It's just about impossible to get onto the island unless you go around to the beach we were on. Even then it's a climb unless you have a shield at your back with over-powered tee-kay."

"And?"

"We chucked them all into the water. Figured if the current didn't get them, the Atlanteens would. Either way, they'd be out of our sight for a time and nobody died. Just as the queen requested."

"Thank you, Lieutenant. I want you—"

"Captain, we've found the prisoners!" Castellan looked up to see numerous shields helping people out of the four buildings. There were too many and none of the prisoners looked to be in good shape. She cursed because the *Vestigo* would be hard pressed to hold what looked to be more than sixty psi, and all of them appeared to need assistance getting to safety. Before Castellan could give an order, Olivienne called out from where she searched through the huddled group.

"He's not here!"

"Sheddech." Castellan grabbed the closest prisoner, which happened to be a skinny woman near her height. "Do you know where they would have taken the sub-con-nate?"

The psera's cheeks were sunken and she appeared exhausted. "Aye, Captain Tosh. We heard some chatter daes ago. My guess is they probably have him at the offi-cer's quarters near the watchtower. Keep along this road," She gestured toward the one Castellan's team had followed to get to their current location. "And you should find the place."

Castellan peered closer at the woman. She looked vaguely familiar in the light of the illeostone lanterns. "Do I know you?"

"Yes, ser. The name is Sleega Gant. I served as your bombardier down in Ostium before your promotion."

Horror filled Castellan at Gant's words. This was no young and vital soldier she left far to the south rotos ago. This was someone who had been starved, probably tortured, and kept in the dark for far too long. Castellan withheld her pity though, sensing a soldier's pride beneath the pain. "Thank you, Bombardier Gant. You all need to be strong a little longer. I'll make sure you get to our dirigible safely so you can put this behind you."

"Behind us, ser?" The woman scowled. "The only thing I'd like to be behind is the trigger of a rail gun with Havington firmly in my sights. Him *and* those wasteful weaslets, General Tenet and Lieutenant Commander Bello."

She nodded. "I suspect you'll get your chance soon enough. You can start by arming yourself with those rebel weapons and help guard the rest on your way back to the *Vestigo*."

"But, ser, I can help."

"I'm afraid the rest is our mission only. You lot need to get back and I'm counting on your sure aim and loyalty to help the others. Savvy?"

Gant's shoulders drooped and Castellan wasn't sure if it was disappointment or relief. "Yes, ser."

"Go now, arm yourself and report back to Lieutenant Wern here." Once Gant walked away, she turned her gaze to Wern. "I want you to lead this group to the docks. You should be able to make your way around to where the *Vestigo* is holding steady. They've the tools and equipment to lift everyone up to the deck."

"It's going to take multiple boats to get them all there."

"I don't care what it takes. Break radio silence if necessary and have Velten come to you, but I want these people loaded and ready to leave as soon as possible."

"Yes, ser. Is your team going after the connate's sib

then?"

"Tosh?"

Castellan met Olivienne's frightened eyes before answering him. "Yes. I have a promise to keep."

Chapter Sixteen

The way got dark again once they left the cluster of buildings to forge deeper into the island. The road indicated by
Gant took a sharp turn not far from where the prisoner
buildings were located, and Castellan assumed they were
headed toward the nearest shore to Dromea. The trees
opened up and they saw more buildings after another fifteen meens of walking.

Castellan, look. Olivienne pointed toward an illeostone spotlight shining twenty yords off the ground. The
area directly below it was also well lit, with multiple
buildings and a flurry of rebel activity going between each.

I see it. This is definitely the place. She addressed the
rest of the shield team. *Anyone have thoughts or intuition
as to where the sub-connate could be located in that mess?*

Nothing but silence met her question.

*Fine then. They're clearly overconfident as to the
security of this island, otherwise they would have the area
farther out well-lit to make it easier to see us sneaking up.*

Devin chimed in. *So, we'll be sneaking then, ser?*

Calderon gave him a light chuck to the arm. *Put a
stone in your brain, man. We won't be honking up the path
like a flock of gozen.*

That's enough, Specialists.

Tosh, what about the spotlight?

She watched the moving beam for a meen. *It should be
easy enough to avoid. Observe how they follow the same
path with each perimeter sweep. We need to have visibility
beyond that watchtower. I want the team split, with half
field crawling to the right, and the other half to the left.
Report if you find something you think may be the officer's
quarters. Stay out of sight, stay quiet, and keep your mental shields up unless you're contacting me. I want the unit
to break apart like we did in Halcyon Station. The only
exception is that Connate Dracore comes with my group,
and Lear goes with Madlin.*

Yes, ser.

Orders given, the groups moved as quickly as possible along the ground to circle the buildings beneath the tower. Castellan kept close watch on Olivienne. She appeared to be no worse for wear from the evening's activities but one could never be too careful with a sovereign or their love.

Ser, do you think that's the place? Qent pointed at a building set farther away from the rest.

Castellan counted at least eight guards patrolling the perimeter despite the low light. It seemed as likely a place as any.

Tosh, you wouldn't guard a vault empty of cred. He's definitely right. Olivienne's worry radiated through their bond. *How are we going to get him out?*

She took note of the armed rebels she could see and assuming there were even more she couldn't. Castellan reported to Madlin as she pondered the problem. *Madlin, we're at the outer edge of the buildings. Keep going along the perimeter until you meet back up with us again.*

Yes, ser. We should be on top of you shortly.

Madlin gave Castellan an idea and her next words were an answer to Olivienne's question. *Given the fact that the rebels appear to be shorthanded on this blasted island, we could assume there are none stationed inside. We found the same with the other prisoners. And if you notice, the spotlight doesn't touch the roof of the officer's quarters. I sense the roof is metallic so I'll lift us all up and Soleng and Leggett can use their ferrokinesis to put a hole in that's large enough for the unit to gain easy access. We'll leave the same way we entered once we retrieve Kesharan.*

What now? Soleng asked.

Now we wait for Madlin to catch up with us. Castellan pulled out her chrono and noted that it had been more than a half oor since Wern's team escorted the rescued prisoners to the docks. Movement caught Castellan's eye and she saw the rest of her shields approaching low to the ground in the darkness. She asked Madlin, *How long did it take your team to travel from where the dirigibles were moored to the prison buildings?*

Ten, maybe fifteen meens. If you're wondering about

Wern, even with the injured, I'd expect them to be there by now.

Castellan weighed the odds that Wern would call Velten for a quick extraction. Her intuition jangled at the notion. She addressed the entire team. *We're out of time. I expect alarm klaxons to sound again any meen when the* Vestigo *hits the docks.*

You think they will?

I'm certain. That means we need to move quickly to capitalize on the distraction that will provide.

But ser, how will we get off the island?

She turned to meet Madlin's eyes in the low light. No words were needed. Sometimes Castellan didn't have the answers everyone sought.

Tosh?

Let's go. I'll lift Leggett and Soleng first, then the rest on their all clear.

It took five meens for the two guardians to open a section of roof in a safe place, and of a sufficient size to fit each armed and armored shield. They found themselves in a large room, with two doors leading off the main space. Castellan gave her lieutenants hand signals to search.

Empty, ser.

Madlin had better news. *Ser, this door leads down to a lower level.*

Sirens sounded in the distance, startling everyone. Olivienne gripped Castellan's forearm tightly. They heard feet running outside and Castellan called, "Everyone downstairs. Go, go, go!"

The entire team clattered down the steps. Castellan was the last one through and bolted the door from the inside. Then she used her ferrokinesis to set the metal in place. She'd forgotten about her own little used channel when they were above, on the roof. The latch was clearly meant to keep people out of the lower area rather than in and she feared for Kesharan's health and safety below. She cleared the steps in time to hear the frustration in Olivienne's voice. "It's too dense for my apportation."

"I've got it, Connate."

Leggett held her hand out toward the lock and it

melted away. They heard rebels enter the room above them.

"Shields, guard!" Castellan yelled.

As one, they fell into position around Olivienne as she helped her sib out of the cage. "Kesh!"

He threw himself into her arms. "I can't believe Maman let you come on a rescue mission."

They pulled apart. "Maman doesn't know. Are you well?"

Pounding came from above them. "Ser, what do we do?"

The tell-tale loud whumps of railgun fire sounded nearby. "Is that the *Vestigo*?" Olivienne asked.

If it was, they would be close enough to make antorae-stone-boosted contact. Castellan reached out. *Velten, have you loaded all the rescued prisoners?*

Tosh, you've yourself in a right press. We've got enemy dirigibles upon us, most likely coming in from Sof-lin. We can't stay or we'll be shot down. Not to mention, the lot you sent us was more than estimated and has the ship at capacity for lift and speed.

The noise in the main level of their building intensified and Castellan knew it was only a matter of time before the rebels made it through the solid door. She and Velten were both aware that you couldn't risk the many for the few. *Just go. You can outrun those dirigibles.*

What about your team? The connate and sub-connate?

If they're chasing you, they aren't coming after us. We'll figure something out here in the meantime.

I'm not comfortable with it but on your orders, Tosh. I'll get the prisoners back safely.

See that you do.

"Tosh, what are we going to do? How will we meet up with the ship with the rebels on top of us?"

"We don't."

"Ser?" Madlin questioned.

"The *Vestigo* is at capacity, but worse yet, she's got multiple rebel dirigibles bearing down on her. Those were most likely the railguns we heard."

"Ser, what about us?"

Qent was as brave a soldier as any of them but in that meen, Castellan thought he looked younger than she knew him to be. "I'm not sure."

"Can't you use your stone?"

She frowned at Olivienne. "I can't manipulate what I can't see."

"Ser, why don't you clear the entire building from above us?"

"Don't be a fool, Dev."

Castellan held up a hand to stay the stress-fueled argument. "Actually, that idea has merit—"

The ceiling above the center of the sub-level exploded in a shower of wood shards, throwing everyone back. The lone illeostone lantern smashed against the far wall casting them into darkness. Pistol and rifle fire sounded above and one of the shields behind her cried out. "Everyone down! Cover the sovereigns," Castellan yelled.

They couldn't see to fire back, and the rebels knew they had the unit trapped like swimmers in a pond. Eventually someone would get lucky. Another shield yelled in pain and she couldn't wait any longer. "Sheddech, this won't do."

Everyone, tuck down and protect your heads!

With a jerky sweep of her hand, Castellan used her boosted telekinesis to simply clear the building from above them. This time it was the rebels crying out into the wind as they were swept away with the structure. Castellan couldn't see where it ended up. She just hoped it was away from her line of sight.

"Holling, Yazzie, see to the wounded. Madlin and Soleng, get the team to the wall opposite the water. Two guard the sovereigns, the rest take positions to fire outward." She looked around the sub level which was naught more than a square hole in the ground about eight foot deep at that point. There were crates stacked on one end and she used her telekinesis to move them all near the perimeter. Then she sprinted for the wall closest to the side where she estimated the brunt of rebel forces to be.

"Ser, Holling's been hit and it's bad."

Castellan turned back to see Yazzie's form illuminated

by the spotlight from the watchtower. Yazzie knelt on the floor tightening a strap around Holling's thigh above a grievous wound. He'd clearly taken a rifle shell through the big bone and artery, and she knew for certain he'd lose the leg. In that split sec of observation, Castellan dashed the entire watchtower to the ground and yelled for her lieutenant. "Soleng, help Yazzie sear that wound closed with your pyrokinesis. Everyone else not guarding the sovereigns, take positions around the wall and fire on anyone who approaches."

As if to prove their dedication and bravery, she heard the quiet sounds of rifles firing behind her and the hiss of expelled aether from their chambers with each.

Castellan felt someone step up to her side and the sound of a pistol, then realized it was Olivienne. "What are you doing, get below!"

"I've sure enough aim, Tosh. You need me right now." Another of their team yelled in pain and Olivienne intensified her stare to prove a point.

"Fine. Stay by me."

"Yes, ser."

"Ser, I'm out of shells."

"And I'm on my final stone, Captain."

Things were dire but something made Castellan take heart. "Listen, can you hear that?"

"Ser, they've stopped firing."

"Yes, they have." Castellan smiled at Olivienne. "Let's see what I can do to clear the area around us—"

Dirt and stone exploded on the far corner of their pit, the side no shields had been shooting from because it didn't face anything more than a cliff edge and water below. It was also the most open to incoming rebel fire. Two more deep *whumps* could be heard and the other corner exploded. "They're honing their aim," Castellan yelled. "Everyone to this end, including wounded."

Once they'd all crowded together, some on crates above and some protected below, Madlin met Castellan's gaze. "I'm sorry, ser. It appears we'll be letting the queen down todae."

Castellan looked around the tired faces, streaked with

black and blood. Before she could answer, a voice called out from somewhere in the darkness. She didn't need the light of Illeos or Archeos to know who spoke. It was a voice she loathed for a handful of rotos when she was stationed down in Ostium.

"Tosh, it looks like you've got yourself into a small bit of trouble down there with no place to go."

"Looks can be deceiving."

"You should give up now to prevent more unnecessary bloodshed. You know I only want what's best for Psiere. I've been loyal my entire life."

"What I know is that you're naught more than a son of a sint, descended from a long line of useless gits. You wouldn't know loyalty or courage if it bit you on the arse!"

Havington tutted above them. "I've never heard more unprofessional words come out of your mouth, Tosh. Connate, if you surrender yourself and your sib, I promise I'll spare all your lives, save your captain."

Olivienne turned fearful eyes toward Castellan. "What are we going to do? Can you clear them away like you did the building?"

She gestured upward. "Listen. Do you hear the engines? By my estimate, there are at least five dirigibles out there with an unknown number of rebels on the ground. They're smart enough to stay out of my line of sight. And if I lift my head high enough to see, well, I suspect I won't have much of a skull left."

"Ser, Holling isn't doing well and Dozier has yet to wake from a shell graze to the head." Yazzie's words sent a chill down Castellan's spine. The situation had turned desperate yet they remained at an impasse.

"Connate Dracore, I'm waiting on an answer."

Another whump sounded. "Brace!" Castellan yelled, as the area behind them exploded. Shards of wood and pieces of stone and whatever else had been stored in the center of the sub-level pummeled them from behind. Olivienne slumped next to her and Castellan turned to see a bleeding gash on her temple.

"'Vienne!" Kesharan stood from his place below.

Castellan pushed him down none too gently with her

telekinesis. "Stay down, Kesh!" Then she moved her gaze to her remaining medican. "Yazzie, I need some stripping up here!"

A bright roll sailed toward Castellan. She caught it and quickly wound the fabric tight around Olivienne's head to slow the bleeding.

"I need an answer, Dracore! You have thirty secs before I consider you all to be enemies of the new power state and have my people treat you accordingly."

Soleng stepped close to help support Olivienne's slumped form. "Ser, what are we to do?"

Castellan looked around at what she could see with their limited vantage point below ground. She had a plan but wasn't sure if it would work. Even so, she'd need a distraction. "Hold the connate up so I can grab her hand. Quickly!"

Soleng lifted Olivienne's hand at the same time a dirigible came into view above. "Time's up," Havington called out to them. Whump, whump, whump sounded and the entire back side of the space they were in was destroyed.

Castellan dashed the ship from the sky then grabbed the ungloved hand held out to her and raised her head above the ground level to get her bearings. There were easily a hundred rebels ranging around them with weapons aimed and ready. They seemed like vapors because the dust was so thick from shell attacks and the crashed dirigible. She gave a mental shout to her team. *Everyone put your heads down and don't look up no matter what!* All Captain Castellan Tosh could do after that was hope that merging her and Olivienne's channels would work the way she intended. Or work at all.

She watched as the nearest rebel brought his rifle to bear in her direction. Her over-powered telekinesis melded with Olivienne's pyrokinesis. Both were fueled by desperation and the antoraestone, and Castellan drew every bit of power into herself and released it all at once. Her eyes were open to see the destruction and it was one of the single most regretful times of her life.

A wall of superheated flame began as a dome above

their location. It spread rapidly outward, growing in size. The first rebels it touched blackened to ash instantly. The ground at their feet burned to slag and cracked. The wave destroyed buildings, flipped haulers, and struck the dirigibles from the sky with the vengeance of a thousand suns. When it was over, Castellan's heartbeat thundered in her ears. The only sound she could hear was the crackling of flames and crashing waves in the distance.

"Tosh?"

Castellan broke from her daze to look down and to her left. Soleng had wrapped his large body around Olivienne's to protect her from something he couldn't possibly fathom. His uniform was ripped and she realized at that very sec that some of the destruction could be attributed to the fact that he, too, was in the channel meld. He pulled back and Olivienne's eyes fluttered open. She winced and tried to touch her temple but Castellan held her hand fast. She'd never seen something more beautiful in the flickering light of the fires burning on the island and brightening morning sky. Castellan's love was certainly a far cry from the ugliness she'd unleashed meens before.

Perhaps it was something in her expression, but Olivienne frowned. "What is it? What's happened."

Soleng's deep voice was quiet in the wake of destruction. "She's ended it, Connate."

"Ended what?" She continued to meet Castellan's eyes, but the weight of what she'd done left her mute in the aftermath.

"Everything." He paused and shook his head. "Just…everything." With those words, he helped Olivienne stand and Castellan pulled her into a tight embrace.

Fear of who she'd become raged within Castellan's heart, hotter and more frightening than what was unleashed upon the rebels. After all, she assumed there were good psi in their numbers, merely misled by a charismatic man and powerful telepath. But now they'd never know which were the monsters and which were led astray.

No. There was one beast left standing.

"Don't you dare think that!" Olivienne easily read the thoughts so near the front of her mind. Castellan knew truthfully that Olivienne would have read her mood as well with their bond. Olivienne pulled back and met Castellan's wet gaze. "If anything, I'm equally at fault here."

Castellan abruptly stepped back and wobbled on the stacked crate. "You are not!" She cut her hand through the air, aware in her periphery of the other shields taking stock around them. "I made you a promise. Using your channel was my decision and mine alone. I am responsible, period." Anger rose to the forefront but she wasn't angry at Olivienne. She was angry at herself, at the rebels, and especially at Pon Havington for putting her and her shield team in such a position. It was untenable and hopeless.

"Ser," she looked down to see Yazzie kneeling next to Holling. "His pulse is weak. I don't know how long he can last."

Castellan tried to run a hand through her hair and encountered the black hood. In a fit of rage, she ripped it down from her head. "We need off this fecking island!"

"Hey, hey, calm down. We'll figure it out."

She turned to look at Olivienne. "All this power, all the weight and expectation, but it only seems to be good for destruction. This one time, this one meen, I wish I could save a life instead of taking one."

Madlin stood a few foot below Castellan's vantage point. "Ser, you saved all of us. You say you do naught but destroy but the truth is that you alone have saved us often and from things that most wouldn't expect to survive." She shook her head and spared a glance toward where Yazzie knelt on broken stone. "Even if the worst happens and we lose Gren, your sacrifice and power is something I'll never forget." Then she did something Castellan never expected. Madlin saluted, which was quickly copied by the rest of the able-bodied shield team.

"I—um, thank you. I'm only doing my duty, as are the rest of you."

"It's more than that, ser. You go above and beyond in whatever you do and inspire the rest of us."

Castellan stared down at Holling's unconscious body then moved her gaze to Dozier. "I'm not sure that's such a good thing." She shook her head in an effort to stay the negative thoughts and attempted to put together a plan. "We either need a speedy way off this rock, or we need to get Holling to a med center. Sheddech, but what I wouldn't give to have Gem here with us!"

She used her severely depleted telekinesis to lift those still on crates at the edge of the sub-level down to join the rest in the bottom. Anything was better than the land on the outside of the pit they were in. Devin stood from where he'd fallen and attempted to pick his way toward them, across the debris strewn floor. He stumbled and Meza caught him by his arm, right where the uniform shirt was ripped from a shell. Devin cried out in pain at the same time Meza stiffened and her eyes closed.

"What is it?" Castellan asked, sensing something strange happening.

When Meza's eyes opened again, she quickly removed her hand from Devin's injured arm. "Ser, it's him." She gestured toward her teammate.

Devin appeared perplexed. "Me?"

"I swear on it, my channel is telling me he can help."

"I have no idea what she's talking about. I've not any med training beyond what they teach everyone in the rescue and salvo track up at academy. That's what we have medicans for."

Castellan wracked her brain as more specialists gathered closer to where she stood next to Olivienne. She intoned his stats to the best of her memory. "Specialist Ben Devin, four enhanced memory, four telepathy, and three in telekinesis. I don't see how any of that can help."

Olivienne snapped her fingers. "No, his papers listed one more."

Castellan looked at her and Olivienne shrugged. "What? I told you I read all about them while you were going through your channel testing on Instrucia. He also has telesana but it was a low one rating and deemed negligible."

"The connate's right, ser. I've never brought it up because it's an unusable channel so I've never even trained in it."

"What are you thinking, Tosh?"

Castellan gave her a grim smile. "That all channels are unusable until they're not. Much like your teleportation."

"The stone!"

She rushed to Devin's side where he'd come to a stop next to Yazzie. She pulled the stone from around her neck. "Quickly, sit on the ground by Holling and grab his bare hand."

He obeyed but shook his head when he saw the antoraestone dangling from the thong in Castellan's grip. "But ser, even with a power boost, I still don't know what to do."

"I happen to be long-time friends with the most powerful telesana healer across Psiere. I think I can help a little. First, take the stone then take Holling's hand. Yazzie, you may want to step back and give them space."

Castellan took a seat nearby after Devin was in place. "Close your eyes and listen to the sound of Holling's breathing. Feel the skin of his hand in yours and focus on the pulse you can sense beneath the surface."

"How did you know—"

"No talking for now. You have to attune yourself to his body. Just listen to me."

He nodded but didn't open his eyes or answer.

"Good. That pulse you can feel beneath the surface, go deeper. Follow the blood as it flows around his body. Feel the muscles, sense the bones. Tell me what colors you see."

"Everything looks gray right now, ser."

"Keep moving and look for a place that glows red in your mind's eye, that is the area with the most injury."

Everyone waited as a meen went by, then two. Finally, he cried out. "I see it. The place is...ser, it's not good. I don't know what to do here."

"Let your mind be cool, a healing balm. Start with the bone and direct the splintered pieces back into a whole. Move each one and don't leave any behind."

"It feels like when I use my tee-kay. What about the shell?"

"Unnecessary. Expel it."

Castellan watched the sweat bead across Devin's forehead and knew she was pushing him beyond his natural capacity but they had little choice since Holling's life was on the line. The sound of a metal casing hitting the stone below brought Castellan out of her mental musing.

"You're doing well. Once you've repaired the bone, I want you to work on the blood vessels next. They're naught more than tiny little tubes filled with blood instead of hard tubes full of spongy marrow."

Olivienne moved closer and put a hand on Castellan's shoulder. "How do you know so much about the makeup of our bodies?"

"Gem has told me way more during the rotos we trained together than I ever wanted to know."

Yazzie interrupted their discussion. "Captain, he's not looking good."

Castellan and Olivienne looked toward Devin and saw him sway. "Are you okay, Specialist?"

"Got a banging headache, ser, and I'm not feeling well. I don't know how much more I can do here."

Yazzie placed two fingers against the side of Holling's neck. "His respiration and pulse are already more stable. He's lost a lot of blood but if Devin fixed the worst of the injury, I think we can safely transport him."

Devin swayed again and Castellan caught him with her telekinesis just before he fainted. Olivienne looked at her with concern. "Will he be okay?"

"I think so. He probably strained his channel, small though it may be. Perhaps especially because it's small. There would be no capacity there to push so much power."

Olivienne flexed her apportation channel and the anto-raestone necklace appeared in her palm. She handed it off to Castellan and gave her a tired look. "Let's see if we can find our way home."

Castellan stood and nodded. "I like your plan." Her body hurt but not as much as her heart. She turned to address the rest of the unit. "Look around for something we can use here to construct litters for the injured that remain immobilized. We need to make our way to the dock and see if there is anything left that we can use to get to the mainland."

"But, ser, can't you just carry us like you carried us here from the ship?"

She shook her head at Sehg's suggestion. "Even I can become depleted. I probably have enough left in me to get us out of this pit and that's it. While I'll replenish quickly, I don't want to tax myself if I can avoid it because I have no clue what the channel merge did to produce that fire blast. Nor do I know if this was all the rebels."

"Ser, there was a building near the docks that we determined to be barracks of a sort. Even if there are no ships available, we should be able to shelter there and come up with a plan."

"Good thinking, Lieutenant."

In total, it took more than a half oor for the unit to circle around the island to the location at the dock. Besides the buildings and motos in the vicinity of the watchtower that Castellan destroyed, they also had to traverse a large area strewn with debris from the downed dirigibles. What Olivienne found more disturbing than the destruction was that there wasn't more of it. So many things and Psierians had simply burned to ash.

When the unit arrived at the dock, they found naught more than a small, armored fishing vessel. The kind that was popular in coastal towns. It was unlikely to do any good in their situation.

They took time to get all the wounded into beds in the building Madlin mentioned, then the two lieutenants, Olivienne, and Castellan went outside to assess the situation. Archeos broke on the horizon and they knew Illeos wouldn't be far behind.

"Captain, do you think that Leniste won against the Rebels on the bridge across the islands?"

Castellan glanced at Madlin out of the corner of her eye. "I think that losing five dirigibles and Havington himself certainly aided the General's efforts. My gut says yes but it doesn't help us right now. It's still hundreds of mahls across the strait to Kemit, then another hundred to Gomen."

"Perhaps Maman will have had a vision and has already sent aid."

Castellan crossed her arms, as closed off as Olivienne had ever seen her. "We've got two lives that hang in the balance right now, with more of the team seriously injured. We can't count on the fickleness of the queen's prescience."

Olivienne didn't take offense at the statement. All prescient channels were fickle. It was something she learned at a young age with having such a high-profile and powerful mother. Soleng returned from his inspection of the vessel with Lear. Calderon broke his leg in the final round of railer fire so wasn't up for more than keeping a cot warm in the building at their backs. That left Lear as their only pilot.

"What did you find?"

Lear shook her head. "Sorry, scr. Looks like fully charged stones but there's no way we could carry enough to get us across the entirety of the Solis Sea. It was a twelve oor trip to Ruina with the fastest dirigible on Psiere and this floating plug isn't even capable of half that speed. The capacity just isn't there." She sighed wistfully. "What I wouldn't give for that Maker vessel back on Magna. I suspect that thing could go on forever."

"At least we wouldn't have to worry about the Atlanteens attacking us."

Castellan rubbed her forehead. "According to Leniste, they call themselves the Atlantee. And we're not going to get far enough to worry about anyone at this rate."

Something about the statement gave Olivienne an idea. Who knew what the Atlantee had available to them, and weren't they technically allies now? "Tosh, wait. What if we ask them for help?"

"Who?"

"The Atlantee."

"Leniste clearly stated that Queen Olivara promised the Atlantee queen that we wouldn't involve them in our conflict. She only asked that we be given free passage on the water."

The more Olivienne thought about it, the more certain

she was that her plan would work. "Nothing was mentioned about helping us with passage. I'm going to attempt contact."

Castellan's panicked face said more than words ever could. "Wait, what if not all the Atlantee have received word of the treaty? This could be dangerous."

"I'm more afraid of what *will* happen than I am of what *could* happen." Olivienne looked toward the barracks where she knew Holling and Dozier lay critically injured, then met Castellan's pale gaze. "It can't hurt to try. You should be recovered enough to help with anything gone awry, but I think I'll need your stone to boost my telepathy."

"But—"

Olivienne cut her off before the next protest could form. "I'm doing this, love, and I won't change my mind."

Castellan grumbled. "Somedae you'll listen to your captains."

"And somedae our people will fly to the stars like the Tau, but neither of those things are todae." Olivienne strode down the path leading to the lower dock. There was a much smaller boat tied up and she suspected she'd have to utilize that in order to be close enough to the water to touch.

There was only room for two in the tiny boat so Castellan ordered Lear, Madlin, and Soleng to do whatever they could to make the fishing vessel work for the entire team as they waited. "I suppose I'm to row the boat as well?" Castellan said.

Olivienne grinned at her. "I should probably keep my hands free. Don't you think?"

"You vex me."

"And you adore me, admit it. Have trust, my love. I'm convinced this will work. After all, I'm of the sovereign line and eventually I'll be the one in treaty with the Atlantee."

Castellan wore a considering look as she pulled at the oars. "I suppose you have a point."

They went about forty yords offshore. Sea birds called out in the morning light and a gentle breeze bobbed the boat up and down. It wasn't enough to prevent Olivienne from reaching over the edge to put her hand in the water. She wore the antoraestone necklace beneath her shirt against her skin for safety. Olivienne tried to remember everything General Leniste told her about her mother's contact.

I seek to parlay with the Atlantee in this region.

She repeated the phrase a few times during the course of ten meens and Olivienne heard Castellan shifting impatiently in her seat at the other end of the small boat. She tried again.

My name is Olivienne Dracore. I am next in line to rule the Psierians after Queen Olivara. I seek travel aid from the Atlantee.

They waited another five meens until something caught Olivienne's eye. A moving ripple sparkled in the rising suns' light, heading toward them. It was no happenstance wave but directed with intent. "There." She pointed toward the oncoming surge of water.

"If that hits us, we'll capsize."

Olivienne shook her head. "I don't think it will." As predicted. The wave slowed to a stop well before their small boat and disappeared entirely within ten foot. The swell simply dropped back into the water as if it never existed. She spoke one more time. *Are you here to parlay?*

A figure rose part way out of the water, just enough to show where the small scales transitioned to larger and heavier ones at their waist. Olivienne had never seen an Atlantee in person before, only artistic renditions and stills at academy. The water race was everything Tosh had said. Aesthetically beautiful, strange, and intriguing. They wore only a decorative shell necklace. Olivienne had no way of knowing if the person before her was one of the ones that met with her mother, but the odds were low. After all, it was a lot of water compared to so little land.

Tau-chosen, I am here. What do you need from the Atlantee?

I have a request of your people. Are you in a position to speak or decide on such things?

An enigmatic smile met her words. *Of course. I can*

address anything relating to the Atlantee.
Who are you to hold so much power?
I am Eurynome.

Chapter Seventeen

I believe your progenitor was the last one to put flesh and mind so boldly into our water. You come from good stock, Tau Chosen. She looked past Olivienne to where Castellan stood in a crouch, her pistol out with the fingers of her free hand dangling in the water. *You must be her protector mate. I promise no harm will come to you, please put away your weapon. I am the Keeper of the Trident, Queen of the Atlantee in this region.*

Olivienne's mouth opened with surprise as she turned to meet Castellan's gaze. "This is the queen my mother spoke of!"

Castellan holstered her pistol but kept her fingers in the water. "Go on, love."

Olivienne turned back to Eurynome. *My name is Olivienne Dracore. It is an honor to meet you and I look forward to learning more about your people in the rotos to come.*

Much like Kinsa, Atlantee facial features were foreign to that of a Psierian and Castellan couldn't read Eurynome's expression. But the tilt of her head indicated the possibility of humore.

Do you have a request for me, Olivienne?

If it wouldn't strain the current bounds of the pact you've created with my mother, we seek aid in reaching the land across this sea as quickly as possible. We have critically injured. She paused. *I suppose a healer in your midst would work just as well.*

The Atlantee do not have magic healers like your doctore. However, the entire world of water is at my beck and call and I believe we can transport you safely. How many of your people require aid?

"What do you think, Tosh?"

Castellan considered the issue. "We don't have a lot of options right now. If Queen Eurynome can transport seventeen of us without risk, I think we need to accept. Though I'm not sure how well our wounded would fair riding across the sea on the back of a great whal."

Rest assured, Captain—

Olivienne and Castellan both jumped at Eurynome's voice in their heads. *How?*

I can hear the thoughts in your head even as you speak them aloud. I would not risk your people so.

Castellan suggested, *We initially thought we could take the fishing vessel moored near the dock but lack the propulsion for such a feat.*

Eurynome made a face that conveyed her displeasure well enough despite being a disparate race. *I have no talent with the metals of our world. Natural minerals work best.*

What will you do?

I'll create a vessel from molten sand and use that to push you along the waves to the other side.

Castellan considered the speed that the *Vestigo* travelled on the way to Ruina. Twelve oors seemed like a long time to be trapped inside a glass vessel on the open water. Musical chittering interrupted her thoughts.

We will not be travelling as slow as that, Captain. The waves are capable of great speeds under the right amount of influence. I believe you split your suns rotation into twenty-four increments?

Oors, and yes.

It should take no more than two of your oors to travel the distance.

Olivienne appeared gob smacked. *Truly?*

I would not lie under pact.

Time was of the essence. Olivienne had done her part and assured them travel so Castellan made the decision. *We gratefully accept your aid. How soon can we leave?*

I will need to call the sand, much the way I do to create my trident. My mate, Murroh, can help. With those words, another Atlantee broke the surface and swam near Eurynome. They joined hands and Castellan and Olivienne were treated to the spectacle of Atlantee channels. Or, magic as they called it.

Sand bubbled up from beneath the waves and flowed into the air. Olivienne raised an eyebrow at Castellan and she could only shrug. They'd both heard the reports from

Leniste. It was still difficult to believe that the sea race was capable of such telekinetic feats.

Surprised as they were to see the sand, both women were utterly delighted when it took the shape of a structure and glowed. Castellan and Olivienne turned their heads away from the bright light and when they looked back, a beautiful, clear, greenish glass vessel floated near them. It looked like a mix between a spiral shell and a Psierian sailing ship.

"It's beautiful!"

"It is, but a little open for our wounded."

I will enclose it for safety once your people are inside.

Well enough. Thank you. Castellan nodded toward the queen and her mate. *If you bring it to the dock, we can begin loading our team.* She picked up the oars to row them back but was forestalled by Eurynome.

There is no need for that. The small boat raised with a swell of water and made its way toward shore, followed by the strange sea glass ship.

Madlin, Soleng, and Lear stood on the dock waiting for them to return. Each showing a different emotion in response to the presence of their Atlantee allies. Madlin's expression was as stern as ever. Soleng appeared open and curious. But Lear was frowning and Castellan remembered that she'd come from defense, just as Castellan had. There were a lot of bad memories in defense from Atlantee inter-actions.

"At ease, Lear. Queen Eurynome and her mate, Mur-roh, are here to help."

Leer straightened and schooled her face. "Ser."

Olivienne addressed the two lieutenants. "They've agreed to take us across the Cunis Sea to Annexus. We need to get everyone loaded up."

Madlin looked toward Castellan. "Supplies, ser?"

"Have everyone take care of business before we leave. Queen Eurynome assured us it would only take less than two oors."

"Yes, ser."

Lear stepped closer as Madlin and Soleng went back to the barracks that housed their unit. She swallowed as her gaze moved to the floating glass ship. "How?"

Olivienne stood next to her. "Eurynome says we'll travel at the speed of the ocean, whatever that means."

The pilot's eyebrows went up with shock. "Are you referring to a great wave? They can make something like that from nothing?"

"A great wave?"

"Yes, Connate. I've seen such from the deck of a dirigible. They are massive and can move faster than a railer."

Castellan nodded. "I've heard of such, though never seen one myself."

"How much faster?"

Lear tilted her head back and forth. "Perhaps four or five times railer max. It's incredible and frightening to witness." She shuddered. "You know I like speed, but if I'm completely honest, traveling that fast without controlling the vessel myself is daunting."

Olivienne looked at Castellan, worry clear on her face and Castellan sighed. "Even so, Specialist. We've got lives riding on the speed of this trip."

It didn't take long for all the able-bodied shields to help load those that were out of commission. They brought some bedding aboard to make the trip more comfortable for wounded and hale alike. The sub-connate was quiet and drawn.

"Are you okay, Kesh?" Olivienne murmured quietly.

He sighed and whispered. "I just want to go home."

Castellan understood his sentiment too well and her heart ached for him.

A column of water rose up to the edge of the vessel and Castellan stuck her hand in it. Eurynome gave them one final warning before she and Murroh enclosed the vessel. *Once we ride the wave, you'll be unable to contact us if there is an emergency with your people. Not to mention, a wave this size will be difficult to slow quickly. I will leave air holes in the top of the vessel when I enclose it. Is there anything else you require before we begin?*

Castellan looked at her lieutenants. "Are we clear?"

"The team is ready, Captain."

She met Olivienne's gaze.

"Let's go home, Tosh."

We're ready, Queen Eurynome. Thank you again for your invaluable aid. She sat and watched the sand flow up to cover the top of the shell ship and warned the team to close their eyes during the superheating. Only a few small holes were left to allow air circulation. Castellan took a seat next to Olivienne. Many of the uninjured shields stared wide-eyed in all directions as the water beneath the vessel swelled and pushed it forward. The faster they moved, the higher the ship, and wave below it, rose.

Perhaps the most disconcerting thing about the unique mode of travel wasn't the height and speed, or the way they had a full spherical view. It was the clear bottom showing the depths of the water below, and the two Atlantee in the heart of the wave they generated.

"Ser." Castellan turned to the right so she could see where Yazzie sat next to an unconscious Holling. "Even if we arrive in Annexus in the time given by the Atlantee, I'm not sure of his chances. He needs a telesana healer."

"Leniste should have multiple available in the city."

"What of the bridge offensive, Tosh? Won't they be drained from the battle?"

Castellan frowned. "Bollux, you're right."

"Do you think Gem will be there?"

A quick probe of her intuition channel left Castellan of middling mind. "I have no way of knowing. My gut is teetering when I think of it." She contemplated the problem before telling Olivienne. "Your telepathy is a smidge better than mine. I think you should try to contact the queen when we get closer. If anyone will hear you, it's her."

She added more, mind to mind. *Between her stone and mine, I think you have a shot of getting through. It will do much to assuage her concern as to the health and safety of her children.*

Castellan pulled out her pocket chrono. "Let's say you start in about an oor?"

Olivienne nodded before turning her attention to her sib. "How are you doing, Kesh?"

"Okay, I guess." His lip was split and swollen, and the cuts and bruises showing on any bared skin stood out in sharp relief in the bright sunshine.

Castellan knew he was putting on a brave face. Though Kesharan was on the cusp of adulthood, he hadn't yet crossed over. In fact, he was a bit more sheltered than most given his position as sub-connate. "It shouldn't be too long. The Atlantee queen assured us of a fast journey."

Qent wiped the sweat from his brow with a dirty sleeve, leaving a streak of black ash in its place. "Gah, but it can't be soon enough. The suns' light coming through this glass ship is hotter than, well, the suns! I fear we'll cook like a sea squim before we make it to shore."

"'Vienne, I know you can bring heat with your pyrokinesis channel, but can you funnel it away too?"

"Truthfully, I don't know. I've never attempted such before." She closed her eyes. "I can feel the heat all around us in this glass tank. Let me see if I can—" Olivienne gritted her teeth then smiled. "There!"

Castellan wiped her own brow in the noticeably cooler ship. "What did you do?"

"Pyrokinesis is about manipulating heat, fire, and the like. I used my channel to move the heat from one side of the glass to the other. I'll probably have to do it periodically until the trip is over."

Castellan gave her a tired smile and leaned her head back against the glass wall, letting the swaying of their trip atop the great wave lull her into a light, tormented sleep.

Olivienne tugged Castellan's sleeve and she sat up straight. "It's been fifty meens, Tosh. Should we attempt to contact my maman?"

"Yes." Castellan removed the stone from around her neck and handed it over.

Olivienne shut her eyes and cast her thoughts out into the nothingness, trusting in the strength of the stone she held, as well as the one in her mother's possession.

Maman?

They were moving with incredible speed so she kept trying every few meens, hoping to get a response. *Maman? ??*

Can you hear me?

Olivienne?

Yes! We're on our way back to Annexus, but we've got critically wounded.

"Did you make contact," Castellan asked.

"Yes."

Kesharan?

Olivienne couldn't feel any emotion in the telepathic exchange but she knew her mother would be worried about Kesh. *He is safe and Havington is dead, along with many rebels.*

Thank the Makers!

We should arrive in— She broke off the exchange and turned to Castellan. "When are we supposed to arrive in Annexus?"

Castellan looked at her chrono again. "Perhaps another forty-five meens? Eurynome wasn't exact with her time but we've traveled a little more than an oor."

We are estimated to be less than an oor out. Do you have a telesana healer available?

I'll have one ready.

Castellan reminded her, "Ask her to pass word to Leniste and Renou that we'll be a strange sight coming into port."

Good. Please let the generals know that we'll be approaching the docks in a strange glass vessel, courtesy of Eurynome.

The Atlantee queen?

Olivienne winced as her channel strained at holding the long-distance communication. *The same. Will speak later, must go now.*

Be safe, love.

"What did she say?"

"They'll have a healer waiting for us." Both of them looked at the three reclining bodies near the back of the vessel. Dozier had yet to wake from the blow to the head, Lazaro was in a significant amount of pain from his badly broken leg, and Holling was unconscious as well, taking shallow breaths but still alive.

The port city of Annexus could best be described as controlled chaos. There were a few dirigibles moored at the transportation hub seen in the distance, and even more fishing vessels near the docks. The glass ship dropped lower and lower in the water as the pushing wave slowed, until they traveled forward at naught more than a gentle pace with nary a wake behind. Haulers, some painted with the medican sign, awaited them. More prominent was the large group of black-clad shields milling around looking tense, but alert. The queen and king stood in the middle.

Olivara strode straight to the water's edge and crouched down to submerge her hand. She and Eurynome shared a communication, the contents of which none of them knew as they were all still aboard the Atlantee vessel. Olivara stood again after a meen and the ship pushed forward.

Intuition struck her and Castellan called out. "Close your eyes."

Secs later, a breeze blew inside from the newly opened top. They were up against one of the many docks so she instructed the team to unload the wounded directly into the medican's care, saving Holling, Dozier, and Calderon for last.

"My Queen, we need someone with telesana for these three. Things are dire. Oh, and I should tell you that we're probably a good seven oors ahead of the *Vestigo*. They're carrying all the prisoners that Havington kept on the island."

Olivara nodded but Castellan saw that the queen wanted nothing more than to run to her children. Unfortunately, there were priorities that the leader of Psiere had to follow.

"Never fear, Captain. I've brought along two, one you well know."

Renou stood next to the queen as a familiar face pushed through the crowd.

"Gem!" Olivienne pulled their friend into an embrace. "Quickly. I believe Holling is the worst, but the other two may be easier." Another doctore stepped through the crowd of shields onto the dock. The man looked vaguely familiar, but Castellan couldn't put a name to the face.

He called out to Gemeda. "I'll work on the other two if you wish to take care of the medican." Holling was recognizable enough with the symbol of his specialty sewn onto his black shirt.

Healing assignments sorted, Olivienne and Kesharan took the opportunity to greet their parens. The other doctore spoke to Castellan on the way by. "You may not remember me, but I was the one that healed you in Pentole a few rotos back."

She nodded. "That's why you look familiar. Many thanks for that dae."

"It doesn't appear as though your life has slowed much but I'm certainly glad to see you whole and hale upon our second meeting."

"More healing, less chatting!" Gemeda said.

Castellan walked to where Gemeda sat cross-legged upon the dock. She was cutting away more fabric from Holling's trousers to get a better view of the injury. "Good to see you too, Gem."

Gemeda glanced up at her with a tight smile and Castellan easily read how worried her friend was. "I'd be happier if you stopped bringing your people back to me broken."

The comment, though light-hearted, struck Castellan to her core. She let out a weary sigh. "I tried not to. I did."

Just as Castellan could read Gemeda after so many rotos of friendship, the ability also ran the other way. "Something happened."

Castellan pressed her lips together and nodded, afraid to speak in that time of visibility.

"Let me get your medican squared away and we can talk later, yeah?"

She sighed. "Much later I'm afraid. I'm sure I'll be tied up in the debrief for a time with all that's happened."

"That's fine. And just to warn you, I'm not sure how much of his leg I can salvage. It's obvious that he lost a lot of muscle, tissue, and blood vessels. I can't heal what doesn't exist." She tilted her head and added, "Though it does appear as though someone has already tried."

The end of Holling's career as a shield was yet another guilt piled atop the teetering heap in Castellan's mind. "I saw that and assumed as much. Do what you can. We'll deal with the rest later. As for the partial healing, we have a one rated telesana on the team. He received the antorae-stone and a crash course in telesana while in the field just to get Holling this far."

"Captain."

Castellan stood at the general's call and made her way to where the three elder psi were gathered with Olivienne and Kesharan. "Ser?"

Renou checked the time on her chrono before stuffing it back into her pocket. "General Leniste is slated to return from his position at the bridge road in thirty meens. You have that amount of time to refresh yourself before we convene in my office on this base. Anyone can direct you there if asked."

"What of the bridge offensive?"

"Successful. But now is not the time. Savvy?"

Castellan swallowed. "Yes, ser. And my team?"

A black-clad lieutenant stepped forward and Renou gestured toward her. "This is Lieutenant Felde. She'll work with Madlin and Soleng to get your shields settled together in a barracks, then her team will take over Olivienne's security detail."

Castellan didn't need to see Madlin or Soleng's faces to know they'd be bristling. "Why—"

Renou held up a hand and spoke to both lieutenants directly. "Temporarily. You and your unit have gone above and beyond expectation. I see you and I know you're all feeling every ince of your bodies right now. Rest and heal so you can be up to snuff again when we head north."

"North?" Madlin said.

"Back to the capital, of course. For now, consider yourselves on holidae. But first I want your entire unit to check in at the field hospital for a full evaluation. You're dismissed."

"Yes, ser!" They saluted and glanced at Castellan.

Madlin and Soleng gave her a nod then left, taking with them the rest of the shields that were not injured enough to ride in the medican hauler.

"Tosh?"

Castellan looked at Olivienne and noticed the king, queen, and sub-connate had left, taking with them three quarters of the shields. "Maman says they have a room where we can refresh before your meeting."

A quick glance toward the dock revealed that everyone was gone, probably rushed to hospital once Holling, the worst wounded, was stable enough for travel. All that remained was the strange glass ship. Someone had looped lines around the spires near the front and back and had pulled it tight to the floats to keep it from slamming against the dock. "What will you be doing when I debrief?"

"Having my own meeting with Papan."

Castellan knew her love well. Olivienne would need to speak of all that happened to them on that island. If only her path were so clear. The more she thought of what she'd done and how she'd used her power so mercilessly, the heavier her rank insignia grew upon her collar. She kept her thoughts locked down tight so as not to broadcast them unintentionally to anyone else, especially the powerful telepaths in her life. "Well enough then, love. Let's go wash off the worst of the grime."

Thirty long meens later, Castellan pushed through the door into the office she'd been directed to. Inside she found Olivara, Renou, and Leniste seated around a meeting table. She saluted then took her own seat.

The queen spoke first. "In this debrief we'll cover the results of the bridge offensive, the current intel coming from the shield and defense clairvoyants and prescients, and lastly, we'll learn of the events on Ruina. Germain, please start us off. How many enemy dirigibles did defense bring down?"

He sniffed. "We didn't have a final count of dirigibles but it sure enough looked to be all but a handful of the ones Lieutenant Cando reported on. We were aided a good bit by the large tonal oscillators installed on our ships. As you know, our biggest concern going into this were the ground forces the rebels had under their control, namely those poxing automatons."

Renou prompted, "You obviously succeeded."

"Yes. One of my smarter bombardiers knew about the mechanics of the automatons and found a way to jam the signal from the rebels. It helped immensely that they were also foolish enough to meet us near Annexus. I suspect Havington didn't want to lose control of the bridges so he front-loaded their defense toward the Endara side."

"Casualties?"

"Twelve lost their lives and one hundred and seventeen were wounded. Most of those were minor enough to not need extended field hospital stay. We drained all of the doctores with telesana to do it but I've been told they'll be at full strength in a few daes."

The queen frowned and Castellan recognized the pain of losing her people written plainly across Olivara's face. "What of the dirigibles?"

"A few of ours hit the sea, which was responsible for most of the casualties. Havington lost all but one. We got confirmation from Captain Dondin of the *Gryphem* that Ser Enik Gannon was spotted on the stern observation deck of the lone retreating dirigible."

"Bollux." The curse slipped out before Castellan could still her loose tongue. She'd hoped that all the rebel leaders had been taken down.

Renou met her gaze. "You have something to say, Tosh?"

"Gannon is a loose end. He doesn't have the power or influence that Havington had, but he may be more dangerous because of that lack."

"The fact remains that he lost his cred, his benefactor, and most of his people. My hope is that once we've cleaned up this mess and reunited all of Psiere, we can finally put to rest much of the distrust and mystery those rebel sympathizers have for the current leadership of our land. All said and done, that will make it even more difficult for Gannon to recruit followers."

Leniste shook his head. "You know it won't be as easy

as all that. There is a lot of pain out there. Healing from this rebellion will take rotos or more." Everyone goggled at the typically gruff general. He growled. "What? I wasn't born yesterdae. I've read my share of texts and spent time on the defense lines facing off against Atlantee and rebels alike."

"I never doubted you, friend." The queen sighed. "The rebellion has damaged the land, the people, morale, and our entire society. Psierians have lost their trust in what's right and what's wrong. Not only that but making peace with the Atlantee will upend everything we've known for generations."

Renou nodded. "Travel will open up in some ways and in others it will become more limited. I think we can better address the ramifications once we get detailed maps of the continental shelves."

"It's one of the many announcements that will go out in the coming daes. But we're straying from the agenda. Let's get things back on track, shall we? Camen, you're up."

General Renou cleared her throat. "Everything coming from the joint task force we put together points to insufficient rebels left to hold their current power structure on Dromea. Lieutenant Kensata had a vision of Havington sending most of his rebels to the bridge when they reported our forces amassing in Annexus."

"Perfect for us, wasn't it?"

Olivara smiled at Leniste. "It certainly was. We can make plans to apprehend the rest tomorrow. I want you to assign two commanders to lead troops across the span and round up any remaining rebels. Make sure they've got sealed power sinks and empathy in abundance. People on Dromea are sure to be frightened. I want to get word to everyone down there that things will get better." She turned to Renou. "Camen, put together the security force for me to take a trip south later this lune."

"That seems a bit risky so soon after—"

"Risky or no, they need to see that I care! All my people need their queen and I won't back down from the pathetic remains of any rebel force left."

"I'll start planning after this meeting."

Olivara placed her hand atop Renou's where it rested on the table. "Thank you." Then the time Castellan had been dreading was upon them. "Captain, tell us of the events on Ruina."

"Tosh, you said Velten and crew were a number of oors behind you and your own group arrived in an... unconventional way. How did that come about?"

"We—" She paused to suck in a centering breath and a subtle probe caressed the back of her mind. She didn't react to Olivara's attempted intrusion but shut her down just the same. The queen may be the most powerful telepath on Psiere but the stone hanging around Castellan's neck was plenty powerful enough to prevent a breach of privacy. Too much had happened that was out of her control and every time Castellan touched on the events with Havington in her mind, she spiraled deeper into blackness. There was no way she would allow anyone else to be privy to that.

Castellan swallowed thickly. "We altered the mission from the original plan we conceived of before leaving Annexus." She went on to detail the events leading up to finding the prisoners.

Olivara leaned forward and rested her elbows on the table. "Was Kesharan with the rest then?"

"No, that's the point where we split with Velten's team. There were significantly more hostages than we'd anticipated. I instructed Lieutenant Wern and his team to escort the prisoners back to the *Vestigo* because they'd been starved and worse. We got a tip from one of the hostages about the location of the sub-connate. We found him but got pinned down in the process."

Leniste's raised his thick eyebrows. "Did they have so many rebels on the island that you couldn't counter their defense with the power of your stone?"

Castellan looked down briefly, then met each one of their gazes around the table. "We were trapped in the sub-level of an officer's quarters with no sight to the enemy outside. I'd instructed Velten to do whatever she needed to do in order to get those prisoners loaded. Unfortunately, that garnered the attention of the remaining rebel dirigibles assigned to Ruina."

"So, you were pinned down and enemy dirigibles were heading toward your ship."

"Yes, ser. Given everything that was going on, I ordered Velten to get back to Annexus as soon as possible and told her I'd find another way to extract my team."

Leniste nodded. "And you did."

She sighed because it had all come down to those final meens. "I didn't. The small group of rebels on the island were easy enough to take care of once I cleared the building from our heads. Unfortunately, Havington and five more rebel ships flew over Ruina on their way to aid in the bridge defense as we sheltered in that hole. When those blasted rail guns began firing down on us..." She trailed off because she could still feel the shaking beneath her feet and smell the smoke of burning buildings. The smell of burning flesh. Castellan picked up a nearby cup of water to garner a little time to collect herself.

"Tosh? What happened next?"

Castellan met Olivara's violet gaze. "Havington gave Olivienne an ultimatum. He would spare everyone but me if she were to surrender. But the rebels kept firing on our location, honing their railguns. One wall exploded and something struck Olivienne in the head, rendering her unconscious. Havington wanted an answer and she could no longer give him one." She shook her head. "With both the connate and sub-connate in mortal danger, multiple shields critically injured, I did the only thing I could to end it."

Perhaps Olivara could sense the darkness in her turmoil despite the mental shields, because she gentled her voice. "Tosh, there is no judgement in this room. I promise that whatever you did in that ugly situation to end it and bring my children and your shield unit home was necessary."

Castellan smiled mirthlessly. "It's not on your conscience now, is it?"

Leniste growled, "Tosh, that was out of line."

"Yes, I was. Olivienne and I had discussed the possibility of using the antoraestone again in a manner similar to that above King's Marsh. I told her I'd take full responsibility and I will. With no hope left for any of us, I combined my channel with Olivienne's. I suspect Soleng was in there as well because we were both holding her up, see?"

"I don't see at all. What did you do?"

The effects of their channel merge were hard to explain but she tried anyway because she knew she wouldn't have to do it again. "Soleng isn't powerful like Olivienne or myself but he's a decent rating in both pyrokinesis and ferrokinesis. That, mixed with Olivienne's six rating pyrokinesis, my seven-rating telekinesis, and that blasted antoraestone produced a wave of superheated flame that exploded outward from my position at ground level."

"Were you able to damage the dirigibles then?"

She laughed brokenly. "Damage. You could say that. There was nothing left."

Renou sucked in a breath. "Of the five dirigibles?"

"Of anything. The soil was scorched and cracked. Motos were blown backward and charred, dirigibles down, and the rebels, they—they were more ash than bone. There was no opportunity to discern true rebels from ones who were merely led astray by Havington." Reliving her darkest time had taken its toll and Castellan used the thumb and forefinger of her right hand to rub deep into her eye sockets in an effort to stay the tears.

Olivara leaned close and gave her hand a squeeze, much the way she'd done with Renou a short time ago. "If you need a meen, Tosh, we'll understand."

"A meen. I've had nothing but meens from the sec we left that island. Ruina was certainly named well." Castellan knew she sounded half mad but maybe that was okay because there was something broken inside her. She continued with her story instead of dwelling upon her failings. "We evacuated everyone to the dock to explore our options. Three of our wounded were critical and the only viable water vessel left didn't have enough power to return us to Annexus."

"What did you do?"

"It's what Olivienne did. She came up with the idea to contact the Atlantee and request travel aid. You know the rest of the story from there." The office was silent for a meen as Olivara and generals digested her information.

"Tosh—Castellan, we'll understand if you need some time. You've gone through something that no one else has, not once but twice. Healing will need to happen for everyone, not just those trapped on Dromea by Pon Havington and his rebels."

"Renou is right, Tosh. Give yourself time and a few therapeutist appointments and you'll be fighting fit in no time."

"Germaine, a little empathy please. She's not an automaton." Olivara turned to her with sad eyes. "Whatever you need, I'll be sure it's available. I owe you a debt of a lifetime for what you've done for my family. Psiere owes you a debt."

Castellan stood from her seat and drew herself up to full height before saluting all of them. "After considering everything that's happened during the past roto, I think that debt can be taken care of in full if you honor my request."

"What is your wish, Tosh?"

She reached into her uniform and withdrew the antoraestone necklace. The pendant grew warm in the palm of her right hand as she stared at the shiny surface.

Leniste was first to speak. "Tosh, what in the—"

Castellan cut him off while meeting Olivara's intense gaze. "I am officially resigning my position in the Shield Corp as I'm no longer fit to wear this." She dropped the necklace onto the table in front of Olivara, then carefully placed her rank insignia next to it with her left hand. Castellan's palm ached from where she'd gripped it too tight on the walk from their temporary room and sat with it in her hand throughout the meeting. No one had even noticed that it was missing from her collar. She finished her action by saluting again.

Leniste's face flushed with anger. "You'll do no such thing!"

Renou gazed at her intently, perhaps trying to understand why she'd make such a reckless and career-ending decision. And the queen...

Castellan tightened her mental shields to prevent yet another intrusion attempt from that faint if familiar touch. That she addressed directly. "Queen Olivara, please respect my mental privacy." Castellan stood firm. "I didn't make this decision lightly and this is the debt I'd like to collect."

Olivara looked as though she'd argue but, in the end, she merely nodded. She'd been trapped by her own word. "Very well. If this is what you truly want."

"It is, my Queen."

"You are dismissed then."

She made to turn back toward the door when Renou called out, "Tosh, at least sleep on the decision."

Renou's gray eyes were shadowed and Castellan knew they'd all been touched deeply by the rebellion in some way. "My dreams won't be any more pleasant, nor will my answer change. I'm sorry, General."

"It's okay, Castellan."

With those words, Castellan abandoned the office and her career.

Chapter Eighteen

Olivienne's meeting with her papan was long over, but she'd yet to see or hear from Castellan. She had no way of tracking her down either with her regular shield team off duty. However, there was one person that her shields could easily locate. She stuck her head outside the door of her quarters. "Lieutenant Felde, where is my mother?"

"I'll be just a meen, Connate."

After a brief code-laden conversation across the voteo, Felde met Olivienne's gaze. "Queen Olivara is in her temporary office not far from here. It will be quicker to walk than call for a moto. Do you wish an escort now?"

"If you please."

"Yes, Connate." Felde whistled to the rest of the shields on duty and they fell in beside Olivienne as she followed the lieutenant through a warren of closely packed buildings. The location was as close as promised and they arrived at the heavily guarded structure a few meens later. Her shield team stayed outside as Captain Torrin led her through the front entrance and down a hallway.

When they got to the door at the end, Olivienne touched his elbow. "Have you seen Tosh?"

He frowned. "She—" He shook his head. "If you don't know then I think it's best you speak with your mother first."

Torrin's words were unsettling and Olivienne grew tired of the mystery of her missing love. She gave the door a sharp rap before pushing through with her mother's call of "enter."

"Something is going on and I'd like to be let in on whatever it is. Where is Castellan?"

Her mother sighed and took a healthy swallow of scotch before waving Olivienne to sit in the other chair. "I was hoping she'd return to you after our debrief. Your confusion and the fact that you haven't seen her tells me that you're probably unaware of her decision."

"Decision?"

"Captain Tosh has resigned her position in the Shield Corp, effective immediately."

Olivienne reeled with the new information. "What? She—" Castellan was her rock, but more than that, they'd agreed on open communication long enough ago that the unilateral decision stung. Olivienne was hurt and was self-aware enough to know there would be no hiding that fact from anyone, especially her own mother.

"Why ever would she do such a thing?" Fear clenched her belly before Olivara could answer. "Was it me? Did I put too much on her with this mission?"

"Darling, no. If anyone pressured the good captain, it was me. The power of the stone was onerous and I should have never asked Tosh to take it."

Her mother's words only added to Olivienne's confusion. "But with it we won this war. Havington and his rebels are gone and Psiere will return to normal at last."

Another sip of the scotch and shake of her head. "Not all of Psiere, 'Vienne. Some will never be the same after the violence perpetrated by Havington and us alike. Not just for the ones that lost loved ones, but for those forced to kill their fellow psi."

"You mean Castellan."

"Yes." Her mother finished the drink and slammed the cup onto the table with a loud *crack*. She stood and began pacing. "The sovereign is supposed to put the good of the nation above all else. The few for the many."

Isn't that what they'd always done? "But, Maman, I've never known you to do less than such."

"I'm afraid that in this case, I've fallen short. But Makers forgive me, I'd make all the same choices again, offer up Castellan's conscience and worse to have you and Kesharan back safe. I understand her choice and her sacrifice as well as her pain, but the loss of life was worth it to me."

"To me as well."

Her mother sighed and poured another drink. "To paraphrase your captain, it's not either of us that will pay for that decision. That lies solely within the realm of Castellan's heart and mind and I fear it's too heavy a burden for her to bear."

Fear struck Olivienne. Too much? She'd known other psi who lost battles with depression and grief. Healing the body was relatively easy but that wasn't the case for healing the mind. Olivienne knew that fact well after lunes of speaking with her father about her own guilt and grief. "What do I do?"

"I don't know, 'Vienne."

Olivienne was speechless. Her mother was never shy with her opinions or advice. Meddlesome to an extreme. "What do you mean?"

Olivara stopped and spun to face Olivienne, radiating anguish. "It means that I don't know!"

"But—"

"I don't always have the answers and I'm not infallible. I'm trying my best here, love, but I'm afraid I've failed your future par." She shook her head. "You were right with what you told Keshien rotos ago."

The pain in her mother's voice was hard to hear but the statement left her curious. She couldn't remember any specific thing she'd said to her papan. "What was that?"

"You told him that Castellan was the most honorable person you'd ever met, that her spirit shined purer than any other."

"Oh." She vaguely remembered gushing to her father about Castellan right after admitting their love for one another. "You remember that?"

Olivara moved closer and took both her hands. "Of course. I remember everything if it has to do with the path of your health and happiness. And we both know that Castellan is part of that path."

Olivienne pulled her into an embrace. *We'll get through this. Tosh is strong and she's not alone. Perhaps Papan can help her the way he's helped me these past few lunes.*

Perhaps. Or maybe it's you she needs until she finds her feet again. Be patient with her, darling. Her mother squeezed her tighter.

"She's been nothing but patient with me, I can do no

less than to honor that love in return." Olivienne stepped back and straightened her shirt. "Now, I suppose I need to make good on that pledge and go find her. No one seems to know where she's disappeared to."

"I think I can help with that." Olivara closed her eyes and Olivienne knew she was drawing on the stone in an effort to search for Castellan's mind. "She's near the cliffs at the southern end of the city." She opened her violet eyes and it was like looking into a mirror. "It's a ways off. Take my personal moto and you can probably make it in time to see the suns set."

"I will and thank you." Olivienne took a step forward and placed a kiss on her mother's cheek before turning on her heel and exiting the office.

It took some work to convince Lieutenant Felde to agree to an escort small enough to fit in the moto outside. Even so, Felde called for another moto on her voteo so the rest of the unit could follow behind them. Less than ten meens later they stopped along the roadway. Olivienne saw someone sitting right on the edge of the tallest out-cropping. She knew it was Castellan from the shock of pale hair alone. Beyond that, the slumped figure bore no resemblance to the strong soldier she had grown to love.

A part of her feared Castellan would do something rash so close to the edge. But the logical voice in her head said the distance wasn't so high that Castellan couldn't save herself with levitation should she fall. But would she want to?

Olivienne directed her shield team to stay at the moto, much to Felde's displeasure. Thoughts, fears, and pleas ran through her head as she approached the woman on the cliff.

Castellan spoke without looking at her as soon as she drew near. "If you're here to change my decision, don't bother."

Olivienne took a seat next to her, admiring the color of the sky as Illeos chased Archeos toward the horizon on their right. "Love, I've come to tell you that I'll support whatever you decide. Just the same as you've always done with me." Castellan focused her pale gaze on Olivienne. There were dark circles beneath her love's eyes, as if she'd been awake many oors. Perhaps she had. Castellan looked wounded, but from an injury that was beyond the skill of any medican or doctore.

"I'm tired and I don't want to be in Annexus anymore."

"I know, darling. And we'll head back to Tesseron as soon as our people are fit for travel. We won't leave any of them behind."

If anything, her words only served to make Castellan draw farther into herself. "We should never have gone to Ruina. I keep wondering if things would be different, better, if we'd only stayed and waited for an alternate plan."

Olivienne shook her head. "I don't think we could have avoided much. After all, it was prophesy that took us to Ruina and prophesy that brought us back again."

"But still—" Castellan ran a shaking hand through her hair.

She recalled something her papan told her when she said much the same thing after King's Marsh. "We've been lost in a maze with many paths to the center."

"And?"

"Meaning since the beginning we've been wandering left and right, choosing each direction with the knowledge we have at the time. I think that no matter what choices we made, we were always destined for this standoff with Havington."

Castellan pounded her thigh with a fist. "There were so many lives lost, 'Vienne! Another path could have prevented that."

"Or, another path could have seen even more death and destruction. Another path could have executed my entire family if Havington had won. Papan pointed out that if we hadn't stopped those ships from continuing their journey to the battle at the bridge, they would have arrived long after we thought we won, taking our forces by surprise." She paused to let that knowledge sink in for a sec.

"Leniste's people would come out on top."

"I'm not so sure about that and neither were my parens. Pon Havington was smart. He'd hid his agenda and rot from all of us for decarotos. The blasted man had plans within plans. No, there were no guarantees."

A broken laugh was drowned out by the crashing waves below. "No worries of that now. I took care of the man and his machinations."

"No, you didn't."

Wide, fearful eyes looked up at her. "What do you mean?"

She placed a hand on Castellan's wrist, hoping to soothe her. "I mean it took an entire shield team to reach and rescue Kesh. And love—you didn't end it all on your own."

"Well, it sure as sheddech wasn't anyone else unleashing unimaginable power on our hapless enemy!"

"That power wasn't all yours."

Castellan quieted. "I told you I'd take responsibility if it came down to that again and I have."

"You don't get to make that decision for me. I was as responsible for the destruction as you were. My power, yours, and that blasted antoraestone. But you know what? I'd do it all again if we stopped him from hurting Psiere, tearing apart one more family or killing another psi. You saw those prisoners, love."

She sighed. "I remember."

"Psierians are a proud people. We're strong, innovative, and capable of great things. We may not know where we came from, but as a people we've got vision enough to see where we're going."

"You don't understand."

"You're right. I'm not a soldier. But I've been fighting for our people just the same. Even I saw that the events on Ruina went well beyond any we've faced before, up to and including King's Marsh. But we did what we had to do because there were no other options. We can wish and what-if for rotos to come but that won't change anything. This war was a stone thrown into the lake of our people that will cause ripples for many rotos to come. All we can do is move forward one step at a time and soothe the water as we go."

Castellan straightened and lifted her chin to meet Olivienne's gaze with a little more certainty. "Your observation is wise and more than a little out of character."

Olivienne laughed. "Yes, well, I'm good at remembering what I learned from my papan. He's got a keen understanding of the world around him." She paused then offered a tentative suggestion. "Perhaps it would help for you to speak to him? He's known a lot of pain in his heart and carries his own share of guilt. He's also got wise advice, as you heard."

"Maybe."

The humore from meens before fled on Castellan's next exhale. She leaned against Olivienne's side and the connate wasted no time wrapping her in an embrace.

"My heart hurts." Castellan's breath hitched and Olivienne stayed silent. In all their rotos traveling together, she'd never once seen her captain cry.

"I know love. I know."

"I didn't want to do that. I wouldn't wish such flame on anyone, enemy or other. I just—" Another breath shuddered free. "I didn't have a choice."

Olivienne pulled her tighter as Castellan cried into her neck. "None of us did, darling. But you're not alone. I've got you."

Castellan gasped. "You still respect me after all that? After what I've done?"

"Oh, my dear Tosh, you're incapable of commanding disrespect. I don't have to put you on a pedestal to see that you're the most adept, honest, and dedicated person I've ever met. I will always trust you to do the right thing when the hardest times come."

"You have a lot of faith in me."

"I have faith in *us*, my darling captain."

A long sigh blew the loose hairs that escaped Olivienne's braid. "I'm no one's captain now. I gave it all up."

"Yes, well..." She waited until Castellan pulled back to meet her gaze and winked. "You also gave up being my lover at one point." That earned a small smile. "I'll be honest and say I don't think I could do what I do without you by my side."

"You don't need me in order to work as an adventurist."

"You're right, I don't. I need you in my life in order to
be happy and heart full. You've made me a better sovereign and psi with your support, wisdom, and love. I hope
you know that."

Castellan pulled away until just their shoulders
touched and gazed at the colorful sky. "I don't know what
to say."

"Say you'll at least consider coming back." Castellan
looked as though she'd protest and Olivienne held up a
hand to stay her words. "You don't have to do anything
right now. Take the time you need to think about what you
want and where you're going. Just don't throw it all away
quite yet, okay?"

"Did your mother tell you to ask that?"

She spoke from her heart. "No. This request is a
purely selfish one. Some future ruler I am, putting my own
needs above those of others."

"You're allowed to be selfish, 'Vienne. But you're
right in that it's not me in this alone. It hasn't been me
since that leviathan stole you below the waves. Let me
take this break to do some hard thinking and I promise to
consider our future before I make another rash decision.
I'm sorry for worrying you."

"Nonsense. You're entitled to whatever path forward
you see. I'm only asking for you to step back and look at
all your options first. Put some distance between you and
what we faced on that blasted island. I'll support however
you need and promise to give you the time and space to
think it over, honoring whatever decision you make."

Castellan gave her a smile that was finally more hopeful than sad. "I appreciate that." She discreetly wiped her
eyes then lifted herself into a standing position using her
levitation channel. "I'd like to go home now."

Olivienne raised her own hand for help up. "I told you
that we're stuck here until the team is better."

"I didn't mean back to Tesseron. My home is you and
I'd like to spend some time together to remind me of all I

saved instead of those we lost."

The admission left her speechless for a sec. "Okay."

They were halfway back to the moto when Olivienne finally organized her thoughts. "Tosh," she said.

Castellan met her gaze. "Yes?"

"I feel the same way. Let's go home."

Castellan was surprised that it took Gemeda two daes to track her down. Despite not having an official duty, Castellan kept plenty busy in the aftermath of the rebel engagement. Leniste had taken a number of Defense Corp platoons as well as scores of automata across the long expanse of bridges into Endara proper. Unit after unit of dedicated soldiers, her previous loyalty, went off to collect the rest of the rebels running loose. It was on Leniste to reassure the people that things were on their way back to normal until Queen Olivara could take the tour herself. But there was plenty of repair work for those left behind in Annexus.

Castellan rested on a pile of construction material after helping the engineers repair one of the nearby docks. It was a familiar task and well within her expanded power rating. She glanced toward the approaching small-statured woman and took another bite of her middae meal.

"I've been looking for you everywhere. It's as if you've been hiding from me."

Castellan chuckled. "Clearly not everywhere since I've been here all morning.

Gemeda frowned and sat next to Castellan. "I even asked your future par and she told me you were off helping a team of engineers." After a pause and vexed look, Gemeda grumped. "Do you know how many groups are working on this Maker forsaken city?"

Two more bites finished the roll and Castellan dusted off her hands. "You're certainly in fine form this morning.

Gem shoved her shoulder. "Be serious! I've worried about you." Her gazed moved up and down Castellan's body, taking in the loose shirt and trousers tucked into comfortable boots. "Are you off duty? It's been so long since I saw you without that black uniform, I forgot what you looked like."

"There is no duty to be off from. I resigned my commission daes ago."

"What? When was that?"

Castellan sighed. "At the end of our debrief meeting, the dae we arrived back in Annexus."

"Oh, Tosh."

Gem was her oldest and dearest friend and Castellan knew she wouldn't lecture. "I'm not sure what the future holds for me now. I agreed to give the captain role some thought once I've had time and mental space away from Ruina. I promised Olivienne."

"But you don't want to."

Castellan glanced to her left. "I'm not sure. I loved this post, truly. You know me well enough after all these rotos that it ticked a lot of boxes for me. But the weight of what I did is heavy. Some daes it's hard to breathe when I think about it. And my team...I just don't know any more. Penn requested a transfer back to the Divinity Corp, and Holling—"

Gemeda rested her hand on Castellan's forearm. "I'm not going to lie and tell you that everything will be fine, at least not like it was before. We both know the scars left by battle. But your medican, he's a tough one. Have you spoken with him?"

"No."

"Why not?"

"I—" Castellan ran a hand through her tousled hair. "I've been afraid to. I'm the one who led the mission that cost his leg. I ended his career."

"It's not on you to take Havington's evils into your heart or your conscience. Havington and his rebel blackhearts cost Gren Holling his leg, *you* saved his life."

"That doesn't lessen my guilt."

"I suppose not. I know he's been speaking to a therapeutist as well as a Shield Corp advisor about his future."

Castellan looked at her with surprise. "What do you mean? I would think he'd be out of shields without the use of his leg."

Gemeda shrugged. "Normal active shield duty, sure. But there are many jobs he'd be uniquely suited for. Holling has gained a wealth of knowledge and experience while serving in Olivienne's unit. Perhaps it will help ease your own guilt if you can aid him in planning out his future."

Her suggestion had merit. Castellan thought of all Holling's qualifications as well as his curiosity and empathy for greater beasts. Was there something out there for him better than what he'd been doing? Perhaps. "I'll give it some thought. Thank you."

"Good. Now, I've heard whisperings that you and Olivienne will be heading back to the capital soon. Would you two care to share evening meal with me tonight? I'm afraid I'll be in the field a bit longer, helping to heal soldiers and prisoners alike."

"I think 'Vienne would be amenable. I'll let her know when I return to our room after I've finished here for the dae."

"Good. How about nineteen hundred? There is a quaint eatery in Annexus proper called Esca. It's away from the docks and this poxing defense base."

Castellan laughed. "Is it any good?"

"Better than defense rations."

"Fair enough." One of the engineers waved at her from near the docks. Castellan stood and brushed off the back of her trousers. "Hard work is never done. We'll see you then, Gem."

Gemeda waved with her fingers before wandering off and leaving Castellan to her voluntary duties.

The eatery in the city proper was as tiny as Gemeda promised. The three friends were shown to a small dining alcove in deference to Olivienne's security needs. Even though Castellan was no longer on duty or a member of Olivienne's shield team, she had special permission to carry her pistol at all times.

Castellan's original shield unit was under orders to remain off duty until the night before their scheduled departure to Tesseron. That meant Lieutenant Felde and her temporary team escorted them to Esca. Gemeda was already seated in the eatery but jumped up to give Olivienne a hug as they approached. Lieutenant Felde stepped forward to block the action until Castellan grabbed her arm.

Felde gave her a cross look but Castellan explained. "Doctore Gemeda Shen has permanent access to any sovereign. She is the one who healed Queen Olivara and the Atlantee queen during peace talks this past lune."

The lieutenant bowed and met Gem's gaze. "My apologies, Doctore Shen. I've heard of you but never seen your face. I would have remembered one so well sculpted."

Olivienne covered her mouth to prevent a laugh from escaping and Castellan shook her head at Felde's casual compliment.

Gemeda sniffed and gave a little bow back. "It's no problem, really. I do try to stay below notice most of the time so it's understandable that I get overlooked."

Felde sent one more volley toward the seemingly oblivious doctore. "Surely a psi as talented and mesmerizing as you would never go unnoticed."

Gem narrowed her eyes. "Lieutenant."

"Yes, Doctore Shen?"

"Have you seen the officer's clubs where only those of sufficient rank may enter?"

The lieutenant blinked. "Uh, sure. Why do you ask?"

"Think of me as an officer's club. One whose minimum rank is captain." Gem winked at the tenacious woman and offered her a kind smile.

"Oh. My apologies then for my inappropriate advance."

Gemeda reached out and squeezed the woman's hand. "No need for apology. My ego was well and truly stroked, so thank you."

Olivienne could no longer hold in her giggling once the three of them were seated. "By the Makers, you have men and women falling for you wherever you go. How do you get through your daes so put upon?"

Even Castellan laughed at that. "She's had plenty of

practice. I assure you."

"*Pssh*, like you're one to talk, Tosh!"

"In my defense, it was naught more than dallying with drones while I waited to find my queen."

That only set Olivienne laughing again. "I'm no queen yet, darling. Do I need to worry about you in the meantime?"

Castellan leaned closer and gave her a sweet kiss. "Never. Not for as long as we live and beyond." Olivienne met her gaze and the air grew heavy between them. They moved toward one another again but were interrupted by a finger snap near Castellan's right cheek.

"Enough of that! No tasting the honey while your poor friend is left without a hive."

Castellan pushed her hand away. "You are full of hot air. I know from past experience that you can find yourself a companion quite easily."

Gem ignored her retort and smoothly changed the subject. "Can we all look at the food list now? I'm fair famished after another dae of healing."

"You're a spoil sport!" Despite Olivienne's protest, the three of them studied the list and were ready when a server came around to take their orders.

After their drinks were delivered Olivienne started again on Gem. It wasn't bright inside but Olivienne dramatically shaded her eyes with one hand as she peered around the eatery. "Hmm, perhaps your own source of sweetness could be in this place."

Gemeda pushed her hand down. "I'll have you know that I don't need to pick such low-hanging fruit. I just so happen to have plans after our dinner tonight."

"Plans?"

"A nightcap."

Castellan grinned. "And have you had a nightcap with this person before?"

Another sniff from the doctore. "Mayhap."

Olivienne rubbed her hands together. "Maybe I can guess. Is it Velten?"

Gemeda snorted. "No! That dalliance is well and truly over. We are too tied to our respective careers."

"That's what she said!"

Castellan grinned. "I'm going out on a limb to say it's another captain."

"Oh you!" Olivienne slapped her arm. "You're just saying that because of what she told Felde earlier."

"No, I'm saying that because I've known Gem a long time and I trust my gut feeling on this."

Gemeda smirked across the table. "You've a big head, Tosh. How could you possibly know who I'm having a nightcap with later when I've said naught about it to anyone and we've been discreet?"

"Who do you think it is, Tosh?"

Castellan took a sip of her vineo and did her level best not to start laughing at either of her dinner companions. Olivienne for her curiosity, and Gemeda for her indignance. She piqued both their tempers when she responded with, "I think I'll keep that knowledge to myself for now." Then, Castellan smoothly changed the subject. "Did your mother say when she was planning to tour Dromea?"

Olivienne gave her a hard stare before answering. "Not for a few wekes. Maman conceded to both Renou and Leniste's wishes to verify all the rebels are caught before she makes the railer trip south. For now, we're returning to Tesseron so we can decide how we want to present the discovered Maker information to the people of Psiere."

"And plan for your oathing ceremony."

Castellan made a face at how things were happening so fast around them.

"What was that look for?"

"Nothing, love. It's just hard to believe we're on the cusp of the rest of our lives. Some daes I feel like we've been on this journey forever and others I'm amazed I get to wake each morning with you."

Olivienne looked as though she'd steal another kiss but was stopped by a server bringing their dishes. It took another oor for the trio to finish their meals and make their way outside. Three motos were already waiting in front of the eatery. Two for Olivienne, Castellan, and their on-duty shield team, and a lone moto for Gemeda.

Gem held out her arms. "Ah, my dears, this is where

we part. I'm afraid I'll be too busy to see you off tomorrow."

The three embraced and Olivienne slid into the open door of their moto as Gemeda walked away. Castellan called out, "Hey, Gem?"

Her friend paused and looked over her shoulder. "Yes?"

"Be sure you tell Captain Torrin I said hello." Then, as Gemeda stood sputtering in front of the eatery, Castellan slid through the doorway after Olivienne and closed it behind her. Laughter filled the moto as it pulled away.

Chapter Nineteen

For security and speed's sake, Queen Olivara took a railer up to Tesseron while Olivienne and her team made the trip on the *Vestigo*. Velten's crew were no worse for wear upon their arrival in Annexus with the captives from Ruina. The entire shield team, other than Holling, had been fully healed by doctores with telesana in the wekes before the return trip. Even Specialist Penn accompanied them after agreeing to stay on with the connate's team until their arrival back in the capital. Because of Holling's injury, he was confined to the *Vestigo's* med bay for observation for the entirety of the trip.

Castellan waited for them to get underway proper before taking her leave from Olivienne and Velten on the bridge. She glanced at her pocket chrono. "I've something to do but I will return in time to walk with you to the mess." Olivienne gave her a curious look and Castellan responded silently. *I'm going to speak with Holling. I've put it off too long.*

Are you sure you don't want me to come?

I'd rather you didn't for this discussion. If you don't mind?

Not at all, darling. Perhaps you could speak with Penn, too.

Maybe. It depends on how my talk with Holling fares.

Okay. I'll see you later.

Castellan nodded and left, her boot heels ringing on the deck. Within ten meens she stood outside the med bay. Castellan drew in a deep breath and squared her shoulders. Though she'd never admit it to anyone, she felt nude without her uniform. Resigning her position meant she was without more than a mere career. Castellan was left rudderless and lacking purpose, a feeling she'd never experienced in her adult life.

The door opened and Yazzie pulled up short before she could collide with Castellan. "Oh! Sorry, ser. I didn't realize you were coming in."

"No harm, Almeta. And call me Castellan, if you please. Or Tosh. There is no longer need for rank or title, or any of the deferment that comes with either." Yazzie blinked slowly, clearly unused to hearing her former captain address her so casually. Castellan held back a smile. She didn't mean to shock the woman but it was important that they all get used to her new status.

"Yes, ser—uh, Castellan." She made a face. "Sorry, but that sounds all sorts of wrong. I'll just call you Tosh, if that's okay."

That did make her smile. "Well enough."

Yazzie glanced toward the door that swung shut on its own after she pushed through into the passageway. She lowered her voice to barely a whisper. "I just want you to know that none of us blame you. Not even Gren. We were in bad straights back there and you got us out. It was just a rare turn of events that saw him lose his leg."

Castellan swallowed and nodded. "Thank you for telling me."

"Have a good dae, ser." Then Yazzie saluted and spun on her heel, most likely headed back to one of the bunk rooms allotted for their team. Castellan snorted and pushed inside.

"Captain Tosh! Hey, I'm sure happy to see you."

"You are?"

Holling shrugged. "I know you've been busy with the dock repairs and official business but I wanted to take a meen to give thanks for all you did back on that island. If not for you, well, the lot of us would be prisoners or worse of that Havington. We'd have never made it back."

His statement was like a flame scorching the tenderest part of her heart and she couldn't keep the guilt-fueled words from escaping. "But I was the reason you were there!"

"Ser?"

"I led us all to that Maker-forsaken island and nearly lost the lot of you. Not to mention…" She swallowed down the lump in her throat. "I cost you your career. No, Gren, you owe me no thanks. And you certainly don't owe any sers. I resigned my commission with the Shield Corp wekes ago."

Though he was seated in one of the comfortable beds, Holling straightened as much as possible. He narrowed his eyes. "Why did you go to Ruina?"

"It was my duty."

"No, ser. It wasn't any of our duties, yet we volunteered anyway."

She shook her head to deny his words. "I made it our duty and led the entire team into unimaginable danger."

Holling slapped the bed next to his hip. "Pardon me, ser, but you and Connate Dracore told us all we could stay back if we wished. You said it was volunteer only but the entire unit wanted to help you right all those wrongs and get our people back. We knew the risks and made the trip anyway. Why did you go to Ruina?"

His repeated question gave her pause. Why did she go to that blasted island? Was it prophesy or duty to Psiere? "I don't know."

"But ser, you *do* know. Our unit shared the same drive to defeat Havington and rescue the sub-connate. Connate Dracore was no soldier, yet she stood up the dae we were to depart and vowed to fight for all of Psiere. None of us could do less."

Castellan had never seen him passionate for anything but the greater beasts and his words gave her pause.

Holling drew in a calming breath and slowly released it. "What I'm trying to tell you is that we were all doing our duty when we went to Ruina. You're our captain, sure. But no specialist follows blindly. They taught us that in Shield Corp training. This—" he gripped the smooth stump poking from his shortened trouser leg. "This was not your fault. I'm proud that we were able to do what needed done and without any of us lost. I told my therapeutist that I'd have traded both my legs and more, my life, to see that man dead and our fellow psi home safe. That's the Maker's honest truth."

His speech was a lot to take in all at once. It turned much of what Castellan had feared or assumed on its ear. She was certain he'd blame her as she blamed herself. Castellan sank into a nearby chair and sighed. "I don't know what to say."

"Say you'll give me a recommendation."

"Come again?"

Holling shrugged. "The word of a Shield Corp captain on active duty carries a lot of weight. They're not retiring me from the corp. Rather, they're asking for a commendation and I was promised they'd find a place for me where I can still contribute to the well-being of my sovereigns."

"I—"

He continued excitedly. "Did you know that not all guardians serve as, well, guardians?" She shook her head. "Some work in the palace in direct service to the queen in other capacities, such as administres, clerks and the like due to security clearance around a sovereign. You'd remain in your corp but working in a less active capacity."

Castellan had read every bit of material, rule, or regulation regarding an active-duty shield unit but admittedly didn't know much about the corp outside that specialty. His words sparked a career idea. She'd have to speak with Olivara but the more she thought about it, the more the notion twanged her intuition channel. Each sec that ticked by expanded her certainty. "Hmm…"

"Ser? You have a strange look upon your face."

"I've an idea for an essential duty that I think you'll like. One that would also require higher than average security clearance and advanced adventurist knowledge. Things you're easily qualified for."

His eyebrows lifted with surprise and he smiled. "Yeah?"

"Yes, but I'll need to speak with Queen Olivara first. Do you trust me with your future?"

"I think I've proven that I do."

His words caused a familiar twinge of pain but it quickly dissipated on the back of her grand idea. Not only could she keep Holling in the Shield Corp, but perhaps there was a way to keep Ciera Penn as well. "I appreciate that. You've helped me more than you know todae. I'll get back with you as soon as I speak with Queen Olivara."

"Thank you, Captain."

"I'm nobody's captain now, Gren."

"On the contrary, ser. You're more my captain in this meen than you've ever been. If you quit now, you'll be letting more than yourself down."

She didn't answer him because there were no words left. Castellan could only nod and leave the med bay the same way she came in.

Her next stop took her to one of the barracks cabins where off duty specialists were housed. She found a handful of the team inside. Soleng, Meza, Leggett and Devin were throwing cubes at a table as Penn read from a book on a bunk in the corner. Everyone stood and saluted as soon as she entered. She waved them off. "At ease. I'm not an officer anymore." Castellan shook her head and grinned. "Save your energy for the next captain, yeah?"

Devin responded. "But ser, we don't want another captain." Meza elbowed him but nodded along.

"Be that as it may, I'm still not an officer. I only came by to speak with Ciera for a meen."

Penn came closer. "Ser, is there something I can do for you? My transfer is already approved, in case that's what you're here for."

"No, I—" Castellan stopped and gave the rest of the group a significant look. Soleng took the hint and herded them out.

"Come on you lot, it's about time for middae meal anyway."

She nodded at him on the way out then turned her gaze to Penn. "Please, have a seat." Once the younger woman was settled, Castellan spoke. "You know that they're letting Holling stay in the Shield Corp?"

"Yes, ser. But mine isn't the same case as Gren. There is no physical reason for me *not* to be on active duty. I've just—" She sighed and rubbed her hands together anxiously. "I've lost my taste for adventure after Ruina."

"Is it adventure that you grew tired of, or violence?"

Penn cocked her head. "I guess I associate all of it with my job as a Shield Corp Guardian. But if I could separate the two, I'd say that I've grown weary of death and destruction. This past roto has been hard and I miss the sheer joy I experienced in discovery."

"And if Olivienne had no more war-like skirmishes, what would you say?"

The specialist contemplated Castellan's words for a few secs before shaking her head. "No. I don't think I could take that chance. I've been speaking to a therapeutist. The entire team has."

"I know. Myself included."

"Well, my therapeutist said that what I've suffered has been traumatic enough to cause intense anxiety when faced with any dangerous situation. I'm afraid my future in the Shield Corp was sealed at that diagnosis. I can't guarantee I'd perform my expected duties to protect the connate when needed. My only option was to transfer back to something sedate, like what I used to do in the Divinity Corp."

It wasn't the first time Castellan had heard of such a thing. It was rare but not unheard of for soldiers to suffer mental trauma and be unable to continue in their career. "Yes, I'm familiar with that injury. Your need to transfer is understandable because no matter what you think, mental trauma *is* a physical disability. But that's not what I'm here to speak with you about. I'm currently putting together an idea for Holling to continue his service in the Shield Corp. One that will take into account his unique qualifications and experience serving with Olivienne's unit. I think the post I'm considering would be well-suited for you, too. It's more of a discovery role."

The specialist's eyes widened with Castellan's statement. "Post? And this is something multiple psi could do, not just Holling?"

"It is. But I can't say more about it until I speak with Queen Olivara. I don't want to get yours or Holling's hopes up if the plan is for naught. I only want to know if you'd be interested in such a placement, instead of back to the Divinity Corp."

"And there would be no chance of violence?"

"Not any more likely than if you were stationed at the Temple of Antaeus."

Penn stared off toward the far wall and rubbed her earlobe. She met Castellan's gaze again after a meen. "I'm interested in this mysterious post provided it meets my mental fitness requirements."

Castellan clapped her hands, happier than she'd been in daes. "Excellent! I'll let you know as soon as I speak with the queen and find out if she thinks my idea has merit."

"Okay." Penn stood. "I suppose I should catch up with the others in the mess." She made it to the door then turned around. "Thank you, ser. I'm aware that you've got your own struggles coming out of that battle but I want you to know that you didn't fail any of us. I will never forget my time serving under your command." She saluted then pushed out the door.

Castellan sat in stunned silence before remembering her own pledge to walk Olivienne to their middae meal.

There was much work to be done before their arrival in Tesseron. First and foremost, on her list was to write a position proposal for two specialists and hope Olivara would say yes. Because, like a canid with a bone, Castellan couldn't get her plans out of her head. Olivienne thought the idea was brilliant when Castellan finally filled her in but it wasn't either of them that would say the yay or nay of it.

Despite the fact that the *Vestigo* was significantly slower than the queen's railer, they were able to fly straight to Tesseron and arrived within two oors of the cathedress, right around fourteen hundred. It was due to Castellan's impatience that she requested an audience with Olivara as soon as they got their gear stowed away in Olivienne's royal residence.

"Do you want me to come with you?"

"No, I think I'll present my idea alone. But maybe…"

Olivienne gave her a flirtatious smile. "Yes?"

"Maybe we can order our meal in this evening and spend some time with some vineo and a good soak after."

Laughter spilled from between her lips. "If Maman likes your idea as much as I like that one, I'm sure it's as good as approved. I'll make the arrangements for later."

Olivienne gave her a little shove toward the door. "Now, go get your work done so we can play for the rest of the dae."

"Yes, ser." Castellan grinned and gave her lover a salute then left to make her meeting with the queen.

Less than thirty meens later Castellan had already laid out her plan. Olivara sat comfortably upon her lounger. She held a cool glass of vineo fruit juice with one hand and rubbed her bottom lip with the other. It was a similar motion to what Olivienne did when in deep thought.

"You said you spoke with Holling and Penn about this?"

"I didn't give them my idea. But they both stated they'd be amenable to a position that would allow them to stay in the corp and contribute to the greater good. They trust my judgement in regard to their future careers and knowing where their skills could best be applied."

Olivara nodded. "It's an unusual request but also an excellent idea. I've been speaking with Keshien about this, trying to come up with the best possible option for staffing that station and others. The information gathered there will be invaluable."

"Olivienne and I have done the same during our off times."

"I'll make it happen. I'm going to speak with Camen tonight and instruct her to put people on it right away. She'll be the one to give notices to your specialists about their new placements. Oh, and speaking of Renou, she wants to meet with you tomorrow sometime about filling those three spots on your shield team."

"She told me. I know I left you all in a bind by stepping down the way I did so I agree to help find the replacements necessary to be sure the team is fully staffed."

Olivara paused and stared at Castellan, though unlike so many times before, she didn't feel the push of mental intrusion. Instead, Castellan felt another kind of pressure from those familiar violet eyes boring into her. "You've done well, Tosh, and your team's faith in you is deserved."

Castellan protested but stilled her words at Olivara's raised hand. "No, I know of your arguments and guilt. But

even your stubborn head must admit that you've truly
earned their loyalty with your service and honor. Please
keep that in mind regarding your own future career as
well."

Olivara's point had merit, not that she'd admit such in
that meen. Castellan clearly had a lot of thinking to do. "I
will."

"Good. Before you leave, I do have a few topics of my
own to go over. Please remind Olivienne that we have a
strategy meeting tomorrow to plan for the release of our
people's history. We should create a united front when I
tell all of Psiere about our origins. Oh, and my adminstre
set a meeting tomorrow afternoon with your parens about
the consoral ceremony schedule."

"But that's lunes away. Shouldn't we focus on reunit-
ing the land first?"

"Trust me when I say a royal consorage will go a long
way toward doing just that."

Castellan made a face. "I've grown weary of political
machinations."

Olivara took a sip of her juice and shrugged. "People
want the truth but they also want to be happy and hopeful.
Your consorage to my daughter is about more than pledg-
ing your lives to one another. It's a fact I thought you
understood by now when it comes to royalty."

She sighed. "I suppose you're right. I'll let Olivienne
know. I'm sure she'll be thrilled." Olivara laughed and
Castellan groaned internally. She could only imagine what
her maman would be like in person. She'd already
received a scathing missive when enroute back to Tesseron
about not informing her family that she was alive.

"Now, if I know my daughter, she'll have you locked
in that house as soon as you return for the evening so best
you be off."

Castellan felt her cheeks warm with her words. "Olivienne and I will see you tomorrow at nine hundred oors for
the first meeting. Good dae, my Queen."

The sovereign scowled. "It's Olivara."

"Yes, ser," Castellan responded, before spinning on
her heel and striding from the room.

"Blast you, Tosh!"

Castellan jogged up the walk toward their residence and both guardians on duty gave her a salute. Lazaro grinned. "Good evening, Captain Tosh." She huffed at the rank but didn't bother correcting him. She supposed it was payback for ignoring the queen's request meens before.

Lear held out her hand. "I'm to relieve you of your cycle key, ser."

"What?"

Lear looked at her fellow guardian. "What was it the connate said, Laz?" She turned back to Castellan and pitched her voice higher to mimic Olivienne. "Be sure she can't leave once she arrives back at the residence. I've got plans for her that will fill the evening."

Lazaro tilted his head forward and winked. "We assume she means some sort of strategy meeting."

Lear kept her hand out and wiggled the fingers.

Castellan snorted and dug the cycle key from her trouser pocket. "Yes, I'm sure that's what Olivienne has planned." Once the key was turned over, Castellan made her way up the steps and inside. The guardians' laughter was cut off when the heavy door shut behind her. "'Vienne?"

When she got no answer, Castellan took a step toward the stairs that led upward from the foyer. She opened her mouth to call again and her pistol belt abruptly disappeared. Castellan peered down the hall, then moved her gaze up to the landing high above. Olivienne stood there with the belt in hand, wearing a mischievous smile.

"You won't be needing this now." Olivienne glanced over her shoulder toward the open door behind her and the belt disappeared.

"That better be hanging from my hook."

"What if it's not?"

Recognizing the prod for what it was, she replied, "If you can't secure my pistol appropriately, then perhaps I'll need to secure you."

Olivienne laughed and apported the top button from

Castellan's casual shirt. "Promises, promises." Then she turned and walked into their bedroom suite.

Castellan took her time going up the stairs, unbuttoning her shirt as she went. She lifted an eyebrow as she took in the scene through the doorway. "Oh ho, what's this? Do you have concerns that I'm unable to hold you in place with my channel now that I've given up that stone?"

"On the contrary, love, the ropes are for you."

"Come again?"

Olivienne waggled a finger at her. "Oh, my dear *former* captain. I figured we could celebrate since you're no longer in command. We may as well see what that's like across the board. Besides, it may do you some good to let go of that tight control you have."

Castellan sputtered at the preposterous notion then she sighed. Perhaps her lover's idea had some worth. "I'm amenable," she said hesitantly.

A wide grin met her acquiescence. "Good. There are rules for this evening."

"I was a soldier for the past fifteen rotos, give or take. If there is one thing I can do, its follow rules."

"Good. Rule number one is that I make and break all the rules." That statement made Castellan laugh but she motioned for Olivienne to continue.

"Second, no touching me *or* using your channels unless I give you permission."

That part of the game sounded decidedly less fun. If there was one thing Castellan enjoyed, it was putting her mouth to Olivienne's soft flesh and hearing those delightful mewling cries of pleasure. Not to mention, she couldn't always control some of her channels. They were instinctual. She opened her mouth to protest but only managed, "But what if—" before Olivienne held up a hand.

"Do you agree or not?"

"Of course, I'll try..."

"No exceptions, Tosh. And to be sure you follow my rules," Olivienne opened a drawer in the stand next to their bed and withdrew a palm-size box that looked to be fully coated in wax. "I've brought along something to guarantee compliance." With a flex of Olivienne's pyrokinesis, the wax around the box clasp loosened enough for her to open it.

Castellan felt the immediate dissipation of her channel strength as soon as she saw the power sink. "How in the blazes did you get that?"

Olivienne smirked. "Velten. She figured out that wax would seal them away and make the mineral safe for transport. She let me take this one upon request."

"Devious. You are much too devious when it comes to tormenting me."

"Mayhap. But now, I believe we should start with a calming bath involving my finest bottle of vineo and some casual foods from our favorite eatery."

It took less than five meens for them to undress and slide into the deliciously hot water. Castellan groaned. "I didn't get much of a workout on the dirigible this morning but even still, this feels perfect. It's been so long since we could relax without a care for mystery, prophesies, or war." Olivienne was reclined on the opposite side of the tub and both held glasses of southern vineo. It was sweeter than some of the others from the cellar, but still refreshing.

"I agree. I feel as though we've been running from one place to another for the past few rotos."

Castellan smiled. "What's this, is my infamous adventurist finally tiring of all the adventure, or, Makers-forbid, slowing down?"

That drew laughter from Olivienne's vineo-stained lips. "Absolutely not. But there are many pleasures I enjoy in life. One of them is sleeping in a sturdy bed without a guardian on the other side of the door to hear every word and thought."

"I suppose that is an unfortunate side effect to having full-time protection."

Once they'd finished their food and were down to just the smallest bit of vineo in the glasses, Olivienne set hers aside. "How are you feeling, love?"

"Relaxed, loose, and all-around better than I have in lunes. Though I'll admit to you and no one else that I'm concerned about the meeting with my parens tomorrow. You know how my maman is."

Olivienne laughed. "I find your mother's concern delightful. Certainly, a far cry different than the meddling from my own."

Castellan nodded to concede her point. But when all was said and done, objectively she knew both their parens loved them and that was what mattered most. She'd deal with Cassiene's ire when or if it came.

"You're thinking too hard. Your first order is to kiss me."

"That simple, hmm?"

Olivienne crossed to Castellan's side of the tub, sliding the front of their nude bodies together. "Less talking, more kissing."

Castellan quickly moved her own glass out of the way. "Yes, ser—"

Touches above and below the water, tongues meeting and twining together, all of it served to heat the couple faster than Olivienne's channel had been known to do. When they finally pulled apart, Castellan was breathing hard and questioning every bit of the stamina she'd bragged about on many occasions. She was reassured that Olivienne seemed to be just as affected. "Should we take this someplace dryer?"

Olivienne didn't answer. She abruptly stood and Castellan delighted in watching the water running off every curve and angle of her body. Dark hair splayed around her shoulders, tendrils sticking to Olivienne's neck and breasts where they'd gotten wet during their passionate activity in the water.

"Darling."

"Hmm?"

"Tosh."

Castellan finally looked up to meet the violet eyes that dominated her dreams. "Yes?"

"My next order is for you to dry me, but *only* dry. Nothing more."

A small whimper escaped at the thought of moving her hands everywhere across the smooth skin of her lover, but Castellan would never give in. "I can do that." To prove her point, she pulled herself up as well, then stepped out of the bath and grabbed a towel. Olivienne removed the stopper from the bottom and held her arms out.

"Be thorough now, and I'll put in a good word for you after."

The comment made her laugh. "A good word? Whomever would you need to profess my talents to?"

Olivienne responded, "Your new commander, of course. After all, if you've left the Shield Corp, you'll need to be searching for a new duty or risk going mad." She lifted a leg from the bath as the water drained and Castellan moved the drying cloth down the toned expanse.

"I thought you were my commander?"

"For now, anyway."

Castellan moved on to the other leg and her breathing grew more rapid being so close to Olivienne's treasure. "Not for always?"

A dark brow lifted and Olivienne smirked. "I mean, it could be arranged. I don't know if you know this, but my mother *is* the queen."

"She may hold the throne but you are the one who rules my heart." Castellan knew as soon as the words left her mouth that they were outrageously sweet and wasn't disappointed when Olivienne burst into laughter.

"Is your slick tongue good for more than just compliments?"

Castellan winked as she dried the final few drops from the top of Olivienne's foot and stood holding the towel. She'd mostly air dried while performing her duties. "There is only one way to find out. What is your next order, Connate Dracore?"

Olivienne's gaze traveled the length of Castellan's body and her intense look gave Castellan chill bumps. "I want you on that bed, ready to bend your will to mine."

Feeling a bit of humore along with anticipation, Castellan saluted her then marched nude into the bedroom. Olivienne's intentions were obvious, though it wasn't a role she was familiar with. Castellan lay back upon the bed and extended her wrists and legs out toward where she knew the soft ropes to be located. "What would you have me do next?"

"Do I need to tie you, or can you be trusted to stay in that manner?"

"I—" Castellan hesitated. There were many things in life that she'd been exposed to where she could definitively say how she'd react. This wasn't such a situation. "Truthfully, I have no blasted idea. I've never done this before."

"That's answer enough then."

Castellan wasn't sure if she liked that particular grin on her lover. It spoke of much mischief or torture to come. She couldn't wait.

It didn't take long for all four limbs to be secured. "Can you move?"

Castellan gave an experimental tug to her restraints. "Not really."

"Perfect." Olivienne said as she crawled up the bed toward Castellan's head. She purposely rubbed their bodies together as she did in the bathing tub. Even the kiss was familiar and warm. Just as earlier, the heat between them built until Castellan thought she'd conflagrate. Olivienne abruptly pulled away and Castellan sagged.

Olivienne traced patterns across Castellan's chest, shoulders, nipples, and stomach. "Tell me, did you get enough to eat earlier?"

The change of topic was confusing. "I'm well sated. Why do you ask?"

"You're telling me that you wouldn't be interested in something sweet if it were offered to you?"

"You know I've never been one for sweets, love."

A smile met her response. "I've got a multitude of sweet words from you that say different." Olivienne swung her leg across Castellan's torso and straddled her stomach. Castellan clenched at the wetness against her skin. "With enough effort, I'm certain I could persuade you to taste some of my nectar."

Her breathing increased and Castellan panted. "I don't think you'd have to try hard at all."

Olivienne didn't give Castellan a chance to say more. She swiftly moved up Castellan's body until her knees were on the pillow to either side of Castellan's head. Olivienne's moist, pink folds were just out of reach above her lips. "'Vienne, you torture me!"

"Do you want this?" Castellan nodded and Olivienne lowered herself ever so slightly, then pulled upward again at the last sec.

"Do you want me?"

Castellan met her gaze and answered from her heart. "With everything that I am or ever will be."

"Good." Then Olivienne lowered herself to within reach. "I expect you to be thorough."

Castellan's words of acknowledgement were muffled as she put her mouth to work. Olivienne was already so aroused Castellan could feel the skin tightening against her tongue and she knew release was imminent. The time finally came when she took that delightful clitoral nub gently between her teeth and lathed it with her tongue. Olivienne screamed and shook above her as Castellan switched to a sucking action.

She continued to work her lover until a weak hand moved from the wall above them to caress her temple. That was a signal Castellan learned a long time ago that meant Olivienne was overly sensitive and needed a reprieve. Castellan tilted her chin up to breathe properly, cognizant at the way her own body and need throbbed with her heartbeat. She checked in to distract herself. "Are you okay, love?"

Olivienne moved backward again and collapsed on the bed next to Castellan. "Never better. That was particularly intense."

"You don't say?"

"I do. As a matter of fact, I think this bit of privacy is what we've needed for a time now." Olivienne paused and Castellan knew she'd become aware of how tense and on edge her body was. The heat in her face alone told Castellan that she must be flushed, but the panting and squirming within her bonds were a definite clue as to the extent of her arousal.

Olivienne leaned close to Castellan's right ear. "I think it's time we took care of you."

"I—I would be most appreciative."

Olivienne wasted no time in moving her hand down Castellan's body and straight through her sopping wet folds. Intense pleasure caused Castellan to pull the ropes taught. Pressure within her head built rapidly with each slick caress and Castellan tried everything within her power to hold off the impending explosion.

Olivienne must have sensed her attempt at control. She leaned even closer and whispered into Castellan's ear. "Love…let go. I've got you."

That was all it took. Pressure increased past the breaking point. Castellan closed her eyes as spots danced in her vision. A wave of intense pleasure crashed through her body again and again until Castellan's voice became raw from her hoarse yells. She sagged in her bonds and Olivienne pulled her fingers away, causing one more great shudder to wrack Castellan's body.

"Are you okay?"

It took a meen for Castellan to catch her breath enough to speak. She panted as though she'd run halfway to Dromea and back. "Just a sec." It took a few more calming breaths for Castellan's heart to slow. She opened her eyes and grinned at Olivienne. "I thought all the danger was behind us. I had no clue you'd try to do me in with pleasure alone."

Olivienne burst into laughter. "I'd say you're in a sorry state indeed if I could accomplish that. What kind of soldier are you?"

"Clearly, no kind."

"No, I think you just needed this release, perhaps in more ways than one."

Castellan contemplated her words. "Perhaps."

Olivienne loosened the ties from Castellan's arms and legs then took a few secs to rub the reddened skin. "How do you feel now?"

The question was loaded and Castellan took serious stock of her body and mind. "Better. You were right earlier when you said you were ready for a break. I think I needed this recharge and quiet as much or more."

Olivienne opened her mouth to speak and Castellan already knew the question. She pulled her lover closer and kissed her to stay the words. "No, I've still not decided on my future. But I will tell you that time and distance from that wretched place is definitely helping. I'll let you know as soon as I make a decision about anything." she said, when they broke apart.

"Promise?"

"On my honor, I do."

"That's good enough for me. Now, how about we seal that power sink away and do this again in a more creative way?"

"Is that your way of saying you'd like to be held down next?"

Olivienne sniffed. "Mayhap."

Castellan grinned. "Well, then, I think you have the best ideas. You find a candle and I'll grab the striker from downstairs." She got up and headed to the door, laughter following each step.

"Tosh! Perhaps put some clothes on?"

"Why ever would I do that? You've told all the shields not to disturb us for the evening."

Olivienne covered her eyes but managed to speak around her laughter. "Yes, but Maman has been known to stop in whenever she pleases, usually to the mortification of whatever lover I've got here at the time."

Castellan drew herself up and threw her shoulders back. "Well, then, if she insists on looking through a spy-glass then your mother better get used to seeing ships." And with those cryptic words, Castellan left the room to search for something to make a spark.

Chapter Twenty

"I'm not going to lie, Tosh, it was hard enough to fill this role before you appeared in our sights. But now that you and Torrin have set a high standard for all Shield Corp captains to come, well it's nigh unto impossible now."

"I'm sorry, ser."

Renou waved away her words. "I'm not angry with you in the slightest. I understand why you made the choice but it doesn't change the difficult strait you've put us in."

The general's words served to pile more guilt atop Castellan's heaping stack. Logically, she knew Olivienne's team needed a captain. To think otherwise fell into the same careless trap that Olivienne herself had floundered in when they first met. "What did Lieutenant Madlin say about a promotion."

Renou scowled. "Hard to get an answer past your lieutenant's laughter. Perhaps you've been too lax with your team. You know I don't tolerate insubordination."

Castellan swallowed, fearing for Madlin's career after such an action. "I'm afraid that particular trait is all from Olivienne."

"Hmm, I suspect you're right."

"What did you do?"

A paper was thrust toward Castellan. "I did nothing. I understood Lieutenant Madlin's response to be a rejection of promotion. I got the same one, albeit in a more respectful manner, from Lieutenant Soleng, despite the fact that he's nowhere near ready for such a role."

"Oh."

"The velum in your hand is a list of everyone due for promotion with the qualifications to lead a Shield Corp team."

Castellan read the names on the sheet. Most she didn't know but a few were familiar. "So, what are the next steps here? I've no experience with the Shield Corp process as I've mostly been involved with much lower-level advancements when I was with defense. This sort of thing is above my grade."

"Tosh,"

She looked up at Renou.

"We've already asked everyone on that list. They all turned down the assignment."

Shock at the announcement rattled Castellan. "Why would they do such a thing? This is an excellent post filled with adventure and new experiences."   '

"I suspect that right there is part of the reason."

"And the rest?"

Renou ran a hand through her short, stele-gray hair. "I told you that you're a hard one to follow. Some are intimidated by the hybrid nature of the task. Others don't want to try to lead a team after you've been their captain."

"By the Makers, I'm not some peerless psi or soldier! I tie my boots, make mistakes, and sleep on the top of the bunk like everyone else."

"It's more than that, Tosh. Think on it. Not only will the next captain be tasked to lead an advanced, highly specialized unit that has been places and seen things no other Psi have seen, but they'll be following in the footsteps of the most powerful psi we've ever recorded."

"But—"

Renou held up her hand. "The same unit whose former captain will be looking over their shoulder the entire time because they are to consor with the sovereign they've been tasked to protect."

"When you put it like that..."

"Tosh, I even asked Cando, despite the fact we both know that would most likely end in disaster due to my heart daughter's penchant toward jealousy."

Castellan sighed and frowned. "So, what are we to do?"

"The way I see it, we have three options. We forcibly promote someone who is not well-suited or capable for Olivienne's hybrid shield team, which is not ideal. We let the team run as-is without a captain until a better candidate comes along, which is also not a great plan. Or..."

"Or?"

Renou gave her an intense look. "Or you stay on in a

temporary capacity until a better candidate comes along."

"But won't you need to assign a team to me as well, once Olivienne and I consor?"

"That depends on you."

"How do you mean?"

The general shuffled a few papers on her desk but Castellan suspected it was more to stall than any real need to organize. "This is a topic that has been discussed many times with the king and queen, as well as the relevant Shield Corp heads. It was decided that if you plan to settle into a career here in Tesseron then technically you'll need a team the same as any other royal. However, if you continue to travel with Olivienne on her adventurist missions, there is no reason that team can't serve in a dual capacity."

"And what of those times we need to go our separate ways? I've never had my own security."

Renou smiled at her. "It's true, you haven't. But once you become a royal through consorage it will be mandatory. We can either expand your current team, or add a special micro unit to be stationed here in the capital. On the event that you two travel separately, the micro unit will go with you, otherwise they can be utilized to fill in for team leaves of absence or guard the residence."

It was only nine hundred oors and Castellan already felt wrung-out like a wet cloth. She ran a hand through her hair, not caring in the least that she had at least two more meetings after the one with Renou. "You're making it bugger-all difficult to get out."

"I'm not trying to. But even you must see that the circumstances we're faced with here make this a delicate balancing act. No matter what, we are unwilling to compromise a sovereign's safety."

Castellan glared at her. "And you think I am? I would never leave her unprotected. Never!"

Renou reached across the desk and patted Castellan's hand where she'd crumpled the edge of the vellum in her fist. "I know that and so does the queen." She sat back. "How about this? There are no missions upcoming and it was decided that only Queen Olivara and a contingent of representatives from the Imperium will be traveling south to tour Dromea. That means we can leave things the way they are for now. You and Olivienne, as well as the rest of your shield unit need this break from action. We can revisit this in four weke's time. What say you?"

Castellan considered all the facts on the topic and had to concede that promoting someone unsuited to the task would only end in disaster. Olivienne's adventurist job wasn't the safest and any captain coming in had to see the unique dangers and pitfalls of such a career. Castellan's shoulders slumped as she leaned back in the chair, defeated. "I'd say that's as good a plan as any. We can revisit lists and qualifications after things have had a chance to settle."

"Excellent." Renou slapped her desk and stood. "Now, I believe we've both got another meeting with the queen, king, and a few royal coordinators about releasing the history of Psiere."

She stood as well. "True enough."

"Need a ride back to the sovereign estate, Tosh?"

"No, ser. I've got my cycle."

Renou grabbed her satchel and placed a few stacks of documents inside. "Good machine, that. Truth be told, I'm right jealous of yours."

They walked out of Renou's office. "Why don't you get one?"

"I don't know if you've noticed, but I'm not young anymore and I don't benefit from enhanced awareness like my heart daughter. I wouldn't want to leave Pendar all alone should I do something foolish like die. I'll be sticking with motos for the foreseeable future."

Castellan laughed. "That's a good enough reason as any I suppose."

They parted ways at the door to the Shield Corp headquarters with thoughts of Olivienne's protection and their future running through Castellan's head.

"My Queen, you can't just come out and say it so plain as that."

Olivara wasn't one to be told no often, and certainly

not by one of her administres. "Whyever not?" Olivienne felt sorry for the woman who swallowed and looked around nervously.

"Erm, Psierians may panic."

"Poldia has a point, my Queen."

The queen leveled a cross look at Renou. "Not you too, Camen."

Multiple voices rose at once as the discussion grew contentious. Olivienne glanced toward where Castellan stared off into nothing. She was clearly as uninterested as Olivienne.

Do you think they'd notice if we snuck away?

Castellan met her gaze and grinned. *Hard to say. It depends on whether your mother is listening to our conversation right this sec.*

They both looked at Olivara and Olivienne shrugged. *She seems pretty occupied. What if I said I needed to use the lav and you were kind enough to serve as escort?*

"And what is your opinion on revealing the history of our creation and existence of Tau Ceti, Olivienne?"

Castellan snorted. *Looks like we've been caught.*

Maybe she didn't—

Olivara cut into their personal conversation. *She most certainly did. Please focus on the meeting.*

Castellan and Olivienne answered at the same time, thoroughly confusing everyone in the room that wasn't privy to their telepathic conversation and chastisement.

"Yes, ser."

"Yes, Maman."

"And your thoughts, 'Vienne?"

Olivienne drew in a deep breath. She considered all the fantastical things she'd seen during the past few rotos, the places they'd traveled and strange species they'd come across. The knowledge was a bit overwhelming at first, but she knew within her heart that Psierians as a people would never be able to move forward unless they learned the real truth of who they were, and where they came from.

"I think we don't give our people enough cred. We are intelligent, curious, loyal, and honest. Psierians have been kept in the dark much too long and it's time we led them into the light. Perhaps you can utilize the long-range jump system and give wekely public addresses that will travel across Psiere in a matter of meens. Let's call them Royal Announcements of Discovery. It's easier to swallow a whal if you take it in bites rather than all at once. Start with who the Makers are, then who we are as a people. Eventually you can move on to other races, knowledge of the Atlantee, other lands, and more."

Castellan reached to squeeze her hand as Olivienne looked around the room to see how her words had been taken. All in attendance looked to be in various stages of thought or agreement.

Her father nodded and gave her a smile. "Well said, my dear. It's about understanding the people's needs. Our land has gone through a lot the past few lunes. I think learning of who we are and the real truth behind the sovereigns will go a long way toward un-sowing Havington's rotten seeds."

"They're right. My Queen, you said it yourself to me just yesterdae. People want the truth but they also want to be happy and hopeful. The fire of discovery upon the horizon unites the people just as much as a royal consorage. This is good, right even. I feel it in my gut."

General Leniste snorted and chewed his mustache. "You and your gut, Tosh. I swear..."

"Germaine, your people installed the jump stations on both continents. How possible is such a communication?"

"I think with enough preparation, entirely possible. We can put a general news alert out that will inform Psierians of the dae and time your speech will take place. Not only that, but you can publish the wekely information in the broadsheets for anyone who didn't catch the live announcement."

Olivara nodded with satisfaction. Olivienne didn't think her suggestion would be taken seriously but clearly her mother and the rest found merit. Truthfully, Olivienne had no idea where the notion came from. It simply popped into her head and she ran with it when called upon for her opinion. Perhaps she *was* crafted to rule her people, as Kinsa stated.

She startled as Castellan whispered in her ear. "You're thinking too loud, love."

Olivienne leaned closer. "Why are we whispering and not speaking mind-to-mind?"

"Because your blasted mother is always listening to our telepathic conversations."

They both stifled a laugh as the woman in question was busy dictating what information she wanted covered in the first speech to Templar Aislyn. "You make an excellent point. As for my thoughts, I was merely surprised she took it seriously with nary a sec of contemplation."

"It was a grand idea. Your surprise is unnecessary, I assure you."

She sighed. "You know I've always had concerns about my fitness to rule Psiere. My maman is larger than life sometimes and everyone loves her. I see how different the two of us are and wonder if I could do half as well for our people."

"The fact that you are already concerned for Psierians long before you'll be tasked to sit on the Divine Cathedra tells me there is nothing to worry about. I've always seen greatness in you, 'Vienne."

Olivienne bumped her shoulder. "Even when I vex you?"

"Even then. You were made to be the best of us."

"You're not far behind, you know." She referred to Castellan's own health score from the coder.

"That's different."

She loved the scowl on her handsome captain's face. "How so?"

"I was merely made to be the best of me. Am I powerful? Yes. But all that power is for naught if I have no moral compass or something greater than myself to believe in. And I pledge to you that I believe in your ability to lead Psiere into a greater tomorrow. The strength I carry, my intelligence, power, and everything I am, will be by your side."

Castellan's declaration left her stunned with wonder at how she'd evoked such loyalty. Olivienne nodded and clasped her future par's hand tight. When she got her emotions under control, she responded with two small words. *Thank you.*

They were startled from their private world when a few people stood. Castellan pulled out her timepiece. "Looks like the meeting is ending. Would you like to find midday meal somewhere before we meet again with our parens at fifteen hundred?"

"I'd say you're also capable of sovereign-level ideas." She looked toward her mother. "Maman, we'll see you in a few oors."

Olivara was deep in conversation with Aislyn but managed a wave to both of them before they stepped out of the conference room.

"Why are you walking so blasted slow? It's as if you're expecting sentencing to Iuvenis when we arrive."

Castellan glanced around at the on-duty shields flanking their steps. They were on the royal estates so had no need for an advanced guardian team, just a small group. "You know why."

"Are you so worried about your maman?"

"'Vienne—" Castellan abruptly stopped and gestured the team away to give them some privacy. "I don't think I could take her disparaging my career while I'm in the midst of a crisis of conscience about that very thing. I can't." She clenched her fist. "I'd rather sit out the meeting altogether and risk the queen's wrath."

Olivienne caressed the back of her hand, gently prying the fingers open. "I think she may surprise you."

Castellan didn't answer. She swallowed the sick feeling down instead and gazed toward the door that lay a few foot away. "Maman has been like this for as long as I've been a soldier. I find it unlikely she'll change now. We may as well get it done." She nodded toward Madlin and began walking again. Dozier was ahead of them and pulled the door open. She lifted her chin to the specialist as they went through.

It didn't take long to make it to the chamber where the meeting was to be held. Castellan drew in a deep breath and strode forward, pushing into the room with a resigned sigh. The scene inside was not what she expected. For starters, nobody was seated at the table. Instead, her father and the king were positioned near the drink table while her maman and Olivara stood nearer to the door. Like a group of automatons, they turned toward the younger couple at the same time.

Quick as a flash, Cassiene Tosh, the mother she'd always known to be level-headed and tightly controlled in emotion and deed, burst into tears, and threw herself toward Castellan. The strength of her embrace was surprising. Her father followed soon after and Castellan found herself engulfed in the warmth of her family. Emotion rose inside her and she tried her best not to become overwhelmed.

"Oh, my darling, foolish, Castellan. I'm so happy you've come back to us."

"We were worried about you, Lanny."

Castellan pulled back so she could meet her father's gaze. "I'm fine, I promise." Her mother had yet to let go and Castellan grew fearful that something else was wrong. "Maman, are you well?"

Cassiene released Castellan's waist and moved her hands up to cradle her cheeks instead, searching for something within Castellan's gaze. "I'm sorry."

The pit of dread grew within Castellan's stomach. "What are you sorry about? Has something happened to my sibs or parsibs? The children?"

"No, love. I just—" She cleared her throat and took a sec to glance at Olivienne before meeting Castellan's worried stare. "All those rotos I belittled and took you to task for your defense position, and then when you switched to the Shield Corp..." Cassiene shook her head and Castellan thought she could see where her maman was going.

"Turns out you were right all along. I should have stayed where I was, or better yet, become an instrae like you always wanted."

"What?"

Her mother's confusion only rattled Castellan further. "Isn't that—"

A big hand came down to rest upon Castellan's shoulder. "Lanny, let your mother finish."

Cassiene gave her a watery smile. "I'm trying to tell you that *I* was wrong. I gave you all that grief and hassle and I was wrong. If you weren't the person that you are todae, or hadn't become such a capable and strong psi and gone where you did, things would have turned out poorly for all of us. Your strength and perseverance brought you back." She turned to Olivienne and pulled her into a hug as well. "Brought both of you back. And I'm so grateful you never spent a meen listening to me or bending to my will."

"Oh." Castellan found herself gob smacked for the second time that dae.

"Can you ever forgive me?"

That snapped her out of her daze. "Maman, there is nothing to forgive. No matter my corp or career, I say with certainty that you and Papan contributed and guided the best parts of me. I've found life and purpose to be much like unharnessed aether. We go where we will and the Makers only know if there is direction behind it all. And if we're lucky, we'll meet people along the way who share our passions and drive."

Castellan looked away for a sec and noticed Olivara, Keshien, and Olivienne watching their reunion with gentle smiles. "I've found all that with Olivienne and I count myself lucky that I ended up where I did."

"Well said, Tosh. And speaking of sharing passions and drive, are we ready for refreshments to aid us in planning out your consoral ceremony?"

Castellan laughed and rubbed her eyes at the queen's words. "That depends, is it your personal supply of scotch?"

Olivara threw her smile around the room, looking much like a felid who found good hunting. "Even better. It's Renou's. She made a bet with me some time ago and I won." She apported the decanter into her hand and held it up to show the small group. "Pendar makes it himself. And for you, Cassiene, we've got a fresh pressing of a new juice variety. We found the seeds a few rotos ago, strangely preserved. The horticulturists at academy have been cultivating the bushes and I received a few bottles from their first yield."

Castellan's maman smiled, delighted to be included by the queen. She and her father made their way back to the other side of the table to collect their refreshments. Olivara had clearly discovered that Cassiene suffered from a physical ailment whenever she drank spirits. Castellan met Olivienne's eyes. *Was it you who told her?*

No. I'm as surprised as you are. But I'm glad because I find your mother delightful and would never want her to feel left out.

She surprised me todae.

I told you to wait and see.

So, you did. Thank you for your support.

Darling, you've done as much and more for me during the past few rotos. We're in this together and I'm glad to help.

Castellan leaned close and kissed her. It was short given the fact that all their parens were in the room with them.

I will never take you for granted.

Good to know.

Olivienne giggled when they looked up to find themselves being observed.

A little more than an oor later they'd finalized the timing of the consoral ceremony. Olivara conceded that giving hope was good but it would be disrespectful of the grand scale of lives lost in the conflict with the rebels for them to rush into a nationwide celebration.

Instead, they set the official date for six lunes out. That was enough time to repair the worst of the damage from the fighting, reassure the people of the southern continent that all of Psiere was beloved by the queen, and guarantee decent weather for the event. While the ceremony itself would be held within the Temple of Archeos, it was tradition for celebrations and festivals to take place in every city leading up to the event.

"Do you need to rush off somewhere for your duties?" Cassiene asked, once the meeting was at its end.

Castellan was surprised by the question. Normally her

mother would be the one wanting to escape the social situation. "Actually, I'm free from all my duties at this time."

Her father came to stand next to them. "Because the war is over?"

"No, because Captain Tosh resigned her commission after the events that saved my family and the rest of Psiere from Pon Havington," Olivara said.

Though Cassiene Tosh could be loud, logical, and prone to raging on occasion, Tello Tosh was quite the opposite. Castellan's father was a man known for being positive, happy-go-lucky, and generally calm in most situations. She'd never once heard him yell, which made his reaction all the more surprising. "You did what?"

"Papan?"

"I think your father is just surprised. Right, Tello?" Olivara said.

He nodded, giving Castellan a wide-eyed stare.

She looked back and forth between her parens. "What's going on here? I thought you'd both be happy."

Tello's deep voice broke the strange tension in the room. "Lanny…you weren't the only one on the front lines facing off against Havington's forces. They sent every fighter they could spare from across the corps, as well as engineers and medican staff to southern Endara."

Castellan shook her head. "You don't understand. You don't know what happened."

He put both hands on her shoulders. They were strong and had roughened skin from a lifetime spent handling dirt and stone. "Everyone knows what you all did down there, and the losses Psiere suffered. The broadsheets have spent wekes writing about it."

"You said fighters. Am I to understand that Tessior was there too?" Castellan never entertained the notion that her sibs or their families would be anywhere near the main fighting in the south. A pit of unease formed in her stomach.

"And Temera, as well as Aeryn. Tellesen had to stay in Portorium to direct dirigible spotting forces so close to the capital, and the children were all with us."

"What he's saying, love, is that Queen Olivara misspoke." Castellan smirked when she saw Olivara frown in her peripheral vision. "You didn't just save her children. You shielded everyone in Havington's sights. Your actions, however brutal and traumatizing, ended a conflict that had already gone on too long and threatened every person we love."

"But Maman, you weren't there. They never stood a chance with what I brought to bear."

Her mother's gaze turned fierce. "If you think for one sec I wouldn't have leveled the same force twice again to protect all of you, you're wrong."

"You would?" The notion of such a thing was baffling.

"Absolutely."

"As would I." Olivara joined them. "Perhaps it has something to do with being a mother but there isn't much I'd hesitate to do for my children."

It seemed like something a sovereign ought not to say. "But, what of your people?"

"Tosh, my children are my people, and the other way around. I can love you all as the queen, and there are definitely times when the good of the many outweighs the good of the few. If you lost your foot escaping from a sharc attack, you're allowed to feel a multitude of things. You can be happy you escaped, grateful you have most of your body intact, and still mourn the loss of your limb."

"But some of those people could have been innocent or coerced."

"It's well within the realm of possibility. But I stand by my statement. If it helps, Leniste and his advanced psychic investigators have been able to ascertain that Havington traveled with a handful of dirigibles staffed by only his most loyal followers."

"I—" Castellan ran a hand through her hair. It seemed as though she couldn't find firm footing anymore. The dae had thrown too much at her to process comfortably.

"Castellan, you should trust your instincts more. I always have."

She stiffened at Olivara's words. "Those same instincts saw the sub-connate captured on that island."

Olivienne moved closer and rested her hand on Castellan's forearm. "Tosh."

Olivara looked away for a sec before addressing everyone in the room. "I'm not going to lie. I was ready to rage and blame the world the meen I found out he was stolen away. But looking back now—" Olivara sighed. "It was the right call to make. We needed those power sinks. And the path you followed took you to Ruina and ended the entire rebellion. Multiple emotions, Tosh. I can mourn the loss of life and be angry that Kesharan was taken, but ultimately, I don't blame you. It was the logical call to make."

Olivienne responded quietly. "Captain Velten said the same thing."

Oddly enough, it was the king's words that resonated the most. "We know you're hurting right now, Castellan. Grief is quiet and cutting. It can pull you through each dae in agony, or drag you down and mire you in place. There is no fast way out of it, only time, and we all heal at a different pace. Don't be so hard on yourself, hmm? Look for the balance in your actions and accept that you can't always be in control of every situation."

She met his deep-set eyes and nodded, not letting on how affected she'd been by his speech. The thoughts he put forth touched on everything she'd been feeling. Mired, low, quiet, and cut up inside. And here was yet another person saying she needed time.

Trust him. Papan understands more about grief that anyone else I know.

I remember his story you shared. He's just given me a lot to think about.

She nodded at the king. "Thank you, ser. I'll heed what you've said."

"Good. Now, I've got some free time myself and learned before this meeting that we have a new group of machines created from maker schematics in for review. Would anyone like to visit the storage facility with me?" He glanced at Olivienne, then Tello. Castellan's father brightened at the idea.

Cassiene moved next to Castellan and hooked their arms together. "I'd like to spend a little more time with my daughter." She gave her par a little nudge. "Why don't you go ahead, love."

They turned their gaze toward Olivienne and she smiled. "I've got something I want to speak with my mother about. You should show Cassiene the gardens, Tosh. They've bloomed since she was here."

Plans set, Castellan led her mother out of the meeting room, toward the exit closest to the gardens. She left Olivienne with a telekinetic caress. The king and her father walked down the hall outside in the opposite direction.

Once they were in the gardens proper, they walked along the path in silence. Castellan knew her mother had something on her mind but she was stubborn, much like Castellan herself.

"I meant what I said you know."

Cassiene never turned her head and Castellan recognized the familiar method of emotional control. "Maman, you always mean what you say."

"Not always, Lanny. Tello and I spoke about you and your abilities often as you were growing up. What you have to understand is that I wasn't pushing you toward those other careers because I thought they'd be a good fit. The truth is, your father and I saw your potential a long time ago and we feared for you."

Castellan pulled her to sit at a bench that had been placed near a decorative fountain. "I don't understand."

"You know your avia Tosh was a prescient, right?"

"I didn't know that." She grinned. "I only know that your mamanar vexed you often."

Cassiene laughed. "It's true that I never had a great relationship with Tello's mother. She spent most of her time going on about her stage daes but occasionally she'd have an episode that was more right than wrong. From what Tello says, the entire family learned to listen."

It wasn't a story Castellan had heard before but she was unsure why her mother needed to tell her now. "What does this have to do with me or my career?"

Cassiene picked at the hem of her shirt. "She had the strongest episode anyone had ever seen the first time she held you."

Castellan sucked in a breath. "What did she say?"

"She said your true path was one of greatness but that the way was fraught with danger and heartache." She shook her head. "And when your talents and intelligence developed so strong and so early, I knew she was right." She met Castellan's gaze. "It's as the queen said. I would do anything to protect you, even push you into a path I knew wasn't true to keep you out of the military corps."

They were quiet for a meen until Cassiene laughed ruefully. "In the end it didn't matter at all. Call it destiny or prophesy, or just random circumstance, but you ended up in the place where you could do the most amount of good."

She clasped Castellan's hands. "I know you're second-guessing yourself right now, questioning your own actions, but you shouldn't. You did something only you could do, lifted a weight that was beyond the rest of us, and we are grateful."

"But how do I live with this guilt? How do I carry on down this supposed best path when the way is blurred with tears from what I've done?"

"My darling daughter, I can't tell you how to carry the weight because it's not something most of us can comprehend. But I want you to think of all the people you've met in this life." She pointed toward a gardener on the far end of the sprawling expanse of blossoms and greenery. "Take that woman. Or even one of the guardians I saw lurking about after we arrived in the garden. Which one of their lives would you trade to remove the guilt you feel?"

Castellan leaned away from her mother at such an abhorrent suggestion. "None of them! I would never trade my pain for someone else's life. I find the idea of such a thing anathema."

"But isn't that what your self-castigation is all about? You thinking if you'd done something different, changed your path or altered course, that you could have avoided feeling the guilt and pain that eats at you. And yet, if you changed anything about what has already happened, *everything* would have been different. More lives would have been lost, perhaps those closer to you or me. Havington may still be alive and our queen may be dead. Every little thing we do cast ripples upon the pond of life until all the water is moved on the surface."

The memory of ash and bone assailed Castellan and she attempted to swallow the lump in her throat. Tears followed soon after. "Maman, it was the most horrific thing I've ever seen and I was responsible."

"Did you know that Aeryn was one of the medicans that treated the prisoners you rescued?"

Castellan shook her head.

"Lanny, she said they'd been starved, beaten, and tortured. If you think that Havington wouldn't have done the same to everyone else rejecting his false claim of rule, you're sadly mistaken. That could have been me or Tello, even the sovereigns. I'm not saying what you did or saw wasn't horrific because I wasn't there. What I am trying to tell you is that it was the right thing to do at the right time, even if it hurts."

"But how do you know?"

Cassiene tapped her chest. "Because you've always been here. I trust your judgement more than anyone else. Your gut said it was correct and you did what you had to do. War isn't polite or gentle and death isn't pretty. I'm going to tell you something that I've never told you before."

She looked up to see tears in her mother's eyes. "Okay."

"I respect you the most when you falter and question your actions."

The words were like a shock of cold water. "By the Makers, why?"

"Because you're powerful, maybe too much so sometimes. But you also practice conscientious compassion. You've always been one to analyze your behavior and understand your place in the world. A psi that doesn't question their own actions on occasion will never learn and grow. And if you take nothing else away from our talk todae, I want you to know that I'm proud of every part of you. The dark and the light."

With that admission, Castellan broke down in tears as

her maman held her tight. It was a healing time for both of them, a turning point in their lives to come. Castellan found that she was proud of her maman, too, and thought that maybe, just maybe, she had a path forward past the pain.

Chapter Twenty-One

Olivara gazed at her daughter. It wasn't the headstrong woman of old standing in front of her, but rather someone who had grown into responsibility and compassion for their people as only a sovereign could do. She knew Olivienne had her doubts over the past few rotos about ruling Psiere when the time came, but Olivara no longer saw those doubts in the violet eyes staring back at her. "Do you have something on your mind, 'Vienne? Or were you trying to give Castellan some time alone to speak with Cassiene?"

"I'd say a bit of both. As you know, two of my guardians are transferring out to a new assignment once their additional training is complete." Olivara nodded. "All of us have been through so much and I wanted to commemorate our time together."

"What are you thinking?"

Olivienne unbuttoned the top few buttons on her high collar and grasped the cord hanging around her neck. Olivara knew it was one of the three temple keys from her daughter's mission two rotos before. The pendant was an intricate representation of the highly familiar temple symbol. The interwoven circle and triangle were made of two different metals. The triangle appeared to be copere and the circle made of stele. It was a little more than an ince across and prominently featured a viridian gemstone set in the center. "I would like to have replicas made for the entire team."

Olivara turned the pendant in her palm, studying the design. "They're heavy. I've never seen them you know? Just the sketches that Keeley Greene took north with her. They're quite beautiful, not something I'd expect from the Makers. The green stone is striking but doesn't appear to be native to Psiere. Karillite is the closest I can think of in color if you were looking to match it."

"Actually..." Olivienne cautiously met Olivara's gaze. "I was hoping to use shards of antoraestone for each. I know enough were confiscated from Havington's rebels down on Dromea."

"'Vienne—"

Olivienne held up her hands. "Before you answer let me ask you this. Who have you trusted with my safety, with the delicate knowledge we've faced during the past few rotos? The specialists who have proven their loyalty in a multitude of ways."

"Why is this important to you?"

"You know how Castellan carries guilt for what happened down on Ruina?" Olivara nodded. "I do, too. Leniste already had a team selected for the rescue mission but when I found out that Kesh was down there, I all but forced my way."

"As you do." The words weren't said with malice, but rather with a small smile.

Olivienne dipped her chin in a little nod. "Yes, well, we gave the entire unit the option to stay behind and as one they refused."

"It's literally their job to follow and protect you, no matter where you go."

"Maman, they weren't just doing their jobs. I know them. Maybe not as well as Castellan, but I've spent a lot of time trying to understand my team. They wanted to go just as badly as I, knowing the danger and uncaring as long as it meant getting our people back. Sure as anything, they've earned a whole lot more than my thanks. My only wish is that Savon could have been here to share in our victory."

"I know, my darling. I approve."

"So, if you've questions about their loyalty—I'm sorry, what?"

Olivara laughed. "I said I approve. I trust you and your word." She walked to the table where there was a stack of velum and a stylus. A few secs of scribbling on the page and she presented Olivienne with a name and teleo code. "They can help you with casting the replicas and I'll arrange the stones with Leniste."

Olivienne took the sheet from her grasp then pulled her into a tight hug. "Thank you." When they separated, she gifted Olivara with a grateful smile.

"Will you turn in the keys you've been traveling around with to Zane?"

"I've already spoken with Templar Aislyn about them, yes. At least until I head out on another Tau mission where I think they could be of use."

Olivara patted her hand. "I suppose you should include yourself and Castellan in the order for replicas then. You should be honored as much as your unit. But I have one request for you with the design."

Olivienne tilted her head. "Yes?"

Olivara reached into her ever-present waist pouch and withdrew a small nut shell coated in wax. She shook it and the stone inside rattled. "I want this split in two and worked into yours and Tosh's pendants."

Eyes widened with shock as Olivienne's mouth dropped open. "Is that what I think it is?"

"No. Well, not exactly. This is mine."

Olivienne quirked her eye brow, "And where is the one Castellan turned in?"

"It's locked in a compartment hidden within the left armrest of the Divine Cathedra."

Olivienne sputtered for a sec. "Wha—how—what do you mean a hidden compartment? I've never heard of such a thing!"

Olivara burst into laughter. "You haven't heard of it because the knowledge is only held by queens of Psiere. Passed on from mother to daughter with each generation that comes of age."

"Oh. Does Papan know?"

Olivara shook her head. "This compartment is something nobody should ever know about. It holds the master key to the familial coder, two spare archeostones, and a sealed container with instructions to only open it if something catastrophic were to occur and our population fell below twenty percent."

Olivienne gaped at her like a swimmer on land.

"Surely it must be from the Tau."

"I think that's a fair guess now."

"I can't believe nobody has ever opened it."

Olivara reached up to run the back of her fingers across Olivienne's cheek. "And let us hope that we never have to."

Olivienne's understanding of the truth came through Olivara's telepathy and empathy channels. She'd vexed and challenged Olivienne all her life but she was entrusting her daughter with the future of their nation. Olivara's heart beat for Psiere and she knew that Olivienne's did as well.

"I know I haven't said it enough or acknowledged all that you do, but I appreciate you. When the time comes, hopefully only after many decarotos have passed, I can only hope to be half the queen you are."

Olivara handed back the pendant. "You will be one of the best. Call it a gut instinct."

That made Olivienne laugh. "Who are you, Tosh now, with her intuition?"

"No. I'm a mother who knows her daughter and sees the greatness she's capable of. You will lead us into the future and I suspect it will be one of not only distance but longevity."

"I'll do my best, Maman."

"Good. Now, don't forget to teleo Vinsun about that pendant order. And if you want a ceremony for their presentation before your previous guardians are sent to leave for their next post, let me know. I'm sure Renou would be more than happy to put something together."

"I will, and thank you."

Olivara nodded. "If that's your only request, how do you feel about a little competitive target practice while we've got some unexpected and more importantly, uninterrupted, time together?"

"I'd say you better bring your best pistol because mine has been hot lately."

"I'll take that challenge. Shall we make it a wager?"

"I'm amenable. What did you have in mind?"

"A bottle of that Ostium vineo you love in exchange for a decanter of Pendar's scotch."

Olivienne sucked in a breath. "We only have a few bottles of that pressing left!"

She grinned and narrowed her eyes. "It's only a problem for you if I win."

Olivienne responded with a clenched jaw. "Fine! We'll just see who gets to drink what at the end of the dae."

Lunes passed and it was the evening before Gren Holling and Ciera Penn were set to depart to their highly secretive next post. The entire shield team, including the two former specialists and Castellan, stood in a line facing the Divine Cathedra where Olivara sat. King Keshien stood to the left of the throne and Captain Torrin stood to the right and just behind the queen. A position that Castellan had taken the one and only time Olivienne sat in that seat.

Olivienne stood between the throne and the line. Templar Zane Aislyn, General Leniste, General Renou, and the rest of the sovereign shields ranged around the chamber, watching with interest.

Olivienne looked at Holling with concern. You would never notice he was missing one leg given the fit of his uniform and attentive stance. "Holling, are you good to stand at attention for a few meens or would you like a seat to be brought over?"

He grinned at her then reached down to rap at the thigh of one leg with his knuckles. The hard surface beneath his trouser fabric became obvious. "No, ser. The prosthetic that came out of the Engineering Corp has me good as new." He paused and amended his comment. "Well, I won't be running any footraces and the cold makes it ache some, but other than that I can stand just fine."

"Good to hear it." Olivienne gave her mother a nod then addressed her unit. "You may wonder why you're all here tonight. This isn't just a farewell for our psi in arms, our family and former unit members." She paused and grinned at the lot of them. "Though I'm told there will be refreshments after."

Olivienne met Castellan's curious gaze. She'd done a

bang-up job of keeping this surprise all to herself.

"We're here because I wish to honor you. This team, more than most, has sacrificed themselves and surpassed every bit of expected bravery during the past few rotos. You've gone places and seen things that no other psi could comprehend, let alone experience. I appreciate and respect your hard work, your dedication. Because of that, I had pendants made that are replicas of the temple keys we retrieved on our first missions together. I want you to understand what the lot of you mean to me and to know that we are all a family no matter where we go."

Olivienne moved her gaze down the line of Shield Corp soldiers, starting with Tosh and ending with their most recent addition, Mohdra Sehg. He shifted nervously, looking extremely uncomfortable. "Do you have a question, Specialist?"

Everyone in the line turned to look at him and his cheeks pinked. "Erm, ser, I wasn't there for those earlier adventurist missions."

She smiled at him. "It's true, you weren't. Those were carried out with our late and dear, Lieutenant Commander Gentry Savon. But Specialist Sehg, you have continued on with us in his place, performing as brilliantly and bravely as he would have. I know that Castellan agrees with me that you've earned your position within this unit." She looked toward her love, who nodded and agreed.

"You certainly have, Specialist."

"I can't give Savon a pendant, but I can honor you."

He swallowed and was quiet for a sec. Then he saluted her. "Thank you, Connate Dracore."

Olivara stepped down from the dais where the Divine Cathedra was installed. Two of the queen's shields approached with satchels. Olivienne recognized one as Lieutenant Cando and smiled, no longer holding the jealousy that ate at her before. The unfamiliar specialist stood by Olivara as Cando followed Olivienne down the line, starting with Lieutenant Madlin. The process was simple enough. Lieutenant Cando reached into the satchel, withdrew a decorative box, and held it up for Olivienne to remove the pendant. Olivienne then placed the pendant around each of her team members before presenting them with the container.

Once finished she stood next to Olivara and smiled. "Go ahead, you can look at them."

"Ser, what is the stone in the middle? That doesn't look like any of the original keys we found. It looks more like obsidae."

"That's a good question, Dozier. It so happens that all of you have been gifted with some of the largest antorae-stone fragments taken from Havington's rebels. They are a sign of our belief in you."

Olivara nodded. "Let's officially call it a symbol of sovereign trust, shall we? I like the ring of that. Much like sovereign oath, our trust is a serious matter. Now, if my daughter will join Captain Tosh, I've my own gifts to give."

Olivienne stood at Castellan's side and waited for her mother to approach.

The process was repeated for the two of them and she saw Castellan's eyes widen when she noticed the significantly larger stones in the center of their pendants. It was as if storm clouds boiled across Castellan's face. "What is the meaning of this?"

Olivara held up a hand to stay Castellan's wrath. "Be at ease, Captain. That is half of my own stone, the other is embedded in Olivienne's pendant. Your previous stone has been permanently locked away along with the stain of its service."

Castellan's shoulders dropped. It wasn't enough for most to notice, but then Olivienne wasn't most people. She knew her love's body better than any other. With a quiet voice she spoke. "Is this okay?"

Castellan spoke just as quietly. "The stone?"

"Our pendants and the stones within weren't my idea. But I approved it. Can you accept?" Olivienne knew that much had improved with Castellan's spirit and conscience during the past two lunes, but she had to be sure she wasn't hurting her with such a gift.

Castellan drew in a steadying breath and gave her a quiet smile. "Yes."

Olivara clapped her hands twice. "Excellent! Now, as my daughter stated, we have food and drinks down the hall in the first conference room so we can send your specialists off properly. I believe that the families of Specialists Penn and Holling are already waiting."

Castellan stepped forward and held up her hands before anyone could move out of place. "If I could have everyone's attention, please."

Olivienne wondered if she were going to thank the team as well. She watched as Castellan shared a glance with General Renou and her curiosity was piqued. "Tosh?" She didn't have to wait long for an answer.

"I don't know if any of you realized, but I didn't correct Queen Olivara when she addressed me by my former rank."

Feet shifted, sounding loud in the large space. Olivienne held her breath. As far as she knew, Castellan had yet to decide on her future career plans. But she'd had a meeting with General Renou earlier in the dae and Olivienne wondered if they'd found a position for her. She mourned because adventurist missions would never be the same without her partner in discovery and danger. A sec later, Castellan met her gaze and Olivienne felt an outpouring of love. But more than that, she read the promise in Castellan's eyes and rejoiced at the words she knew would come.

"After much consideration, and lunes of healing with the rest of you, I've decided to resume my position as Connate Dracore's shield team captain. Your captain." As one, every specialist let out a cheer, even the staid and serious Lieutenant Madlin.

Olivienne threw her arms around Castellan and gave her a kiss. When they pulled apart, she turned back to the gathered people. "We didn't need more to celebrate but once again, my captain likes to go above and beyond. Go on now, refreshments are waiting." She waved the specialists toward the door but they didn't move. Each one saluted Castellan.

Captain Castellan Tosh saluted back. "You're dismissed."

Torrin waved to his unit in attendance as well, quickly

followed by Captain Gorne of the king's unit. "Go on, celebrate with the rest of them. If we're not safe here with this many shields in one place, I don't know where we would be." That lit a spark under the rest and black clad soldiers filed out of the main chamber toward the conference room mentioned by the queen.

Leniste clapped Castellan on the shoulder. "Well, Tosh, you've certainly made a whole mob of people happy todae. What convinced you to stay?"

Castellan shook her head as she gave Olivienne the lightest telekinetic caress to her cheek. "Well, I realized that it would be a disservice to Psiere not to perform to the best of my abilities. And frankly, ser, my abilities have done the most amount of good for queen and country right where I am."

He chuckled and put his hands in his pockets. "Well said, Captain. Glad you finally came around, if only to prevent Renou from stealing another one of my promising defense officers in an effort to square peg your round hole." Then he turned on his heel and made his way over to speak with Olivara, Keshien, and Renou.

Olivienne burst into laughter at the expression on Castellan's face. "You look so perplexed right now."

"I know he was my ultimate commanding officer for many rotos but even now he still comes out of nowhere and I can only make an academic guess at his meaning."

"I think you should take it as a good thing and not dwell on his words too long or you'll spoil the celebration."

A few meens later, the couple walked through the doors into the large conference room. A quartet of musicians played in one corner and a large selection of food was spread out along tables on one side of the room. Specialists milled about, chatting amicably with their counterparts in the other sovereign units. Olivienne overheard the conversation between Holling and Meza.

"Come on, Hol. I promise not to tell anyone."

"Sorry, Mez. But the destination of our next post was sworn to secrecy by Queen Olivara herself. Me and Penn can't say, even if you guess correctly."

Meza looked down for a sec. "Will we ever see you again?"

He grinned at her, looking as excited as he did when he first joined Olivienne's unit and Olivienne knew that Castellan's idea for their posting was the right one. He held out his hand. "Take my goodbye." Meza clasped it. "And return it when I see you next. If the Maker's will it, we will meet again sooner rather than later."

She threw her arms around Holling and gave him a big hug, which was quickly followed by the rest of the shield unit who had been watching out of the corner of their eyes. Then they did the same to Penn.

"I'd say this is going well. Are you finished eaves-dropping?"

"I wasn't—I—" Olivienne swore and pushed Castellan's shoulder. "I just want them all to be okay, you know?"

"Trust me when I say I do."

Olivienne hesitated for a sec. "Thank you."

"For?"

"I don't think I could have done this without you. My entire life has changed in the span of just a few rotos and I'm not the same person who regularly went off on her own. That woman didn't know the value of trust, team-work, or long-term companionship. You've changed me and I don't want to do what I do alone."

"You never have to worry because I feel the same way. I just needed to be certain I could do the position jus-tice and not constantly worry I was making the right choices. We had a saying in defense that second guessing will get you first dead."

"True enough."

"Good evening Connate Dracore, Captain Tosh."

Castellan held out her hand and clasped it with Lieu-tenant Cando. Then Cando held out her hand to Olivienne. She smiled at the other woman and took it gratefully. "Thank you for your assistance in there. I wish you all the best on Maman's shield team."

Cando leaned in and lowered her voice. "A little bird told me this team may be a good place for advancement."

Castellan tilted her head. "Oh? Torrin seems pretty healthy and capable to me."

"Well, ser, our dear Captain Torrin has been seeing some Maker-touched telesana doctore. I hear they're quite serious."

Olivienne burst into laughter. "That little minxle! We clearly need to have a visit with Gemeda soon and get the updates right from the source." She noticed the smile teasing Castellan's lips. "How do you feel about such a thing?"

"I think it's grand. It's about time Gem settled down and made an honest psi out of someone. Plus, that means she'll be stationed in Tesseron and we'll get to see her more often."

"You make good points."

Castellan turned back to Cando. "And you. I'm certainly glad you landed where you did. It's a well-deserved promotion to the black uniform. I expect nothing but great things from here out. Savvy?"

Cando winked at her. "Yes, ser. Now, I'm not sure if you've seen the spread but I noticed a few jugs of stone brew on the drink table. Would you two care to share some with me? I've always been fascinated by the Divine Mystery and I'd like to speak with you both."

Olivienne was pleasantly surprised by her request. "I've heard of stone brew but never tried it."

Castellan grimaced. "I assert that nights of stone brew have never led to good-headed daes."

"Excellent! Lead the way, Cando. Discovering new things is what I excel at."

Cando grinned. "Yes, ser."

"And then she says, 'I've never given it much thought and it seems wasteful to walk by again when you're already here. Good dae.' right before exiting the establishment. By the Makers, Tosh literally walked away from someone asking about love at first sight with zero clue the woman was making a play."

Olivienne and Del Torrin burst into laughter at

Gemeda's story.

Castellan grimaced. "I was fresh out of academy and knew nothing about nothing. I was also distracted because the lot of us were waiting for upcoming assignments to be posted."

Torrin took a sip of his scotch. "I'm notoriously thick when it comes to romance but even I would have picked up on that one."

"Don't worry, love, I like you just the way you are."

Castellan gave Olivienne a grateful smile. "Thank you. At least I can count on support from one part of my life—"

"The denser you are, the more I benefit since I won't have to compete with a crowd of pseras and pseros for your affection."

Olivienne's words elicited a gentle warmth instead of the intended annoyance. "I can definitively state that there would never be any competition with you in the vicinity." She leaned forward to give Olivienne a kiss and wet droplets hit her cheek. She looked up in time to see Gem wipe her fingers on a cloth next to her water glass.

"Was that necessary?"

Gem grinned. "Oh, absolutely. I want to sit here and enjoy post dinner drinks and conversation with my friends, not watch the two of you snog as though you're just becoming acquainted."

"Speaking of acquainted," Olivienne gestured back and forth between Gemeda and Torrin. "When did this all come about?"

Castellan burst into laughter. "I can't believe you took so long to ask."

Olivienne shrugged. "I've gotten better at curbing my curiosity."

The two people being questioned glanced at one another and Castellan witnessed real affection between them. Perhaps Captain Del Torrin was finally the one to tame her wild and wandering friend.

"Well, you know I've been spending a lot of time in the capital of late. Specifically, near Queen Olivara." Gem lifted one corner of her mouth in a half smile. "Truthfully,

I don't know how it happened. At first this big behemoth of a shield vexed me something awful. But the more time we spent together the more I came to appreciate his many fine attributes."

"More like you were attracted to his large—"

"'Vienne!'"

Olivienne smiled innocently. "Heart and wise insights. What did you think I was going to say?"

Torrin scrubbed a hand across his face, dark skin hiding a blush that Castellan knew must be present. She shook her finger at both troublemakers. "The two of you are incorrigible. But I'll gladly accept my fellow captain as bait if it means he's caught my closest friend here in Tesseron for a time."

"What can I say? I can't let you be the only one haring off and finding yourself a par. I figured it was time for me to start scouring the ranks."

Olivienne snorted into her scotch. "You and your captain fetish."

Thick brows drew together as Torrin looked at Gemeda. "Captain fetish?"

"Ignore them, darling. They're being crass and acting in a manner unbefitting of a sovereign couple."

"Who is they? I never poked fun at the two of you," Castellan said, indignantly.

Gemeda ignored Castellan's protest. "Speaking of pars—"

"You're the only one that was, Gem."

"Are the two of you nervous for your upcoming ceremony?"

Castellan wanted to say she hadn't given it much thought but truth be told, most of their daes of late were spent in planning of one sort or another. There were speeches to memorize, fittings, dinners, and most importantly, working with a designer to create their tattoos of consorage. "I, we—"

"Tosh is nervous. I am not."

Castellan made a face. "I never said that! I think I've been too busy to be nervous. It's a good thing I've got excellent lieutenants in charge of bringing the new guardians up to expectation because I've bloody well spent all my time getting stuck by pins and parading in front of a slew of broadsheet reps."

Olivienne scowled. "I'll concede the planning of it has been a bit tedious. To make it worse, Maman directed me to sit in on Imperium meetings as she does her extended tour of Dromea." She paused and said to Torrin. "Speaking of which, how the blazes are you here? Shouldn't you be south with the rest of the shield team?"

He chuckled. "We made a bet that she lost. My prize was not having to go down to that blasted continent."

"You made the good end of that deal. They're just past the warmest part of the roto right now. It probably feels like a swamp everywhere except the mountains."

"It's not the heat. I mean, that part certainly isn't ideal. It's those Maker forsaken howlers. I hate them. I lost track of how many things I've had stolen for each and every trip I've taken down there."

Castellan met Olivienne's gaze and made the same howler face that sent the unit into laughter rotos ago. Olivienne reacted as she did back then. Castellan responded to Torrin. "At least it wasn't a voteo. We had to listen to random screeching for mahls until I instructed the team to adjust the frequency on their handheld units."

Olivienne laughed. "Poor Lazaro never lived that one down."

"Anyway, to give your question a serious answer, I'd say I'm less nervous now than when we first oathed to one another."

Gem burst into laughter then quickly covered her mouth. "That doesn't even make sense."

"It's true though." Castellan defended. "Everything about the first ceremony was foreign and strange. Not to mention the lead up with both of our families. But now," She met Olivienne's violet gaze and felt nothing but love and a sense of peace. "Now it feels a lot like coming home after lunes away. I'm ready for our next adventure together."

Those mesmerizing sovereign eyes shimmered with emotion. "I couldn't have said it better myself."

That time they did get to kiss before Gem could interrupt again.

Chapter Twenty-Two

"Stop fidgeting."

"I think the clothier made an error in measurement." Castellan tugged at the high collar of her long coat. Silver buttons ran up each side of the double-breasted front and Olivienne thought the brilliant white fabric looked quite stunning against her tanned skin. The tapered white trousers tucked neatly into knee-high polished black boots. "She didn't because it fits you perfectly. I think you look dashing."

"I don't see why I needed a new suit for this. My dress blacks would have worked quite well."

Olivienne shook her head at the familiar argument. "Darling, white is tradition for sovereign ceremonies because it's a color not held by any of the corps. It shows that we will be impartial and rule fairly when the time comes." She held up her hand as Castellan opened her mouth. "I know a mere color can't guarantee fairness but again, it's tradition."

Castellan turned and scowled at her. "Why aren't you dressed yet?"

"Because I was having too much fun watching you." She reached up to caress the medals on Castellan's chest. In deference to her rank and responsibility, the clothier had included everything from her regular dress uniform on the consoral outfit. Castellan even wore her sword. It was cleaned and polished for the ceremony.

"Don't tease todae of all daes."

"You aren't still nervous, are you? Papan cautioned you may suffer a faint."

"For the last time, I'm not going to suffer a faint when we pledge to one another. I managed just fine in our oath-ing."

Olivienne giggled. "Barely. And he wasn't talking about the ceremony, love. He was referring to the tattoos of consorage that happen immediately after the celebration."

"Oh. Eh, I'm sure it will be fine."

"Your words to the Tau's ears—erm, ear holes?" Castellan chuckled. "At any rate, I hope you're right." She brushed a little dark lint from Castellan's sleeve and stepped back. "I'm off now to change. I'll meet you here in fifteen meens for the procession in."

Castellan grinned at her. "Yes, ser."

The quarter oor seemed as though it took ten times as long. Castellan sat on a lounger, her leg jiggling up and down as she played with the sword in her lap. One couldn't sit upon a lounger while wearing such a device. She pulled out her chrono and checked it for the sixth time. Another sovereign tradition was for the couple to be alone during their consoral ceremony preparation. On one hand, it made Castellan happy not to have a bunch of people around making her nervous. Conversely, she thought maybe some company would have helped the wait pass by faster.

She checked the time again. It was quarter of thirteen hundred and she knew the Grand Chamber would be nearly full. There were no psychometrist warnings for this particular dae. It had been a peaceful seven lunes since Havington and his rebellion were brought down. Though Castellan wasn't sure if it had more to do with the queen's wekely Announcements of Discovery, or her long and public tour of Dromea. The entire country of Psiere seemed eager to celebrate something, anything, that didn't stink with the pall of war.

"You're thinking awfully hard."

Castellan looked toward the doorway and froze in shock. Despite the fact that their ceremonial outfits were both white and of a similar style, there were enough differences between the two of them that allowed each woman to be utterly and simplistically unique. Olivienne also wore a long coat with a high collar. But instead of two rows of buttons, Olivienne had a single row down the center. And not having any medals or awards to speak of, the clothiers tried to balance out their outfits by including silver decorative threadwork across the left and right side of Olivienne's chest, as well as similar design stylings on each shoulder.

She had a polished black waist pouch to match her boots. It was symbolic of her life as an adventurist as much as Castellan's sword represented her rotos spent in the military corps.

"You're beautiful!"

Olivienne's cheeks pinked at the atypical outburst and Castellan didn't regret her loose tongue in the slightest. "Thank you, love." She turned them toward the large, polished mirror so they could see one another in full. "You know, it's funny how we aligned so well with my parens."

Castellan knew of the queen and king's ceremony from long ago, but she'd never seen any stills of the dae. "How do you mean?"

"When maman and papan said their vows of consorage in the Grand Chamber, she wore her pistol and Papan also had a waist pouch."

"I thought the queen was a judex before ascending to the Divine Cathedra?"

Olivienne grinned. "Oh, she was. But Maman made a name for herself with her pistol long before she began her career in the Codice Corp. Did you know she still holds the Tesseron festival record for shot accuracy and distance?"

"I did not."

"I always wondered how she felt when I followed into the corp of my father rather than something more sedate and, well, befitting of a sovereign."

Castellan held Olivienne's hands. "Any corp or rank you could achieve would be worthy of your title, 'Vienne. As a sovereign, it's your duty to know the people and understand our society."

"I'd wager you weren't thinking such noble thoughts on that railer down in Ostium."

She snorted. "We won't speak of our contentious start. Not on such a portentous dae. Savvy?"

"But my love, without that friction, without every spit and spark between us those first few lunes, it's likely we wouldn't be standing where we are now. We are but ripples in the lake of our land. I consider myself lucky for my wave to move along at the same pace and space as yours."

Her words startled Castellan. They were adjacent to the advice her own maman had given her about changing past events. "Maman said something to me lunes ago that stuck. Don't ever tell her I admitted this, but she's a big part of the reason I was able to move past the horror of Ruina."

"What did she say?"

"Every little thing we do casts ripples upon the pond of life until all the water is eventually moved on the surface."

Olivienne reached up to tuck a strand of hair that had come loose and fallen across one of Castellan's eyes. "What does it mean?"

"To boil it down, it means that no matter how badly we'd like to go back and alter the worst events of our lives, it would also mean altering the best. Despite my sorrow and guilt about both King's Marsh and Ruina, I wouldn't want to take away my memories if it meant never having you. Not if it cost me everything I love most about this life."

"Tosh..."

"Yes?"

"I appreciate the sweet words, and better yet, the emotion behind them. But you don't have to try so hard because we've arrived."

At first, Castellan couldn't make sense of her words. "Come again?"

"Darling, we're here together and it's time."

Then a knock sounded at the outer door and she startled. One quick check of her chrono revealed they had five meens until the ceremony. She smiled and poured even more love through their bond. "We certainly have. Ready, love?"

"Even sirens couldn't keep me away."

"We won't need to make it through something so drastic." Castellan took one step toward the door and paused to look back at Olivienne. She held out her hand. "Together?"

"Always."

Olivienne's entire shield unit stood outside the doors and snapped to attention as soon as they left the private suite located on the top level of the Temple of Archeos. Each guardian wore the dress blacks that Castellan longed for. The only thing that seemed out of place was the pendants they wore on their uniform like badges of honor.

To our guardians, they are. The pendants I mean.

Are you eavesdropping now? Watch yourself, 'Vienne. You're not the queen yet to be meddling so.

Olivienne stifled a laugh behind her hand.

Madlin and Soleng moved to stand in front of the royal couple. Both saluted but Madlin spoke. "Captain Tosh, Connate Dracore, we are to be your escort into the Grand Chamber. Do you accept?"

Castellan and Olivienne answered in unison. "We accept." It was a formality more than anything but tradition must be observed. Castellan thought her team was happy to be part of such a historic ceremony. She met Soleng's gaze and he gave her a grin and wink.

The shields split with three pairs in front of them and three pairs behind, leaving a lieutenant to each of their sides. The escort paused outside the large entryway into the Grand Chamber less than two meens later. Madlin glanced to her right at Castellan. "Ready, ser?"

Castellan looked at her love, who was silent for a few secs. Olivienne finally whispered, "Is it okay to admit that my knees are a bit weak?"

She moved so her lips were next to Olivienne's ear. Castellan kept her voice quiet in deferment to Olivienne's fear. "Jump and I'll lift us." As soon as she said the words, Castellan remembered a previous utterance that was similar. It was on the Island of Navis when faced with one of the first black bladder ships produced. One adventurist and a handful of soldiers put their trust in Castellan to catch them before they could fall into the Caerula Ocean.

Olivienne's lips parted, clearly having remembered as well. "You promised that once before."

"Did I lie then?"

"No."

"I've not changed, 'Vienne."

Olivienne gifted Castellan's cheek with a brief caress. "That's one of my favorite things about you."

Soleng prompted them. "Sers?"

Castellan gestured forward. "Let's go. The sooner this is finished, the sooner I can remove this stiff-collared business."

A few shields snickered but quickly quieted as they marched through the doorway.

Silence fell across everyone in attendance as the double column cleared the doors and marched up the wide aisle leading directly to the dais where Templar Zane Aislyn and Queen Olivara stood. The uniform cadence of sixteen pairs of boots echoed in the chamber.

Castellan glanced to her left and right and swallowed hard. One thing their minimal oathing hadn't prepared them for was the massive crowd that would turn up for a royal consorage ceremony. With no threat or danger, it was open to everyone who requested an attendance ticket. Olivienne even said there was a lottery for folks that didn't make it into Tesseron often. Castellan supposed that witnessing the consoral ceremony could be a once in a lifetime event. She saw her own family standing near the king and sub-connate.

"Tosh, are you with us?"

She hadn't even realized they'd stopped walking. She straightened, guiltily. "Of course." Someone sneezed nearby. It sounded like Qent. Escort duty complete, the Shield Corp guardians moved off to the side where they had seats of honor for the event. They stood the same as everyone else in attendance, waiting for Olivienne and Castellan to ascend the stairs.

Unlike the less significant oathing ceremony, the Queen of Psiere and the head templar needed to provide pricks of verification on the altar. It was proof of legitimacy for a sovereign consorage. Perhaps not wanting to draw things out, Olivara and Templar Zane Aislyn moved to stand across the altar from one another. Each placed their palms into the hand-shaped indentations set within the top of the pedestal. The space around their palms glowed so bright Olivara and Zane looked away. Once it flickered out, they removed their palms and stepped back.

Olivara held up her hands and spoke to the gathered crowd. The unique acoustics within the pyramidion meant the sound carried to all in attendance, from one wall to the other and across again.

"Permission has been granted and received. Olivienne Dracore, as your queen and mother, I will remind you that any pledge you make in your heart to a par should be matched equally to the pledge you owe our people. Live your joy and remember to pay it forward when your time comes to rule all of Psiere. Do you accept the constraints of your privilege?"

"I do."

Olivara turned to Castellan and a bead of sweat trickled down her temple. "Castellan Tosh, as your queen, I will remind you that any pledge you make in your heart to a sovereign should be matched equally to the pledge you owe the people of Psiere. For you are a future royal yourself and thus expected to carry our values and burdens as if you were born to them. Do you accept the constraints of your privilege?"

"I do."

She nodded and stepped back. "Let us begin."

It seemed like lifetimes ago since they found themselves in that exact position. Castellan met Olivienne's gaze across the pedestal and it was as if the entire room fell away from them. She smiled. *I love you.*

Olivienne smirked. *You forgot your lines, didn't you?*

I did not!

"As travelers and companions, seekers, and sibs, we are but secs of time in a life measured by oors and rotos. All things of Psiere have their own pace of existence, from trees to ships, sharcs to stones. And there is no more serious a pledge than one comprised of two lifetimes that have come together. What is your covenant?"

Olivienne spoke first, per the ritual. "I am the tree with branches tall and roots deep. I will shade and shelter those nearest to me."

Castellan answered. "If you are the tree, I am the bird

deep within your branches. I will warn of stele and famine alike, protecting those nearest to me."

Templar Aislyn recited the next line. "And what of your vow to Psiere?"

Unlike the previous oathing ceremony, this was the time that Castellan and Olivienne were required to speak as one. They'd practiced their timing and cadence until there was nary an error. Olivienne called out one final warning.

Don't falter now, Tosh.

Focus on your own tongue, 'Vienne.

What made the twinned vow more challenging was the fact that they couldn't make eye contact. They each had to turn their heads to the right to look out across the crowd in opposite directions from one another.

"We vow to Psiere that our course will be steady and steerage firm." After that line they were able to turn their heads back, but still had to speak at the same time. "I oath to you, and give you my loyalty, honor, and truth. In return, I ask for fairness, love, and respect."

They placed their palms into the pedestal indentations. Castellan closed her eyes as the light grew brighter than she remembered from before. A loud chime sounded and shining rays from Archeos and Illeos fell through two different skylights to bathe them upon the dais. Gasps went through the crowd and Castellan knew it wasn't as fantastical as it may seem to the rest. Everything had been well timed with the suns' path across the sky.

Templar Aislyn held up her hand to stay the murmuring crowd. "By the Makers will, and within the great Temple of Archeos, the suns shine down on this permanent bonding, one that can only be held by a sovereign and their par. Your pairing is now complete with the exception of your consoral tattoos that must occur before the next suns' rise. Consentisne?"

Joy and love ebbed and flowed straight from Olivienne. They spoke the final word together. "Assentior." Castellan knew her life was only just beginning.

As soon as they stepped from the dais, Olivienne and Castellan exchanged cheek kisses. Olivara and Zane followed them down the steps. While the first few well-wish-ers in a never-ending line were all family, the next forty meens went by in a blur of smiles and embraces. Castel-lan's own papan shed a sea's worth of tears but still had a hearty embrace and back slap waiting. One difference from their oathing that Castellan appreciated was the lack of broadsheet representative questions. Just as before, a group of musicians played the "March of the Sovereigns" as the newly consored couple, led by their shield escort, made their way out of the temple to the surrounding gar-dens.

Tables were set up all around and more musicians played off to the side of the grand lawn. Castellan reached up to unclasp the top three buttons of her collar as soon as they stepped from the path to the green surface. "That's much better."

Olivienne burst into laughter. "You're ridiculous. I've seen you wear more constricting clothing for longer."

"Different material. I'm positive the inside of this is nothing but sand and nettles."

"Who knew my par would be so dramatic." Olivienne paused and smiled with wonder. "I quite like the sound of that."

"Of what, me being dramatic?"

"No, my par."

It hit her then that she was consored to the future Queen of Psiere. That Castellan herself was the future king. She opened her mouth to respond but no words came forth. "I, uh, I—"

"It's okay, darling. I suspect it will take some getting used to for both of us. In the meantime." She hooked their arms together. "We should get some food because I'm famished."

Castellan saw both their families approaching through the crowd and gestured toward them. "Shouldn't we wait for our parens?"

"Olivienne and Castellan, Cassiene and I were just talking about the delights of babes and I told her I couldn't wait to be an avia."

Olivienne tensed next to her. *Nope. We're definitely*

not fortified enough for this conversation.

Right. Food it is.

"We'll return as soon as we sup, Maman!" Then they ran across the lawn toward the waiting tables of food, laughing as they went.

Epilogue

"You wanted to see us, Maman?"

"Please, both of you come in and close the door."

Olivienne moved forward so Castellan could follow her into the small study. They sat on a lounger across from her parens. "Is something the matter? Tosh and I have gone on a few missions since our consorage and have had no issues with the team or protection for the two of us."

"I've read the newest stack of velum you discovered in that cave near Montesilva. Some of the schematics are like nothing I've ever seen."

She laughed at her father's enthusiasm. "I thought you were deep in the middle of the Atlantee history provided by Queen Eurynome's diplomatic liaison?"

He harrumphed. "Well, yes, as King I have my duties to crown and country but I can't study the histories all the time, 'Vienne. I'd go mad. And I read your adventurist papers for pleasure."

Olivara patted his hand. "I'm afraid your father will always be an adventurist at heart. I suppose that's why our news thrills him as much as it worries me."

"News, my Queen?"

"Yes. If you remember, I made the journey to see your Tau friend, Kinsa, two lunes after your consoral ceremony."

Olivienne laughed. "I do. And I told you that you'd like him. I think you'll like Nessie even more, whenever you find the time to travel again."

"Travel is why we called you here todae. Kinsa sent us a message via, uh, droon?"

"Drone, dear. His recorded message of voice said it was a drone." Keshien explained, "It's a small, autonomous, flying mechanical construct. A truly fascinating device."

Excitement swelled within her at all the new information. "What did Kinsa say?"

"Well, they wanted to officially congratulate the two

of you on your pairing. They also provided a map, coordinates, and the background histories of the people on the next continent east of Psiere. Kinsa says they are peaceful and more advanced than us, though without flight capability."

Olivienne froze. She glanced toward Castellan, then back at her parens. "What are you trying to tell us?"

Olivara reached to clasp her hand with Keshien's. "I'm saying that the fire of discovery spreads through our people and we would be remiss not to explore the world that's been opened to us with those archeostones."

"And?"

Her father answered. "'Vienne, are you ready for another far-off expedition? As a sovereign, you've got the weight of diplomacy behind you. I can think of no better to undertake this next big adventurist mission."

"Are you not worried about the danger of such a long journey?"

"Tosh, this is a chance of a lifetime!"

"Love, they all are. We've already encountered many such things. But my job is seeing to your safety and traveling to an unknown land filled with a new race of people could put us at a significant disadvantage."

Olivara shocked her when she defended the mission. "Actually, part of the missive we received from Kinsa assured us that the peoples in the next land are cultured, kind, and pacifistic in nature, though the Fae may appear a little strange. They are also abnormally long-lived."

Olivienne's mind reeled with all the new information. "Will they remember the Tau Ceti? Where do they come from? How far away is this land?"

Laughter interrupted her questions. "Oh, my daughter, that's why we called you here. Why don't you pour yourselves glasses of vineo and we'll give you all the details."

Olivienne recognized the familiar looking bottle as the same one her mother won from her during an impromptu pistol challenge. "Isn't that out of our crate from Ostium?"

Castellan looked back and forth between her and the vineo. "Is that where it went? You told me we must have finished it without knowing."

"Well, I couldn't admit that I lost it in a shooting match with my mother."

All four of them laughed as Castellan poured their drinks.

"So, what is the timing of this adventurist mission?"

Olivara leaned forward. "We've got a contingent of psi from various corps that are completing supplemental training."

"Do you plan to rotate the current crews at the towers on Magna?"

"Yes. Rotate and expand. Keshien and I thought that may be a good time for you to depart as well."

"What about the staff that are scheduled to come back to Tesseron?"

"We only want you gone for two wekes this first trip. That's enough time to make contact and report back. That will also give the original tower teams time with the replacement crews for handover instruction."

Olivienne looked to her right. Castellan's gaze was heavy and deep. "Are you ready for another jaunt?"

"With you? Always."

She turned to her parens. "I'd say you have your answer. When do we leave?"

"You've one lune to plan. Captain Velten will take you on the *Vestigo*. It has plenty of space for the extra crew on the way to Magna and back."

Castellan leaned against her shoulder. "It will be good to see Holling and Penn again."

Olivara shook her finger at Castellan. "I have to give you credit, Tosh. That was a brilliant idea staffing the research station with your shields. From what I hear, your Nessie is quite taken with them both. The lieutenant with the scientere subspecialty that Camen assigned with them said it's the best position she's ever had. And by the Makers, the amount of information they've translated and sent back...we may have to add another building to the area and send more psi to aid in their research."

Castellan smiled and took a sip of her vineo. "I'm just glad that they're happy."

Olivienne knew that Ruina still ate at her from the

inside, but much of the guilt had finally subsided after a roto of healing. "Me too, darling." She paused to top off both their glasses. "Now, drink faster. It will hardly seem as though I lost this bottle at all if we finish most of it."

"I won fair upon fair, 'Vienne. And I say you must share the bottle around."

She held up the vineo to taunt her mother. "You know what they say. A bottle in hand is worth two in the crate."

The vineo suddenly disappeared from Olivienne's hand and reappeared in Olivara's. "You're forgetting something important."

"What's that, Maman?"

"The queen's word is law."

The ocean stretched as far as the eyes could see in every direction. It was an odd feeling after spending their lives tethered to Endara and Dromea. Castellan stood next to Olivienne on the observation deck watching the setting suns. Archeos was half gone on the horizon and she knew Illeos wasn't far behind. The deep reds and oranges of the sky bathed Olivienne's face where she stood with her eyes closed.

"You know, you'd see more if you were looking. We came out here to watch the suns set."

"I was just thinking about that. We've spent a fair lot of time staring behind us on one conveyance or another. Dirigible, railer, boat."

"It's true."

"But why? Why do people find so much comfort staring behind them rather than appreciate the excitement of what's to come?" She opened her eyes and Castellan grew lost in those dark violet depths.

She contemplated the question for a meen. Olivienne wasn't wrong with her observation. Castellan moved her gaze back to the horizon. "Perhaps it's because we already know where we're going. It makes no difference whether there is surprise at the end of the dae or no, we're still going to make the trip. But sometimes..." She turned to see Olivienne watching her intently. "Sometimes it's nice to remember where we've been. I don't know about you, but the suns' set is a reminder of all the beauty we carry with us from those places."

She paused. "Did you know that it was common for those in the Defense Corp to whisper the names of fallen soldiers at the end of the dae? It was said to bring closure and peace. I don't think any of the other corps do that."

"I've never heard of such a practice. And I like that notion of remembering beauty. You've gotten quite wise since you became a royal." Olivienne reached up to trace Castellan's tattoo of consorage around her neck and she shivered.

"That tickles." She looked at Olivienne's tattoo in the fading light. Theirs was created with special iridescent ink, just like the king and queen's. "Well, if I'm to serve my sovereign and become her advisor in our latter rotos, it's important I start acting the part. It wouldn't do for citizens to think me thick."

"My love, after everything you've done for our people, no one on Psiere will ever look upon you with such disregard. But speaking of serving your sovereign, she's got a few orders for you tonight. What say you?"

Illeos sank below the horizon. Olivienne's face was bathed equally in faint bluish-purple light and shadow. Castellan leaned close so she could whisper in her ear. "I say yes, ser, then suggest we go someplace more private. I hear the connate was given the nicest cabin aboard ship. Perhaps we should check it out?"

Olivienne slapped her arm. "You're ridiculous!"

"So, is that a no?"

"It's a yes, you fiend. The suns are gone, why are we still standing here?" Rather than wait for Castellan to answer, Olivienne led her toward the door into the ship.

Castellan gave one more look behind her and sighed. No suns set was ever truly the end of the dae. It was merely the enterprise of morning yet to begin. Despite no longer serving with defense, she whispered into the breeze, "Gentry Savon," before following Olivienne inside.

Acknowledgments

I have so many people working magic behind the scenes and I appreciate all of them more than words can say. Patty and Natty, you two are instrumental when it comes to making sure only the best version of my story goes to print. Then there is my fab beta reader, Anne. I learn more from you with each new novel. And finally, I would like to thank Lyss. I would be nothing without those folks who are as invested in my characters as I am. You inspire me.

About the Author

Award winning author and Michigan native, Kelly Aten-Keilen brings heroines to life in a variety of blended LGBTQ fiction genres. She specializes in speculative fiction, focusing on extra-ordinary women who are as flawed as they are compelling. She's not afraid of pain or adversity, but loves a happy ending. Kelly's goal with each new novel is to make people #Think, #Feel, and #Discuss.

"Some words end the silence, others begin it."

Email: killerwit68@gmail.com
Website: http://www.katenauthor.com

Books by K. Aten

Arrow of Artemis Series

The Fletcher
The Archer
The Sagittarius

In the Blood Resonance Series

Running From Forever
Embracing Forever

Other Titles

Rules of the Road
Waking the Dreamer
Burn it Down
Children of the Stars
Remember Me Synthetica
Elemental Attraction
The Last Scion of Ra

FLASHPOINT
PUBLICATIONS

Bringing rainbow stories to life.

Flashpoint Publications welcomes submissions from writers of every color and books featuring characters of every color. In addition, Flashpoint Publications encourages job applicants of every color whenever a staff position becomes available. We believe that EVERYONE is entitled to a seat at our table.

www.flashpointpublications.com

Milton Keynes UK
Ingram Content Group UK Ltd.
UKHW021117030324
438552UK00008B/82